D1706811

Destiny! In the Land of the Morning Calm

DESTINY!
IN THE LAND OF THE
MORNING CALM

A KOREAN WAR NOVEL

TOM ARTHUR

Two Harbors Press

Two Harbors Press
212 3rd Avenue North, Suite 290
Minneapolis, MN 55401
612.455.2293
www.TwoHarborsPress.com

The design of the South Korean flag (the "Taeguki") is the Chinese design of yin and yang. The four trigrams represent the four Taoist philosophical ideas: harmony, symmetry, balance and circulation. They have many meanings such as, clockwise from upper left: sky, moon, earth, and sun. The circle shows the yin and yang in perfect balance. The vertical Korean characters translate "destiny of a soldier" The cover photo, taken in 1953 by the author, shows crewmen at a 105 howitzer. The center figure holds the lanyard; the man at right on the radio relays the fire command, as the other three brace for the shock and noise.

ISBN - 978-1-936198-42-9
ISBN - 1-936198-42-8
LCCN - 2010928848

Printed in the United States of America

Dedicated
to
Jane, Lisa, Julia, and Jillian

*We thought we were doing the most important
things in the world . . .
maybe we were.*

Col. Gordon E. Murch
Spoken to his son, years later while traveling
to the Arlington National Cemetery

TABLE OF CONTENTS

Korean Peninsula Map...viii
Preface...ix
Introduction xi

Chapter One: Lakes, Woods and Swamps....................................1
Chapter Two: A Police Action...23
Chapter Three: A New War..43
Chapter Four: Worry and Foul Weather.....................................51
Chapter Five: Selective Service...58
Chapter Six: Real McCoy 62
Chapter Seven: Able Battery and Hard Knox..............................69
Chapter Eight: Jody Was There 78
Chapter Nine: The Garand and Agony Hill 81
Chapter Ten: Holiday Time 88
Chapter Eleven: Back to Basics 99
Chapter Twelve: Leave Time 106
Chapter Thirteen: Basic and Beyond 110
Chapter Fourteen: Between Schools 115
Chapter Fifteen: Murch and Leadership 121
Chapter Sixteen: The Raven and Easy Eights 130
Chapter Seventeen: The Garage 139
Chapter Eighteen: Time Winds Down..142
Chapter Nineteen: Limestone and Solstice Weathers.....................148
Chapter Twenty: Chosen for Chosin 160

Chapter Twenty-one: The Furlough 165
Chapter Twenty-two: The Great Northern.. 172
Chapter Twenty-three: Stalemate Explained 184
Chapter Twenty-four: The Hungary i 196
Chapter Twenty-five: Target Practice 203
Chapter Twenty-six: Goodbye Mama, I'm off to Yokohama 207
Chapter Twenty-seven: Sukiyaki and the Sermon 216
Chapter Twenty-eight: The Dream and the General 224
Chapter Twenty-nine: An APA to Inchon..234
Chapter Thirty: Finally, Part of a Team 242
Chapter Thirty-one: The 105..252
Chapter Thirty-two: Fire Direction Center and Otto........................262
Chapter Thirty-three: March to the Sound of the Guns 276
Chapter Thirty-four: The Fragment...288
Chapter Thirty-five: They Came Out of the West..............................297
Chapter Thirty-six: New Plans 308
Chapter Thirty-seven: FO Frenchy...314
Chapter Thirty-eight: The Window and Long Tom..............................326
Chapter Thirty-nine: Over Enemy Lines 340
Chapter Forty: The Corsairs...350
Chapter Forty-one: Back to the OP..365
Chapter Forty-two: Big Noise in Winnetka 373
Chapter Forty-three: The Colonel Bogey 380
Chapter Forty-four: On Patrol..401
Chapter Forty-five: Where Do We Go From Here?.........................419
                         Epilogue...425

Acknowledgements 429
The 21st Century Army: by Colonel Julia Arthur 440
Glossary 444
Bibliography 447
About the Author 455

Korean Peninsula Map

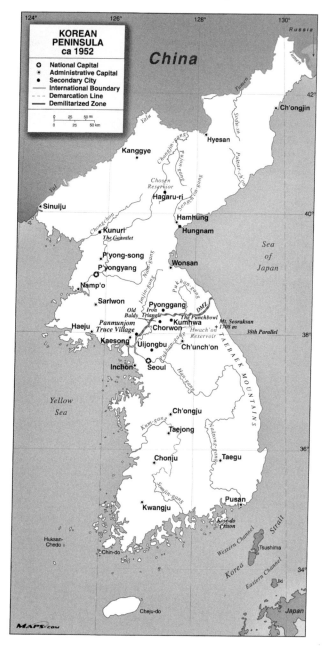

Preface

This is a work of fiction. Although I fed off people I've met, Frenchy, his friends, and relatives are based on no persons living or dead. The same is true for all of the characters on the ore boat, at Fort Knox (with three noted exceptions), at Oakland, aboard ship, at Camp Drake, and throughout Frenchy's Korean experiences.

Except for the well-known generals and world leaders, there are only three real people woven into the story. The speech I had Maj. Gen. R.W. Stephens give to Frenchy's class was in reality his open letter to my basic training unit. The fictitious Rabbi describes a real Marine Lieutenant at the Yokosuka Naval Hospital, who survived his terrible ordeal and reached the rank of Lieutenant General!

My third real person emerged because of a happy set of coincidences. Lt. Col. Gordon E. Murch was Commandant of the Ft. Knox Leadership School both in my time and in the book when Frenchy was there. Murch was very favorably described in S.L.A. Marshall's chapter, Murch's Battalion, and was praised in other books on the Korean War, for his leadership both before the breakout from the Pusan Perimeter (the Bowling Alley Battle) and at the time of the CCF Intervention (the Task Force Dolvin Battle).

I wanted a toehold on the personal life of this heroic soldier. The chance came in July 2008, when my wife, Jane, granddaughter, Jillian, and I attended an intergenerational week at The John

C. Campbell Folk School, Brasstown, North Carolina. I mentioned my interest in Murch to retired West Point Colonel, Bob Comeau. Soon afterward, Comeau e-mailed the phone number and address of Colonel Murch's son, Bob Murch, who gave me the information that made it possible to place his father in Frenchy's path. At one point in the story, after meeting with Frenchy, Murch says, "If you're late for something, trooper, blame it on me." Bob Murch told me his father called all young soldiers "troopers." Even in 1950 the word sounded so old army—1930s vintage. The Murch episode was such a happy discovery.

Amanda is fictitious and a very special character. In Jungian terms, she's an archetypal anima figure *for me*, her creator. Folks ask why I gave a French girl an English name; actually, I didn't know any better. To use an army expression, "No excuse!"

Interwoven in Frenchy's adventures is a short history of Korea and the Korean War, as fought by men of my generation, men who suffered close to the same number of casualties in Korea as our forces later did in Vietnam—a war that lasted twice as long. There were more casualties in two or three days at the Gauntlet and the Reservoir in Korea than have been suffered in Iraq between 2003 and the end of 2009.

How strange it was to become wrapped up in the study of Korea—that forlorn, ripped-apart peninsula of the early1950s—and to realize that South Korea's industrial output now ranks twelfth in the world, that South Korea's lady golfers are dominant players on the LPGA tour, that the Chinese hold a huge share of our Treasury debt, and that the magnetic thing we put on our cars saying "Support Our Troops," says on the back "Made in China."

I hope you enjoy my guy, Frenchy.

Tom Arthur
Glencoe, Illinois, and Palm Desert, California
January 2010

Introduction

I am pleased to write this introduction. However, most of what I have to say is an epilogue that includes my comments regarding today's military, today's wars, today's artillery, and today's frustrations. It is found at the end of the book and is titled 21ˢᵗ Century Army.

Although the Korean War was a tragedy that occurred before I was born, I have gone through some of the same training as Frenchy, which may make the story easier for me to relate to than it may be for some readers. However, the actual reasons for my involvement are: the author is my Dad—whom we all call "TA," and I'm an Army Reserve Officer currently serving on active duty.

My mother grew up on a cattle ranch in the Flint Hills, south of Wichita, Kansas, and majored in Agricultural Economics at Oklahoma State. By the time I was in high school, she had an exciting agricultural investment job with a major Chicago bank, which steered me to consider following her career. Together we visited Texas A&M University.

During that campus visit, the housing office representative told us there were 28,000 students enrolled at A&M and only on-campus housing for 8,000. When Mama balked at off-campus apartment living, the housing office rep told us to check with the Corps of Cadets. They still had housing. I had grown up with great stories of Artillery Officer Candidate School, the First Cavalry, 105 howitzers, FOs, and the military lingo, so I signed up for the corps, got my campus dorm room, and sixty new friends—freshmen women in the Corps of Cadets.

The Texas Aggie spirit is strong and not just on the football field. In World War II, there were more officers from the Texas A&M Corps of Cadets than from the Military Academy and Naval Academy combined. Gig 'em Aggies—we were there!

While at A&M, I lettered in riflery and was on the team that won the Southwest Conference Championships in 1980 and 1981. My senior year I commanded one of the two units of women in the Corps and wore my traditional senior boots. As a Distinguished Military Graduate, I was eligible for a Regular Army Commission. A civilian at heart, I declined and accepted a Reserve Forces Commission.

Now, twenty-nine years later, as our military enters its eighth year of Overseas Contingency Operations in Southwest Asia, I'm an Army Reserve Colonel on active duty, serving as the Deputy Chief of Staff Comptroller for the 75th Battle Command Training Division in Houston, Texas.

I want to stress TA's interest in the concept of limited war. The world leaders were struggling with this concept in 1950, but since then we've had Korea, Vietnam, Grenada, Panama, Desert Storm, Somalia, Bosnia, Kosovo, Afghanistan, and Iraq.

Julia Arthur
Colonel, United States Army Reserves

Chapter One
Lakes, Woods and Swamps

They called it a "hoochy" from the Japanese word for thatched hut—a crude word for a crude, dilapidated place. It was dug into the south side of a North Korean hill, and then built out with timbers and many stacks of sandbags on the three exposed sides and part of the roof. It had been badly damaged by artillery and mortar fire a few weeks before but was now rebuilt—stronger than ever. Arnold Desprez lay on his cot in the hoochy, feeling cozy enough, knowing that safety was in high places; the real hell was the crater floor a few hundred feet down below to the north. A trip to that place was called a patrol, a reminder that frontline men like him were expendable—available for sacrifice to gain an objective, like when the high command spoke of an *acceptable* number of casualties. He shook his head, thinking *while old men are talking, a few thousand young men on both sides of these front lines have to bear this conflict pretty much by chance and are required to suffer and die for everyone else! So be it.*

That savage attack by enemy artillery and mortar fire had uncovered forgotten remains of soldiers from earlier fighting. As he often did, Arnold pondered how he came to be in such a sorry, godforsaken place. He thought of the people involved. . . .

1

Top of the list had to be the former popular artillery captain who—like Arnold's father—fought at the Meuse-Argonne. The man struggled and sometimes failed in business and politics and then, in 1945, found himself President of the United States! He said, "I felt like the moon, the stars, and all the planets had fallen on me." Arnold's Commander in Chief was Harry Truman.

As he took war command of the Far East United Nations Forces in June 1950, another great leader spoke of his appointment as "Mars' last gift to an old warrior." The incomparable Douglas MacArthur, a five-star general, with great confidence and against all advice, planned and led one last brilliantly successful attack, only to be bluntly fired by the President seven months later.

Of course, Arnold could hardly judge or understand those two—to him they were people often named in intercessions, news leaders; one considered a scrappy upstart, the other a demagogue.

Then he thought of other leaders who had met up with him and supported him: an infantry colonel courageously led his battalion here in Korea during the longest retreat in the history of American Armed Forces; a brigadier general first met him over a beer at an army camp in Japan; and a Republic of Korea colonel, speaking little English, presented him with an automatic pistol taken from a North Korean major Arnold had killed.

But ever on his mind were younger people befriended along the way, including the tall French girl who loved him, a foxhole mate who fell dead at his side, and now the second lieutenant who shared the hoochy with him.

As for the man himself, how did he merit those sergeant chevrons, and how did he end up in this foul-smelling hilltop of dirt, sand, and debris? He was so young—could it possibly be a long or complex story?

He wouldn't be sized up as either a big or a small fellow, just sort of average—his hair a sandy color and his profile strong, marked by a prominent nose and fully rounded chin. There was a sinewy vigor to his frame, combining a lithesome, graceful look with a natural gift of endurance and coordination. No, it amounted to more than that: call it exceptional motor reflexes—useful in many ways, fatefully including expert marksmanship.

He had always been a shy fellow, who didn't mind just listening to others talk. Yet, for all his quietness, he liked people, liked to be with his close friends. In his army days this meant standing around, hearing his buddies complain, since griping sessions seemed to reduce tension and boredom for newly inducted soldiers.

From boyhood, beneath Arnold Desprez' outward appearance, something smoldered—a restrained determination, a petulance, a contrariness. He recognized, perhaps earlier in life than most, that, paraphrasing favorite poet Robert Burns: sometimes our best-laid schemes fail *and leave us naught but grief and pain for promised joy.* He knew full well, from all he read and all he heard and all his own experiences, that it becomes necessary throughout life to face significant adversities, to fight, and give your all to win.

As a very young boy, he sometimes muttered, gritting his teeth, "I want it done right, and the right way is my way." But, as he grew older, he began to look beyond himself and to think about the feelings and actions of others—a broader concern, bringing him slightly out of his shell and making him a more likeable guy.

His father was proud of his son's gritty spirit and did nothing to blunt it, as he would say, "Defend your rights . . . don't be bullied" and—most often—"God helps them that help themselves," never anything like "turn the other cheek." His sweet mother once said, "If a bigger boy is picking on you, hit him with a brick!" So, in awkward times, he was prompted to shake his head and mutter, "Where's mom's brick?"

Pierre and Marie Desprez raised their four children in North River, a small community in northwest Minnesota—sugar beet and potato country. Arnold was born in 1933; his sisters Nancy and Norma were older and Lucey was younger. His position as

3

the only boy probably contributed to his solitary ways. While the girls usually supported him and were basically proud of him, they could be rude and selfish, he thought they sometimes took up too much of Marie's time with seemingly petty, unimportant things.

Marie was the family leader—a retired school teacher, an avid reader, and a radio news fan. At the dinner table, where family business was always conducted, she fed the children current events about the war, politics, and even sports. She might ask "What happened in school today?" The girls proffered many stories, but it took more prying with Arnold. One time he answered, "Nothin' much," leading Norma to say, "Why talk that way? I saw you kick that soccer goal today—speak up! Brag a bit!" Later on, he told his army buddies, "Dinner-time at the Desprez house was like a Troop Information and Education Class."

Pierre had a younger brother, Guy. The two were very different: Pierre had stayed in the farming country and worked at Harvey Brothers, the dry goods store owned by Marie's family, and Guy went off to the College of St. Scholastica in Duluth, working for an insurance company while still in school and then joining the business after graduating in 1926. With roots shifted to Duluth, he specialized in the great local industry—shipping.

Duluth was a growing city on the western tip of Lake Superior, at the mouth of the St. Louis River, opposite Superior, Wisconsin. The Duluth–Superior Harbor with forty-nine miles of water frontage was one of the finest in the world. In 1950, it ranked second only to New York City among U.S. ports in terms of commercial tonnage handled. Coal, iron ore, and grain were leading products. Guy had chosen the place to seek his fortune wisely, indeed.

Before Guy was old enough to start on this successful road, Pierre's life was interrupted by service in France in The Great War. Pierre rarely spoke of his war experiences and when questioned usually responded as briefly as possible. He once said, "With my storekeeper background, I served in the Quartermaster Corps and was in the St. Mihiel Offensive in September 1918 and then the Meuse-Argonne until the War's end that November. We kept a sharp inventory on everything, but if something was missing it was certified 'lost in combat.' Our most important chores were supplying edible food and potable water. We knew how to over-allocate food rations from the division commissary."

Pierre was in the army some twenty-two months, was overseas eleven months and in combat approximately one hundred days. His service was in the 353rd Infantry Regiment, 89th Division, and he emerged in that relatively short time as a sergeant—no simple accomplishment for a country boy.

Uncle Guy and Aunt Ruth had one son, Raul—just Arnold's age. In some ways, the two cousins had more in common than did their fathers: the boys both loved the north woods and farm country as remote and beautiful places to visit but not to live out their lives. Raul figured his future would follow his father's lifestyle, while Arnold knew in a vague way that his path would surely leave North River behind, but the problems of where and when were more challenging to him—all wrapped up in the bigger question of finding a career path.

The two fathers and their sons went moose hunting every October during the rutting season. When the boys were very young, they just tagged along; however, Pierre and Guy piled extra chores on the boys each year and awaited the time when they could stand by and watch Arnold and Raul do the planning and most of the shooting. Finally, Pierre ordained, "For the 1949 hunt, Guy and I decided you two will be in charge of everything: the dates, lodging, canoes, food, food menus, all camping gear, camp sites, shoot locations, butchering, even taxidermy. However, by popular demand, Guy will help with the cooking, and we'll all share clean-up."

In that final year, the four hunters drove straight north from Duluth to the Boundary Waters Canoe Area, rented canoes at Flintlock Lodge, Vermilion Lake, and headed north and east on a new route to Ebony Bay. Arnold felt extra tense, like this trip was special and the culmination of something important—not to be repeated.

They knew that a bull moose could be attracted with various calls and used a hand-made birch bark megaphone to mimic the wail-like call of the cow—the same method used in the old days by Ojibway hunters. Surprisingly, the best way to augment this call was not by remaining quiet and sneaky, but by thrashing in the trees and grass to imitate the big creature's noisy tromping.

Ebony Bay's hillside became the daunting scene of a charge by a 1,300-pound animal during that last hunt. They first heard it and then saw the head and antlers of a bull charging through the tall grass and scrub oak. Guy, Raul, and Arnold all firing, Arnold cocked and got off another round just when the animal turned; then Pierre, who had held fire, shot a broadside, as it disappeared from view. They dashed after the laboring creature, which soon fell.

"Biggest ever—maybe a sixty-inch antler spread," Pierre said with solemn respect, while the four stood over their mighty prize. Arnold resisted claiming to have fired the killing shot, though he was confident he had a hit in the chest area—dead center. He also realized that his father had held fire as a safety move in case the others missed. Pierre was the sort of hunter who was quite prepared to draw a charging animal toward him and stake his life at a range of six feet. Arnold mused, *my father is a simple man, but I love him and am proud of him.*

They winched the carcass head-first up a tree, and the boys butchered in the late afternoon and on into the evening by Coleman lantern, removing all entrails and using care not to puncture vital organs. They cut the upper chest cavity and tailbone with a bone saw, and the fathers condescended to help carry water from the bay to clean and cool down the carcass. Unwanted parts were left for the smaller animals. Finally, with the choice parts squared away, the boys ran bare-tail down to the bay, screaming as they hit the cold waters and washed the caked blood and residue from their hands and arms. Raul screamed, "What a great day!" Arnold fired back, "And how!"

They looked back as they packed out the next morning, watching ravens circling over the kill site while Pierre pointed and said, "Smartest birds ever, they're probably juveniles, charged with signaling friends and relations that there's a feast down below by Ebony Bay."

The canoes carried out the trophy head and more than two hundred pounds of meat for each family. Moose meat was delicious—a lot like beef but more tender, with less fat. Always the introspective one, Arnold said, "The meat will run out, not the memories."

Back in his younger years, Arnold disliked staying inside in winter when days were dark and cold. He went rabbit hunting on cross-country skis, played hockey, and skated for miles on the frozen ponds. He and his friends wore the kind of skates that could be strapped to the bottoms of their boots and easily removed for portaging. Little did Arnold know that these boyhood idylls were preparing him for harsh days when he would carry a rifle in a far-off land; still beautiful, but now a fearful place ironically called, "the Land of the Morning Calm."

The Desprez' side of the family was French–Canadian. Pierre's parents had come down from Manitoba to work the beet harvests and one year simply stayed. With all the Scandinavians in Minnesota, friends joked that Arnold, with his light complexion and blue eyes, could pass for a Swede. Pierre laughed and explained, "No surprise there. The family came from Normandy, a part of France raided some 1,100 years ago by Viking north men, the old cliché asserting they came to rob and rape, but they also settled. Arnold's Nordic ancestors were so fierce French King Charles the Simple ceded much of Normandy to the Viking raiders in the year 911."

This explanation was embellished by boasting that the Duke of Normandy—also known as William the Bastard—conquered England in 1066 and became known as William the Conqueror.

Arnold laughed at those royal names like The Simple, The Bastard, and The Conqueror. He collected more: the Bastard's father was Robert Le Diable, which meant The Devil—devil enough to beget the Bastard by bedding a tanner's daughter. Then there were English Kings: Athelred the Unready and Edward the Confessor, and his favorite, a Spanish Queen, Juana la Loca, which meant Jane the Mad.

He adapted that dubious title to call his sister Norma la Loca, but no one got one-up on attractive and perky Norma, who was just a year older than Arnold; she called her brother Arnold the Moper. The brother and sister then conspired: the eldest sister becoming Nancy the Noncommittal, probably because she had gone steady with the same fellow for two years and was a bit aloof with her younger siblings. Nancy the Snotty had also been proposed. Lucey the Pubescent was tried out around the house by Norma, who now referred to herself as Norma the Normal. Nancy was in school in Duluth and so unavailable for teasing, while younger sister Lucey blushed and complained to Marie who laughed at these antics but said, "Reaching puberty is scary enough; trot out a new name to make her feel good, like Lucey the Lucky, and remember, these fancy royal names shall not be expanded to include the parents!"

Arnold thought—*those family names strike close to home.* In his case, he could be a sulk, a mope. Nancy was indeed the distant elder who, years before, babysat for the others, led the way, and made the path easier for the younger ones. She was austere and perhaps a little arrogant.

In contrast, Norma was his true soulmate—like a fraternal twin. The two had few hang-ups about privacy around the house: helping, joking, teasing, pushing, and shoving. She claimed she was like Ogden Nash's "young belle of old Natchez," who drawled, "When Ah itches, Ah scratches."

Lucey was the family baby—age thirteen—a pretty girl, just blossoming; but now mostly silent, even more mopey than Arnold. He heard from Norma that Lucey was in some stage-or-other of puberty, which translated to none of his business, though in private sister Norma discussed such matters with him.

Pierre had grown up speaking both French and English and tried with some success to carry on the bilingual tradition with the children. Arnold continued his French studies in prep school, his fluency later shaping his life and proving quite a blessing.

In 1947, Arnold entered St. Patrick's Parochial School in Thief River Falls, a town of seven thousand located on the Thief River, which ran down from the marshlands to Thief Lake and finally to the Red River of the North. The Red had an unexpected course: one usually thinking of middle-west water flowing into the Mississippi; but this meandering river and its valley went north, forming the border with North Dakota and going on to Lake Winnipeg, its waters eventually reaching Hudson Bay. It really didn' seem like much of a valley—everything looking darn flat and dominated by rows of sugar beets with rotating fields of barley and wheat.

A sentimental cowboy song was said to have originated there, perhaps when a Canadian soldier left the river valley to return home:

> *Just remember the Red River Valley*
> *And the one who has loved you so true.*

In November of that same year, 1947, the United Nations General Assembly adopted a resolution that called for a general election in far-off Korea, under the supervision of a U.N. commission. The North Koreans refused to cooperate—not surprising, in retrospect, since any fair plebiscite would sweep them from power. Trouble with Communists was old news, even back in '47, so such matters were little noticed in rural Minnesota.

At dinner, Arnold asked, "Why can't we cut a deal with Soviet Russia; there's plenty of space in the world for both of us?"

Marie eyed Pierre who shrugged and nodded at her to take a try answering.

"Well, of course it's real complicated, but to try to answer your question directly, it's hard for us to have common ground with people dedicated to ending our way of life. Marx and Engels did all this theorizing in the past century about how the present bourgeoisie society must be replaced by the resolute working people—the proletariat—who would lead revolutions around the world. Private property was to be abolished so socialism could result.

"What actually happened was different from all that theory: Communist countries all came under totalitarian rule, dedicated through their International Comintern to the spread of their beliefs. Since rule was absolute, those in disagreement were simply shot or sent to places of great suffering, called 'gulags.'"

Norma nodded and finished the picture: "So, after the Second War all countries in the Russian sphere were given Communist leaders controlled by Moscow—including not only the Eastern Europe bloc but also North Korea."

Arnold nodded his head. "Yes, I understand all that, but it just annoys me so. I want the world to wake up and everyone to cooperate."

"So do we, son; so do we."

The mood everywhere was to forget about international troubles, disarm, build homes, and get on with peacetime and prosperity. Anyway, who had ever heard of that Korea place? Forget it.

St. Patrick's School, with its target of excellence, was about right for Arnold, not too big for the provincial kid, but large and varied enough to offer adequate preparatory classes and to stimulate the boy. He loved the literature classes and volunteered to do extra reading.

He was on the hockey team and learned to handle, even seek out, hard knocks and an occasional brawl, tending to overdo the rough stuff—like slamming a skater into the boards. At the prep-school level, with strict limits on body checking, he frequently ended up in the penalty box, leaving the team a man short. But there was no stopping him, as he would say, "When I'm on the ice, I seem to just skate mad." The coach, Brother Herman, would shake his head: "I'll take a bull over a chicken any time. Remember our Lord in the temple with the money changers, how He drove them out, how He overturned their tables? Even He had a temper!"

Arnold figured, *that's a mighty selective reading of God's Holy Word,* but he welcomed the coach backing his scrappy hockey play. Arnold also managed to get in his share of trouble with the nuns, and resented their firm discipline. He disliked anyone bossing him—an attitude to be more thoroughly challenged later on when the leaders were sergeants, not sisters.

During the summers of 1947 and 1948, Arnold and Raul worked as fishing resort chore boys in the Superior National Forest—halcyon times: beautiful country, healthy outdoor work, and a chance to pair up with the resort waitresses.

Arnold readily admitted that Raul was the Romeo of the family. With his dark, curly hair, long straight nose, and an exotic name—sort of like a foreign movie actor—Raul Desprez attracted more than his fair share of the ladies. Arnold realized *I'd do better if I weren't so darn bashful.* Still, both Desprez boys had lots of good times.

For their last two high-school summers, 1949 and 1950, Arnold's uncle found them work on a Great Lakes ore boat. Guy made it sound kind of romantic: "People don't realize what an incredible spot we have here in the Duluth Harbor and what a great opportunity this is. The Minnesota Iron Ranges, including the Mesabi Range that everyone knows about, constitute the largest iron-mining region in the United States. The Mesabi is some fifty miles northwest of Duluth.

"They mine the ore in open pits and ship it by hopper-bottom railroad cars to Duluth or other ports, like Two Harbors, Silver Bay, and Thunder Bay, where they grind and pelletize it. Here's where you boys get involved: there's seven iron ore docks in the Duluth–Superior Harbor where the processed ore, called 'taconite,' is dumped into huge vessels of up to 60,000 tons weight, called 'lakers' or 'boats.'"

Raul scratched his head, "I've always wondered, dad—if they're so big—why they aren't called 'ships.'"

Guy smiled, "You got me, son; all I know is they aren't and never were known as ships. That's all I know. Maybe it's because they're essentially just big barges with various operating facilities at each end. Anyway, their destinations are steel processing ports located across Lake Superior, through the Soo Locks at Sault Sainte Marie, and then to a choice of many ports. The point is, the ore boats are a big part of one of our most essential industries. What can be much more important than steel?

"You're going to make good money, learn a lot, and work your butts off. The food is great and you'll visit new, interesting places. Some trips go down Lake Huron, perhaps to Port Huron or through a series of rivers to Lake Erie to Cleveland, Detroit, Toledo, or smaller harbors. Others take the short Lake Huron passage southwest through the Straits of Mackinac, afterward down Lake Michigan, to the U.S. Steel Works at Gary, Indiana, or to the Inland Steel facilities at Indiana Harbor. This first summer, the destination will usually be Gary—just southeast of Chicago."

Guy's final admonishment was; "No tattoos, no boozing, obey orders, and keep your private parts in your pants—we want no women hollering for their kid's daddy."

Raul rolled his eyes and smirked at Arnold when he heard that one!

The jobs sure sounded great, especially to Arnold for whom it was all new and extra exciting. They were hired aboard *The Hawkeye*, a fine-looking ore carrier—Edwin Pierce, Master, and

Morgan Jones, First Mate. It stood at dockside: pilothouse and deck crew area located at the bow, with the stack, engines, galley, and the aft crew members located and housed astern, both areas painted white. The hull was a deep brown—appropriate, since it matched the color of raw hematite and didn't show rust.

The crew numbered twenty-seven, the boat's length 678 feet, beam 70 feet—a huge boat, yes, but some were larger. *Hawkeye* was independently owned, Arnold figured, by a company that worked with Uncle Guy's firm, thus providing the entrée for the Desprez cousins. The vessel had contracted to serve U.S. Steel.

The first voyage was extra thrilling for the boys, as they went through the venerable ritual of signing aboard—just as Ishmael had signed on the *Pequod* to go a'whaling.

There were hatches over fourteen separate compartments, connected by tunnels at the hull bottom through which the boat's self-unloading belt brought ore forward to where the giant white crane could raise the ore and deposit it on land, sometimes in trucks, sometimes in hopper cars, sometimes simply in a cone-shaped pile near dockside.

Arnold and Raul served as deckhands, their duties directed by a petty officer known as the 'bos'n'—a sourpuss respectfully called Mr. Ross. He immediately taught them to handle lines on the deck when entering and leaving a port. If the port had harbor-men working on the dock, they could throw 'heavin' lines' to those men, then attach the boat's heavy cables to the lines and, in this way, secure the boat's massive cables to bollards along the dock.

The deckhand held the heavin' line with about half of it coiled in each hand. The leading end was fastened to a heavy lead ball—called a "monkey fist," which was spun around to increase forward thrust, rather like a cowboy with his lariat, then heaved toward the dock—making sure the dock workers were watching. As the monkey fist flew and the line played out, the deckhand let go of the remaining coil, except for the rope's end—called the "bitter end." Often as not, there were no harbor men to assist so one of the deck hands had to retrieve the lines after swinging ashore on a boom—sort of Tarzan style. It might seem scary, but Ross had the cousins eagerly practicing before they even left Duluth harbor.

They learned that their trip from Duluth–Superior was referred to as "downbound" with return voyages called "upbound"—all part of a well-established, but strange, boat lingo.

Loading was a precise, gravity-driven process. The hopper cars deposited the ore in cribs high above the boats. Spouts from the cribs were centered over the open hatches, and the ore was allowed to cascade into the boat, the descending ore looking from a distance like a black fluid. The First Mate, Jones, directed this process so the boat kept what he called "a proper ballast" and was not overloaded. From time to time during the loading, the boat had to be repositioned to align hatches and spouts. Jones said, "It's a neat trick—putting on that last trimming run of ore!"

After loading, Ross directed the deckhands as they deployed the winches to close the fourteen heavy hatches. Then, as the boat inched from dockside, its deck and hatches covered with ore dust, the deckhands were required to wash them down with powerful hoses.

The hosing process was drudgery for the deckhands. Every two or three trips the cleaning was more intense—a process called "soogying." With boiling hot water, the hatches and the rest of the deck were blasted with pressure hoses, the deckhands needing boots and other protective gear.

As **Hawkeye** exited the Duluth Ship Canal, it passed under Ariel Bridge, a famous landmark, before it entered the open lake—largest lake in the world! Raul was able to spot his house—to port, high up on the north bluff. Both wondered what adventures lay ahead.

When the bluffs faded astern on the port side, there were less and less signs of civilization, allowing the boys to imagine the thrilling days when the early French explorers rowed west in birch bark canoes to bravely face the land of Sioux and Chippewa. The Apostle Islands on the south and, later on, Isle Royale to the north were lush and green above gray rocks and white water. Arnold never tired of the blue waters and varied shore lands. He wondered what lay over the hills, what would be over the hills for him—surely not the family store or some Duluth desk job, but what?

During the voyage, the deckhands were employed in normal maintenance, such as cleaning, scraping paint, and painting, and, when in port, also helping load and unload groceries and other supplies. For them, it was a normal, eight-hour workday, different from the rest of the crew who usually worked four hours on and eight off. For the most part, those crewmen were able-bodied seamen, called "Abs" once they passed the Coast Guard test in their specialty.

The Coast Guard required fire drills every week, and Capt. Pierce deemed it useful to get that ritual done on the first day downbound. The two neophytes were given safety instructions. Whether standing dockside or aboard, one of the main dangers was the shifting of mooring cables as the vessel took up slack. The massive lakers had vast inertia, not wanting to start or stop; in either phase the ever-tightening, moving cables were snarling enemies of the unwary—entitled to be feared and respected.

One small but revealing event occurred that first evening. Forward in the deckhand quarters, Arnold and Raul shared a double bunk, near one occupied by a wily old hand named McNabb. Arnold saw that McNabb had two pillows and his was missing. Righteous reaction was swift, Arnold's hand slamming down and recovering a pillow, as he phrased a leading question in a steady voice, "Was this mine or the other one?"

McNabb grasped half the pillow, and the two stood face-to-face—a wiry man and a raw youth half his age. McNabb smirked and said, "Think you're a tough guy, eh?"

The young boy bravely replied, "No, not at all, not at all, but I'll stick up for my rights; why should you have two pillows and me none?"

Fortunately, and probably realizing he had acted hastily, McNabb released the pillow, then came forward, actually patting Arnold on his left shoulder, saying with a snear, "I found the damn pillow on the deck; take care of your things and mind your manners!"

"A likely story" Raul said, standing next to his cousin in a show of solidarity.

Arnold had flinched when McNabb touched him with his right hand, thinking he was about to meet a left hook—grab with one hand, hit with the other—an old hockey move.

"We both gotta watch that codger," Raul whispered, "My remark may very well have added me to the old guy's shit list."

"Wow, Raul, when he reached out and touched me, I damn near let him have it; the old bird would probably have made hash of me! The next move is to cool it, right?"

"Right! There may be some feeling that we're dawdling with undeserved summer jobs—a couple a rich boys. He was testing us; let's stick together when we're on the open deck until we can better size him up."

On the second day, *Hawkeye* rounded Whitefish Point and turned due south into Whitefish Bay. More and more slips, wharves, and summer homes came into view on the Michigan shore, but to port—the Canadian side—there remained little but pines and the bare Precambrian rock of the massive Canadian Shield. It was prudent to hit these waters in daytime, since the Bay could lead to ship collisions, as vessels funneled into and out of the Soo Locks.

At the locks, Morgan Jones reported the boat's draft to the Coast Guard Inspector. There was no use trying to fool anyone since the Inspector could read the draft level at the bow, where the long row of numbers met the water line. The Coast Guard regulated all shipping on the Great Lakes and furnished many valuable services, especially disaster services. It took forty-five minutes to clear the four locks, which were needed because Lake Superior is twenty-one feet higher than Lake Huron.

There at the locks, another McNabb episode played out. The boys had swung down to the lock side and were headed toward the forward bollard, when the ten-pound monkey fist on the heavin' line flew from the boat and landed with a thud right in front of them—the dangerous thing barely missing. They looked up to see McNabb in the bow, laughing, waving, and yelling, "It's your job to watch the heaving line; pay attention, you helpless lubbers!"

Raul said, "He was obviously aiming at us—a head hit coulda been fatal. That was his little payback. Don't give him the satisfaction of bitching about it." Raul had it figured—it was a close call and a dirty trick, but there were no more antics from McNabb. After that, on dockside, they surer-than-hell kept an eye out for the heavin' line.

Off Sault Sainte Marie stood a small boat—the "victualer," sent to furnish fresh groceries and local foods as requested by the Chief Steward, all coming from the Great Lakes Fleet Warehouse. Arnold and Raul carried up boxes and crates of fruits and vegetables. This might seem unnecessary after only two days downbound, but laker meals were a traditional high point, an extravagance thought to be essential to compensate for the sailors' otherwise dull and lonesome lives—sans women, sans liquor.

The crew was also served by the mail boat and the bumboat—the latter a sort of floating department store.

Below the town, they entered St. Marys River—a narrow and dangerous run. Arnold watched with fascination as the wheelman stood on a raised platform and successfully managed to keep the massive, high-inertia vessel centered in the river's narrow, winding course. Once in Lake Huron, the bearing was due west—past Mackinac Island and through the Straits of Mackinac. Ore boats tried to stay clear of this area each July during the running of the Chicago-to-Mackinac Sailboat Race, an arduous event with a history going back to the last century.

Ferryboat service connected the lower and upper parts of Michigan and also served Mackinac Island, which Arnold eyed as they steamed by, and Mr. Ross—in a rare friendly moment—explained, "There's only pedestrian traffic going to the island—no cars. You get around using bicycles, horse carts, and shoe leather with the whole island smelling faintly of horse manure. That's Grand Hotel on the hillside—a real old-style summer place for the wealthy, said to have the longest front porch in the world. Then to the right you can see the battlements of old Fort Mackinac, built in 1780 by the British to control the fur trade."

Arnold fancied he'd like to come back there someday—*maybe on a honeymoon!*

From the straits, it was a thirty-six-hour run to the U.S. Steel Works in Gary. The boys watched as the green forests seen all the way down past the Straits gave way to views of houses, towns, beaches, and harbors along the western shore, then the megalopolis stretching almost uninterrupted from Milwaukee all the rest of the way south. Off Wilmette, Illinois, they saw the lighthouse, the harbor, and the spectacular Baha'i Temple. Then they passed Evanston and, finally, Chicago with its skyscrapers, including the Board of Trade Building, the Field Building, the Civic Opera Building, and many others.

At U.S. Steel's Gary Harbor, the ore was gradually moved forward by the self-unloading device and lifted ashore by the crane. Water was added for ballast, and supplies were loaded, the entire process taking six hours and resulting in about the same film of dirt as they faced back when they loaded. Without more, the boat was ready for upbound, and Raul and Arnold again hosed down the hatches and deck.

And so the summer cruised on. Sometimes a weekend intervened or repairs were required, providing for a layover at Gary, allowing the crew to go ashore, known as "going uptown"—more boat lingo. One time the boys took the South Shore Electric Line to Chicago, where they followed Marie's orders and visited the Art Institute and also saw the Cubs play.

Their Cub hero was Hank Sauer—a big, rough-cut outfielder who regularly hit 'em over Wrigley Field's ivy-covered wall and who also chewed tobacco and managed to spit about once a minute. The bleacher bums kept the big guy supplied by throwing tobacco packages to him. Arnold thought about trying a chew but realized it was a messy habit and would be forbidden on shipboard and certainly forbidden at home. Raul never considered such foolery that might stain his perfect teeth—teeth brushed after every meal.

Arnold was becoming more a man of the world. The old-timers introduced Arnold and Raul to their repertoire of smutty jokes and yarns; some were over their heads, but they would laugh and pretend to understand. The war veterans described navy life: some had seen battle, but for most it was the old song,

> *We joined the navy to see the world,*
> *And what did we see, we saw the sea.*

The crew tried many ways to amuse themselves, including poker, pinochle, and sheepshead, the latter a German–American game, especially popular in Wisconsin. No doubt, subjecting Arnold and Raul to those ribald stories was a time-honored way for men in their twenties to impress teenagers and also a way for everyone to pass the time—all part of growing up.

Two odd complaints were often heard: on hot windless days the horseflies were so bad they forced the crew indoors, a reasonable enough gripe, but the other complaint was that the food was too good, that they were eating too much, even going to the galley in between meals and putting on the pounds. It was certainly true that one seldom saw a slim boatman.

Especially when the weather was foul, a crewman would mumble the old saying, "Hell hath no fury like a Great Lakes fall storm." They made sure Arnold and Raul knew all about the terrible storms that plagued the Great Lakes, each year the worst apt to come in November, just before winter ice shut down the lakers. In 1940, fifty-seven men died when three freighters sank in Lake Michigan, but the worst tragedy was in November 1913, when 254 died and eighteen boats were lost.

Another somber one applied to Lake Superior: "The Lake does not give up its dead." This was certainly true. In most waters, bodies sank until bacteria caused swelling and the bloated remains resurfaced, eventually washing up on shore, but Lake Superior was so deep and so cold that the remains froze before those effects could occur and bodies simply glided to the depths.

Storms could explode across hundreds of miles of open water with little warning. Some sailors said they feared Lake Michigan most of all because of the sweeping winds and frequent wind shifts. The usual storm pattern involved cold arctic air heading south and meeting low-pressure storms coming up from the south. Boat companies fought those bad Novembers to get in the last runs before ports like Duluth–Superior were iced in.

He got to know the First Mate, Morgan Jones, and was invited to the bridge at special times to learn navigation. The ship was seldom far from land, and with radar and loran radio beams, there was not much that could go amiss except the weather. However, Jones saw that Arnold was a bright kid, might enjoy a career in marine shipping, and might decide to attend the Great Lakes Marine Academy.

The mysteries of the sextant were explained; he learned how to find latitude by sighting the sun and stars. Jones also provided a chance for him to train with the radio operator. With all this generous help, the First Mate was the first of a whole series of senior people who befriended Arnold and helped his career along the way. Of course, at that time, the question was: what career?

There were other so-called maturing experiences during layovers at Gary when the sailors sometimes went uptown across the Indiana border to Calumet City, Illinois. Calumet was the name given by the French in Canada to the peace pipe of the American Indians. Word had gone out among the hands: "Let's get Raul and Arnold some ladies in Cal City."

"Very funny," said Arnold, "but Raul is already the scourge of the north woods, and I was taught last summer by an eager, thirty-year-old dishwasher!"

Raul parried with his side of the story, "Arnold's friend was actually quite a saucy dish—hard to pan the way she looked."

Then Arnold got the last word, "We spooned until our relationship went to pot." The men could see that the two cousins had rehearsed their yarns—whether true or not.

Regardless, most Cal City fun was confined to its tawdry skin shows—a form of back-street burlesque. The shows had strippers with great show names, like Baby Ruth Barr and Sandy Claws.

Arnold later said, "That first summer on the ore boat was a great experience, but none of us realized that times were a'changing."

Chapter Two
A Police Action

Arnold and Raul completed their third years of high school and signed back on *Hawkeye* for the summer of 1950. The boat went downbound on 17 June and returned to the iron country for another run on 25 June. That very day, forces from the Democratic People's Republic of Korea—in other words Communist North Korea—invaded the Republic of Korea.

President Truman, who had been home in Independence, Missouri, flew back to the White House and met with his aides and the Joint Chiefs of Staff—all star-rank veterans of the recent war. Truman had already made up his mind, as he promptly said, "We've got to stop the sons-of-bitches."

So began the first armed clash between communist and free-world forces, a clash the President feared would likely be the start of World War III. The Cold War had been on since 1945, and Truman had fought several rounds with the Russians before Korea, including the Marshal Plan, the Soviet U.N. vetoes, containment in Greece, and the Berlin Airlift. His policies and his party were blamed for the fall of Chang Kai-shek's Nationalist Government and the takeover by Mao Tse Tung's Red Chinese, though there was little or nothing that could have been done to prevent it.

Arnold and Raul pondered their future: Arnold figured the U.S. would be dragged in, and, with conscription already in place, he would be drafted. Raul, on the other hand, at least hoped the U.S. could stay out, but also planned to continue in school and, if worst-came-to-worst, figured he could stay a civilian for a while by having a college deferment.

The rest of the boat crew, with so many navy vets, followed the war news with special interest, and they posited many what-ifs over coffee and meals as they paid attention to the radio and other news sources.

Everyone soon realized that the leaders in South Korea, and certainly in the United States, were unprepared and caught by surprise. Like most folks, Arnold and Raul hadn't known the sorry history of how, after the defeat of Japan, the United States occupied the south part of the Korean peninsula while the Russians set up a communist regime in the north. Both north and south had many problems, but conditions in the north were clouded in the mist of its isolationist, totalitarian rule.

The U.S. occupation authorities faced unique quandaries. After the Russo–Japanese War of 1905, all of Korea became a Japanese protectorate until officially annexed by Japan in 1942. Inevitably, all leaders of the Korean government and of key Korean industries for two generations had been Japanese—people deeming themselves a superior ruling class, which, by 1940, had swelled to a resident bureaucracy of 700,000 expatriates, who felt fully entitled to lord it over the Koreans, even requiring them to take Japanese names and to speak Japanese. All this dominance, this control of Korea, was completely by force, assuring that the Korean people hated their overlords.

And so the Koreans welcomed the U.S. occupation, no doubt thinking, *our hated enemy's enemy must—somehow—be our friend.*

Having lost the war, the Japanese were to be sent home. Everyone agreed and certainly wanted that, but the problem lay in a leadership gap so vast the American Army of Occupation had to rely on their former enemies to get anything done. To use the Japanese word, *honchos*—bosses—were needed. Although continued Japanese presence in leadership roles during the U.S. occupation was avidly resented by the South Korean people, there was at first no dominant party or coalition fit to take over; after all, how could there be after forty years of tight-fisted foreign rule? U.S. occupational forces were led by generals, colonels, and career diplomats, all facing new situations and feeling inexperienced, frustrated, and understaffed.

The Americans sought out the leadership of Syngman Rhee, the first leader of substance to return from exile. Rhee campaigned as an ardent anti-communist, and in this role, managed to eliminate not only the Reds but all other opposition and establish dictatorial powers.

Ironically, the American occupation of our Korean friends did not go as well as did the occupation of our Japanese enemies, where Gen. Douglas MacArthur headed the effort with spectacular success. He and his staff were headquartered in Tokyo's Dai Ichi Insurance Building, next to the Imperial Palace. Dai ichi means "number one," and the name certainly connected with the imperious Five-Star General. As he left the Dai Ichi each afternoon, people would stand alongside and below the raised entrance to catch a glimpse. MacArthur would emerge between lines of his honor guard, pause atop the entry steps, and for a moment look both ways, like a model on a runway; then, hurriedly pacing on, he would be whisked away in his five-star black Cadillac, all in a performance staged for the Asian audience and its abiding interest in face and prestige.

Like most Americans, Arnold and Raul did not know how the Korean dividing line was set back at the Potsdam Conference by the Americans and Soviets at the 38th Parallel—an artificial and supposedly temporary division of no particular significance except that it was a convenient line of latitude, cutting the Korean

Peninsula about in half and doing so at one of its narrowest places. That same line crosses the U.S. at about the level of St. Louis and San Francisco. However, because of weather patterns out of Siberia and because of its mountains, Korean weather was much more severe than at those same latitudes in the U.S., especially in the mountains of North Korea and along the 38th Parallel, where it could reach thirty below, without including windchill.

Raul said, "Now that I'm alerted to this split-peninsula problem and since I'm a draft-age kid, I've checked it out: we won the Pacific War with the Soviets not helping one bit; so we never should have let them set foot on the Korean Peninsula. Partitions don't work. From one country, we create two haggling neighbors—made weaker by standing alone. Trace it out in history: ancient Israel divided, Germany after the Great War and again in 1945, Ireland in 1921, India in 1947, and nothing worse than our own tragic experience, brother against brother, disaster of disasters—a house divided against itself cannot stand."

Arnold's studied reply: "I hear ya, cousin, but sometimes a bad boundary is better than religious or political chaos. Sometimes these artificial divisions eventually work, as they did in England–Scotland, U.S.–Canada, and Bolivia–Chile. Anyway, in this case, a narrow band of Soviet territory lies directly to the north, right across a river from Korea, so the Reds could hop and skip down the Peninsula before we could do anything, even shouting, 'Sorry it took us so long; we're here now to help out,' probably leaving us lucky to gain dominance of the southern half. Then, too, the bulk of the northern boundary fronted on their allies—Red China. Of course, that 'We're here to help' is a euphemism for 'We're here to steal Korea.'"

For what little it mattered, Arnold's analysis of Korean macro-politics at Pacific War's end was nearer reality than Raul's. When the U.S. XXIV Corps landed in Korea on September 1945, Russian troops were occupying Seoul and other parts of South Korea and, somewhat surprisingly, backed off to the north in accordance with Potsdam obligations.

Of course, any communist promise to cooperate with U.N. plebiscite plans was—as Arnold put it, "pure bullcrap"—and two Koreas resulted. Looking back five years later, in 1950, the notion that the Reds would honor any plebiscite, knowing that more voters lived in the South than in the North, seemed very, very naïve. We had learned a hard truth in those intervening years: if the communists move in, they aren't about to move out absent force of arms.

The North, known as the Democratic People's Republic of Korea, was led by Kim Il Sung, a legendary Stalinist ruler, holding absolute power. Kim was born Kim Song-ju in 1912—soon after the start of the Japanese rule. His family moved to Manchuria and lived there off and on. He attended Chinese schools and became indoctrinated by communist teachers, joined the Party, became a guerrilla leader, and was driven by the Japanese into Soviet territory, where he joined the Soviet Army, was trained and further indoctrinated.

Apparently several other Korean soldiers led guerrilla struggles against the hated Japanese, using the appellation *Kim Il Sung*, thereby suggesting to the Soviets that they simply attach the intrepid name to their protégé and thus carry on the myth of a "great fighter-leader," perhaps as if the English or the Americans introduced some dauntless character named Arthur Pendragon or Paul Bunyan. A despot with an alias was not a new device: few remember Schickelgruber, Jughasvili, or Ulyanov, but none forget Hitler, Stalin, and Lenin—names emitting strength and power.

It was quite a propaganda feat to prop this uneducated vagabond on the Pyongyang throne, since Kim was far from a naturally charismatic leader; instead, like many tyrants, he appeared a small, insignificant man. However, he did have an outstanding record from the communist viewpoint, causing the Soviets to extend and magnify Kim's persona and set him on the North Korean stage as the ideal leader—a big brother, a demigod—exaltedly called "dearly beloved, father leader."

Kim soon squelched all opposition, ousting even the Soviets, establishing a completely closed and stagnant society, millions purged, no freedom, no religion except the worship of Kim Il Sung, and no national goal except support of a huge standing army—unfortunately, an army with a goal!

In the south, Syngman Rhee ruled as a fascinating seventy-five-year-old autocrat who had been tortured by the Japanese and exiled to the U.S. in 1904. Apparently using hand-outs and chutzpah, he managed to graduate from Yale and Princeton (PhD), to become an ardent Methodist; to marry an Austrian-born, Caucasian woman; and to return home in 1945 on the heels of the Japanese defeat.

Rhee was far from popular at home or in the free world. Arnold heard his father sum up the sorry Korean situation: "We got a Commie Moscow puppet in the North and a tin-horn dictator in the South." Others simply said, "He's our guy and we're stuck with him," reminiscent of the days when America looked at Latin America and felt obliged to support banana republic dictators. Kim Il Sung referred to Rhee's government, hypocritically, but with some justification, as the "puppet clique."

As everyone recalled, in 1949 Chang Kai-shek was driven from the mainland, the communists thus claiming China—the biggest domino of them all. Few recalled that in the same year American troops departed South Korea, leaving only a Military Advisory Group, known by the acronym KMAG, of about 500 American military leaders to train the newly-formed Republic of Korea Army, known as the ROK Army. Use of KMAG was a dream growing out of the successful management of Indian troops by the British Raj in the last century, but in repeated attempts by several nations the expedient hadn't worked well since.

The uninformed Americans remained blind to the size, might, and intentions of the North Korean invaders. 90,000 Korean

People's Army soldiers in ten divisions poured across the Parallel, most heading southwest to target the major cities of Kaesong and Seoul, the capital. Soviet T-34 tanks led the attack and proved almost unstoppable.

Although the Soviet forces had replaced the T-34 in their own forces, it was still a very formidable fighting vehicle—considered the best tank of World War II when it outnumbered and crushed the German armor. It was a medium tank of twenty-six tons, low in height, very fast, long-ranged, and equipped with an 85mm gun.

Throughout the first week, news remained bleak. The ROK Forces were heroic in some instances but lacked the training, equipment, and numbers to meet the attack. Gen. Paik Sun Yup, then Commander of ROK 1st Division, reported that his men had never seen a tank! The troops suffered from what came to be called "T-34 disease"—a state of terror when the monsters rolled into view. Still, some heroic ROK soldiers made suicide attacks on the T-34s, using hand grenades and Molotov cocktails. The ROK Army possessed no armor, no heavy artillery, no spare parts, and no ammunition reserves, and, to compound these problems, their 2.7-inch bazookas—anti-tank rocket devices—could not pierce the T-34 armor.

The American public, certainly including the two Minnesota boys, knew none of these rotten—near fatal—details of military inferiority, but most felt, like Truman, that we had to stop the sons-of-bitches. In a calmer public utterance, the President explained that he found immediate intervention necessary to save not just Korea but, more importantly, to save what he termed "the concept of the United Nations."

Knowing there had been a conscription system since 1948, Arnold and Raul realized they were prime targets for a draft right after high school graduation in 1951 and then prime fodder for Korea. Of course, they didn't know the details of U.S. leader-ship or they might have been more exasperated. For example, the possibility of the North Korean invasion had not been seriously debated in Washington on the what-if list of potential dire events. If he had known about that sort of a manifest omission, Arnold would surely have been in one of his dark moods.

Gen. Douglas MacArthur, Supreme Commander of the Far East Command, called FECOM, was instructed to furnish aid, and on 7 July, MacArthur was named Supreme U.N. Commander.

Truman felt that he had no choice in this appointment: the general had served since the Mexican War, been a general in World War I, Commandant at West Point, leader of the U.S. Olympic Team, Chief of Staff, evictor of the bonus marchers, and Military Adviser to the Philippines. He led Aallied ground forces in the Pacific Theater, presided at the surrender ceremony, and then stayed on in Tokyo and did commendable work during the occupation.

But there were more aspects to consider than the impressive resumé: omnipresent politics lurked. The public looked for politicians to blame for China's fall, for the North Korean invasion, for our unpreparedness. Some considered Truman a President by happenstance—a political hack, hand-picked by corrupt "Boss Tom" Pendergast to run for Senate in 1934. MacArthur had a following among conservatives, a man on a pedestal—a far-off, unspoiled hero above the fray. Perhaps he was somewhat like long-serving FBI Director J. Edgar Hoover, but even more of a mysterious untouchable. Republicans found it easy to sneer at Truman, a little harder to be enthusiastic about the remote, cocksure FECOM leader.

He had already been testy and belligerent, close to insubordinate, on several occasions. The generals on the Joint Chiefs of Staff had been junior to him all their careers and had neither the wherewithal nor the desire to boss around their legendary elder. What does the Chief of Staff say to a man still on active duty with five stars—to his four stars—who had been Chief of Staff fifteen years before when he was probably a major?

With Louis Johnson now over his head and found wanting as Secretary of Defense, it could be asked what person or persons were left to control this remote, cocksure, and very able man? The answer was only the guy from Missouri—Harry S. Truman.

Raul and Arnold knew that their fathers were Bob Taft men, but it was a time of great befuddlement in the conservative camp. Adding to the national confusion, as American leadership faced the communist threat, suddenly it became the *McCarthy Era*. On 9 February 1950, Senator Joe McCarthy had given a speech in Wheeling, West Virginia, in which he claimed that the State Department was full of communists, his accusations soon leading to the term *McCarthyism*. Politicians tried to outdo one another in expressing anti-communist sentiments and accusing their rivals of being soft on communism. Folks like the Desprez family were at a loss to know where things really stood: were there communists and fellow travelers in the government in Washington and, if so, how about in the universities, how about in St. Paul, their State Capital? To Raul's credit, he quietly said, "This McCarthy stuff seems like bull-crap to me."

With whom could this remarkable fellow MacArthur be compared: Hannibal, Cardinal Wolsey, and other great leaders who changed the world, men of great power but not chiefs-of-state? Such individuals were unique, seldom found on the world stage. Secretary of State Dean Acheson referred to this "MacArthur mystique, giving him many of the attributes of a foreign sovereign." ROK Gen. Paik Sun Yup said he was regarded by Korean soldiers and civilians alike as "almost a god." Certainly no previous American had such extra powers. To many free-world leaders, these attributes seemed unusual and worrisome in the 1950 summer, and, by year-end, they seemed disastrous—panic-causing. Arnold, Raul, and the other boatmen hadn't thought it through that much, and many weren't old enough to remember those old glory days of the five-star man.

There was no request for Congressional approval of Truman's executive initiatives; and at a news conference, he responded to a question by terming the situation not a war but a "police action." The term stuck but was widely criticized as having a bad effect on the morale of American soldiers suffering and dying in what was obviously a very major war.

In one of history's significant coincidences, in January 1950, the Soviet delegate to the U.N. Security Council, Yakov Malik, walked out of the Council in protest over another matter and was still gone in June, allowing the Council to condemn the North Korean attack and to call for withdrawal. Two days later, a second resolution recommended that U.N. members furnish assistance to South Korea, all without Ambassador Malik being present to bestow the Soviet veto. This permitted the U.N. to intercede in a war for the first and only time when it was clearly on the side of one party and against the other.

Poorly trained and inadequately equipped U.S. troops formed the U.N. advance elements in Pusan, South Korea, and heroically held what came to be known as "the Pusan Perimeter." On *Hawkeye*, Arnold first heard the grumpy bos'n expound, "Them gooks will skedaddle when the good old GIs arrive," but such notions soon gave way to shock and amazement.

What did go wrong with the U.S. Armed Forces? Following World War II, the manifest and logical goal of reducing the size of the military began to clash with the continuing need to maintain its readiness during the Cold War. It was so tempting to balance the budget by cutting military expenditures. In 1949, President Truman appointed Louis A. Johnson Secretary of Defense. The man had served in the Great War, then practiced law, became a bureaucrat and head of Truman's campaign for president in 1948. He shared Truman's enthusiasm for cutting the military budget and also wanted to eliminate the navy and the marines, leading to the so-called *Revolt of the Admirals* and a Congressional investigation, centered on the cancellation of plans for a super aircraft carrier. Along the way, naval and other military strength was greatly reduced, and equipment, arms, and ships were dropped, scrapped, and mothballed to a point below the level needed for conventional readiness.

Inevitably, Secretary Johnson—a slicer, not a builder—took a large share of the blame for the sorry state of troops sent to Korea and the lack of strength to form a naval blockade. He resigned in September 1950, and was replaced by Gen. George Catlett Marshall—former Chief of Staff and former Secretary of State. Truman had gone from a political hack to the most logical choice—a highly regarded statesman.

The first U.S. troops in Pusan came from the occupation forces in Japan, soldiers then about to leave the completely pacified country and return it to full sovereignty as a democracy under the Emperor. Times of strife were past, as it became downright folksy there in the Land of the Rising Sun. There were no simulated combat exercises; marches gave way to motorized transport; armor could not be deployed on the narrow roads and weak bridges; and annual troop turnover exceeded 40 percent. The men had heated barracks, weekend passes, and fraternization on an unprecedented level with *musumes*, meaning young girls, but called "mooses." Soldiers of all ranks were marrying these devoted women and bringing them back to the States—one happy part of an over-indulgent military lifestyle.

These Japan–based troops began to arrive in Pusan on 29 June, and by 1 July, portions of the 24th Infantry Division were committed. The first organized unit was Task Force Smith.

In Japan, Lt. Col. Charles B. Smith, commanding 1st Battalion, 24th Regiment, 24th Infantry Division, was ordered to take his convoy to Itazuke Air Force Base. There, he met Maj. Gen. William F. Dean, commanding the 24th Division. Dean said, "When you get to Pusan, head north for Taejon. We want to stop the North Koreans as far from Pusan as we can. Block the main road as far north as possible . . . Sorry, I can't give you more information. That's all I've got. Good luck to you, and God bless you and your men."

The head-for-Taejon order pitted a poorly trained, depleted battalion, supported only by fleeing ROK soldiers, against nine North Korean divisions led by unstoppable armor. Call it 440 green Americans against 80,000 Asians.

Smith's force also met up with fleeing American advisors—the KMAG. Some of them, thinking they would never get out, said their acronym meant, "Kiss My Ass Goodbye."

War correspondents arrived, and Arnold and Raul followed their discouraging reports. Task Force Smith first met the enemy at Osan where they fired howitzers and bazookas at the oncoming T-34 tanks without effect and were forced to retreat in disorder. Like the ROK forces, these early Americans lacked armor, artillery, anti-tank weapons, naval gunfire, air support, and experience.

All units, but especially the artillery battalions and air reconnaissance and air support units, were further hampered by a lack of maps. Some parts of Korea had never been mapped, and available maps were old and usually prepared by the Japanese. People back home didn't realize that an army must mobilize, must put together thousands of details, mustering men, materiel, food, clothing, transportation, intelligence, and, finally, a plan for action. No modern army can do that in two weeks.

Again, lack of the newer 3.5 bazooka was critical against the T-34 Soviet tanks. To add to the confusion and just plain bad luck, Maj. Gen. William F. Dean, 24th Division Commander, was captured and doomed to sit out the war in a Manchurian prison camp.

There were tragedies aplenty: one was on Hill 303—so named for its height in meters—which lay on the east side of the Naktong River, as it ran south and formed the western boundary of the Pusan Perimeter. It was in the lines held by the 1st Cavalry Division and was fought over in the month of August.

The 5th Cavalry Regiment regained Hill 303 on 17 August, 1950, and, sadly, came upon the bodies of twenty-six brother soldiers from How Company, hands tied and slaughtered with burp-gun bullets.

This episode gained wide publicity, and the Desprez boys ranted when they heard about it. Meanwhile, traffic on the Great Lakes increased, as the nation geared up for war. Steel was suddenly in huge demand.

The enemy attempted to cross the Naktong River on 14 August. This was a determined effort at the Yongpo bridge-crossing, some eight miles south of Hill 303. The 7th Cavalry Regiment, then in reserve, went forward on an hour's notice and eliminated the bridgehead. Among the many documents recovered from enemy casualties, one was a leaflet, sent to the troops in the last day or so, that read:

Kim Il Sung has directed that the war be carried out so that its final victory can be realized by 15 August . . ."
Our victory lies in your eyes. Young soldiers! You are fortunate in that you are able to participate in the battle for our final victory. Young soldiers, the capture of Taegu lies in the crossing of the Naktong River . . . The eyes of 30,000,000 people are fixed on the Naktong River crossing operation . . .

But the tide was turning. How Kim Il Sung's young soldiers fell at the Naktong! At the Yongpo, they fell at the hands of the 7th Cavalry Regiment, which is undoubtedly the only military unit to celebrate Annihilation Day—wiped out under Custer at Little Big Horn, Eastern Montana Territory on 25 June 1876—seventy-four years to the day before the North Korean invasion!

Lt. Gen. Walton Walker, 8th Army Commander, swore that, "Pusan will not be another Dunkirk."

At their usual robust dinner on the ore boat, Arnold asked, "What the hell's a Dunkirk?" He learned Dunkirk was a French port where 340,000 badly beaten troops of the British Expeditionary

Force luckily escaped by sea in May 1940, saved by the British Navy and a flotilla of small craft but leaving their weapons and materiel behind. Arnold was only seven at the time.

Gen. Walker had been a disciple of Gen. Patton who called Walker "a fighting son-of-a-bitch." Walker quoted from Patton's writings and followed what he considered Patton's approach to warfare, though without his mentor's charismatic leadership. However, the mountains, rice paddies, and extreme cold of Korea proved to be a far different tactical environment from the more open and more temperate tank country of Patton's European battle sites. This difference was not fully understood by the U.N. leaders or by the on-the-spot commanders.

Walker, a pudgy little man, appeared popular with his soldiers and the American press but did not get on well with MacArthur and his staff—not surprising, since that group, known derisively as the Bataan Gang, did not get on with most outsiders, including the CIA, the Joint Chiefs, the State Department, the President, and others back in Washington, D.C. Walker was particularly at odds with Maj. Gen. Edward Almond—MacArthur's Chief of Staff. Walker liked to move his jeep at high speeds, chauffeured by a sergeant who had been with him since Europe in World War II.

The important City of Taejon was lost, and battles were centered along the Naktong River in defense of Taegu and Pusan. However, additional army divisions arrived in July and August as well as a brigade of Marines and a brigade of British troops. The situation stabilized, and a strange condition arose: U.N. forces on the defense actually outnumbered the fervently-attacking North Koreans, whose best frontline troops were being cut down and whose supply lines were over-extended. That supply line ran down the only road and rail system from Seoul, as MacArthur well knew. Since July, he had planned to cut that line!

Arnold and Raul continued to tend to their duties, always wondering if something would go right—if there could be some good news in the so called police action. They left *Hawkeye* on

10 September, each returning home for his senior year. Arnold and his classmates took pre-induction physicals; most of them, including Arnold, were classified 1-A, and deferred until graduation.

In a controversial surprise move, on 15 September 1950, Gen. MacArthur planned and led an amphibious landing at Inchon, a seaport on the Yellow Sea some forty miles west of Seoul. Inchon was hailed a brilliant success, in part because most strategists overrated the difficulties caused by the great tides in the beaching area. Speaking of tides, Inchon was the high water mark in the last command of the "American Caesar" and no doubt contributed greatly to his political invulnerability and his famous sense of self-esteem.

The great Inchon move cut the North Korean supply line. Armored units broke out of the Pusan Perimeter, soon united with the Inchon forces, and pushed north. The marines took Seoul on 26 September.

Interestingly, it was later learned that Mao Tse Tung and Chou En-lai, sitting in Beijing, had concluded that there would be a U.N Forces landing at Inchon on 15 September—the precise date being predictable by analyzing tide charts. They warned Kim Il Sung, but the North Korean dictator, full of bravado, ignored the advice.

A significant event occurred on 1 October 1950, when U.N. Forces crossed the 38th Parallel, causing Mao to conclude that he could not stand by and see his comrade neighbor overrun. Chinese Marshall, Peng Dehuai, who led Chinese Forces in Korea, was ordered to a meeting in Beijing. Mao asked Peng and other advisors to state the disadvantages involved in dispatching troops to Korea. Afterwards, Mao said: "You have reasons for your arguments. But at any rate, once another nation is in a crisis, we'd feel bad if we stood idly by."

That moment could well have been when the die was cast. In retrospect, Mao's attitude would seem predictable, but MacArthur, who claimed to understand the Asiatic mind, forcefully took the position that the Chinese would not intervene. There was a feeling among some experts that China had a long reputation as a crybaby that never struck back, and some American strategists were caught up in that unfortunate mindset.

The Supreme Commander's opinion became such entrenched doctrine at the Dai Ichi headquarters that his staff officers were in a state of denial even after some Chinese soldiers had been taken prisoner and readily admitted they were in Korea in great force.

The Dezprez family shared the common American attitude, the common talk, "Darn right we're going after them; why stop at the 38th Parallel?" Similarly, there was little talk in official Washington, D.C., of stopping at that boundary. However, from the initial incursion by North Korea, George F. Kennan, State Department Planner and later Ambassador to Moscow, warned that, if we were successful in expelling the enemy from South Korea, we must stop at the boundary and settle for restoring the *status quo ante* on the peninsula. Truman listened to more hawkish advisors—Acheson and Dulles, as they joined in the irrational groupthink.

Regardless of what the U.N. Forces might do, Syngman Rhee had already ordered the ROK Forces to keep going. And so, the Joint Chiefs directed MacArthur to drive on with the mission of destroying the North Korean Army but with one inhibition: in territory near the Chinese and Soviet borders he was to deploy only ROK troops. Perhaps most people would say, moving on north was no more than human nature, or, as now hawkish Arnold said to his naturally cautious mother, "If you are chasing someone who attacked you from behind a tree, are you going to stop at the tree and let him escape?" With Pierre nodding in agreement, all Marie could do was shake her head.

Under these temporarily favorable conditions, President Truman met General MacArthur at Wake Island 15 October 1950. Wake was a sorry-looking dot in the North Pacific, really a coral atoll of three little islands—2.8 square miles. The deep blue waters of its lagoon held the remains of sunken ships, and parts of Japanese tanks rusted by the airstrip—all in all, a very weird place for two great leaders to meet.

Truman said they were there to discuss the final phase of the war. He had approved MacArthur's instructions from the Joint Chiefs directing the move above the 38th Parallel, but he was alarmed by various acts, claims, and recommendations of the general, who advocated more widespread action. The two had never met—not surprising since the general had not been in the States in many years, and the President was fairly new to the world stage. The President dressed him down, as they rode in Wake's only automobile, the gist being, "I'm the boss, and don't you forget it!"

Arnold queried at the dinner table, "Why should the President of the United States travel halfway around the world to meet with someone?"

He thought the general should just be summoned to Washington; however, Pierre argued that the Far East Commander could not leave his post for the week-or-so necessary for any round trip. Arnold didn't want to argue with his father, but he muttered to himself, *bullcrap; why not have a summit meeting in D.C., invite Prime Minister Atlee of England, Prime Minister Pleven of France, the Joint Chiefs, and perhaps other free world leaders and show MacArthur that he is just the FECOM leader and only one of many able people—world leaders—whose voices must be heard.*

Noticeably, the general did not salute when they first met on the Wake airstrip. This gross slight was highly symbolic. While there were reports that the general was rude, Truman wrote that the meeting was more courteous than he expected. The President did, however, express annoyance that MacArthur was so informally dressed, without a tie and wearing his scruffy, twenty-year-old, scrambled eggs cap.

What a difference between the two! Truman been a National Guard Captain in World War I and had developed a dislike for general-grade military, which carried over in his later life, with the major exception of George C. Marshall. MacArthur, of course, realized full well that he had no equal and that this second-rate politician was beyond comparison. In any case, the meeting was just political theater.

Truman had spoken earlier of a police action at a press conference. What was probably on his mind was a "limited war" concept. To MacArthur, limited war was an oxymoron; you fought to win or you didn't fight—mighty tough words, sounded right on. The materiel and manpower he requested indicated his plan to expand the war. He wanted to deploy Chang's forces, to form a naval blockade, and to bomb Chinese installations in Manchuria, north of the Yalu.

Back home, the generals and the politicians were feeling their way: seeing a plateful of trouble, hoping and planning not to provoke the Soviets enough to start World War III, nor provoke China into attacking Taiwan, nor dilute the European ground troops enough to invite Soviet attack in that arena. The European partners in particular were leery of MacArthur's saber rattling. Many saw Korea as a feint by the Soviets and worried about concern number one—tanks rolling out of East Germany.

More and more leaders believed that what was needed was a force capable of making the punishment fit the crime, applying power adequate to contain the threat. The idea, not yet clearly enunciated, was that one superpower must be allowed to fix perceived problems in its sphere of influence and the other powers must stand aside, no matter how distasteful the fix might seem. Bigger problems like Korea should be handled in limited ways. There would be some unfortunate results, but those would be far better than Armageddon.

On the other hand, MacArthur saw avenues toward success in Korea that were being denied him, causing unnecessary casualties and prolonging the conflict. The State Department and Joint Chiefs were holding him back, forcing him to argue, talk to the press, make his case, tread a fine line, and, sometimes, go over the line and do as he pleased.

At the time, it seemed fairly reasonable to be the advocate of either the Truman or the MacArthur positions. Arnold did not profess to understand his leaders' different approaches. At face value, the President had gone to Wake Island to discuss what to do in the soon-to-end conflict. He also saw that the meeting was considered good politically for Truman's Democratic Party, with Congressional off-year elections coming up in November.

Four days after the Wake Island meeting, Pyongyang, the North Korean Capital, fell. Did it manifest a great triumph or presage a Pyrrhic victory, like Napoleon arriving in Paris after his return from Elbe? Actually, the Emperor had one hundred   days—the U.N. Forces had less time.

Walker's 8th Army pushed toward the peninsula top, toward the newly famous Yalu, a shallow and silted river, 491 miles long, separating North Korea from China, with its headwaters at Paeku-san—the white-headed highest mountain at nine thousand feet.

Arnold and his friends perked up; they would not have to go after all; the war was nearly over. Perhaps they would serve, since there was a draft, but it would be a peacetime situation.

Similarly, 1st Cavalry men were hoping to be in a Thanksgiving victory parade in Tokyo and were planning to wear their yellow cavalry scarves. Although the division had been dismounted since 1910, the horse cavalry tradition was lasting and deemed important, especially in the 7th Cavalry Regiment—Custer's last command.

Meanwhile, six ammunition ships carrying 105mm and 155mm shells were diverted back to Hawaii. On 25 October, Gen. Walker said, "Everything is going just fine."

Still, the speed of the advance worried Walker. To his east, and across the watershed Taebaek Mountain Range, the 1st and 7th Marine Divisions, constituting X Corps, also moved north. MacArthur had split the command: the marines were kept separate from the 8th Army and were led by Army Maj. Gen. Edward Almond, who reported to the Dai Ichi, not to Walker, whom he disliked. X Corps reached the Chosin Reservoir. The cold was extreme, reaching 20 to 30 degrees below zero, not counting wind chill.

Perhaps, the senior military thought of those glorious sweeps through Germany in 1945, of the armored units pushing forward, unstoppable until they ran short of fuel, then holding only until refueled and off again, like the Spearhead Division moving east 101 miles in a single day. Knowing only that it was cold, terribly cold, the men plodding along the dirt trails of North Korea saw no such heroics. With no respite, they were cold twenty-four hours a day for weeks on end! Their first concern was frozen feet—not the enemy.

The 7th Regiment of the ROK 6th Division actually reached the Yalu on 26 October.

Almond, MacArthur's Chief of Staff and a favorite, sensed a chance for glory and did not share Walker's concerns. In any case, both 8th Army and X Corps separately prepared to press on, having all but destroyed the North Korean Army, not knowing as they prepared to move north that a new, unseen, unknown, and more formidable enemy prepared to attack!

Chapter Three
A New War

They said they would intervene, and they meant it. The first appearance of the Chinese Communist Forces (CCF) in strength was at the Battle of Unsan, 1 and 2 November. Chinese soldiers captured days before were perfectly truthful: "I'm a Chinese soldier . . . we're here in great force." Because MacArthur said it wouldn't happen, Allied Command ignored these warnings.

From out of the northwest, they struck the 1st Cavalry Division and the ROK 1st and 7th Divisions at Unsan. The 8th and 5th Cavalry Regiments suffered heavy casualties and retreated to south of the Chongchon River. The Chinese didn't follow, simply disappearing. This very serious encounter, again, was not heeded. The 8th Army drive went on—an insane plan—and the 17th Infantry Regiment of the 7th Division reached the Yalu.

The tragic fact is that the CCF knew all about their unsuspecting enemies, who still headed north into a trap. These fresh, new intruders appeared to U.N. Forces like misty shadows, in unknown numbers, perhaps crouching somewhere north of the Chongchon, perhaps headed home.

No, they didn' go home: while Arnold and the other St. Pat's boys were tending to senior-year studies, the Chinese swept down from their sanctuary beyond the Yalu. Hundreds of thousands came, wearing warm, padded uniforms with no apparent distinctions in rank, sending signals by bugles, whistles, and shepherds' pipes. Well-equipped and self-reliant, many were veterans of the struggles with the Japanese and with the Kuomintang, as Chang's Chinese Nationalists were called.

A Chinese soldier could carry enough rice and other supplies to sustain him for a week without support. They had no armor or heavy artillery, no air power, poor radio communications, few trucks, no systematic logistical support. Their most handy weapons were just mortars and burp guns—but those two were arguably the best basic weapons used by any force in the Korean War. When they lacked sufficient handguns to go around, the second wave would run forward unarmed and pick up weapons of the fallen first surge, as the Russians had done at Stalingrad. It was a peasant army, perhaps one of the last in history.

CCF marching discipline was amazing, comparable to famous marches of antiquity: the Roman Legions doing twenty-four miles in five hours, Caesar marching fifty miles in twenty-four hours. A CCF Army of three divisions marched 286 miles in sixteen to nineteen days. One division marched over mountain roads eighteen miles a day for eighteen days. Marches began at 1900 hours and ended at 0300 the next day. All stopping points were camouflaged by daybreak, after which a scouting party would go forward to pick the next bivouac. In this way, the Chinese moved 300,000 troops into position.

Red leader, Marshal Peng, explained that they employed the tactic of purposely showing themselves to be weak, increasing the arrogance of the enemy, letting him run amuck, and luring him deep into the mountain areas.

What followed was the longest retreat in the history of the U.S. Armed Forces. The 7th Infantry Division made it so far north that it was almost annihilated during this first CCF offensive. Only 385 soldiers of its 3,200-man force survived. From 29 November to 1 December, at Kunuri, the Chinese virtually destroyed the 2nd Division; 4,940 men were lost.

Kunuri lies on the south bank of the broad-but-shallow Chongchon River. Roads run north–south and east–west from the small town, the southern route winding about twenty miles to Sunchon, the west road about an equal distance to Anju. Because the CCF XIII Army Group advanced en masse from the Unsan area in the north, there was an apparent, but false, advantage to retreating due south on the Kunuri–Sunchon road. For the first six miles the road was flanked east and west by rolling hills. Then there was a tight pass, often blocked by disabled vehicles. Years from now, those six miles—from Kunuri to the pass—would be remembered as "The Gauntlet."

The Chinese gave the impression they had not yet reached this stretch in any force. A word has come to be used repeatedly to describe Chinese tactics: the U.N. Forces were lulled. The road was to be 2nd Division's escape route. 9th Corps Commander, Maj. Gen. "Nervous John" Coulter ordered Gen. Keiser to take the 2nd Division out by the south road. There were probably two better choices: form a perimeter and, though surrounded, fight it out or take the west road to Anju.

It was not to be. A division of CCF lined the hills along both sides and also held the pass. It was, indeed, a gauntlet—commonly defined as "a torture in which the victim is made to attempt a run between lines of enemies." The Chinese peasant army clung to the hills east and west and destroyed the highly mechanized, road-bound American forces in a replay of what the Finnish ski troops had done to road-bound Russian armor at Suomussalmi during the Winter War of 1939–1940. Horror of horrors, drivers who made it through the Gauntlet reported "bumping over soft lumps in the road." In a part of one morning, 2nd Division lost 2,000 killed and wounded in the Gauntlet.

Meanwhile, at the Chosin Reservoir, army Gen. Almond was slower than his own marine troops in seeing the danger. Forty thousand Chinese were encircling the area with 100,000 more approaching; although faced by ample evidence, Almond actually ordered the marines to force their way north—an arrogant, blind march to disaster.

Most of the 2nd Battalion troops of the 7th Marine Regiment, 1st Marine Division, were located west of the reservoir at Yudam-ni village, while fourteen miles south and just below the massive reservoir, the 2nd Battalion Command Post was located at Hagaru-ri, together with a landing strip and an artillery base. In between those villages, Toktong Pass was held by Fox Company on Fox Hill where 192 officers and men fought off attacks by battalions of Chinese from 27 November to 4 December. Unable to dig foxholes in ground frozen hard in the minus 15 degrees cold, the Fox men used Chinese corpses to build protective shelters. The enemy had fallen in attack after attack under hand-to-hand combat; small-arms fire, mortars, and artillery; and Corsair runs, resulting in a blanket of dead Chinese so plentiful it was hard to avoid stepping on them. Bodies simply froze. They neither bled nor stank.

The gallant remnants of Fox Company were finally reinforced by surviving troops from Yudam-ni. Three men on Fox Hill were awarded the Medal of Honor.

Those eight days of resistance bought time. The encircled 1st Marine Division fought its way southward under the leadership of Marine Maj. Gen. O.P. Smith, all the time outnumbered and suffering from extreme cold. As Smith put it, since they were surrounded, they were merely attacking in a different direction. They moved through places made famous by their struggles: Yudam-ni, Fox Hill, Hangaru-ri, Koto-ri, Hamhung, and finally to the Hungnam seaport—known as the Hungnam Perimeter.

Winter took the greatest toll. Marine casualties were 718 killed in action, 192 missing, 3,508 wounded, plus an even more daunting statistic: 7,313 losses caused by frostbite or indigestion ailments! At Hungnam, 105,000 U.S. troops, ROK troops, and civilians were evacuated by sea. This was not a Dunkirk, because most of their equipment went with them. Although a retreat—no matter what O.P. Smith called it—it was an extrication from bad planning and even worse intelligence work at FECOM; and, it was a proud moment for the U.S. Navy and Marines.

Arnold and his friends generally knew that the Chinese had intervened with bad results, though details of the 8th Army defeat and the marine escape were not disclosed. All Arnold's hopes of avoiding the conflict were dashed, the American public aghast, the Administration defensive, the Allies pondering the quality of U.S. leadership. Frowning eyes turned to the recent Wizard of Inchon who was quick to say, "Not my fault."

The U.N. Forces were over-extended and high command out of touch. The men at the front—company grade officers, sergeants, and ordinary grunts—could look out and see what was happening and knew the score, having seen and been hit by the new enemy and having taken Chinese prisoners who readily told the Americans about the massive extent of the intervention. However, with field grade and general grade officers at regiment, division, and corps levels, there was confusion. Word came up from lower echelons describing companies surrounded, platoons wiped out—bugles and whistles! But orders came down to hold the line or even to keep advancing.

There was too much trying to emulate Patton—too much trying to go until you run out of gas. The topography and weather were not right. At the higher levels, orders were received from Supreme Headquarters at the Dai Ichi Building in Tokyo. The sainted words remained: "The Chinese will not intervene." Secretary of State, Dean Acheson, referred to this reaction as "Schizophrenia at GHQ."

Gen. Keisler, 2nd Division Commander, had lost control at Kunuri. He radioed Corps Headquarters where Gen. "Nervous John" Coulter was not about to change orders from MacArthur, with whom he had served since World War I.

47

Almond, with X Corps, served as MacArthur's Chief of Staff and was caught up in the same state of denial—a damned travesty. When Almond was presented with captive Chinese soldiers, he referred to them as "just a bunch of laundrymen." Disdain for Orientals was another manifestation of Almond's extreme racial prejudice, the man having ardently opposed integration of the U.S. Armed Forces.

Much blame was placed on Maj. Gen. Charles Willoughby, who was FECOM G-2, in charge of intelligence, and an original member of the so called Bataan Gang of officers who had been with MacArthur since World War II. Willoughby deliberately distorted accurate and convincing intelligence, which brought him the fervent dislike of the CIA and intelligence officers throughout the services.

MacArthur's staff prevented an organized, timely retreat that would have saved thousands of lives. Since the Chinese intervened anyway, it is possible to argue that the outcome might have been better if the general had been given more latitude in attacking the enemies; at least that was his claim and his basis for saying, "Not my fault."

All this must be compared with the action taken by Maj. Gen. O.P. Smith, 1st Marine Division, who defied Gen. Almond and thus the whole MacArthur chain of command, saved his men, and emerged one of the heroes of the war.

President Truman had said there was always the possibility of using atomic bombs. That shook up the British, causing Prime Minister Attlee to fly to Washington and have it out with the President. A new approach was dawning. The British saw the Chinese as rather independent of the Soviets—not a mere satellite. In fact, the war was instigated unilaterally by the North Koreans. There was no monolithic global communism. It was dawning on leaders that since the whole idea in defending Europe was containment, not conquest, why couldn't the same approach apply in Asia?

Thus, in December, there was more of a swing to accepting limited war on the heels of the big-bomb talk. Of course, there had been consideration at high levels about using these bombs all along, but the Joint Chiefs advised that there were really no strategic targets left in Korea worth using some of the country's then-limited supply of atomic bombs. One of MacArthur's proposals was to create a nuclear wasteland north of the Yalu.

While facing the indignation about bomb use in Asia, people in-the-know understood that atomic bombs were the planned defense against Soviet tanks rolling out of East Germany. How else would the handful of NATO divisions contain the swelling Soviet armor?

Back in Korea, luck next ran out for fast-driving Lt. Gen. Walton Walker. He was killed in a jeep accident on 23 December and replaced by Lt. Gen. Mathew B. Ridgway. Actually, it was time for a change in the 8th Army Command, and Ridgway quickly proved he was the man for the job. Although one cannot applaud the death of a true American hero, the change was a good one.

There was despair among the U.N. Forces as the year ended, and in January 1951 MacArthur talked of having to evacuate troops from all of Korea. For sure, there would be no unification of Korea. The Third Phase CCF Offensive forced U.N. troops fifty miles south of the 38th Parallel. Seoul was lost on 4 January 1951. However, Ridgway's counter offensives, Operation Thunderbolt, Operation Killer, and Operation Ripper, turned the situation around, and Seoul was retaken on 15 March. In April, MacArthur, the old Supreme Commander, was finally relieved—Ridgway taking his place, and Lt. Gen. James Van Fleet assuming command of the 8th Army. Van Fleet was a member of the West Point Class of 1909, the class the stars fell on, where 59 of 164 total cadets became generals, with Bradley and Eisenhower becoming five-star generals.

In the spring of 1951, there were a series of offensives by the Chinese and more counter offensives by the U.N. Forces. The emphasis in the U.N. attacks was to kill maximum numbers of the enemy—by exploiting air superiority, vastly superior firepower, and adequate supply lines facing the extended Communist supply lines. Chinese Fifth-Phase battles, between 22–30 April, cost the enemy 70,000 casualties; between 16–20 May, 105,000 more—staggering numbers in a huge failure. Joint Chief Omar Bradley said that Ridgway had "turned the tide of battle like no other general in our history." By June, the Soviets instigated talk of negotiating a ceasefire, and on 10 July, armistice meetings began at Kaesong.

By summer 1951, the conflict had turned into trench warfare in the highlands along the 38th parallel, with killing continuing on a large scale. The Chinese suffered badly as soon as the U.N. Forces became well-trained and gained proper respect for their enemy, meaning that the Chinese peasant army could no longer lull their chastened opponents—could no longer simply out-smart the U.N. commanders. Meanwhile, no progress was made on the battlefield or at Kaesong. It was a stalemate.

Chapter Four
Worry and Foul Weather

When Arnold graduated from St. Patrick's in May 1951, the Korean War was firing along unabated. Four U.S. Army divisions participated in Operation Piledriver to secure an area known as the Iron Triangle, and the U.S. Marines encountered heavy resistance from the North Korean People's Army in the battle for the Punchbowl, leaving three hundred killed in action, 3,831 wounded.

All very worried, the Desprez family contemplated Arnold's future. They pleaded with him to prepare college applications but he protested, saying that he wanted a break from academics, that money paid by Pierre and Marie for tuition would be wasted at this point, and that he worried about family expenses and the faltering family business, sensing that it would be good for business to have his in-uniform picture in the store window. He knew that boys from the class ahead of him were dropping out of college or trade school and going in to the service. Most local boys were volunteering.

It all came back to looking around and seeing that the insurance business in Duluth and similar sorts of office work held no appeal. He wanted to avoid doing the same thing over and over for forty years, then retiring—going out to pasture. He remembered a school friend saying, "My father didn't have forty years experience in the retail business; he had five years experience eight times."

So, what was he thinking? Deep down, what was on his mind? He knew he was stalling, suffering from untimely restlessness, wanting to be on his own, and figuring that his time in the service—however unpleasant, however dangerous—would snap the rut he was in, like kicking over the chess table and starting over. Besides, army service would give him the GI Bill college benefits.

The thought of college now seemed awkward: *maybe I can avoid accounting, business, and agriculture—the usual subjects; maybe, just maybe, I could embark on a liberal arts voyage and study literature and history. The problem is all that good stuff would lead to graduate school. That's six years, and neither the draft board nor our family finances will stand for that. Talk about piling on the problems!*

But it sort of came together—the conclusion was: don't run off to some school you're not interested in, much less some crummy job, when you will have to eventually serve in any case—get it over with!

If military duty were to be his decision, they discussed the possibility of enlisting in the navy—seemed safer, a natural with the Great Lakes experiences, but after family talks, and after conferring with friends and teachers, Arnold decided he would wait until they summoned him. Marie favored that approach, since it would string out the time until he put on a uniform while they talked at the truce table. Meanwhile, he would return to the ore boat where he had the promise of new duties for one final summer.

Somewhat curiously, there was no outward expression of patriotic duty, of service to his country, of doing his part. Of course those sorts of sentiments were percolating somewhere in his sharp brain but not expressed to family and friends, leaving them to ponder, *what the heck is he thinking?*

Raul had enrolled in summer school at the University of Minnesota and planned to join the Naval ROTC. These steps gave him a deferment.

Meanwhile, *Hawkeye* made voyages out of Duluth–Superior to Gary and also Port Huron. Now on his third summer on the boat, Arnold had been promoted to Communications Specialist. The new job pleased him for several reasons: more pay, less physical effort, and a position on the bridge—the nerve center of all boat operations.

The Korean War had brought pressure on the boat companies, indeed on all integrated portions of the steel industry. Production had to increase all along the pathway from mines to ports to lake shipping to steel mills to finished domestic and military goods. The boat companies were losing crewmen, just as they were about to lose Arnold. Spending less time in port, cutting a few corners, and forcing the turbines to put out more knots, the men of *Hawkeye* seemed to smile less and work harder.

Arnold had been told to expect a draft notice in September or October and kept Capt. Pierce informed. Some crewmen urged him to seek a draft exemption, since he was engaged in an essential industry, but he said it was only a summer job and that such an exemption would not be deserved. He said, "If I sound confused, it's 'cause I am confused. I know I've got options, choices, but they're hard choices. If I knew what to study, I might try for a college deferment, but when I review all the possibilities, I keep seeing Uncle Sam pointing a finger at me and saying, 'I want you,' like in the famous poster."

And so the summer of 1951 went by with truce talks and the war going endlessly on. Finally, the vessel left Port Huron on Arnold's final run in mid September, and, as they steamed north, he reflected, *I wanna get home—start the next phase of my life—whatever the hell it's gonna be and wherever the hell it's gonna take me!* They sailed north through the Soo Locks at Sault Sainte Marie toward Lake Superior. As the vessel turned northwest into Whitefish Bay, thunderstorms began with stronger-than-usual winds out of the west. Arnold knew the saying, "The winds played a fast tune on the rigging."

From his radio desk on the bridge, Arnold had a front row view of growing weather problems. They again headed north and rounded Whitefish Point. The water would not be treacherous until they rounded Keweenaw Peninsula, which they planned to reach by 1200 hours, so decisions would have to be made then.

Gale force winds were reported beyond the Copper Harbor Lighthouse on the peninsula. Arnold kept the weather station turned up for all to hear. As they neared the point, Capt. Pierce very calmly said, "Change course for Thunder Bay."

This was a wise compromise: Arnold saw that the choices included turning back to Sault Sainte Marie, plowing on toward Duluth–Superior, or heading as now planned to the harbors at Port Arthur and Fort William, Ontario. There were no other safe havens along the way for a massive ore boat. Perhaps if the captain had been under no pressure, he might have turned back, but the port at Fort William had the added advantage of complete shelter from winds out of the west and ore docks, enabling Pierce to contract for a load of taconite right there, wait out the storm, load, and be off and cruising back downbound!

Arnold's head spun: *how the hell do I get home?* He realized he was in no trouble; he could give his draft board a beautiful, certified excuse, probably the best they would ever receive, but he wanted to get home—*oh well, patience, patience; right now shipboard duty calls.* He kept his mouth shut; they all had more important and more eminent problems.

Past Keweenaw, the boat staggered, as fifteen-foot waves hit the portside, rising above the bulwarks, flooding the deck and hatches rail-to-rail, and smashing against the observation deck.

The Rock Harbor Lighthouse on Isle Royale and leeward shelter were some fifty kilometers north–northwest. As usual in a storm, it was best to keep full steam while they went broadside across the flow of the storm.

Old-timers on the bridge were calm as they faced temperature 40 degrees, barometer still falling, winds at thirty knots, waves high, rain-pour steady. The empty boat had advantages over one loaded with 20,000 tons of taconite. *Wow! Think about being afloat with a full load, no radar, winds and waves twice as high—like it was in 1905 when fifty-four vessels went down! Well, this is bad enough, bad enough!*

Company headquarters in Duluth radioed agreement with the captain; not that it mattered, since a captain had full authority and responsibility.

They all knew that when a laker went down it was a sudden exit: one moment they would appear as a blip on radar, the next moment—no blip. That's because they tended to roll over and sink like a bathtub. The crew was on full alert. The pattern of booms and bangs of the striking waves and the rolls of the responding boat went on and on, rhythmically, by the hour, accompanied by the steady beat of the rain, and the soft flip-flop of the bridge wind-shield wipers. But the boom of the waves dominated, sounding sort of like the guy who hit the gong at the start of a J. Arthur Rank movie, with the empty hull serving as a giant drum. The usual drone of the turbine and the screw was now drowned out by these other noises. Occasionally radio static added to the cacophony.

This was the first time he had carried out specific duties under the pressure of violent noise levels, sounds he had to put out of his mind; it would not be the last time!

Hot tea was served. Arnold figured the cook had brewed batches for forward and aft sections back in Whitefish Bay in anticipation of foul weather. As he tried to steady his mug, Morgan Jones joked, "Too bad we've done away with the traditional ration of grog John Paul Jones would have provided."

"I'm not above sharing a sip of sour mash," the captain replied, "but only after we round Rock Harbor." They all knew there was supposed to be no liquor; it was forbidden by the Coast Guard.

Arnold contacted Fort William and handed the speaker to the captain. "Hello, William; *Hawkeye* is headed your way. We estimate arrival 2300, over."

"Ah, roger, *Hawkeye*; be expecting you, fairly calm here, wind west fifteen knots, over."

"Thanks, William. Be in touch, out."

Arnold then tried to call Rock Harbor on Isle Royale—no answer. Capt. Pierce was not worried, figuring the radio was simply not manned on that little island. Isle Royale was a National Park, probably the most remote and seldom visited of its kind. Some of the crew knew that one reason tourists went there was to see the remains of wrecked ships off its forty-five mile southern shore. *Kinsman Enterprise* went aground there because of a navigational mistake by the wheelman.

They got back to Fort William and asked them to call the island by cable phone and rouse someone at the Park Service. Sure enough, in fifteen minutes they heard from Rock Harbor. The captain replied, "Good to hear from you, Rock Harbor. We wanted to be in touch in case we miss the lighthouse. Hate to clutter your shore, over."

"Actually, *Hawkeye*, we now have you on radar . . . we have your position, let me see . . . about forty-eight degrees, ten minutes north, and eighty-eight degrees, twenty minutes west. Good navigating in this soup, I'd say; over."

"Roger; hold on a moment, please . . . yes, Rock Harbor, you are now on our radar, just as you indicated; please keep an eye on us; thanks; we will be in touch, out." The captain turned to Arnold, "The winds should abate in fifteen minutes, when we are in the lee of Isle Royale. Remind me to call back and thank that fellow."

"If he hasn't gone back to the pub, his girlfriend, or wherever he was," First Mate Jones said with a smirk.

They found the Rock Harbor Lighthouse, the wind did abate, and they found Thunder Bay on the radar. But there was bad news at 2130 hours: a crewman entered the bridge and reported part of the boom had collapsed. Actual damage unknown, but bound to be considerable. *More delay,* Arnold thought. But then again, this could be a bad break for *Hawkeye* and a good break for him. *I'll wait and see.*

By 2230, they spotted the Fort William Lighthouse and called for instructions and tugs. The dockside was lit up, as tugs guided *Hawkeye* to rest. Arnold decided to wait until morning to call Pierre. He knew he could reach Duluth by rail in a few hours, and finally get home in another day or so, but his duty was to stay with the boat.

By mid morning it had been determined that the boom damage required return to Duluth for repairs. Arnold called and advised Pierre of the delay and was informed there was a letter awaiting him from Selective Service, naming 24 October as his doomsday appointment. The storm blew hard most of the day, so *Hawkeye* delayed departure for twenty-four hours. Arnold spent the day helping the deckhands clean up after the storm, thinking that the fair blow was a worthy end to his days on the lakes.

Chapter Five
Selective Service

Once home, Arnold took up the Selective Service System's *Order to Report for Armed Forces Physical Examination*—duly stamped by the local board with orders to report to a Duluth address on Grand Avenue on 24 October 1951.

Arnold noted with special interest—*this is not a notice or a direction, but something stronger . . . it's an order. The greatest nation on earth is ordering me to do something, sort of one-on-one, up close and personal, certainly on a different level from being told to do something by my folks, the hockey coach, or the mother superior.* He sat for some time and studied the half-page message. But with that passing fancy, a confused anxiety set in: *after the 24 October induction, I'll be gone, gone, gone! From then on, I'll have no choice of what to wear, where to sleep, what to eat. No leaving a messy room; no raiding the ice box; no "I guess I'll do this" or "I guess I'll do that," much less, "I guess I'll do nothing."*

He would be kicked around by men called "sergeants." He had seen how they operate in the movies. First and foremost, he knew there would be training, then a long voyage ending up in a strange land of mountains and stinking rice paddies where well-trained, nasty enemies, hiding in tunnels or bunkers or caves on nameless mountainsides would dedicate their lives to ending his life.

These thoughts bounced around his head. He thought about history studies—one of his favorite subjects. Those ancient battles had seemed so romantic, like when the separate and independent-minded Greek States united against the Persians at Marathon. But there was nothing glorious about the senseless slaughter at Cold Harbor, the Argonne, and Iwo Jima, or at those new places like Taegu, the Reservoir, and the Gauntlet.

He compared a combat struggle to an ore boat disaster, remembering that Lake Superior did not give up its dead, thus providing finality—such a quick exit. He thought of the romantic seafaring hymn:

> *Eternal Father, strong to save,*
> *Whose arm has bound the restless wave*
> *Who bids the mighty ocean deep*
> *Its own appointed limits keep:*
> *To you we pray most earnestly*
> *For those in peril on the sea.*

As these sacred words and touching melody swam in his head, he realized they comforted him. He often repeated, *"Eternal Father, strong to save, to you we pray most earnestly."* He didn't have to go beyond that: *God understands my inmost thoughts . . . it comforts me to talk to him, and I know He's glad to hear from me.*

But his indignation about the war continued. In retrospect, newspapers claimed our policies had not made clear that South Korea was considered part of the American sphere of influence, leading Kim Il Sung to believe we would not interfere. That was probably because in January 1950, Secretary of State Dean Acheson, speaking at the Washington National Press Club, had not included South Korea in the defined American vital interests in Asia. *That was like saying the candy store is unlocked!*

Experts said our generals were often one war behind in planning. In Arnold's lifetime, horse cavalry had been sent against armored vehicles, and Naval Officers had wanted battleships, not aircraft carriers. The great Gen. MacArthur had screwed up so badly he was fired!

Yes, he was angry and afraid and figured his fellow draftees were in the same fix! He cursed the now known fact that American diplomats and military leaders, including Gen. MacArthur himself, had repeatedly misjudged the communist enemy.

The most overt manifestation of these official difficulties came early in 1951 when MacArthur challenged U.S. civilian leadership by ignoring directives. His letter to House Minority Leader Joe Martin solidified opposition against him in Washington and London, leading President Truman to replace him on 11 April 1951. The command of U.N. Forces was given to Lt. Gen. Matthew B. Ridgway who had only recently replaced Gen. Walker as 8th Army Commander.

The need to remove MacArthur was controversial and not fully understood. As Pierre put it, "The failed haberdasher has fired our greatest military leader. What a sorry mess!"

But if Arnold had all these complaints and second thoughts, if he were so concerned and critical, why was he not pursuing one of those other choices, like staying in school, instead of just waiting to be called up?

Arnold had a repeating dream: he was back in the Boundary Waters—alone—when a giant moose attacked, just like in the family hunt, but this creature was huge and black. He fired at the charging figure, time after time, but bullets had no effect. The animal was upon him. He couldn't even turn aside and simply fell. He would wake with a start at that point.

He brought up the dream at the family dinner—during their discussion time. Pierre said he used to have dreams where his rifle wouldn't fire; they all chalked it up to anxiety over the impending army times. Arnold shrugged; he wasn't sure that was it.

On top of his personal woes, he could see full well that the family store was not doing well. Times were changing, with troubles blamed on two enemies: Sears Roebuck and Montgomery Ward. He had heard Pierre and Guy argue about the mail-order business. He suspected it was killing his father's store, while his uncle was probably selling insurance to those companies. Yes, times were changing; he and his sisters could and would fend for themselves; they could do that very well.

Finally, the time arrived to stop thinking and dreaming and start moving. Leaving stalwart Marie and the teary sisters behind, Pierre drove him to Duluth. There were bits of advice along the way: it's usually best not to volunteer; be positioned in the second or third row; respect all those of senior rank. Arnold thought, *that would be easy to follow, since everyone will have senior rank.* The list went on: don't get VD or, God forbid, tattoos; stay sober; and please write your mother.

They stayed with Uncle Guy and Aunt Ruth that night in their bluff-side home some six hundred feet above the harbor and the beautiful Lake, with fall colors at their height. The men had some beers in the den where they could admire the moose head over the mantle. They teased each other over which one had shot the fatal bullet, only agreeing that it couldn't have been Raul, because he wasn't there to defend himself!

Pierre dropped his son off the next day at the government building and drove away with tears in his eyes. The swinging entry door was a curtain closing Arnold's youth.

Chapter Six
Real McCoy

Inside was a melting pot of young men of all sizes and shapes—some finding friends; he recognizing no one. There was the usual sort of physical exam, including a private interview, which he figured was to see if his head was screwed on. As he stood at a long urinal holding a cup, he was surprised when the man next to him handed over his cup, saying, "Leave a little in here; I just can't go." Arnold obliged.

Several draftees were rejected, and, to his surprise, after all the worry and anger, he found himself wanting to go, fearing that something would go wrong and he'd be left behind! He scratched his head over this sentiment for days, but the powerful thought lingered—*with all men my age joining up, it's my destiny.*

Those accepted for induction, about forty, lined up in three rows—his first military formation! They raised their right hands and were sworn in accordance with the soldiers' enlistment oath:

I, Arnold Desprez do solemnly swear that I will support and defend the Constitution of the United States against all enemies, foreign and domestic; that I will bear true faith and allegiance to the same; and that I will obey the orders of the President of the United States and the orders of the

officers appointed over me, according to regulations and the
Uniform Code of Military Justice. So help me God.

To conclude the oath, they then took one step forward. Arnold wondered afterward if anyone ever just stood there—not taking that famous step twixt freedom and bondage. He figured the men in civilian clothes he saw standing by would know how to handle such a situation, Arnold guessing they were volunteers, perhaps World War II vets from the Legion Post.

A sergeant escorted them to a bus, which drove them to the Milwaukee Railroad Station. While still on the bus, they were handed their orders, which were also read to them. Their destination was Fort McCoy, Wisconsin, the closest induction center. Each responded "here" when his name was called, except some ass-kisser who said "present, Sir." The sergeant looked up, frowned, then read on. Arnold learned later that sergeants do not like the "sir" word—makes 'em mad—they want to be respectfully called "sergeant" or "master sergeant," or whatever their precise rank happens to be. The damned commissioned officers were the "sirs."

He was part of a list that began, "the following EM . . ." which stood for "enlisted men." The order was his first exposure to the army's endless acronyms: the rule seeming to be: never spell out something if initials can be substituted. For example, the order used the letters EDCSA—what the hell did that mean? It was followed by a date, 24 October 1951. No human being could guess that one! Later, he learned that EDCSA was on all personnel transfer orders; it meant "estimated date of change of strength accountability." That was pretty important to know because if you weren't at the named destination by that date, you were, to cite the most infamous acronym of all, AWOL!

His name was written, "Private E-1 Desprez, Arnold P., US55294297." The "US" part meant he had been drafted; had he volunteered, his serial number would have commenced "RA" for

Regular Army. This was probably why a soldier who was particularly eager was spoken of as being "RA" or "Gung-Ho."

When he finished reading, the sergeant handed out train vouchers and wished them luck. The train took the rest of the day traveling to Fort McCoy in central Wisconsin, between Sparta and Tomah. Arnold rode with three others in facing coach seats. Of course, they visited, all curious and wondering.

"That sergeant didn't seem too bad," said one little guy in work clothes.

"Easy for him," a fellow in a neat sport coat replied. He appeared to be the group know-it-all, as he continued, "The basic training cadres will be purposefully nasty; they'll work at it; it's part of the process of breaking us down and molding us. My brother told me all about what we can expect."

Arnold shivered but kept quiet.

The fourth recruit perked up, "Well, I was a punch-card operator, and I hear there's a good chance I can use my civilian skills in the army and perhaps end up with some stateside job."

Arnold laughed, "That's unlikely in my case; the army doesn't need ore boat deckhands."

The first little fellow seemed disturbed by the whole concept. Arnold asked him what he did in civilian life.

"Tuck-pointer."

"What the hell is that?"

And so it went. Arnold quietly smiled at his new friend the tuck-pointer and thought *how naïve can you get?* Strangely, he had a feeling he was more mature and better educated than most of these guys.

They arrived at dusk and were taken to a large mess hall. After dinner, they marched, or staggered, tired and scared, to an unoccupied barracks building. Arnold knew he would never forget that day.

So army life began. Next day, they were issued uniforms: Ike jackets and trousers, fatigues, field jacket, fatigue hats, and so-called overseas caps, most everything in two sets. Very importantly, there were low-quarter shoes and two pairs of stiff leather combat boots. The new GI was faced with wearing all new footwear; blisters were the rule.

Each name and serial number was stenciled on a duffel bag, which was designed to hold all the new gear. Finally, they lined up at a machine that printed their dog tags. These little metal chips resembled just what they were called; they bore the soldier's name, serial number, blood type, and religious choice. In Arnold's case that was O for blood type—a universal donor—and C for Catholic. He noticed a little notch at one end of each tag and later learned that if a soldier were KIA—killed in action—one tag could be placed between the teeth at that notch, and the teeth jammed shut. The second tag would be taken by a unit leader and used for casualty report. No leader wanted to collect dog tags. "His dog tags were separated" was a euphemism for "he was killed," another way was to say, "he bought the farm."

What sad sacks they were in their wrinkled new uniforms, as they marched around, usually led by a tired old sergeant about his father's age. They had haircuts—undifferentiated bean shaves. They took hours of aptitude and intelligence tests and were read cover-to-cover *The Uniform Code of Military Justice*. There were the usual laughs over the line in the *Code* that read, "penetration, however slight, constitutes rape." Afterward, someone said, "How slight is slight?"

The old sergeant stayed in the barracks with them, in a small rear room. He was mustering out after thirty years of service. One morning, he handed Arnold a razor and asked him to shave the back of his neck. What a difference between this man and the stereotype drill sergeant. Arnold inquired about his shoulder patch, which was a two-inch circle, picturing blue sky, a patch of yellow sand, and a single palm tree. After hearing it twice, Arnold caught the cryptic reply: "The isle of Guam."

Arnold began his career of pulling KP in the consolidated mess, first being assigned to cleaning the garbage cans out on the loading dock. Edible garbage was picked up twice daily for delivery to pig farmers. The dirty empty cans were then inverted over a large hose and the insides were blasted by a geyser of steaming hot water. Everything was cleaned three times a day; KPs were rarely allowed to sit down.

It was at the garbage cans that Arnold met his first army buddy, and, for that matter, it was there that he picked up his new nickname. Joe Cerutti was an incredibly strong "Dago," as Joe himself put it, from Superior, Wisconsin. Joe did most of the lifting when the cans were stuffed with the so-called edible garbage. He could flip them from the loading dock onto the trucks and relished the fact that he could do it by himself. The mess sergeant undoubtedly knew this was rugged work and picked a strong-looking slave for the job.

"Am I glad you're my friend!" Arnold would say with a laugh, implying that he would hate to have Dago Joe for an enemy. But both soon realized they truly were friends. Joe was one of those people for whom ethnic background was a great curiosity: when a new name came up, he would mutter, "Irish, Kraut, Polack," or, if stumped, "what kind of a name is that?" He was quick to give Arnold the nickname, "Frenchy," which would last his entire army career.

It was now perfectly natural for the new friends to team up, eating together and, after work, going to the PX, as the Post Exchange was called. They mostly bought essentials such as shaving gear, Band-Aids for foot blisters, and boot-shining equipment. But there were bargains galore, and Frenchy figured at the next post he would shop for his folks.

In one corner of the PX, there were school chairs—the kind with a wrap-around writing table. He and Joe could sit there and drink a bottle or two of 3.2 beer.

At first they were puzzled by the compound next to their barracks; it was surrounded by a barbed-wire fence, and soldiers inside wore pale fatigues, white arm bands, and no insignia. It was, of course, the stockade. The fascinating part was how well they marched: when doing a column left or column right, they did a skip step and sort of lurched forward. They also had a peculiar way of marching in place. This was known throughout the army as the stockade shuffle.

After five days of testing, processing, and KP, Frenchy and all his barracks-mates were called out and formed in their usual ragged formation. In a command voice, no doubt perfected by many years of drilling soldiers, the sergeant made it short and sweet:

"At ease; give me your attention!"

These were the commands used before addressing a formation, the idea having developed, maybe over centuries, that troops at *attention* or *parade rest* could not take oral information except drill commands. Then the old sergeant gave the speech Frenchy never forgot: "Moving out, 0600, Fort Knox, Tucky. No fence!"

That was it. *That old bird was not longwinded!* Apparently, in addition to Guam, the sergeant had been stationed at Fort Knox, Kentucky, and knew there was no fence around the military installation, at least near the main gate. This seemed like useless information unless you wanted to go AWOL.

Next morning, now heavily laden with duffel bags and usually a small bag for Dopp kits and books, the rag-tag crew was bussed back to the train depot for the 560-mile, twenty-eight-hour journey to Fort Knox. The Fort lay in forested hill country, twenty-two miles south-west of Louisville, a famous old city on the Ohio River, known to Frenchy as the site of Churchill Downs and the Kentucky Derby as well as Louisville Slugger baseball bats.

The site of Louisville was visited by Sieur de la Salle in 1669. In 1778, Gen. George Rogers Clark, on his way to the Illinois Territory, landed settlers there, and the town was founded the next year. By 1951, it was the largest city in Kentucky, with a population of 370,000.

There, in a switching yard, the men received a nice dose of kindness when ladies from the United Services Organization served donuts and coffee. It had been a tough trip: getting through Chicago, the nation's railroad hub, required considerable switching; there was no dining car; sandwiches were furnished in a freight car. The men were nervous and dead bushed.

Chapter Seven
Able Battery and Hard Knox

Frenchy and Joe stood in formation in front of three barracks buildings. On their left was the orderly room—a one-story, wood-frame building that served as headquarters. By its door, painted yellow and black, was a prominent sign, indicating this was Battery A, 68th Field Artillery Battalion, part of the 3rd Armored Division. The sign included a red, yellow, and blue triangular logo with an oval form like tank treads under the number three. Beside it was the logo of the 68th, being in the form of crossed cannons under the number sixty-eight. The words "A Battery" were on another sign, neatly placed above the division and battalion logos.

These were merely the names of outfits from World War II. The 3rd Armored Division only existed as a training unit, not a real division at all. It would not likely again be deployed, its graduates simply moving on to other units, some for more training but most heading directly to Korea to a full-fledged combat outfit.

Behind and to the right of the barracks was the mess hall; across and opposite it was an assembly building, a structure badly in need of repair, shabby and seldom used. All buildings were left over from the last war: roofs leaking, paint cracked or missing—all easier to replace than repair. Military installations were still recovering from the jolt of mobilizing for the so-called police action, which had commenced some sixteen months before. Every structure in sight was overdue for destruction. Second floors could not be given a tried and true GI dousing because water would leak down on the men and their clothing on the first floor, and so it was improvise, improvise, make do.

Things seemed to be run by a first sergeant who looked extremely sharp in starched, faded fatigues. His blouse had obviously been tailored to fit skin-tight around his thin waist. His boots were paratrooper-style jump boots—not government issued—and were spit-shined to a fine gloss. The blouse pocket bore the name "Noonan." On the right shoulder was a big yellow patch with a diagonal bar and a horse's head, indicating he had served in combat with the 1st Cavalry Division; on the left shoulder he wore the red, yellow, and blue triangular patch of the 3rd Armored Division. Since Noonan looked to be no more than twenty-five years old, he must have served in one of the 1st Cavalry's infantry battalions, 8th Army, either during the stalemate or perhaps in the tough-going span of 1950 to 1951. Although they kept the name, Cavalry, the division had been dismounted soon after the Mexican War.

Two other sergeants and a second lieutenant stood off to one side. Names were called out and barracks assigned. Frenchy and Joe grabbed an upper and lower bunk on the second floor of the center barracks. They hit the sack, ending another long day.

"Out of the sack; hit the deck! An old sergeant named McNulty shouted at 0500 the next morning. The latrine on the first floor soon crowded up. Separated by the center-aisle rifle racks, the men on the lower floor were designated first squad and second squad; those above, the third and fourth. The first squad was given latrine cleanup duty. McNulty said that from then on, the men would fix their own cleanup schedule, and woe to them all if the latrine was not kept in good order!

Each man was also responsible for his own area and a part of the common areas on his floor. Brooms, mops, buckets, and trash bins were furnished; it was surprising how most men endeavored to do at least their share and more of the almost constant cleanup.

The latrine was usually so congested, Frenchy was glad he had an electric razor; it saved him valuable time each morning. In fact, the congestion was so bad, it appeared that the obsolete barracks had been designed probably some fifteen years before, to house about half as many men.

McNulty explained that the entire barracks constituted a platoon and that each platoon had four squads. He selected squad leaders who were designated Lance Corporals. Dago Cerutti was named for the third squad. This was an easy selection for the same reason that Frenchy had once said, "I'm glad you're my friend."

When the men lined up in formation, Dago was taught to be at the left end of the third rank. When the troops were given "left face" and then "column of twos from the right, forward march," he would turn his head and shout "stand fast" until the first two columns were about to pass, then shout "forward, march."

These were heady new concepts for troops with only about a week in the military. The confusion at Fort McCoy was being gradually replaced by proficiency at Fort Knox. Marching techniques were part of what was called dismounted drill, a phrase left over from the horse cavalry days. Drill was taught by a book called FM (for field manual) 22–5; its contents would apply to a soldier all his army days. The *Manual* itself explained that the first army field manual was written in 1779 by Maj. Gen. and Army Inspector Gen. Baron Friedrich Von Steuben, a Prussian officer whose aid had been enlisted by Benjamin Franklin.

The second day at Fort Knox was a big one. Field gear was issued: helmets, helmet liners, packs, tarps, tent poles and pegs, web belts, canteens, utensils, bayonets, entrenching tools, bandage pouches, division patches, and M-1 rifles. Most gear was stacked in a prescribed manner on shelves behind their bunks. Rifles were stored under lock-and-key in the center-aisle racks.

Names were stenciled on the helmet liners, which were worn most of the time, instead of the fatigue hats issued at McCoy.

That evening, they were expected to sew on the 3rd Division patches. The peak of the triangular patch had to be two finger widths down from the shoulder seam. For many, this was their first attempt with a needle and thread.

An early formation was taken by Sgt. Bratton, another barracks leader like Sgt. McNulty. With all the trainees assembled, one of the men asked Bratton a question about sick call. The sergeant grew red in the face, scowled, and then shouted, "How should I know? I'm not your fucking chaplain! Get this straight: in the army, it's hooray for me and fuck you."

That was all. The sergeant made no explanation nor sought any reprisal; it was just everyday language for him, since no sentence was complete without some expletive. To Frenchy, who was brought up to believe some language was out-of-bounds, the remark had a physical impact—*so awful, so insensitive!*

This was the first in a series of crude acts by Sgt. Bratton that made it clear to all the troops that he never should have been promoted, that his rank must have been given under extreme combat conditions. Perhaps he committed some heroic act requiring primitive reaction. His situation also reflected on the leadership training or lack of training he had received since entering the army. Face it: it was not a seasoned army.

Frenchy admonished Dago, "Watch that jerk; stay clear of him. There'll be more Bratton problems before the sixteen weeks are up."

Able Battery got its first dose of corporate punishment after the noon mess. There were stragglers when the whistle blew for afternoon formation. First Sgt. Noonan was displeased. "When the whistle blows, you will form up on the double. You will move! Move! Move! Prepare to fall out, and be ready for the whistle . . . fall out!"

They scrambled back into the barracks. Then the whistle; pushing through the doors; leaping off the stairs; back in formation; fall out; the whistle! On and on, until fifty men were repeatedly lining up in fourteen seconds. "Not bad," Noonan conceded. But falling in and falling out continued to be one of his favorite little tortures. If one person were late, all paid. All this fairly stupid behavior was known as corporate punishment. It was believed that to form the men into a team, promote cooperation, and instill prompt, cheerful obedience, corporate punishment had to be dished out. Therefore, various reasons for the punishment had to be found, however lame and undeserving—like the fall-in, fall-out drill.

Frenchy and Dago realized that these confrontations were part of the training process, inevitable and old as armies. The noise, the yelling, the chewing-out became impersonal—water off a duck's back. Simply grin and bear it.

The troops went to dress-right-dress and sharpened their ranks. They marched into the cruddy assembly building and took seats. After a delay of some minutes—no doubt planned in advance to create some suspense—one of the sergeants shouted "atten-hut," and all jumped to their feet.

From a side door, in strutted a short, stocky captain who had not appeared before the troops until that moment. Frenchy had learned about second and first lieutenants with gold and silver bars and captains with two connected silver bars, sometimes called "railroad tracks," the three ranks constituting company-grade officers. The new arrival stood on the dilapidated stage and looked out at the men, as if sizing them up.

The rank of captain was a good one. Senior officers would fondly recall their days as captains, a time when they commanded companies and had a close-enough relationship to know the names of all their men and would be responsible for providing food, medical attention, leave time—the whole package.

Then, in a sharp, shrill voice, he commanded "seats!"

"Men, I am Capt. Birdsall, Able Battery Commander; you will serve under me for the next sixteen weeks."

Frenchy noticed the reference to "Able" Battery. The army used the phonetic alphabet: able, baker, Charlie, dog, easy, fox, etc. The captain continued, "I will set you straight on a few confusing names. You are taking infantry basic training; don't be confused by the unit names. There are three combat arms: infantry, artillery, and armor. Infantry troops go back to the days of the Roman Legions; they hold the line, attack, and defend. When we can, we ride in trucks; when we cannot, we walk. We are not bound by roads, as our brother units sometimes are. If we were a real combat unit, we would be called a "company." A "battery" is an artillery term. *Armor* means "tanks," but an *armored division*, like the 3rd Armored Division, does have infantry troops.

"Fort Knox is the Armored Center of the United States Army, but, like I first said, you will receive infantry basic training.

"Under our command system, you are a company; I am your commander. We are part of the 2nd Battalion. Its headquarters is up the hill behind you. It is commanded by Lt. Col. Roger B. Evans. The Assistant Division Commander is Brig. Gen. John T. Cole; Division Commander is Maj. Gen. RW Stephens. Gen. Cole may drop in on some of our training sessions; if he does so, look extra sharp.

"You should also know that 3rd Armored won its name Spearhead while leading the attacking forces across Europe in World War II. It landed on Omaha Beach in Normandy, was first into Belgium, first to fire into German soil, first through the Siegfried Line, first to capture a German city. One of the Division's most famous accomplishments was a one-day advance of 101 miles—the longest in military history. Our outfit has a proud past; we must carry on the tradition!"

The captain then introduced his officer team: two second lieutenants on their first assignment after completing their own training. Their route to a gold bar could have been military school,

ROTC, or Officer Candidate School, probably at Fort Benning, Georgia, or there at Fort Knox.

He called First Sgt. Noonan, who introduced McNulty and two other sergeants, each being in charge of a barracks and one being the meathead Sgt. Bratton, who rose with his usual frown. Noonan then introduced the Mess Sergeant, the Supply Sergeant, and the Battery Clerk, Cpl. Dan Fox.

Frenchy was learning that there were two sets of leaders: the enlisted men who had most of the contact with the trainees, and the officers who seemed to stroll around and do nothing.

He was, however, impressed with the captain, though he wondered how many troops had absorbed all the talk about batteries, companies, and battalions plus the names of all the brass. *It must be a formality to describe the chain of command so we can't say we were never told, sort of like when they read the* Uniform Code *back at McCoy. And that stuff about the101-mile advance, that's pure gung-ho stuff—like a pep talk between periods in a hockey game.*

The command structure within the battery was explained. Troops were to take questions and problems to their barracks sergeant, not the first sergeant or the lieutenants. Those in Sgt. Bratton's barracks saw that it was useless to check with him so they usually took their troubles to Cpl. Fox, who understood the Bratton problem.

Back on stage, the captain continued, "If you are sick, go on sick call, but remember that malingerers will be found out and will regret it. Missing training for any reason is a bad idea; being there and paying attention could make the difference between life and death."

He explained that every soldier could go to chapel on Sundays. The only order preventing chapel would be KP. Dry cleaning and laundry were covered, along with KP and guard duty. Then, the captain became more solemn: "You all get the same pay—which isn't much. There is no lower son-of-a-bitch than someone who steals from his own comrades. If you catch a thief, bring him to the orderly room; however, I don't want the thief able to walk, so carry him there; and explain how he fell down the stairs!"

Finally, Capt. Birdsall admonished the troops once again. What they would learn could save their lives and the lives of their comrades. Cooperate and graduate! He nodded at the first sergeant, and the command "atten-hut!" was given. The captain kept them standing there, as he very deliberately took his clipboard and helmet liner and strode off the stage, and the sergeant took charge.

KP duty began the first day. The roster was posted in each barracks with the kitchen police assigned in alphabetical order. KPs had been excused to hear the captain, but were usually on duty all day in the mess hall. This meant they would miss a day of training; too bad, but the army at that time had found no alternatives.

The work was not as bad as in Fort McCoy's consolidated mess. The men got to know the mess sergeant and had a chance to eat like horses. They helped serve the food, cafeteria style, swept and mopped the floor after every meal, and washed all utensils, pots, pans, etc. They did little of the food preparation; there was even a machine to peel potatoes. When working in the serving line, it was an old stunt to see a buddy coming and put Jell-O on top of his mashed potatoes and gravy.

Guard duty was at night. The duty roster began in reverse alphabetical order, so Pvt. Aaron would not be double hit. Pulling guard was important training and could last for years—until the soldier became an NCO. The ten Orders of the Guard had to be memorized. They began this way:

To take charge of this post and all government property in view.

To walk my post in a military manner, keeping always on the alert and observing everything that takes place within sight or hearing.

There are many stories about guards. Everyone had to be challenged, regardless of rank. One order specified that the guard would pass on orders from "the commanding officer, officer of the day, and officer of the guard only." That meant that a master sergeant or a colonel strolling by must be challenged. After all, the First General Order was *take charge of this post!*

There were stories of pickets in the Civil War who would chat back and forth with enemy pickets seen on the other side of a stream or some other nearby place, and also accounts of commanding generals, such as Gen. Patton, being challenged, and, rather than being annoyed, commending the guard for doing his duty.

Inevitably, GIs conjured up so-called supplemental orders. One was a takeoff on order 2: "to walk my post in a military manner and take no shit from the company commander."

But it was really no joking matter. In combat, lax behavior of a guard could jeopardize an entire unit. Sleeping on guard was a court martial offense, punishable by death.

When off duty, the boys sometimes walked to the service club. It had various facilities: barber shop, hot food, reading rooms, and the usual 3.2 beer. They would sit and drink, like the old days at Fort McCoy. In the entrance was a massive mural, which included a portrait of Patton wearing four stars. Frenchy didn't realize Old Blood and Guts had gotten that far.

Chapter Eight
Jody was There

Frenchy and Joe made friends in their barracks. One was a little skinny guy named Bingo Heusting. He couldn't have weighed more than 120 pounds and looked particularly incongruous in his steel pot, which of course came in only one size regardless of wearer. Bingo was a college graduate, was a whiz at the numbers work and helped others with technical matters and with memorizing the General Orders of the Guard. He even helped some men write letters home. Strange as it might seem, some men had never been away from home and had never written a letter.

Big Joe marveled at how much harder everything must be for Bingo, yet the little fellow was the kindest and best-liked guy in the barracks.

Another buddy was Bernie Weinman from Green Bay, Wisconsin. Bernie's 201 File noted that he had studied piano. He was called to the orderly room, handed a drum, and told, "Weinman, you're the battery drummer."

Bernie had it down in a day or two, and by the end of basic, he was a virtuoso. The drum kept them in step with the heavy beat on the left foot: *brrr-rump, pum-pump, brrr-rump, pum-pump*. During basic, they marched hundreds of miles, and Frenchy recognized how much esprit de corps the drum added on a march.

The drum replaced the cadence calling of the unit leader—usually First Sgt. Noonan. FM 22–5 described cadence as "a uniform and rhythmic flow of words." The human voice, however strong, would give out in a manner of minutes, but beating the drum seemed to have little tiring effect on Bernie, and if he did want a rest, he would simply stop for a while, and then pick up the beat once again.

They also learned the Jody marching cadences. Jody was the proverbial guy left behind to steal your girl. Sgt. Noonan was terrific at singing these chants. The most basic was:

>*You had a good home but you left . . . (you're right)*
>*Your gal was there when you left . . . (you're right)*
>*Jody was there when you left . . . (you're right)*
>*Sound off. . . . . (one, two, three, four)*
>*Sound off . . . (one, two, three, four)*
>*Break it on down . . . (one- two . . . three- four)*

The proper foot was to come down with the words "left" and "right." Some Jody versions were a good deal more sentimental, even sad:

>*If I die in a combat zone,*
>*Box me up and ship me home;*
>*Sound off . . . (one, two, three, four), etc.*

Or, bringing it right up to date:

>*I don't know; but I been told;*
>*North Korea's mighty cold;*
>*Sound off . . . (one, two, three, four), etc.*

Noonan added a new song—to be sung one line by each of the three platoons, then all together on the last line:

>*Old soldiers never die,*
>*Never die, never die;*
>*Old soldiers never die.*
>*They just fade away*

If your feet weren't sore, marching was fun and obviously necessary—often many miles a day. Jody added a spark—a chance to yell! The sergeants and lieutenants marched alongside Weinman, the drummer. It was important to remember that the leaders marched just as far as the troopers.

When they neared an intersection, Sgt. McNulty gave the order, "Road guards post, fore and aft." McNulty had been in the navy in the big war.

They usually marched with rifles at sling arms; but sometimes at right shoulder arms or left shoulder arms. At double time, the rifles were at port arms. As part of the marching, and dismounted drill in general, the troops learned that drill commands contained two parts: the preparatory command and the command of execution.

FM 22–5 said, "Correct commands have a tone cadence and snap that demand willing, correct, and immediate response." The command of execution had to be loud, short, and crisp. It was given at a higher pitch, without using the lips or tongue. Thus, "march" became "harch"—a crisper sound from the back of the throat—and "attention" became "ten-hut."

Each leader did his best to work on his command voice, and, over time, his rhythm, volume, and pitch would improve. It was like a singing lesson—the noise must come from the chest. Noonan excelled; his orders and chants were rhythmical, tuneful, and powerful.

After hearing Noonan, the efforts of movie actors, like John Wayne, sounded feeble, indeed. In all his war movies, John Wayne never learned how to salute; he must have thought it was smart to be really casual about it, as if he were above it all. In the real army, saluting was taken seriously and done by the book or not done at all. In an area where soldiers were working together, one salute during each detail would be sufficient.

Chapter Nine
The Garand and Agony Hill

In the second week, training with the M-1 rifle commenced. At first, they sat at long tables in a classroom, rifles lying before them, while 1st Lt. Spiro, the rifle instructor, stood and faced them at a similar table on stage. They took their weapons apart and reassembled them; Frenchy soon could do it blindfolded, unless mischievous Dago Joe hid one of his parts.

The M-1 was semi-automatic—this meant you could keep pulling the trigger and firing one round at a time. It was gas operated: as propellant gases escaped from the barrel, a small amount flowed down a port into another tube below the barrel. There, the gas drove a piston back toward the bolt, an action that both pulled back the bolt and ejected the spent cartridge.

A clip holding eight rounds could be inserted into a slot in front of the withdrawn bolt. When the bolt opened after the rifle fired, a spring on the clip forced a round into the space in front of the bolt before the bolt could close, all in less than a second. In this manner, a soldier could fire nine rounds as fast as he could pull the trigger, assuming he started with one round in the chamber.

When the weapons were stripped down, Lt. Spiro held up the piston device—a steel tube. He sighted down it and said, "Oh, my, it's bent."

He then pretended to try and straighten it, saying, "Should I bend it straight?" This was a little joke; the piston was designed to have this curve. He continued, "The M-1 was invented by a tinkering genius named John C. Garand, and so is often called "the Garand." It has a classic elegance of form in which the blue steel and the walnut butt and lower housing are shaped to form and function. Gen. George S. Patton said, 'In my opinion, the M-1 rifle is the greatest battle implement ever devised.'

"Well, that may be a stretch. Mr. Garand himself would probably say, 'Thanks for the endorsement, George, but, you're a military history buff, how about the Medieval Longbow—the weapon that gave the English all those victories over the French in the Hundred Years War, including Crécy in 1346—a turning point in military history?'"

Frenchy had fired 30-caliber rifles since he was a kid—except not with the semi-automatic function. He quickly knew the basic statistics, since it fired the same ammunition he had used in his Springfield .30-06 rifle back home. A ".30-caliber" meant three-tenths of an inch; the effective range was five hundred yards; its weight unloaded was 9.8 pounds.

There was one woeful aspect: when there was no round in the chamber, the Garand was to be left with the bolt closed. However, after expending the last round or any time, such as inspection, when the bolt was drawn back to the open position, the problem was how to close it—not a laughing matter.

To close the bolt, the soldier had to place the edge of his right-hand palm against the lever at the end of the operating rod to hold back the bolt, then stick his thumb into the open chamber and push down the clip spring to release the bolt. The palm against the lever would hold back the bolt, and the thumb and the palm would then be removed simultaneously. It took practice and coordination. If the thumb didn't get out of the way, the closing bolt would slam the poor thumb forward against the chamber wall. Result: pain as if you hit your thumb with a hammer.

No big deal, but the result was a blood sore under the nail known as an M-1 thumb! It wouldn't disappear until the nail grew out months later. It would soon stop hurting, but the brand of incompetence remained. Sooner or later most basic trainees screwed up and got an M-1 thumb. John C. Garand must have been cursed many a time.

Another manifestation of incompetence was to call the M-1 rifle a "gun." Sgt. McNulty was delighted to find a way to humble Joe Cerutti when the big guy referred to "my gun."

"Pvt. Cerutti, you may not know where your gun is."

Joe gave him a puzzled look.

The sergeant pointed between Joe's legs. "Your gun is down there! Now, where is your rifle?"

Duly chagrined, but trying to repress a smile, Joe held up the Garand, "Here, sergeant."

"Here is what?"

"Here is my rifle, Sergeant."

"Much better, but I think a little catechism is needed, don't you?"

Now fully aware that he was being teased, Joe replied, "Oh yes, Sergeant."

"Ready, now. With appropriate gestures, repeat the following:
This is my rifle; this is my gun.
This is to shoot; this is for fun!"

No one seemed to get a bigger kick out of the episode than Joe. Soon after, while marching, Sgt. McNulty shouted,

"Pvt. Cerutti!"

"Yes, Sergeant."

"Can you properly identify your rifle and your gun?"

"Yes, Sergeant."

"Do so."

"This is my rifle; this is my gun.

This is to shoot; this is for fun."

It was great to hear everyone from the officers on down laughing at this little episode of chicken-shit. McNulty later slapped Joe on the back and said, "Good for you. No sense picking on someone who can't take it."

"Yes, Sergeant; thanks for all the instruction. However, I see that we're having all this rifle practice; when do we get the gun practice?

McNulty was ready for him: "Practice with your gun is not in the Table of Organization and Equipment; it's not obligatory, though desirable, and is being reserved for leave time."

Battery A took the long march to the firing range, which was located in a valley at the foot of Agony Hill. When they finally got there for the first time, Lt. Spiro explained that there were two privies: one for the trainees and one for the officers. He explained that this was necessary because "the officers had different shaped butts." Frenchy saw some of the men gaping in wonder, and thought, *could anyone really believe that silly remark?*

The lieutenant then introduced a demonstrator, said to be an expert, who fired from the three basic positions: standing, kneeling, and prone.

Frenchy noticed that, when standing and kneeling, the demonstrator kept his right elbow up in the air, even higher than his hand. He thought, *Screw it, I've shot for years with my elbow much lower; I'll do it my way.*

There was a watchtower centered on a line of firing positions. Out in front of each firing position, they saw paper targets in wooden frames along trenches at one hundred, two hundred, and five hundred yards.

They practiced at all distances using the three positions, with much better scores from the prone. The weapons were first sighted-in at one hundred yards. Each rifle fired a little differently; so range and windage had to be calibrated by adjusting little knobs on the rear sights, located just above the trigger housing.

Over the PA system from the tower, Lt. Spiro, the range officer, would announce,

"Ready on the right? . . . Ready on the left? . . . Ready on the firing line? . . . One round ball ammunition, lock and load." His assistants would signal ready after each question; then the command followed: "Commence firing!"

The men took turns firing with a partner alongside. After firing, the targets were lowered; they were quickly raised again with the score indicated. If the target was missed altogether, a red flag, known as "Maggie's drawers" was waved.

They were taught by the acronym BASS, which stood for breathe, aim, slack, and squeeze. This was clear enough, except, perhaps for the "slack" part: every trigger had some slack in it, and this had to be taken up deliberately before the final squeeze. Otherwise, the trigger finger would pull the rifle off its aiming point. In spite of these teachings, some men would flinch, close their eyes, or fail to keep the rifle steady. It helped mightily to have a strong left arm, but exceptional hand-eye coordination, practice, and confidence were the most important traits of a marksman.

During a ten-minute smoke break, Frenchy was surprised when he was approached by Lt. Mason, who spoke to him and said, "*Alors, on vous appele*, Frenchy."

"*Oui, monsieur. Ma famille est Québécoise.*"

"*Oui, je comprends ca, à cause de votre accent.*"

Frenchy smiled; he knew his accent was different from the old country. With curiosity, he wondered, *Where did a guy named Mason learn French with more facility than I have?*

"Mais vous, monsieur, vous n'avez pas un nom français?"

"J'ai étudié le français à l'université et j'ai passé une an-née avec une famille á Paris."

"Je comprends, monsieur." Frenchy responded.

"Alors, Frenchy, il ne faut pas utiliser la politesse militaire avec moi en français. Si je peux vous aider, faites-moi le savoir."

"Merci monsieur."

By the time of his last *merci monsieur*, the two had gathered a little crowd. It was fairly plain to see that the lieutenant had spoken favorably to him, and this was not lost on Sgt. McNulty. However, most of the troops could not recognize the language and could not imagine what the hell happened.

Later, Frenchy explained to Joe that the lieutenant had learned French in school and in Paris where he had lived for a year with a French family, and he went on to say that Frenchy did not have to follow strict military courtesy when they were speaking French. Finally, the lieutenant offered to help him, if needed.

"You know, Joe, I hardly remember seeing Lt. Mason around the battery area, never saw him give commands, chew someone out, you know."

"Yah, you mean he's bashful and has shown no particular lead-ership qualities—just sort of stands around."

"That's it. The guy must be an ROTC Officer, studied in France, college graduate, put in his summer camp work at Fort Benning, did the maneuvers—whatever the hell they do—but never went through a real grind. Still, he was nice to me so I accept him as he appears to be—someone who can help me."

Joe shrugged his shoulders.

Frenchy, who had handled firearms from the time he was ten, had no problem qualifying as an Expert Sharpshooter and Marksman and was awarded a pin for this honor. He and the drummer, Bernie Weinman, were the best shots in the Battery. It was with consid-erable pride and growing interest that Frenchy made the trek up Agony Hill and back to A Battery after each day's training.

If he were on a high by his firing range success, one day a low followed: Sgt. Noonan selected him to clean Battalion Headquarters that evening. *What a bum deal! He probably picked me because of that confrontation with Mason—showing that being friendly with the lieutenant doesn't win points with him.* After chow Frenchy headed up the hill, as a rainstorm began.

He hadn't been to Battalion Headquarters before. It was a large, rotting building, like the others: a central room lined with little offices for the senior NCO and the officers. Cleaning was a snap: sweep, mop, empty the trash—done in a half hour. A lieutenant, pulling Duty Officer, was the only other occupant. They visited; and the lieutenant told him he could stay until the storm passed.

Then they heard faint cadence calls. A look out the window and he knew for sure he was not going anywhere: Able Battery was marching with field gear in the rain!

The officer muttered, "What the hell? Out in the rain? Unbelievable! That's a training unit, not combat troops."

The rain did cease, and Frenchy strolled—very slowly—back down the little hill. *A good day followed by an incredibly lucky evening. Thanks after all, Sgt. Noonan.*

Back at the barracks, he found the troops trying to dry out, the floors wet and muddy. It seems Sgt. Bratton had been left in charge, found the men in need of punishment and had turned them out in the rain. However, a car had stopped and a man in civilian clothes rolled down the window and called to Bratton. The car had a blue license, meaning property of a commissioned officer. They heard Bratton say, "Yes, sir; yes, sir; yes, sir!"

That ended the punishment; obviously Sgt. Bratton had been chewed out for marching the men in the rain. Much later, Cpl. Fox told Frenchy that Capt. Birdsall received call from a major, expressing concern over the march. The nickname "Dingbat Bratton" had spread around the barracks—originator unknown. Dingbat was a quieter man after the affair in the rain.

Chapter Ten
Holiday Time

Basic training was to be in its eighth week at Christmas time, and upcoming holiday time naturally led to speculation in the barracks about leave time. Frenchy had no expectation of going home—too far, too expensive, and too complicated—so he wrote to forewarn the family that this would be his first Christmas away.

On Friday, 7 December, by coincidence, the tenth anniversary of Pearl Harbor Day, Capt. Birdsall stood before the assembled troops with an announcement:

"Lt. Col. Evans, commander of the 68th Field, has asked me to announce that Monday, 24 December, will be a training holiday. Sunday being our usual rest day, I have determined to issue passes starting after inspection on Saturday to all those worthy of leave time, as determined by your barracks sergeants. If you plan to leave the Fort, you must notify your sergeants by Monday, 17 December. This is critical because the Battery Clerk must prepare the passes, and I must sign them. In addition, the Mess Sergeant must have a head count on what promises to be a very fine turkey dinner for those of us who remain on post. It will be with all the trimmings and some fellowship.

"I wish to add some personal comments. This is the first extended time away from home I dare say for most of you, and it's perfectly natural to feel homesick. I will also remind you that last Christmas several of us were halfway around the world in Frozen Chosin. I urge you to stay here—no, I will require you to stay here with us unless you have a definite place to go. Your sergeants will question you in this regard. By the way, a bar in Louisville is not "a definite place to go."

"I am well aware that this is no big break which Col. Evans and I are now presenting you; however, if it were not for Christmas, there would be no leave time. Troops traditionally receive a furlough after basic training. For you, that will be in late February, and I'm making no promises. I don't know what I will be doing then, much less what you will be doing.

"Also remember, if you are not here for duty call on Wednesday, 26 December, you're AWOL! There will be no grace period and, absent a serious emergency, no excuses. First Sergeant, carry on."

Many a nickel tinkled in the pay phones that evening, followed by, "Operator, I want to make a collect call." Frenchy waited his turn and called North River.

"Hi, Mom."

"Arnold, dear, is everything all right?"

Spoken like a true mother, he thought. As he heard Pierre also listening on the Desprez family's only telephone, Frenchy pictured them standing there with their heads jammed together. He explained that he was fine and getting more than enough to eat; then he summarized the captain's announcement.

Pierre greeted the leave time news with some enthusiasm and asked if he could wire his son at Able Battery. Frenchy said he was sure that was possible and a good idea, since he could not be easily reached by telephone.

Just two days later, he was called to the Orderly Room where Cpl. Dan handed him a telegram and said,

"Well, Desprez, I reckon this will qualify as a place to go; you're a lucky boy!"

Frenchy smiled and said, "Reading other people's mail, are you? But thanks, Cpl. Dan."

He took the opened envelope and read the wire then and there. This was a calculated act, because if he left the Orderly Room, he would be subject to whatever chores Sgt. Noonan might have in store.

A R N O L D S T O P H A V E B O O K E D R O O M S A T S T A R HOTELWESTPOINTSTOPWILLARRIVEINFORD NOONFRID AY12/21STOPADVISEONHOOKUP
LOVEP&M.

Frenchy scratched his head. Cpl. Dan said, "You ever get a telegram before, Desprez?" Seeing a shake of the head, he went on, "Don't ask me why, but these telegrams don't separate words or use punctuation. *Stop* means "period." Who are P and M?"

"My folks, Pierre and Marie."

"Okay, like I said, it's clear enough. They are arriving, in a Ford, at West Point, Kentucky, at noon, Friday the 21st; they want to know how to meet you. Since you pay for a telegram by the word, I'd say your folks sent a pretty clever message."

"What should I do?"

"Let me check a minute." The clerk went through a door into the sanctum of the Battery officers. To his momentary shock, the corporal soon emerged with Capt. Birdsall and his ami from the firing range, Lt. Mason. The captain took another look at the telegram and said, "So, Pvt. Desprez, your parents are coming to see you all the way from Minnesota—a very long drive; you're lucky to have such a devoted family. Here's what you should do: have them drive to the Fort, going to the main entrance."

Then, knowing that his junior officer wanted to make the arrangements, he paused and turned to Mason, who picked up: *"Allô, Frenchy, tout va bien?"*

Frenchy whispered, *"Oui, Oui monsieur, merci."*

The captain smiled, the corporal gasped, and Mason continued. "I will leave instructions with the gate MPs to direct your family to Able Battery. Unless they're late, they will probably be here about noontime; we will all be in our Class A uniforms; you and I can show them around, have lunch in the mess hall, and you're off!"

Mason looked toward the captain for any further words, and the Battery Commander then added, "As you know, you'll find West Point on the Ohio just north of the Military Reservation. Star Hotel's a rickety old landmark—a small place—visible from Dixie Highway; let's call it adequate.

"I want you to understand, the parents of each soldier are important to Gen. Stephens, to Col. Evans, and, of course, to us. The lieutenant tells me you're a hell of a shot and that Sgt. McNulty has favorable reports about you. Keep up the good work."

He handed the telegram back to Frenchy who thought, *I gotta get this right*. He took the telegram, then a step backward, held a salute, and said, "Sirs and corporal, I thank all of you on behalf of myself and my family."

The officers returned the salute, and Cpl. Dan chuckled, perhaps flattered at being included in the little speech.

That evening, another telephone call instructed his folks on the Fort Knox details, while he learned that sisters Lucey and Norma were coming, but Nancy would be with her fiancé's family. Fiancé! News to him, but not unexpected and about time. After Frenchy returned to duty, the rest of the family would drive farther south, at least to Mammoth Cave, then head for home in another week. It was all a good excuse to head for warmer weather.

Finally, his request to bring Big Joe with him was readily accepted and they promised to write, inviting Joe so that the big guy also would have proof of "a definite destination." This last little step had unforeseen consequences.

And so it came to pass: inspection on Saturday, 22 December, was perfunctory; Frenchy wore his Class A uniform consisting of

Ike jacket, shirt, tie, and trousers bloused in his combat boots, which were spit-polished to a high gloss; the family arrived in the Ford wagon at about eleven, finding the son they knew as Arnold standing anxiously in front of the Orderly Room; and, after hugs and tears, the women hanging back, Pierre strode boldly to the Orderly Room with his son. The lieutenant and the corporal were there; Pierre saluted, saying, "Retired Sgt. Pierre Desprez reporting, Sir."

Salutes were exchanged and the women introduced.

Frenchy was now thoroughly choked up. As he led them to the Mess Hall, Lt. Mason jabbered in French with his parents and returned salutes from dozens of scurrying troops. Pvt. Joe Cerutti met them by the barracks, looking spectacular in his uniform—like a recruitment poster!

Frenchy contemplated why he was so emotional: in addition to seeing his family after two months, he took pride in his uniform, his buddy Joe, the lieutenant, the whole damn worn-out place!

During lunch with the troops, no one put Jell-O in the mashed potatoes. The Mess Sergeant greeted the family, and Marie eagerly accepted his offer of a tour of the cooking and storage areas. She was amazed at the cleanliness. The sergeant explained the KP process, then added, "At Christmas we have a nice custom: the men of Jewish faith volunteer to pull KP. The opposite occurs during High Holy Days."

Frenchy introduced the family to Sgt. McNulty and First Sgt. Noonan, but avoided Dingbat Bratton. Frenchy thought, *Shunning the man probably adds to his paranoia, but rehabbing Bratton will have to be an opportunity for somebody else, not me.*

The old Ford station wagon, which had made so many trips in the North Woods, held all six passengers well enough, especially since Pierre had long ago rigged a luggage rack on the roof. Frenchy took the wheel and drove around the post, stopping at the main PX, where the family wondered at the startling low prices.

The boys bought little gifts and then made purchases on behalf of the others, since only military people could use the PX.

The heart of Fort Knox was handsome, indeed. The parade ground was surrounded by the various red-brick headquarters buildings. Each had a sign out front, using the omnipresent brown letters on a yellow background plus the 3rd Armored triangular insignia. Impressive pieces of materiel sat here and there: famous tanks, guns, howitzers, and vehicles from past wars. They drove by the site of the U.S. Bullion Depository, then out the main gate (no fence!).

The next stop took everyone else by surprise. Across the Dixie Highway and a little north of the Fort gate, Frenchy pulled into a used car lot, explaining that he had saved over five hundred dollars after three summers on *Hawkeye* and wanted his father to help him pick out a car. He reasoned that with men regularly shipping out from Knox there would be a steady supply of decent cars right there. He hoped to remain at Knox another three months and could then drive home before going overseas.

Pierre advised Marie, "What the hell, I'd rather have him in charge than in the back seat with some drunk at the wheel."

Turning to his son, he added, "But no car of yours moves from this lot till your Uncle Guy advises he has an insurance binder on the vehicle—a binder adequate in his judgment to protect you!"

It took an hour with much tire-kicking, odometer-checking, and test-driving. Joe had a chance to visit with the ladies and already seemed to zero in on Norma the Normal, while Pierre and his son zeroed in on a 1946 Chevrolet—a four-door, maroon, quite handsome, driven 35,000 miles. Frenchy showed his father the deciding factor: a windshield decal indicating it had been owned by a Fort Knox officer—some comfort, since the owner could at least afford to put oil in it.

Pierre said he was giving one hundred dollars toward the purchase. The salesman asked $450; Frenchy countered with $400 in cash, closing the deal. Yes, he could leave Big Red on the lot until next weekend. There would be no paperwork delays. Guy was to call Friendly Sam, the car salesman, and advise him regarding the binder. This was best, since it remained hard to get ahold of a basic trainee.

The Star Hotel faced the Ohio River just north of the Dixie Highway, painted white with eight thin columns supporting a second-floor porch and intricate railing, all topped by a single, off-centered gable. Surely a unique structure, it seemed designed by a committee of amateur carpenters some fifty years before. A stairway greeted them awkwardly close to the door front, with dining room and bar to the left and two parlors on the right—both decked out in Christmas cheer. All second-floor bedrooms faced either front or back off a narrow hall. Frenchy remembered when the captain used the word "adequate," which now seemed a pretty accurate description. The cluttered parlors and bedrooms featured old and overstuffed furniture, however at least all clean—no dust, no mildew. Marie called the Star, "antiquish, country Victorian"— *whatever that meant.* He suspected she had invented the description; after all, women knew about such things.

They dined well; in the off-season time the Desprez family dominated the little hotel. Marie figured the Star was more popular for its food than its beds.

Next morning, Joe lumbered down to breakfast, now dressed in Levi's and a tee shirt—muscles rippling, a Charles Atlas. "Boy, I'm glad you're my son's friend," Pierre said with a grin. Knowing Frenchy put him up to this, Joe responded, "That only applies when we're cleaning garbage cans; Frenchy better watch out!"

Marie piped up, "Why this 'Frenchy' talk? My son has a nice American name, 'Arnold'—nothing more needed."

Joe lowered his head, bit his lip, and sheepishly replied, "I know, I stuck him with it ma'am, and I do apologize. You know my nick name is 'Dago.'"

"How horrible!" Norma interjected, "Worse than 'Frenchy,' even; that's an epithet—an ethnic slur."

"I know, I know; but that is so only if intended and taken that way, but now my own dear mother will say, 'Dago, bambino, it's a time a for da lasagna.'"

Norma laughed and fought back: "What bullcrap!" She already knew that Mrs. Cerutti was a school teacher and wasn't even Italian. She pointed at him, "Okay, Mr. Ethnic; but you'll be 'Joe' to me, and you can call me 'Norma the Normal,' because I alone in this crazy family am normal."

Everyone laughed. That was the opening salvo of much teasing between the two; and by day's end, Norma quietly placed her hand in Joe's, where it remained a good part of the time.

Meanwhile, Pierre offered to lead the family on walks along the Ohio River, to Louisville for a show, or maybe a riverboat ride. However, Frenchy and Joe were fresh from marches down and up Agony Hill and were more interested in sleeping late and resting, "recharging our batteries," as Joe put it.

Frenchy added, "Do your gallivanting after we're out'a here."

Joe proved to be the entertainer, specializing, as always, on ethnic matters. He would name a food, and the family was expected to guess from what country it originated. Golobki, paella, borsch, frijoles, and haggis were some easy guesses.

"All right, wise-ass," said Frenchy, "What is Ouzo?"

Joe bravely guessed, "A Portuguese cheese."

"A fairly nice try; it's a Greek aperitif. I can see the bottle from here behind the bar and thought it would stick you; for not knowing, we ought to make you down a shot of the stuff."

Joe admitted defeat and took up country-by-country differences in the quality of toilet paper. Lucey blushed. He moved on to the differences between heaven and hell. The punchline was, "In hell the Italians are the soldiers; the Germans are the policemen; and the English are the cooks."

The boys then started a story from basic training, but got to laughing so hard they had to stop and start over. It seems there had been a class on personal hygiene that centered on venereal disease. The instructor was a pink-cheeked second lieutenant, who said, "It is perfectly normal and commonplace for a man to go his whole life without engaging in sexual relations."

In the back of the classroom, a black soldier from way down south, totally shocked by what he considered an absurd statement—an absolute impossibility—blurted out, "Oh no, sah!"

Of course the classroom erupted with laughter, as did the boys when they told the story. Lucey blushed, but her father roared the loudest. Joe tried one more:

"A sometimes fatal disease is 'gonakorea.'"

"Oh! Not funny, not funny!" Marie responded sternly.

On Christmas Eve, Pierre came a little bit out of his shell about The Great War. He talked about the time during the St. Mihiel Offensive when they took the town of Euvezin, establishing 89th Division Headquarters in the local chateau and remaining there from 14 September to 26 September 1918. He remembered the exact dates. The Germans shelled them the entire time, finally forcing the Americans to move to other buildings where a hillside lent more protection. He added that the 354th Regiment was in the Lucey Sector.

Everyone then looked at younger daughter, Lucey, and Pierre nodded, "Yes, I found shelter there and liked the name, so the town of Lucey was, indeed, the inspiration for this Lucey right here. Our eldest daughter, Nancy, is also named for a French town. *Norma*, however, is an opera."

Joe's reaction to the words about Norma was startling; he shook, covered his face with his hands, and leaned forward.

"What is it, Joe?" Frenchy asked. There was a pause, as Joe collected himself.

"Well, this *Norma* thing just caught me by surprise; I hadn't put two and two together. You see, we're big opera buffs at home, especially Italian opera. Bellini wrote *Norma* over a hundred years ago; it's about the Roman occupation of Gaul. Norma is a High Priestess—a French Druid—who is betrayed by the Roman

Pro-Consul. With a change of heart, he joins her as they are both burnt at the stake."

Norma rose and stood behind him, hands on his massive slumped shoulders.

"It's no secret that Joe and I have kind of hit it off this weekend. So now it seems two thousand years ago, Italian boy goes up in flames with French girl. Well, this is now; I'm no Druid; and you're sure no Pro-Consul!"

Joe reached up and touched her hands, cheering up at once, "Right, right, but I want you to hear our record of Maria Callas singing "Casta Diva"—*Norma's* great aria; it's unbelievable.

Attention shifted back to Pierre. With everyone's attention, he became particularly serious—for him, downright eloquent, "Well getting back to my days under fire at Euvezin, on the other side of the hills, in the opposite trenches, perhaps where the shelling came from, a mustached soldier a few years older than me served as messenger—a dangerous job.

"This Austrian vagabond attained the rank of corporal and was decorated with the Iron Cross, both Second and First Class. In later life it was the only medal he wore, and he looked back on his battle experience, which he called *fronterlebnis*, as the most formative influence of his life. Why did God let so many millions die and not let an artillery shell destroy this person of all persons! Like friend and foe—on both sides of the lines in those terrible days, he was under artillery, mortar, and small arms fire for months on end!"

There was a hush; it seemed that Pierre had pushed his talk too far; his lips trembled. Lucey finally asked, "Who was this man, daddy?"

The reply was a whisper, "Adolph Hitler."

The boys had bought small presents for everyone at the PX. You can't splurge when you make eighty-seven dollars a month. They exchanged gifts under a tree in the west parlor and enjoyed Christmas dinner there as well.

About 4:00 Christmas afternoon, Pierre rose and said, "Good times must come to an end," a signal he would drive the boys back to Fort Knox, leaving the women at the Hotel. Packed and ready to go, the only delay was the kiss Joe planted on Norma. Frenchy thought, *Never have I endured such an emotion-charged Christmas. What will the next year bring? I could be a goner by next year—statistically it's a good possibility. What the hell! Be positive, not a moper!*

Chapter Eleven
Back to Basics

Frenchy retrieved his new car, Big Red, the next Saturday. Soldiers in basic training were not allowed to have cars, but he thought he would challenge the regulation. What could they do? As a partial subterfuge, he parked up at Battalion Headquarters.

Soon after the holiday, a crisis arose: Bingo Heusting's entrenching tool was stolen. Each soldier had been allotted a short shovel with a blade that could be turned 90 degrees to form a pick. It was obvious to Frenchy that little Bingo, being the wimpiest guy in the barracks, had been specially picked for the theft.

Frenchy was furious—one of his rages! But what could he do? After some pondering, he and Dago Joe knocked on Sgt. McNulty's door with a plan. Next morning, McNulty's wake-up call was extra early, and center barracks was first in formation. McNulty shouted, "At ease; give me your attention; Pvt. Desprez has an announcement."

Frenchy trotted forward, still so hot under the collar that he overcame his natural diffidence and made his first speech:
"Someone in my platoon is missing his entrenching tool. You all remember what the captain said to do with a thief? Well, perhaps this was just a mistake; anyway, we're all for sticking together and avoiding big trouble. The man who is missing the tool happens to be

one of the smartest soldiers in the camp. He has a sort of brand—a mark—which he puts on all his equipment.

"That's a pretty good idea. Of course, it wouldn't do for me to say what mark, or where. It also has been explained to me that sometimes the Supply Sergeant has extra gear to replace mislaid items. I reckon during mess sometime today would be a good time to quietly return the tool. Tomorrow, Saturday, being inspection day, Sgt. McNulty has agreed to look for the tool, if it's still missing; but I figure it will be returned before then."

That evening, the missing tool was found on the rifle racks. There was no further action. However, the sergeant commented to Frenchy on how fortunate it was that Bingo had marked the tool.

"No, Sergeant, how fortunate someone thought Bingo had marked the tool."

Another event occurred during basic, which taught Frenchy an important lesson. Many soldiers on the first floor were blacks from the rural South. Some had been brought up with little contact with white folks, much less the type of close encounters they were now experiencing. One, a tall skinny boy named Parker, was the platoon loudmouth—very strident and offensive. Trouble brewed for a week or so between Parker and a short, stocky Irishman named O'Hare.

It was decided to stage the fight behind center barracks. One of the black soldiers asked Frenchy, Joe, and Bernie to attend—a wise move, since this was to be a one-on-one and not blacks-against-whites.

A circle formed. Parker asked, "How you wanna fight?"

O'Hare looked tough and experienced, really a stronger man than skinny Parker, but he made a bad mistake: he answered, "Anything goes!"

They put out their dukes, then circled, looking for a few seconds almost like prize fighters, a fake here, a fake there, feeling each other out. Then, almost in a blur, O'Hare was down, and Parker was kicking him in the head. Blacks and whites pulled Parker away. O'Hare, cut and bloody, skulked off. Frenchy and his buddies agreed: "Never fight a black man!"

Training went on. The infiltration course involved crawling across a field, as 30-caliber heavy machine guns fired live ammo with tracers over their heads.

They threw hand grenades. The thing was shaped like a little football, about four and a half inches long and two inches wide with a safety handle—sometimes called the "spoon," which curved around it and was held on by a steel pin connected to a ring. Frenchy learned that he could hold the grenade comfortably in his hand, firmly grasping the safety handle. When ready to use it, he could pull the ring, which extracted the pin. No hurry, he could then hold the grenade in this manner indefinitely, but if he didn't hold that handle, in about five seconds it would snap off and the grenade would explode!

They took turns entering a pit where an instructor knelt beside them. At his turn, Frenchy crouched down, took a grenade, held it like a football, pulled the pin and threw a sort of spiral.

"Great toss," said the instructor, "longest throw so far."

Well and good, thought Frenchy, *but I sure as hell wouldn't want your job! What happens when some dingbat drops a grenade?* He later told his friends that the word came from the French word *pomegranate*, coined in reference to its size and shape. When he commanded the 8th Army, Gen. Ridgway had always carried a grenade hooked to his paratrooper suspenders about level with his right shirt pocket. This certainly brought attention to the weapon and the man and seemed a better touch than Patton's outlandish pearl-handled revolvers and white bulldog.

They learned about gas masks the hard way. Using their masks, they were first subject to mustard gas—a WWI killer, and then they endured tear gas both with and without the masks. They had classes in CBR—chemical, biological, and radiological warfare.

They had bayonet drill in which they learned various moves like the horizontal thrust, horizontal butt thrust, and vertical butt thrust, all moves made while doing some tough-guy yelling. These were all well and good and all worth knowing, but Frenchy figured he would likely be bigger than some Asian opponent, so the long horizontal thrust would be best for him to use to pierce the enemy before a smaller guy could reach him. It might also help to have spent years scrapping with a hockey stick. Bernie Weinman put a damper on these fierce theories when he said, "Hey, in this day and age, when do two enemies meet with empty rifles and fixed bayonets? That's highly unlikely. Basil Rathbone loses his duel with Errol Flynn only in the movies!"

They charged across a valley while live artillery whistled over their heads and shells landed on the hillside to their front. He was told the guns were 105 howitzers. Another time, they attacked a mock aggressor village.

Then they encountered a new army innovation: the concept of retreat. Probably since King David's day, it had not been considered wise to teach men to retreat. It put bad thoughts in their heads. However, it had been found in Korea that when huge waves of CCF would mass attack a thinly-held hilltop, the best course would sometimes be to kill them by the hundreds, as they struggled up, and then on prearranged command the defenders would disappear off the other side. The Chinese would have the hill but would have many dead and wounded, and likely be tired and short of ammunition, food, and water.

That was the time for the artillery to pulverize the hill, then to lift their fire, as the U.N. troops with fresh reserves charged back up the hill. Thus, a retreat became a proven, tactical device, leading to ultimate success—in no way a bug-out.

With air supremacy, these enemy attacks were sometimes met by Corsair or AD Skyraider bombing runs, including napalm bombs. In this manner, the Korean hills along the current MLR (as the main line of resistance was called) were left barren and pockmarked with shell craters and fox holes. Here and there black, burnt-out areas showed the napalm effects.

With these principles in mind, half of Able Battery would be positioned on a hill in the Fort Knox Training Area. The other half would attack, and the doctrines of attack, retreat, and counterattack would be acted out. When Frenchy was halfway up the hill in the attacking group, he glanced up: in a leafy bush, not six feet away, he saw a set of white teeth grinning at him—it was one of the defenders, Burley from the first floor!

Frenchy knew that in real combat he would have been a goner for sure. He remembered seeing those teeth—just the teeth—a black man's shinny teeth! Like in *Alice in Wonderland*, when Alice saw the Cheshire Cat in the tree; then the cat disappeared, except for its teeth. He loved the *Alice* books, especially the poems, and would have brought them along, except for the likely ridicule.

They were exposed to, but not thoroughly trained in other arms, including the 45-cal. automatic pistol, light and heavy 30-cal. machine guns, the Browning Automatic Rifle (BAR), 50-cal. machine gun, the so-called grease gun, the recoilless rifle, the Bazooka, and the 60mm and 81mm mortars. The M3A1 grease gun was particularly interesting: a shortrange, 45-caliber submachine gun made with a combination of machined and stamped parts so it resembled a child's toy. Frenchy fired it at tin cans on a hillside and was able to walk the cans away from him, always firing from the hip. The Chinese Type 36 was a direct copy.

The trainees learned that the clever Chinese also had both a 61mm and a devastating 82mm mortar. If the Chinese captured any of our 60mm or 81mm shells, they could use 'em, but their slightly larger shells wouldn't fit in our mortars. He pondered, *How many of our troops have been hit with our own ammo?*

A final training event was the bivouac—consisting of three days in the woods. Each soldier had been given one canvas shelter half, two tent poles, a length of rope, and several tent pegs, and when these parts were united with those of a comrade, a pup tent resulted. It was best to sleep with heads slightly up hill, with a shallow trench dug around the tent to ward off rainwater . . . but no need to fear that—on Frenchy's bivouac it snowed!

Each squad dug a slit trench downhill from the tents. These toilet trenches were about the width of a bayonet, about six feet long, as deep as possible. The soldier could thus put a foot on each side, lower his trousers, and let fly in the open breeze. Fancy trenches had a forked stick stuck in the ground. A toilet paper roll would be put on one fork with an empty coffee can kept over it to protect against weather.

The officers and NCOs were there, too, but they used larger tents and covered slit trenches. The officers' butts were not exposed—more proof that rank has its privileges.

While on bivouac, they ate C-rations. These were canned meals left over from the last war. Some were palatable, like the spaghetti and meatballs; but others, like sausage patties, were greasy and hard to take. Other smaller cans contained crackers and jelly and cocoa—all decent. For breakfasts, the cooks dished powdered eggs into the mess kits. Utensils were cleaned in boiling water after every meal.

At one formation, Sgt. Noonan surprised the troops by muttering, "Brrr, its pretty cold out—just above freezing." He paused; they thought maybe he was done; then in a stronger voice he said,

"Now picture it 50 degrees colder, high winds, and Chinese mortars . . . weeks on end—not just three days!"

The troops were quiet for a while after that.

Some had never roughed it like this before. Frenchy figured, all told, he had spent months living outdoors—*no sweat!*

Chapter Twelve
Leave Time

After the halfway point at Christmas, weekend passes were issued—good for Saturday, after inspection, until Sunday night. The boys would take Big Red to Louisville's USO building for Saturday night dances. Young Louisville girls would stand on one side of the room and readily dance with any of the troops. While there was much talk about doing more than just dancing, overnight relationships did not seem feasible, perhaps because Frenchy and his new friends lacked the savoir-faire of cousin Raul or perhaps because the girls were well-chaperoned. They stayed at the YMCA and packed as many bodies in one room as permitted. Louisville was friendly to soldiers.

On his second USO outing, Frenchy was approached by a pretty girl he had not encountered before.

"I heard them calling you 'Frenchy,'" she said, receiving a nod and a short explanation concerning his North Woods background; she went on, "I have a friend who is too bashful to come to these dances. Her family is from France, and her father is on a sabbatical, teaching French literature at the University of Louisville. Maybe the two of you would hit it off."

Gazing at her, Frenchy thought of the famous quote, "Why don't you speak for yourself?" But then, *What the heck*, he said, "Sure, that would be nice."

They introduced themselves; her name was Anne Robards, and she said her shy friend was Amanda Fontenot. How could they make this blind date happen?

Anne returned from the pay phone, said she had called Amanda, who was hesitant, but game. The next day, the girls would be at St. Mark's 11:00am mass, out in Iroquois Park—a nice area south of downtown.

He thought, *What could I do but say yes? Now what am I in for? The girl had been found at home on Saturday night and wanted to meet in church?* Fortunately, he had a clean shirt.

St. Marks was found at the edge of a park developed in the 1890s by Frederick Law Olmsted, the great landscape designer. Anne and her friend were by the church door. Amanda was as tall as he, skinny, small breasted, with a slightly receding chin— *Well, an all-right chin, just not a jutting chin. I guess you'd call it a pointed chin, not a rounded Desprez chin.* After he had a chance to scout out her legs, he decided they were A-OK. She had beautiful brown hair—just past shoulder length—which tended to cascade over her face—fine, unblemished skin, long straight nose, perfect teeth.

Frenchy remembered his sisters growing up and saw in Amanda what had until recently been an awkward, ungainly, overly tall girl just now growing into a very attractive woman. As for the bashful part, of course she was bashful—she was a stranger in a strange country. He was bashful; she was bashful, too; *What the hell, we might just sit and stare at each other!*

Even though Frenchy considered himself a weed in the pope's garden, he made enough of the correct liturgical moves to get through the service. Matchmaker Anne disappeared, and they went to a coffee shop for lunch. Her family was from Normandy—

what a coincidence, but he decided for now to skip the story about William the Bastard. Her parents had decided to spend at least a year in the U.S., where both taught French: papa at the University, mama at a high school. Frenchy and Amanda thought about going to a movie, but decided they could get better acquainted if they went to her home, which proved to be a nice apartment about five blocks from the church. Since October, this was his first experience in a private dwelling.

The parents greeted Frenchy with kindness and interest. The father, Jean, was a lanky man with a mustache, slightly resembling Charles DeGaulle; the mother, Sofia, seemed sweet, maybe a little tacky in a dark dress and sturdy, practical shoes—perhaps *couture de classe moyenne*. He realized he had seen them from a distance at St. Marks, where they must have decided not to make contact with the young people.

They visited in French and English, selecting English as best and deciding right away that they could hardly call him Frenchy, which the father equated with being called a frog.

They talked about books and there found the common interest, to the surprise of all, a very common interest. "Arnaud," as they dubbed him, listed his favorite childhood books. They were familiar with *Alice . . .* and *Treasure Island*—not too surprising, both being hatched just across the Channel. The parents had read many British classics—like Sir Walter Scott and Conan Doyle—but not many American titles. What could they get from the library for next time?

Frenchy chuckled: *So I made the cut, and there's to be another rencontrer!* If they wanted American classics, he suggested Longfellow and Poe, specifically "The Midnight Ride of Paul Revere," "The Raven," and "Annabelle Lee."

They talked about the military: Jean compared the American experience in Korea with the French struggle against the Vietminh in Indochina, explaining that the French had a battalion of elite troops serving with the Americans in Korea. The French Battalion had made a bayonet charge and taken Heartbreak Ridge back in October 1951. Their leader was an incredible soldier: Lt. Gen. Raoul Magrin-Venery of the French Foreign Legion, in Korea using the nom de guerre Raoul Monclar. In World War I, he had been wounded seven times and received eleven awards for valor. Monclar accepted a demotion of four ranks to lieutenant colonel so he could lead the French Battalion and fight under the already-outstanding American Col. Paul L. Freeman of the 23rd Infantry Regiment.

Jean wished his country could do more, but French forces were strained by problems in Indochina and North Africa. Frenchy was surprised, a little shocked, to hear Jean talk frankly about the decolonization of the French Republic.

They even talked sports, with Frenchy urging them to attend at least one baseball game—to watch The Louisville Colonials, a triple-A team with a fine record. The Fontenots nodded at him, he thought a little quizzically, until Jean replied, "Oh yes, yes, the American pastime: beginning this spring, we surely shall go, as you say, out to the old ballgame."

He left in the late afternoon with Amanda walking him to his car, where, to his surprise, she grabbed hold of his head, pulling him toward her and kissed him. In part just to keep his balance, he grabbed hold of her solid frame, while she completed her little ritual with the French word of parting, "*Merde!*"

He knew the expression, not the most polite, but used all the time and literally translating to one of the most uncouth, four-letter words. He had the presence to respond, *Merde!*

What a crazy world. I meet someone at mass, talk litera-ture, war, politics, and sports, end up with a kiss and a dose of French slang; ooh-la-la, those French!

He drove carefully down the Dixie Highway—known as "the Dixie Dieway"—and back to the Fort. He walked toward the middle barracks, thinking with no regrets, *I guess I have a girlfriend.*

Chapter Thirteen
Basic and Beyond

In the gab sessions of middle barracks, second floor, Frenchy and his friends sized up their situations. They were due to graduate Saturday, 23 February 1952. What then? It was so cold in Korea it was extra hard to dig trenches, bunkers, and underground living quarters, harder still to fight. Winter storms swept down from Manchuria, and the sea effect caused huge snowfalls. Bad weather hampered air and naval support for the U.N. Forces.

Even so, the Chinese had to endure the same problems and many others as well. Their replacements had to march down from the Yalu, mostly at night, often unable to carry food enough for the long march and unable to forage off the frozen valleys and mountains of North Korea.

There was every reason to be cynical about the Armistice talks, now in their seventh month, and there was the commencement of talk about trouble controlling the North Korean and Chinese soldiers in the U.N. prison camps—a problem soon to become a catastrophe.

Obviously, if there were something else to do or someplace else to go, have at it. Lt. Mason checked Frenchy's test scores, saw that he would be eligible for Officer Candidate School, and then counseled with him. Both knew it would be better if he were older.

Besides, his active duty commitment as an enlisted soldier was for just two years; if he took a commission, his active duty time would extend by more than six months. Mason and Capt. Birdsall found an alternative—they arranged for him to be put on orders for the eight-week Armored Leadership School. The next class would start soon and would train him to be a non-commissioned officer and tank commander.

Mason, himself, was to have a leave and then off to Armed Forces Far East (AFFE), meaning Korea, with a Military Occupation Specialty of infantry platoon leader—atop the danger list. During their last visit—mostly in French—Mason explained that he had gone to Claremont College, majored in French, spent a year in Paris, taken an ROTC commission, and trained at Fort Benning. He was from Matoon, Illinois, had two elder brothers and a widowed mother. Frenchy still figured his lieutenant friend was more than a little unsure of himself. The work with the basic train-ees had done little to improve his readiness; he seemed to have had no experience asserting himself, no experience being tough, chewing out someone—a vital skill for a company-grade officer. They were both bashful introverts. Time would tell, but Frenchy felt like saying, "Kick some ass; show 'em who's in charge; you've gotta lead."

The drummer, Weinman, wanted special services—like a drum and bugle corps—but was scheduled for AFFE. Dago Cerutti signed up for jump school. He would have a leave and then go to Fort Bragg, North Carolina. Separating was hard on both Frenchy and Joe. It was typical army: you meet some guys . . . you like 'em . . . they're gone. It could be worse; they were in a dangerous business. But neither Frenchy nor Joe were then headed for harm's way, unless you called jumping out of airplanes "harm's way." Anyhow, Frenchy had a hunch Dago Joe would show up again; if not with him, with the Druid Priestess—Norma the Normal.

The biggest surprise and so-called, all-time super boon-dog-gle was Bingo Heusting's assignment: Counter-Intelligence Corps, at Fort Holabird, Maryland. Bingo confessed that the appointment had been made before he entered basic. No one seemed to know exactly what CIC was about except that it was well known that CIC men wore civilian clothes, had expense accounts, and checked up on things. They must be counterspies—liked comic book heroes. *What a break!*

As to the sergeants, it was understood that Noonan was up for promotion to master sergeant—top rung of the enlisted ladder.

McNulty planned to resign from the service; in response to the prospect of doing a second tour in Korea, he said, "Been there, done that." Frenchy had briefed him on the Great Lakes Maritime Academy, Traverse City, Michigan, where he could take advantage of the GI Bill and be trained in various disciplines, such as deck officer, pilot, and maritime businessman. They promised to stay in touch, as Frenchy smiled and shook his head, thinking about that former fear of sergeants.

A long-discussed plot against Sgt. Bratton now ripened. Bingo wrote a letter to the Post Inspector General, explaining that he had not written until then for fear of reprisal. However, he wished the IG to know that he had studied psychology in college and felt that Sgt. Bratton was mentally unfit for duty with a training unit. He simply recommended Bratton be given an interview with a trained psychologist. Some specific instances relating to Bratton's eccentric behavior were cited. The letter praised Able Battery's other leaders—the first sergeant and other cadre—and tried to make clear Bingo was not complaining about strict leadership. The letter was typed with the secret connivance of Cpl. Dan. Also, Frenchy, Joe, Bernie, and others signed so it ended up sort of a petition, with a carbon copy to Capt. Birdsall.

Frenchy and his friends never learned what happened, but they were proud of their efforts.

The graduation ceremony was in the main post theater, and, naturally enough, consisted mostly of a series of inspirational talks. Maj. Gen. R.W. Stephens bestirred himself to attend, apparently to the surprise of the other officers. The young trainees could not know that this plump, bald, two-star general had commanded the 21st Regiment, 24th Division in Korea—very tough duty. It was his first combat command; he was popular and outspoken and had been awarded the Distinguished Service Cross in July 1950. He had also received other decorations, including the Silver Star, and the Croix de Guerre.

The Post Band played the National Anthem, after which Capt. Birdsall introduced the trainees to the senior officers simply by pointing to the audience, referring to the Division's Special Order and stating that all present had completed the prescribed course in a satisfactory manner. With the Division Commander present, the two colonels were short and snappy.

Most of the men in the audience had never attended a graduation ceremony, never held much of a job, and never been promoted to any sort of higher rank, so they surely were inspired by Maj. Gen. Stephens, whose closing remarks were as follows:

"You have just completed a very important phase in your army career—I think the most important phase.

"You are leaving Fort Knox with a challenge and an added responsibility. Your challenge is to carry on in the outstanding manner of those who have preceded you in the 3rd Armored Division and have given this Division a combat record equaled by few other units.

"Your responsibility is most important in these trying days for your country and the remainder of the free world—to be ready and willing to defend your homeland and freedom.

"I am proud to have been your Commanding General and hope that we will serve together again some day. Good luck in your future assignments, and may God bless you."

After they fell out and formed up in their usual formation, the band struck up "The Caisson Song," a march so popular that it was used by all army units, not just artillerymen. At the point where the words go, "shout out your numbers loud and strong," the troops shouted, "one, two."

Frenchy had invited Amanda and her parents to the ceremony and was glad to see all three standing with other spectators; they applauded and waved. Frenchy had been a little troubled by Gen. Stephens seeking to compare the bunch of rookies now present with the Spearhead Division, which, after all, had advanced across Europe 101 miles in one day! That was the equivalent of going two-thirds of the way across the east–west Korean front line! However, he thought the ceremony had been a good one, and that tradition was important. The hard thing was to leave Joe, Bernie, Bingo, Lt. Mason, Sgt. McNulty, and many others, even crabby Sgt. Noonan.

He dined that evening with Amanda and her parents at the Service Club. He had seen them on weekends in Louisville, where the four met and got more and more acquainted. They first drove by the U.S. Bullion Depository—a fortified structure used to store much of the Nation's gold reserves. Then he took them to the PX, where, like all civilians, they were wowed by the low prices. Amanda said they had rented the books Frenchy had suggested, and the family was eager to have readings and to hear his comments.

Chapter Fourteen
Between Schools

And so, with graduation from basic, Frenchy became a Private E-2: no new stripes, no outward signs of change, but a slight pay hike and the strong hope that non-commissioned officers would no longer go out of their way to be nasty.

Indeed, Cpl. Dan Fox went out of his way to be a help and in so doing proved that the name Fox fitted him well. Leadership School didn't start until 2 March, leaving Frenchy a week with nothing to do. He had no place to go and did not want to take leave time. If he stayed on post, he might be stuck pulling KP or serving as a guard in the stockade.

Instead, with Lt. Mason's help, Lt. Spiro, the rifle instructor agreed to take Frenchy as an extra assistant instructor for that week. Temporary duty was arranged as well as a room in the transient barracks where Dan lived.

That week Frenchy went out to the range at the foot of Agony Hill in style—riding from the Range Office in the back of a three-quarter-ton truck instead of pounding gravel. He posed and demonstrated the basic positions for firing the M-1. He was careful to keep his elbow raised—army style. He had confessed to Lt. Spiro that he liked to use a different style. The lieutenant didn't seem to mind, telling Frenchy, "I'm sure you know,

Desprez, there's the right way, the wrong way, and the army way. Demonstrate the army way; and when it counts, suit yourself. After all, maybe there's a fourth way—the Desprez way."

Out on the range, there was soon a strange problem: hearing a sergeant at the far end of the range yelling at a soldier, Frenchy trotted down the line, and found the sergeant nose-to-nose with a man who appeared unwilling to shoot. Frenchy put his hand on the sergeant's shoulder and said, "Please, let me talk to him."

Somewhat startled, the sergeant stepped back. Frenchy took the soldier's arm and guided him a few paces away.

"What's the problem?"

Tearfully, the boy responded, "I've never shot a gun. I've never killed anything. When the time came, I froze. It just seemed so oppressive, so deadly, like a live thing!"

Frenchy explained that he had shot since he was big enough to hold a rifle and had killed hundreds of animals. He thought firearms, properly used, were fun and important. No one wanted to kill a man, but for him, and, indeed, for everyone on the range, such an act was a long way off—if ever! Putting his arm on the boy, he asked, "Are you against fighting for religious reasons?"

"I don't know, maybe."

Sensing that this was a case of sheer terror and not a planned protest, Frenchy guided him back to the firing line. Meanwhile, Lt. Spiro, who had to climb down from his tower, came jogging up. The sergeant motioned to him to hold off; all was quiet on the range. Frenchy checked to see if it was clear to fire; he helped the boy level his rifle, as they lay side-by-side. Both put their fingers in the trigger housing, and it was actually Frenchy who pulled the trigger.

"Fire again," he said.

With both fingers in place once more, he whispered, "Pull."

Wham! Off went one round. It didn't hit the target, but it was a start.

"I'll work here for a while, if that's Okay, Sir."

The sergeant smiled; the lieutenant said, "You bet!"

Lt. Spiro paused momentarily and then shouted, "As you were; back on the firing line!"

Frenchy spent the morning with the frightened fellow, who actually hit the target a few times.

"If they let me, I'll work with you again. Meanwhile, always do what you are told; learn about all these weapons. You must realize that if I hadn't intervened, the sergeant would have been forced to discipline or report you. That's why he willingly stood aside when I came up, as I hoped he would; he wanted to avoid trouble for you, sort of find a way out of what could be a big problem.

"Remember, if someone fails to obey orders, he is subject to company punishment or to trial in one of three levels of courts martial with punishment at even the lowest level still imposing up to six months in the stockade, therefore leaving the convicted soldier's record permanently tarnished. If a soldier has a disciplinary army record, his problems carry over to civilian life. Obviously, a dishonorable discharge or a Section 368 discharge will brand the fellow forever. You must obey orders. Am I getting through to you? Obey orders! Damn it, obey orders!"

Frenchy wanted to scare the poor guy so he laid it on pretty thick, but he then softened his words, "However, if someone objects to becoming a combat soldier for religious reasons, there is a formal process to go through; sometimes the army will put a conscientious objector, known as a CO, to work in a hospital or some job like that where he is both serving and helping others, but not fighting. The catch is that the proposed conscientious objections have to have a provable relationship to prior lifestyle; for example, a Quaker might make a more likely CO than a former bartender. In your case, I think you were mostly just scared."

The boy nodded earnestly. Frenchy went on, "When you get back to your barracks, they will ask what the hell happened. I suggest you laugh and simply say 'boy, did I have the jitters; that marksman straightened me out.' You understand? Work out a little answer in advance.'"

The soldier nodded and beamed so earnestly that Frenchy gave him a hug, started to turn away, then, pointing his finger, said with a smile, "By the way, it's a rifle, not a gun!" Then he thought, *My Lord, I was acting just like a sergeant, kinda putting the poor guy on the spot, laying it on the line—my first mild ass-chewing!*

That wasn't quite the end of it: when the truck squeaked to a halt back at the Range Office, Lt. Spiro took Frenchy and the sergeant aside.

"Desprez, the sergeant tells me he was having trouble handling the situation and gives you full credit for stepping in. I saw the rest. I'm proud of you both; we all must understand that there is a time to be tough and a time to step back and let others solve problems. You two combined to save that boy.

"I'm dropping a note to Col. Murch, Commandant of the Leadership School, telling him what happened. The colonel is a remarkable soldier—a great leader in Korea, both before the breakout and after the CCF intervention. That's all the help I can give you, Desprez; you're at the bottom of one greasy pole; I'm near the bottom of another."

The lieutenant, then the sergeant, shook his hand, followed by salutes all around.

Back at the rifle range the next day, he again helped the frightened boy for a while, and then turned him loose. Frenchy could only shake his head, shuddering and wondering if the poor fellow could survive the grenade pit and the infiltration course—especially the grenade pit.

Throughout the week, Frenchy helped many of the trainees adjust their rifle sights and was also allowed to practice. His scores improved; the lieutenant wished he could recruit Frenchy for the Corps rifle team, but he was on other orders, important orders to the Leadership School.

Frenchy had been spending weekends with Amanda but decided to stay on post the next weekend. He had chores to do and really didn't know how to get a pass in his in between status. After work during the week he had made trips to the tailor shop, where he had his shirts cut thinner so there was no bag around the middle, making him look sharper and trimmer—showing off his waistline. He did the same with his Ike jackets, also adding brass hooks, which he could attach to his belt so the jacket could never ride up and look messy. He did the same trimming with his fatigue shirts and had the lower sets of pockets on his fatigue trousers sewn shut so they would be flat, closed, and much sharper.

His father had given him an additional fifty dollars for Christmas, and Uncle Guy had sent a like amount. Most of this was spent at the PX. He bought additional shirts, socks, and the jockey-type shorts he preferred to the GI boxer style.

The big deal purchase was a pair of ten-inch Corcoran Jump Boots. These had a stiffer, more rounded, better looking toe and took a better shine than the government-issued combat boots. He knew that some day he would buy still another pair, but, Lord, they were expensive! Corcorans showed a soldier who cared about his appearance, thence cared about his performance and his job. His model of the *idéal soldat* was Sgt. Noonan.

Finally, he bought a B-4 bag. It would flop open and hold, fairly neatly, his pressed uniforms and many other belongings, all much better than the trusty duffel bag.

He had already bought an iron, mostly to touch up his uniforms so they could be worn more than one day. He had also bought heavy rubber bands for blousing his trousers. To improve the blousing, he bought sets of light-weight chains, which were worn inside the trousers just where they were bloused. The chains gave an even, smooth look where the trousers met the combat boots.

Now, with all the new paraphernalia, he looked, at least from a distance, like a seasoned trooper, even an officer, for they wore exactly the same uniform. Indeed, some company-grade officers wore the same uniforms they had been issued on entry. Field-grade officers had probably outgrown their original-issue gear.

The big difference between him and those officers was he wore no symbols of rank, since he was a mere Private E-2. But he knew that Amanda didn't understand those things and that he would look extra sharp for her next time he could get a pass.

That Friday, Lt. Spiro and his crew wished him well, and he returned to his temporary barracks.

Chapter Fifteen
Murch and Leadership

Frenchy arrived at the Leadership School about 1500 hours, Sunday, 2 March, having gone to church and then lunch with the Fontenots in Louisville. That trip had been made without benefit of a pass, but he rationalized *with no roll call, I'm not technically AWOL.* However he characterized it, he joined the ranks of generations of young soldiers who had done the same thing.

The new school was also part of 3rd Armored Reserve Command. It resembled a smaller and freshly painted version of old Able Battery. Spread out around a parade ground were a headquarters building, classrooms, two barracks, and a mess hall. The flagpole was centered on headquarters at one end of the parade ground, and, upon reporting in there, he was directed to East Barracks.

He had just entered when the cry "Frenchy" was heard. There was his friend Burley from the first floor—the guy he had likened to the Cheshire Cat. He thought, *There goes my chance to opt out of the nickname. What the hell, no matter.* They shook hands, and Frenchy threw his B-4 bag and duffel down on the next bunk. There were handshakes all around, which kept occurring whenever a new man straggled in. They were all less reserved, less bashful than when they showed up for basic; now they were trained soldiers, starting out on a new mission, with new associates, but already bonded by their past training.

Morrison Burley, known as "Maury," was one of the black soldiers from the first floor. Frenchy didn't know him well but remembered him as pleasant and quiet, like himself.

"Maxwell and Copeland from Able Battery are here, too. Did you apply for OCS?"

Frenchy shook his head, "No, they just expect to make a tank commander or a future sergeant out of me." He unpacked, made his bunk bed and heard an explanation from a sergeant on display of clothing and other gear.

They went to the East Barracks and chatted with Junior Maxwell and Mike Copeland. Then the four Able Battery men went to the mess hall. They found they were lucky to show up late; early birds had been put on KP.

Frenchy sized up his new friends. All were older, had at least some college, and had been selected for OCS. Maury said he was a graduate of Prairie State Agricultural and Mechanical College in Prairie View, Texas—a Jim Crow school.

"What's that?" Frenchy asked.

Junior and Mike looked askance, but Maury laughed and explained that "Jim Crow" was sort of a euphemism, taken from an old song. The southern states had special laws, called "Jim Crow Laws" to segregate Negroes in separate schools. Nowadays, Jim Crow schools were supposed to be equal, but, of course, they weren't. His father was a professor at Prairie View. He wanted to get into the Combat Engineer Corps or possibly the Signal Corps—both long shots; the army needed combat officers: infantry, armor, or artillery.

Frenchy spoke about his days as a communications assistant on an ore boat. The others were impressed, and Maury suggested he try and sell himself as a commo expert. Frenchy nodded, having already had that in mind.

They fell out the next morning at 0630 and were surprised to see a lieutenant colonel standing to one side. After the sergeants found all present and accounted for, the colonel led them in a run around the campus. In the eight weeks they were there, he often ran with them and proved that, though he might be forty years old, few were in better shape. After chow he introduced himself in the assembly room. His name was Gordon E. Murch. While he did not say so, he was formerly Commander, 2nd Battalion, 27th Infantry Regiment, a part of the 25th Infantry Division.

Murch had seen it all, his record showing one of many paths to excellence: he was born in 1913, went to high school in Bloomington, Illinois, but joined the army in 1930 at age seventeen, during times of hardship for most Americans. He was sent to the 21st Infantry Regiment, Schofield barracks, Hawaiian Department, a post afterward noteworthy for being hit in the Pearl Harbor Attack. He was later assigned to Jefferson Barracks—an old military post on the Mississippi, just south of St. Louis, where he boxed, played football, and developed a hatred of mules.

Murch made sergeant in 1936, tech sergeant in 1940, and master sergeant in 1941, when his 1941 Certificate of Appointment was signed by one Walton H. Walker, Colonel, 36th Armored Infantry— the same man who commanded the 8th Army in Ko rea during the Pusan Perimeter, Inchon, the Breakout, and the CCF Intervention, then died in a ditch.

Next on Murch's record came officer candidate school and a commission as second lieutenant in July 1942. The new second john attended war games in Louisiana and the Armored School at Fort Knox.

In April 1944, he was sent to England as a tank commander, then to Normandy, D-Day plus five. He was in XII Corps, part of Patton's Third Army, which sped across France, the Ardennes, and finally Germany. Murch was awarded the Bronze Star "with V."

He received a regular army commission as a first lieutenant, then captain in 1947. He was posted to Japan in 1948 and joined by his wife and son. In July 1950, he was called off the golf course and sent to Korea.

Tom Arthur

The 27th Infantry—known as *Wolfhound*—was an advance unit, arriving in Korea on 10 July 1950, its 2nd Battalion commanded by Maj. Murch, who was soon promoted to light colonel. He was thirty-seven years old.

At that stage the frontline positions were unsettled but with U.N. Forces on the retreat and forming the Pusan Perimeter. The 27th first went to the Uisong area, some thirty-five miles north of Taegu. It was forced back on 22–25 July, and relieved ROK troops at Hwaggan. At that point, the 1st Battalion made a carefully orchestrated retreat, and, as anticipated, the North Koreans attacked the abandoned position. In so doing, the NK forces were caught in the open by combined fire of tanks, artillery, and mortars, plus automatic and small arms fire from the 2nd Battalion. The North Korean attackers retreated, and Murch's Battalion took thirty prisoners.

Finally, Murch put all available armor in line to cover another retreat, which headquarters ordered with a cryptic, *how able*, meaning "haul ass."

On 18 August, the 27th was ordered to attack the North Korean 13th Division along the road north from the Village of Taegu, a traditional clearing house in an agriculturally rich area, which was proving to be a key point in defending the Perimeter. The Wolfhound Regiment sought to restore the line with the ROK division to its right. Murch's Battalion was on the east side of the road, some eighteen miles north of Taegu. Commencing that night, the North Koreans made seven assaults on the 27th in what became known as the Battle of the Bowling Alley. A regiment of the ROK 1st Division to the left of the 27th began to fall back, but its Division Commander, the outstanding Gen. Paik Sun Yup, personally halted the retreat and led his troops back into line. Yup later referred to the battle name Bowling Alley, "I must say, I found it difficult to understand the Americans' humor when they referred to a grisly battlefield with such a lighthearted name."

By whatever name, that battle, including Murch's leadership role, saved Taegu and kept the Perimeter intact.

Murch's Battalion went north with the breakout after Inchon, thence north across the 38th Parallel and on past Pyongyang. Chinese were first encountered at Unsan on 1 and 2 November. By 25 November, Murch's Easy Company was assigned to Task Force Dolvin, a specially formed unit of two tank battalions, a ranger company, assault gun platoon, reconnaissance platoon, engineer battalion, and Easy Company. Lt. Col. Welborn G. Dolvin led his Force north along the east bank of the Kuryong River, which flowed out of the north to the Chongchon River. The route was south of Unsan and north of Ipsok.

The 27th was behind Task Force Dolvin, with support elements and the artillery to its rear. In spite of the presence of Chinese, Murch's men felt fairly safe at that time. Then the Chinese struck Dolvin with great force and also drove through a seam to the east of both Dolvin and Murch, forcing Murch both to aid Dolvin and to protect the rear elements. With his E Company suffering farther north as part of Task Force Dolvin, his F Company was wiped out, and his G Company suffered forty-nine casualties. Murch himself used small arms to defend his headquarters.

Easy Company, with Dolvin, won a Presidential Unit Citation, and its commander, Dusty Desiderio, was awarded the Medal of Honor posthumously.

Murch was praised for leading the successful extrication of these U.N. forces, in a battle lasting three nights. One officer said, "Our brilliant commander, Col. Murch, was responsible for the uniformly fine performance of the 2nd Battalion from the onset of the Wolfhound involvement in the war during his eight turbulent months in command."

Murch received a Purple Heart for a non-incapacitating wound in the back. His eardrums were punctured; his executive officer had his foot shot off. Murch was also awarded the Silver Star four times with three bronze oak leaf clusters, the Bronze Star, the Legion of Merit, and, his favorite, the Combat Infantry Badge.

Of course, Frenchy knew nothing of these harrowing experiences and great leadership. He could see that the School Commandant had been in combat in the 25th Division by the patch on his right shoulder, consisting of a red leaf with gold border and gold lightning bolt. The man was average size, well put together, friendly, and, judging by the way he ran, in good condition.

Schooling began with a pleasant event: the teaching of Chief Warrant Officer Hodge. He gave a series of classes on the Army Method of Instruction, referred to as MOI. The rules were simple enough: a detailed outline was required and had to be available should a senior officer or other inspector come into the class; graphical training aids, of course called GTAs, were to be used, meaning, for example, that if a topic had three points, there would be three bullet points displayed as the instruction progressed. After the points were discussed, they would be covered, then all uncovered in the summary.

Each student was required to give an instructional on any subject of his choice. Bashful Frenchy managed to pull off a major success with a brief account of ore boats. He cut the silhouette of a boat out of cardboard and pinned it to a hanging blanket—showing the stack at the stern and the pilothouse at the bow as well as the locations of the crane and the hatches. It did occur to him that many of the college boys in his audience had never had a real workingman's job. He gained confidence.

CWO Hodge said, "Fascinating, fascinating, good report" and asked questions about where the ore came from and about some of the ports he had visited. Frenchy gulped when he then noticed that Col. Murch had quietly entered and was standing in the shadows by the entry door.

The best speech of all was given by Pvt. Harold Judy, one of those college boys. He described the Battle of Cannae, Second Punic War, when Hannibal, the great Carthaginian, utterly defeated the Romans in 216 B.C. Hal Judy used drawings to show Hannibal's staged retreat, then movement from each flank of reserves and cavalry, and final envelopment and slaughter of the outmaneuvered Romans. He then came up with what Frenchy later called "Hal's tour de force." Hal continued: "One of the two Roman Consuls leading his massive army of 87,000 to defeat was named 'Lucius *Paullus*'—a name that stuck in my head; I then remembered that the German General who lost about 250,000 men at the Battle of Stalingrad, some 2,159 years later, was named 'Friedrich *Paulus*'—what a coincidence! I guess it's sort of a bad luck name."

The colonel couldn't let that one go: after Hal Judy's talk, Murch walked to the front and explained that Cannae was surely taught at The War College in Carlisle, Pennsylvania, and of course at The Military Academy as well. Hannibal's guile had been employed in many battles and used as recently as World War II, when armored leaders like Patton, Guderian, and Rommel were well aware of the classic tactics. He confessed that he had never heard Pvt. Judy's little Paullus-and-Paulus comment, which he found very clever. He then paused as if contemplating whether he should say more, then charged on:

"Unfortunately, Marshal Peng Dehuai, CCF Commanding General knew the game all too well. You see, the Chinese have a long tradition as military strategists, beginning with the legendary Sun Tzu around 500 B.C. Back in winter 1950, on our 10th Corps' road north to the Chosin Reservoir, there was a very strategic point where destruction of a bridge at Funchilin Pass would have slowed the advance of our marines. Maj. Gen. O.P. Smith—one of our greatest heroes—was surprised that the bridge *was not destroyed by the retreating red forces*. An ancient Chinese ruse is called "entice the tiger to leave the mountain." That's how William the Conqueror won at Hastings in 1066. In retrospect and too late, Smith saw that the Chinese *wanted* us to keep coming, not be slowed down, just as Hannibal wanted the Romans to keep coming—same idea over two thousand years later. A shame Smith's bosses couldn't get it."

The colonel closed his apt talk by thanking Pvt. Judy. Then, he said, "I'll have a word with the ore boat man after class, please."

My Lord, thought Frenchy, *what have I done?*

The colonel waved him to a seat and said, "Relax, Desprez, I really came to hear your little talk."

He explained that he had received a nice letter from Lt. Spiro and then had looked at Pvt. Desprez's 201 File.

"I noted several things: you had a perfect score on the AFQT, that's the Armed Forces Qualification Test, and you qualified for application and interviews leading to possible acceptance in Officer Candidate School. You chose not to apply. You are an Expert Sharpshooter and Marksman—probably born with a rifle in your hand."

Frenchy smiled at this point and nodded.

"I also notice that you are only eighteen years old—you have plenty of time to consider an army career and get some more schooling under your belt. By the way, I joined when I was seventeen."

"I hope I've done the right things, Sir."

"Oh, I expect you have. Now, Desprez, I'm just a field-grade officer, in grade less than two years, in no position to wave a magic wand at you. I could, however, do something like hold you here in some clerical job, or the honor guard, post newspaper, that sort of thing. You would be safe, not get shot at; but years from now when people ask "What did you do in the army?" you would probably mutter and try to change the subject.

"No, I recommend we just send you on; I see the makings of a soldier in you; we'll see what the future brings."

The colonel jumped to his feet and extended his hand. There wasn't time to salute or say anything very clever. Frenchy thanked him, and they walked out of the classroom together. They then exchanged salutes, and the colonel added, "If you're late for something, trooper, blame it on me."

And so, the Leadership School moved on, most of it interesting. Frenchy figured that the dark side of the School was definitely KP—definitely! The cause was a scrawny little corporal, probably pushing forty. He was frowning, unkempt, a loud mouth. Here was a man who had obviously gone up and down the ladder of enlisted ranks, maybe three or four times, and was now simply putting in time for retirement-after-twenty. His intelligence didn't approach the level of his victims and probably contributed to his need to persecute.

Frenchy could already spot the main problem—the plague of the enlisted ranks—alcoholism. He knew the type: go on pass; binge drink; end up AWOL, perhaps virtually comatose in some sleazy bar or whorehouse; be court marshaled and busted back to private; get another chance from sympathetic officers and NCOs and perhaps gain back his stripes; then repeat the cycle. Counseling and medical care for in-service alcoholics was just coming in—way too late for the sallow, bleary-eyed, assistant cook. It was a problem of his generation—more noticeable with professional athletes who were newsworthy, but nowhere more rampant than in the enlisted ranks, where the off-duty thing to do—often thought to be the only thing to do—was to drink, night after night.

Chapter Sixteen
The Raven and Easy Eights

The Fontenots faced their friend Arnaud with enthusiasm, all having done their homework and being prepared to discuss some of his favorite American classics. He had become a sort of test case—now deemed part of their American adventure—so they needed to see and understand what he had selected, what appealed to this bright, likeable, teenage boy, yet, as they knew, still an inexperienced high-school youth, sprung from rural Midwest sod.

The works of Henry Wadsworth Longfellow were favorites of the Desprez family, and among his earliest recollections was his mother reciting "The Midnight Ride of Paul Revere," an account of how Paul Revere rode out from Boston, in 1775, to warn the countryside that the British were coming—perhaps a cliché to Americans, but new to the Fontenots. After he read the poem, parents and daughter applauded with sincere appreciation.

Frenchy did not present the poem as a masterpiece; he and his French friends recognized that Longfellow was less popular than before and seemed, perhaps, too sentimental, a little corny—starting out, as he did, "Listen my children"—compared to other poets of his and more recent generations.

Sofia said that French people had to admire a nineteenth-century poem depicting how the stage was set in this small, dramatic way first for withdrawal of the British from Boston and finally for their defeat at Yorktown eight years later. Her thoughts led to a discussion of the War's end when the blockade of Adm. de Grasse and the French Fleet was the decisive element at Yorktown.

Amanda's father went deeper into the American Revolution, which he called a bourgeois struggle compared to the French proletarian Revolution twenty years later. Jean felt that the Magna Carta—the rise of parliamentary government in the thirteenth and fourteenth centuries—reforms after the English Civil War of 1642–1649, and the democratic concessions forced on later kings and queens had saved the English from the destructive class struggles endured by the French and later by the Russians. Even more than France, Russia had suffered under despotic leadership for many centuries with no human rights progress until it was too late to avoid the 1917 catastrophe, which, in turn, bred the alien culture of communism.

Frenchy thought, *I might have added that too much power corrupts whether at le Palais de Versailles, the Winter Palace of the Tsars, the Kremlin, or the Dai-Ichi Building.* He really enjoyed this intellectual banter.

"The Raven" by Edgar Allen Poe proved more familiar to the French family; after all, Poe had been immersed in the classics and many of his stories were set in Europe, some in Paris, like "The Murders in the Rue Morgue." Amanda, however, asked, *"Qu'est-ce qui se passé? Qu'est-ce que le symbolisme de le grand corbeau?"*

Everyone nodded; that was the crux: What was happening, what was the "ancient bird of yore" supposed to represent, what did it symbolize? Was it a prophet of doom, some sort of demonic figure? That was a tough question, which all four bounced around. Perhaps it was all a dream suffered by the poor demented narrator who, after all, said in the first stanza, "While I nodded, nearly napping . . ."

They saw that the narrator would ask impassioned questions, knowing the bird would say, "nevermore;" then the narrator would become enraged and order it "back into the Night's Plutonian Shore"—in other words, "go to Hades, to the underworld." The narrator both wanted to remember and to forget his lost love, Lenore, and the Fontenot's and Frenchy all agreed that by the poem's end, the man was in a frenzy and reduced to madness, as shown in the last verse:

> And the raven, never flitting, still is sitting, still is sitting
> On the Pallid bust of Pallas just above my chamber door;
> And his eyes have all the seeming of a demon's that is
> dreaming,
> And the lamp-light o'er him streaming throws his shadow
> on the floor;
> And my soul from out that shadow that lies floating on
> the floor
> Shall be lifted—nevermore!

They decided that the mood and rhyme scheme were paramount and each person could read into it whatever symbolism struck his or her fancy without searching for some hidden meanings. Jean said that the high climax, which a reader should scream was "that lie," in the preceding verse:

> Leave no black plume as a token of that lie thy soul
> Hath spoken!

They also noted that "The Raven" dealt with Poe's favorite topic—the death of a beautiful woman. Jean pointed to where the Raven was asked:

> Tell this soul with sorrow laden if, within the distant Aidenn,
> It shall clasp a sainted maiden whom the angels name
> Lenore—

Then, the raven cuts him off by saying, "Nevermore."

Amanda figured the "distant Aidenn" referred to *Le Ciel*—to Heaven—and that Lenore was not her real name but the name the angels gave her. Frenchy nodded, adding, "Poe liked that device. In another poem, he wrote, "a maiden there lived whom you may know by the name of Annabel Lee." It's a real tearjerker—the first poem I ever memorized. Poe says:

> She was a child and I was a child,
> In this kingdom by the sea,
> But we loved with a love that was more than love—
> I and my Annabel Lee—
> With a love that the winged seraphs of Heaven
> Coveted her and me."

Amanda wiped a tear, as Frenchy went on to describe that the angels were so jealous:

> "That the wind came out of a cloud, chilling
> And killing my Annabel Lee."

Sofia looked at Amanda and said, "Come now, jealous angels? Really, let us be practical; tell me, Amanda, why the name, 'Lenore?'"

"*D'accord, mère*; he needed a word to rhyme with nevermore." That broke the tension. They laughed. Frenchy summed up by explaining that Poe's whole life was kind of a mess: he married his thirteen-year-old cousin in 1835; he wrote "The Raven" in 1845, and his wife died two years later. So she was not *the lost Lenore*, except, perhaps, as Poe knew she would die soon from tuberculosis. Poe died soon after, at age forty. Jean added, "Poe had a great influence, especially in horror fiction, crime fiction, and detective fiction. You Americans love our French words, *mystery* and *the macabre!* By the way, did you know that Noah released a raven and a dove and that the raven did not return to the ark?"

That brought on a discussion of ravens in many cultures—mostly as an evil creature, associated with death and doom, but sometimes as a hero, a trickster, or a messenger. In North American cultures, the raven was even seen as creator of the world and deliverer of the sun. Frenchy came down on the side of ravens being good guys; he remembered seeing them, as they flew boldly and unafraid up in Lake of the Woods territory, especially the time they signaled in circles over the moose carcass—shrewd and opportunistic.

Wow, thought Frenchy, *I'm getting in pretty deep with these people.* In fact, he was holding his own and gaining a valuable respite from KP, tanks, and guns.

It was not all intergenerational; Frenchy and Amanda went off to movies or other events. They would end up necking in Big Red. Frenchy tried to avoid going too far, but Amanda's groans, her sighing *"tres excité,"* and the way she clung to him made cooling down more and more difficult for both. Finally, when they parted, she said, "Next time, come equipped to be *mon amour; Je pratique que le safe sex."*

He protested, "Your parents . . . I'll soon be gone, and I feel a responsibility to them . . ."

"No, no. They know already that you are a good boy and that I am the aggressive one. I know you are going soon; that is why we must start now! This is *my* decision; I will have it *my* way. I'm not the utterly innocent person you may have believed. I have plans; you wait. It will be meaningful, not be *une liaison grossier.*

The next work week was important: the soldiers learned tank driving and basic tank maintenance, just an introduction, since every hour spent driving a tank required many hours of maintenance, meaning there was no time to make vehicle experts out of the Leadership School men. Fort Knox was the Armored Center for the U.S. Army, the training of future tank leaders was tried and true, and curriculum planners knew that tank maintenance was mostly learned on the job, not in a school.

The men were trucked to the tank park and talked through the M4 Sherman medium tank, named after Union Gen. William Tecumseh Sherman. The machine was well named: when war tactics before the use of the combustion engine are studied, Sherman's famous March to the Sea comes about as close as possible to twentieth-century-style armored blitzkrieg.

So we sing the chorus from Atlanta to the sea,
While we are marching through Georgia.

In World War II, production of the Sherman exceeded 50,000. Surprisingly, it was not a first rate tank, even back then. Its 70mm gun was not in the same class as the famous German 88, either in size or in muzzle velocity, and it could not go one-on-one with the German Panther or the massive Tiger. Still, its chassis could be used for other armored vehicles, including self-propelled artillery, and, most importantly, it did not easily break down and was manufactured in huge numbers—truly a product of American mass production—something unequaled by the Axis Powers. By the Korean War, it was obsolete and replaced by the M26 Pershing, by the M46 Patton, and, toward the end of the War, by the M48 Patton—all heavy tanks mounting 90mm guns and shielded with heavier, more competitive armor.

Frenchy stood and listened to lectures on the Sherman, learning that it took a crew of five: commander, gunner, loader, driver, and co-driver; the co-driver also serving as bow-gunner and using a light 30-caliber machine gun. There was also a 50-caliber machine gun in the turret. The Sherman stood nine feet high, so just climbing up on the thing and getting back down were chores. Frenchy thought, *You'll never be a tank commander if you fall off this damn thing and break an arm!*

They took turns driving the Sherman. School troops called it the "Easy Eight," apparently because it was model number E8. It steered like its ancestor—the early farm tractor—using long levers, one for each hand, called "laterals." To turn right, the driver pulled back on the right lateral; this would break the right drive wheel and stop the right-side tracks. With the left tracks continuing, the vehicle would turn on the proverbial dime.

Frenchy thought, *How primitive, how awful it must be buttoned-up in this thing, perhaps worse to be the commander and usually have your head out above the hatch. When the gun is fired, the noise and smoke must be tough. And they're training me to command one of these damn things!*

He also knew that the anti-tank bazooka had a shaped charge, designed to make a small hole through several inches of armor. The shaped charge was counterintuitive, since it was the opposite of a regular pointed projectile. It used a pointed brittle shell as a nose, fronting a hollow conical projectile that operated in accordance with the mysterious Monroe effect discovered back in 1888. On impact, the conical recess greatly increased and concentrated the explosive force. The device was developed in 1942 for the bazooka with startling success, though not fully understood results.

The molten plasma from the shaped charge plus the red-hot fragments thus torn from the tank's own armor would spew around and likely kill the crew, set off the tank's ammo supply and gasoline, or create other mayhem. Frenchy rubbed his chin, *So, the tank commander seems to have a choice of being picked off in his exposed position by a sniper or having his lower extremities cooked by a bazooka!*

Then, too, combustion engines had to breathe, as in any vehicle, making the rear deck the breathing point and vulnerable to air attack. Ground mines, buried in the roadbed, could knock off a tread and stop the vehicle, sometimes clogging the road and halting all that followed.

The most bizarre anti-tank weapon was the famous Molotov cocktail—derisively named for Soviet Commissar V.M. Molotov by the Finns when they fought the Russians back in '39. In simplest form, it was a glass bottle filled with petrol or any flammable liquid with a soaked rag wick. The Nationalists used it in Spain, the Finns in the Russo–Finish Winter War, both sides throughout World War II, and the South Koreans against the T-34.

Barracks talk had it that Korea was bad tank country. In the south and in the west there were hills, mountains, and rice paddies; in the north and throughout the east there were mountains. Thus, the whole country virtually confined armored vehicles to roads and trails, highly susceptible to mines and anti-tank ambushes. Most bridges were not built to support the huge things—anyway, blow a bridge, or stop the lead tank in a defile, and you likely stopped the whole column.

Bad news? Yes, there were plenty of nasty things to say about the armored service, but Europe, on the other hand, was the tank country where he'd been told the Spearhead Division advanced 101 miles in one day. Since there still were armored divisions there, perhaps graduates of the Armored Leadership School, at least those not going on to OCS, would be able to sit out the cold war in some nice German town with no one shooting at them and with fabulous leave opportunities. *Oh well; it's fine to dream.*

On Thursday of his fifth week in the Leadership School, he went through the Tank Leaders' Reaction Course. Frenchy stood with his head above the hatch, an instructor crouching next to him. He had a map in hand showing a destination. After giving the driver instructions on an intercom, away they went. He chuckled at how easy it was to take the correct trail, because it was the one most traveled, and an Easy Eight left a mighty cut-up trail.

Then, on his starboard side he saw a wrecked airplane—a real L-19, which was a sort of souped-up Cessna Model 170. There was fire coming from the engine area. A soldier—obviously posing as the pilot—ran toward him, waving him down. Frenchy ordered the tank to stop; the man yelled, "My plane crashed. I was delivering important dispatches to Division Headquarters, and now I need your help getting them delivered."

Frenchy hollered back, "Sorry, I have my orders; I'll call my battalion and give them your location and tell them what you said. Drive on."

Over a hill, the tank stopped. The instructor pointed, "That's an enemy tank dead ahead!"

Sure enough, there was a tank out there. Frenchy yelled, "Gunner! Enemy tank ahead—fire!"

After some simulated firing, they proceeded, soon entering a forested area. Around a few corners, he saw a soldier, carrying a carbine and leading what appeared to be two aggressor prisoners. He could tell they were aggressors by the special helmet liners they wore for the exercise.

What the hell do I do? He ordered the tank to halt, as the men kept coming and reached the tank. The two aggressors produced mock grenades and threw them in the bow-gunner's cockpit. His final problem—flunked cold!

The instructor said that the school solution was to order them not to approach the tank. "You can't let strangers near your precious vehicle, *your* vehicle, which *you* command! You should dismount the bow-gunner, have him search the three and ascertain that the man with the carbine is really a friend. The next best solution would be to just keep going."

Well, I get the picture: you can't sit on your ass . . . you gotta move . . . you gotta do something, even if it's not quite the best solution. You gotta do something!

It was all a great experience, reminiscent of the thrill of the moose hunt. It also recalled the time he saw Burley's teeth smiling at him on the hillside. He now had two dry runs at being done in, *But, what the hell, I'll bet everyone screwed up that last problem.*

Toward the end of Leadership School, when they were junior instructors, he played the downed pilot. He started a fire in the wrecked plane and acted his part to the hilt—no bashfulness at all!

Chapter Seventeen
The Garage

By the Saturday afternoon after the Tank Leaders' Reaction Course, he had equipped himself with needed supplies for the planned tryst with dear Amanda. At the Fontenot apartment, Amanda kissed him and asked, *"Avez-vous préservatif?"*

"Oui, oui, le meilleur, très cher."

What next? he wondered. *This seems to be her show—all her plan.* She took up a large handbag, and they went out the door, into his car, and thence a short drive to a nearby house in Iroquois Park, then down a driveway and back to a separate two-car garage with a second-floor apartment.

"Anne Robards' family lives here; they're out-of-town, and she is kindly letting us use the garage apartment. Just leave the car here."

He recalled that pretty Anne had fixed up his first date with Amanda, just after Christmas time. He chuckled, *That girl seems to furnish complete services—from dancehall, to church, to bed!*

Amanda gave him a quick kiss and hurried up the outside stairway. The key was in the lock. There was a bedroom, a bathroom, a small refrigerator, champagne glasses, and flowers on a table. She found French champagne on ice and said, "Drinks now or later?"

"Later," Frenchy said emphatically.

When he returned from the toilet, she had taken a nightgown from her bag, laid it on the bed and began undressing. Although she had turned off the overhead lights, they could still see fairly well by the bedside lamp. With her skirt and blouse off, she came to him, standing eye-to-eye, as tall as he was, then helping him with his shirt and feeling his arm muscles and whispering, "*Comment tu te sens?*"

"*Je me sens très bien, très excité.*"

He kissed her and reached for her waist and bottom; but she quickly turned and slipped away, finished undressing, faced him, and posed in the soft light—long, slim, pale, hair streaming over her face, and just plain gorgeous! Staring at him, she crossed her arms and cupped her breasts, massaging them for a moment, her hands then sliding apart and working down to her hips, slowly running them up and down, for a moment her fingers touching, just brushing between the legs. Next, turning, finding the gown, guiding it over her head, hunching her shoulders to help it fall in place; then, pulling down the bedcovers, she lay back and watched his fumbling preparations, finally extending her arms as he lay beside her. . . .

She whispered, "*Mon petit chou, mon trésor, embrasse-moi.*"

They kissed, at first just little teasing pecks, and hugged, first side-by-side; but there could be little foreplay after weeks of touching and caressing and then her undressing ritual—leaving no time. She parted her legs, pulled up her gown, and guided him. It was an aggressive act by both, neither gentle. She was strong, at first controlling his movements, but quickly giving way to her own passion. There would be other times for tenderness—this time was so good, so powerful, *très excité!* She held him, unwilling to free him—tightly, very tightly—savoring his weight, gripping with her long legs, groaning.

"*Mon Dieu! C'est vari que je t'aime!* Yes, I do love you!"

"Yes, and I love you, *je t'aime, ma chère!*"

"*Arnaud, chéri, tu es mon meilleur beau souvenir.*"

Still breathing hard as he lifted up and rolled to her side, he grew thoughtful: "*Mon Dieu*, we're under such a gun! You're a wayfarer for a short time in a foreign land, while I'm a country boy from the land of sugar beets and woods, a private in the rear ranks, soon off to a field of blood. God knows what will happen to me—much less to us—so impossible, *très impossible*."

They lay side-by-side, reality truly setting in: they had only four more weeks. They both knew it—four weeks! She broke the spell, "*Je voudrais le champagne*." Soon they were squared away, first sitting up in bed toasting—"*à ta santé*"—and sipping; then setting aside their drinks, touching. . . .

"*Comment tu te sens?*"

"*De nouveau—excité!*"

Loving again—slower—then more talking. Finally they dressed, cleaned up the room and left.

It was a weary and very thoughtful boy who drove back down the Dixie Dieway.

Chapter Eighteen
Time Winds Down

Frenchy had made good friends at Leadership School: Junior Maxwell, Mike Copeland, Maury Burley, and Hal Judy. Since the four were older, he was frankly flattered that they welcomed his company, but he also knew they were curious about what he was up to on the weekends. While he had been pretty tight-mouthed about *l'affaire* Amanda, it was obvious to the others that he wasn't running off all alone to Louisville to watch the Colonials play ball.

Hal suggested they have a banquet in town at some hotel, but a basic problem quickly arose: even though Maury Burley might be perfectly fit to fight for his country, he would not be welcome in a Louisville hotel. Frenchy ranted and raved, finding the situation strange and grossly unfair; ironically, Maury was the one trying to calm him down. Junior's idea of a two-day outing, not just a party, proved to be a better plan anyway: they would go to the Hotel at Mammoth Cave National Park, a place run by the National Park Service, which would welcome them all.

This great idea expanded when Junior contacted his aunt in Bowling Green. Frenchy then revealed that his girlfriend would come along with her friend, Anne Robards, as chaperone. *Some chaperone!* thought Frenchy, but the plot thickened when Jean and Sofia Fontenot decided to join them. Frenchy concluded having them along was probably for the best.

There was more elaborate planning. Frenchy felt that Hal Judy was perhaps the best match for Anne—sort of class-with-class. He felt strangely protective of Anne, like she was a sister, *Well, not quite like a sister.* Junior's Auntie dug up three Bowling Green girls who would drive up and be blind dates for Junior, Mike, and Maury. What an outing it would be!

Meanwhile, Leadership School entered the final phase, where class members served as assistant instructors for basic training recruits. Frenchy taught map-reading. Of course, he had to prepare by writing a lesson plan and presenting his talk to Chief Warrant Officer Hodge. He used topographic maps, which they called "topo maps." They had contour intervals shown every forty feet and heavier lines every two hundred feet, a scale of 1:24,000. Buildings were indicated by little squares. Smaller areas of the maps were shown by two-digit numbers of so many minutes of latitude and longitude. By eyeballing a third number to each of these numbers, a precise location could be described—called designation by coordinates.

Such information was vital in combat but was sadly missing at the start of the Korean War. He was told that now, in the stalemate, everything was surveyed and locations along the U.N. Main Line of Resistance and the Demilitarized Zone were pretty much down pat.

He would ask his troopers, "What are the blue areas?" They answered "Water—rivers, lakes, or ponds." The thin blue lines were rivers. Then, a harder question, "Which way do the rivers run?" Someone would figure out that contour lines always point upstream; they discussed why that was so. Next, they figured out that when the contour lines were close together, the terrain was steep; when far apart, fairly flat. He added flourishes of his own, "How would you climb that hill? What if the hill were mined? What if there were machine guns guarding the summit?"

The men came to his teaching post marching in small groups. He gave commands: "Detail halt! Left face, at ease, relax; Give me your attention." This was all new, and he found himself enjoying finally bossing other troops and using dismounted drill techniques. He also decided he could try to sell himself as a map expert.

Sometimes the brass came around. One day Lt. Col. Murch appeared with a high-ranking foreign officer and his staff—all decked out in ornate uniforms—tan poplins festooned with red and gold epaulets, ribbons, and piping. He was told later they were Turkish. Trying to act normally, he proceeded with his usual lesson, as the scary big shots stood and watched. He sent the men on to the next post.

The colonel said, "Drive over here, Desprez." He trotted toward the group, "Pvt. Desprez reporting as directed, Sir."

He felt confident, but cautious. For the benefit of the visiting brass, he was asked the expected questions: how long had he been in the army; how old was he; where was he from. Murch turned to the dignitaries, and the obvious leader—certainly a general of some sort—proffered a question, which a subordinate translated: "Did you study maps in your home school?"

"Yes, Sir," he replied, explaining that he came from farm country at the edge of the north woods where most people were familiar with topo maps.

Murch could not resist interrupting, and asked the translator if his general spoke French. When it was learned that the general knew some French, Murch said, "Give it to him in French."

Frenchy repeated the answer as best he could, now with a smile. There was some laughter and banter among the guest officers; finally the translator said, "Colonel, the general does not believe all your privates read maps like an artillery officer and speak French." Everyone laughed.

The colonel patted Frenchy on the shoulder and said, "Carry on, trooper." One step back, a salute held until returned, and the group moved away.

Destiny! In the Land of the Morning Calm

That same week, Frenchy spent a whole day sitting in the crashed L-19, reading and occasionally playing the part of the downed messenger, an enjoyable goof-off time such as any young soldier would welcome and figure he deserved.

That weekend, he met with Amanda and her parents. The topic was Alexandre Dumas, the great French novelist and dramatist. Jean had given him the English version of **The Three Musketeers**, and he had gotten through a good chunk of it while sitting in the L-19. Surprisingly, he learned that the author's name, Dumas, came from the liaison of Dumas' grandfather, the marquis de la Pailleterie, with Marie Cassette Dumas, a black woman of San Domingo. The author's father, also Alexandre Dumas, enlisted in a dragoon regiment and rose from private to general during the French Revolution. However, the father died when young Alexandre was only four, leaving the family desperately poor.

Jean related with pride the rise of Dumas and how he came to write great historical novels, then handed Frenchy **Les Trois Mousquetaires** and said he expected him to put down the translation and read the original French version. Frenchy gamely said he would try with the assistance of Amanda and a French dictionary. He also said,

"Please don't count on me going from private to general; that's harder nowadays."

He related his adventures and misadventures on the Tank Leaders' Reaction Course. Sofia then bemoaned the fact that all the talk from **Les Mousquetaires** to the Easy Eight Tank was about war and more war. They all agreed she was right, and Jean promised to take up the topic of Mississippian-aged limestone strata at Mammoth Cave when next they met. They all laughed when Sofia said that idea was not promising either.

Through all of the literary talk, the two young ones were eyeing each other. He figured the parents weren't fooled about what was going on; in particular, Sofia could see the rapturous look in her daughter's eyes when her Arnaud was visiting. Perhaps the mother thought of how she would feel if her lover were going to war in a few days, especially since her brothers had been involved in La Résistance, giving Sophia's family many anxious days and the realization that life may be short, hard, and tragic.

Amanda set the stage by saying they were going out for a while. They kissed and hugged in the car for a moment, then went to a Dairy Queen, bought chocolate cones, and parked in a schoolyard where, having something else in mind, they quickly munched down the cones.

When he tried for their usual embrace, Amanda pushed him away, took the Kleenex box, opened the door, got out, and climbed in the back seat; he followed, walking around the Chevy's front and circling to the passenger-side back door. She waved him back, saying "*attendre*, wait." He obediently stood by the door, watching her lift her middle, tug and pull up her dress and struggle with her panties, muttering in French that she should have taken off *le slip* before she got in the car. The panties clung resolutely to one shoe until she finally could kick them off. She was so tall, with so little room, it required time and some experimentation to get situated and fairly comfortable for what they planned to do: her dress pulled well above the waist, her bobby sox and loafers still on, her right leg against the back seat, her left leg spread on the floor against the front seat, her butt flat and angled to the front of the seat, her head probably too jammed in the corner for comfort.

Still standing, he looked into the car, viewing her progress: seeing first the long white legs: starting with the thin calves, leading to pale, barely-visible inner thighs, the evening darkness hiding anything more, her hands touching and pulling and arranging the dress—all a delirious sight, but it was those pale thighs—those pale inner thighs. . . .

It was even more awkward for him: he considered taking off his trousers and shorts, but that seemed like too much exposure, especially just at dusk in a public parking area, so he settled, somewhat out-of-order, for dropping them all the way down; then, remembering he needed to deploy equipment in his pockets, he had to pull them back up partway to find and fumblingly unwrap his little *préservatif*, then roll it on—steps requiring both hands and allowing his trousers again to drop ankle high, sort of hog-tying him and forcing him to hobble in at the open door where he finally reached her outstretched arms.

With her usual strength, she took charge, grabbed hold and positioned him so she could help him find his way. He struggled to hold back, and, as before, he let her rapidly increasing groans rhythmically direct the progress of them both.

It was a real workout, but soon over; they gasped, like they'd completed a race, then quieted down, at which stage, recovery operations began: he had to pull out, then back out the open door, bare-tailed and bent over, completely exposed in a most awkward, ungainly, laughable state; next, pull up his trousers partway, peel off the rubber, throw it in some nearby bushes, and, finally, pull up and buckle his britches.

Manifesting the major advantages of a dress for such occasions, she clutched Kleenex between her legs with one hand, quickly slid across the back seat, then out the door, and followed his example with a quick wipe and a toss in the bushes. Standing beside him, hands on hips, dress finally back in place, she joined him in laughter at the efforts, antics, and passions of going out for ice cream cones. He said, *"parfait chocolat,"* and she responded, *"oui formidable!"* He took her home, but as an encore to the romantic comedy, when he walked her to the door, she halted, giggled, muttered *"le slip,"* turned back, and retrieved her panties from the back seat.

Chapter Nineteen

Limestone and Solstice Weathers

The Mammoth Cave excursion proved to be a melodrama in three acts: afternoon, evening, and next day. Anne Robards and the Fontenots drove from Louisville, while the boys drove the sixty miles from Fort Knox down Route 31 in two cars—Frenchy's and Junior's.

The cave was old hat to the blind dates coming from Bowling Green—just twenty miles away and the site of other cave entrances, so the dates planned to arrive in late afternoon after the others had been in the cave. They were also arriving in three cars: the dates for Junior and Mike in one car, Auntie Maxie in another, and, probably later, Maury's date, someone named Soul who was said to be Miss Maxie's manicurist.

The five soldiers took three rooms at the Mammoth Cave Hotel—a large wood-frame building with a nice veranda looking out over a green lawn, the Visitors Center, and the parking area. They flipped for the single, Hal winning, Frenchy not pleading to swap. Each room had a double bed, lavatory, corridor shower, and toilet—daily rate: three dollars and fifty cents.

A park ranger met them, and when the Fontenots, the two girls, and the five soldiers were all assembled, he walked them down a tree-lined gulley to the cave entrance and prepared to lead what was called Historical Trip Number Three. Trip price: one dollar and twenty cents.

The ranger welcomed them to the longest cave system known in the world, with some 150 miles of explored corridors, all part of a thick layer of Mississippian-aged limestone—marine deposits, some 350 million years old. On top of the limestone was a layer of almost-impervious sandstone and shale, capping and stabilizing the entire structure over countless millennia, and allowing groundwater to percolate through the cracked and soluble limestone rock—a form of calcium carbonate—thus carving the vast caverns, tunnels, and side tunnels, and forming the bizarre rock formations.

In some parts of the cave, water dripping from the cave ceilings left behind small deposits of calcium carbonate, which gradually formed icicle-shaped stalactites. Similarly, stalagmites formed from those same drips on the cave floors, and if the two formations joined, a column was created. And so, over those millennia, the cave was being constantly carved and reformed. *Fascinating*, thought Frenchy, now truly attentive to these wonders.

Amanda greeted him with an extra warm kiss and locked arms, obviously claiming him as her property, while the other men viewed the tall French girl with awaited curiosity.

The cave entrance was not spectacular, the ceiling low, the place dim and cold. In fifteen minutes, they entered the Rotunda—a large room 140 feet below surface, with a circular, gradually receding ceiling. The ranger pointed to some wooden posts, evidence of digging along the trail, and explained that nitrates—called "saltpeter"—had been mined there by black slaves back in 1812, to be used in making gunpowder. He started on, but Amanda, who had been holding extra tightly to Frenchy's arm, halted and grasped the guardrail. He saw she was somewhat distressed and figured he knew the problem; in fact, since they had been intimate for about four weeks, he'd been expecting it. She must have planned the garage meeting like a bride.

"*Désolé, Arnaud amant; je me sens faible—des crampes.*"
She smiled somewhat weakly and said, "*Ma mère sera contente que je suis pas plein.* I'm going back."

Anne came up and the two women exchanged intimate words and stood together for a minute or two. Amanda smiled, nodded, and cast her hair over her shoulder—he'd come to know that was her little sign of courage and confidence. Turning to him, Anne said, "Let her go alone, as she wishes . . . she'll be fine." However, a ranger insisted on accompanying her.

And so they moved on without Amanda. They saw Gothic Avenue, Bridal Altar, Indian Mummy, and other signs of prehistoric occupation within the cave. The ranger added touches of humor, a theatrical component, which had been a tradition since the cave first opened in 1812. He described sites of pre-Columbian habitation. Frenchy was fascinated on learning about blind fish in the rivers, recalling his biology studies of species adaptation. Jean Fontenot seemed impressed in much the same way.

Jean explained that he had a colleague back at the university in Paris who was an expert in the famous Paleolithic cave paintings, discovered just a few years before at Lascaux in southwest France. They showed aurochs, stags, horses, and other animals, all 17,000 years old. The paintings showed shading and three-dimensional forms—aspects previously considered modern techniques. Frenchy thought, *Wow, we may have the longest cave, but it's kind of drab. Those cave paintings would surer-than-heck beat this place!*

His overall impression was dark, gloomy—rather sad now without Amanda. He looked for the famous stalactites and stalagmites and was advised, "Not on this trip; take the Frozen Niagara Trip." *A cave doesn't quite make it without stalactites!*

As they returned to the earth's surface, Frenchy saw that Anne seemed to be getting on well with Hal, the two walking arm-and-arm. He felt pleased, yet, deep down, was he a little jealous? He'd always been impressed by Hal, the guy who knew about the Punic

Wars, and Anne sure was pretty . . . he wanted everyone to have a nice time.

In the Hotel they found Aunt Maxie and the two blind dates. Junior's Aunt must have been stuck with that nickname when she was a kid named Maxwell. She was now a sketch: loud, outspoken, married three times—full of piss and vinegar. She hugged her nephew and introduced him to Brenda. Mike Copeland figured out he was paired with Grace and walked over to her. Frenchy smiled: it appearing that Miss Maxie had selected the plainer of the two for her nephew. Grinning broadly and probably feeling the same way, Mike stood by Grace; Frenchy then thought, *So what . . . they're all Okay.*

Mike said, "Where's Maury's date?" Junior smiled: "A sure case of prejudice, I'd say, Maury." Everyone laughed. It was nice that they could joke about things like that.

Meanwhile, Miss Maxie explained that she had asked Brenda and Grace to come up with a black date. They hemmed and hawed and produced no one. Miss Maxie asked her manicurist, Miss Soul Weathers, to find someone. "How about me?" was the surprising answer, "I'll do my share for our nation's finest."

Judas, thought Miss Maxie at the time, *my volunteer is a twenty-eight-year-old, plump divorcee with two kids. May I, in good conscience, turn her loose on a friend of my nephew, whether he be black, white, or green? . . . What the heck, yes, let's do it!*

Later, she thought of the old ditty from the Second War:

> Put on your old gray corset;
> If it don't fit force it;
> 'Cause the Navy's anchored in the bay.
> When the sailors come ashore,
> Be a patriotic (lady)
> For the good old U.S.A.

No liquor was served at the hotel and restaurant, but there was a big picnic area, and coolers, paper bags, and six-packs soon appeared. The Fontenots joined the group, with Amanda looking better. Then a cute black Ford coupe swung up Mammoth Cave Parkway to the parking lot. "There's your girl," Miss Maxie shouted to Maury, "Go help her with her things; she'll figure out who you are." Thus, Soul Weathers came walking up the path, guitar in hand and with smiling Maury toting a bag.

A happy change occurred in the group. Soul Weathers seemed to take over immediately: she greeted everyone in turn and had something nice to say with each introduction, and, when asked where the name came from, she explained, "It's worse than you could imagine. Ya see, my Christian name is Summer Solstice. Get it: Summer Solstice Weathers—the longest day of the year. I don't need to tell ya my birth date. Just another too-fancy, colored-folks name. So I'm stuck with it; could have been worse, like Stormy Weathers. I think that's the name of a stripper."

She visited with Maury and later on said, "My, my, I have here a real middle-class guy: college boy, gonna be an officer, gonna try to save the nation; he strikes my fancy."

It had been earlier decided that each of the five soldiers would speak after dinner—just prepare and deliver a short speech about their friendships. They all enjoyed the house specialty—Kentucky fried chicken and country ham, served in a private dining room. Maury presided and led off, "My, my, I have here such a pretty lady, mother of two, gospel singer; she's supporting our troops; she strikes my fancy." He turned to Frenchy and said, "Mammoth Cave, being made by God, not man, has no Jim Crows in it—just bats and blind fish."

Mike stood and had Grace also rise. In a more serious bent, he came up with something new: "My Scottish ancestors defeated the hated English only twice: at Sterling Bridge under Wallace in 1297 and at Bannockburn under Robert the Bruce in 1314. After that second glorious victory, the Pope sided with the English, causing the Scottish Barons to meet at Arbroath and send an appeal to Rome—known as The Declaration of Arbroath, now considered the Scottish equivalent of our Declaration of Independence. I'll read a translation of part of the original Latin:

> . . . as long as but a hundred of us remain alive,
> never will we on any conditions be brought under
> English rule. It is in truth not for glory nor riches,
> nor honours that we are fighting, but for freedom—
> for that alone, which no honest man gives up but
> with life itself."

Everyone was touched by this eloquent, yet unfamiliar, passage, especially the Fontenots.

Junior rose, holding a small piece of paper, not smiling and obviously taking his speaking assignment as seriously as had Mike, so the mood remained quiet and unchanged.

"For me, it's sometimes hard to rationalize our job in the army, where we are called 'warriors,' with our duties to our God. Perhaps this little passage from the Old Testament will help:

> The Lord, your God, is in your midst,
> a warrior who gives victory;
> he will rejoice over you with gladness,
> he will renew you with his love. . . .

"Then, too, Jesus said, 'Render, therefore, unto Caesar that which is Caesar's.' And so, my friends, I will go off to the Conflict—the horrible Conflict, knowing that God is a warrior and that God is love."

This was a side of Junior not before revealed; it touched a religious chord more and more felt by the young soldiers but so hard to express. As he sat down, amid a moment of quiet, some said, thanks and some said, amen.

It was then Hal's turn, and they all figured the Punic Wars expert would have something elaborate in store: "First, I promise to say no more about the Punic Wars. When I heard that Frenchy was about to recite a poem, I thought it would be nice to read a couple of passages from Shakespeare. This is Caesar talking, from *Julius Caesar, Act II, Scene II:*

> Cowards die many times
> before their deaths: the valiant
> never taste of death but once.
>
> Of all the wonders I have
> yet heard, it seems to me most
> strange that men should fear;
> seeing that death, a necessary
> end will come when it will come."

"Fine words," said Jean, no doubt pleased that he knew the famous passage. Then Hal went on, "King Henry the Fifth addressed his men this way before the Battle of Agincourt. I will change a few words to fit it to us on this day:

> This story shall the good man teach his son
> And these days shall ne'er go by,
> From his day to the ending of the world,
> But we in it shall be remembered
> We few, we happy few, we band of brothers.

"Are we not brothers?" Hal shouted, putting his arm on Maury's shoulder. "Here! Here!" They shouted raising their glasses.

Then Jean interceded once again and laughingly said, "I will not drink to the Battle of Agincourt, where the flower of French chivalry fell to the English long bow, as they did in three great battles during the Hundred Years War. But I will drink to "The

Declaration of Arbroath" because at that time the French were allies of the Scots; more important, I will drink to you five soldier-brothers, now alongside the French, the Scottish, and the English—all on the same side in the U.N. Forces."

There was a second round of "Here! Here!"

Over-charged with emotion from the other readings, from everything that was happening, from being with his best friends and dear Amanda, Frenchy stood and began to describe a seventeenth-century English poet named Richard Lovelace. People snickered nervously at the name until they saw how serious he was. The poet was a Cavalier—a Royalist—who dedicated his life to serving the doomed King Charles I. Lovelace fought, was jailed, released, and fought again. From prison he wrote his mistress, "Stone walls do not a prison make, nor iron bars a cage." There was no better example of the romance of the lost cause: Lovelace and King Charles lost the war, and the King lost his head! Obviously thinking of dear Amanda, Frenchy then read the poem, "To Lucasta on Going to the Wars:"

> Tell me not, sweet, I am unkind,
> That from the nunnery
> Of thy chaste breast and quiet mind
> To war and arms I fly.

> True a new mistress now I chase,
> The first foe in the field;
> And with a stronger faith embrace
> A sword, a horse, a shield.

> Yet this inconstancy is such
> As thou, too, shalt adore:
> I could not love thee, dear, so much
> Loved I not honor more.

It didn't go as planned. He had selected perhaps the greatest poem ever written about leaving a loved one and going to war, yes, an appropriate choice, but just too much for the two lovers to handle at that time and place—way too much!

Frenchy started crying as he read the last stanza and barely got it out. Also on the last line, Amanda whimpered, moaned plaintively, and then threw herself in her mother's arms, sobbing loudly, inconsolably. The men were touched by the poem but momentarily bewildered by the lovers' responses; then Maury put his arm around Frenchy, and Anne crouched by Amanda.

Soul stood and more or less took over: "Perhaps this had to happen. I'm jus' the outsider, but going to war ain't a happy time, and we can't pretend otherwise. Nor is the separatin' of good friends and loved ones ever easy. Let's all join hands, an' I'll try a song."

She sang "The Lord's Prayer" and blasted the ending, "For thine is the kingdom, and the power, and the glory, forever! Amen!"

It was beautifully done but left more people in tears. She turned to her guitar—a moment for tuning—and then she said, "Do you know 'Swing Low, Sweet Chariot?' Let's try it together." Amanda lifted her head and shook her hair. She looked at this strange woman with such a deep voice—*how like the great La Baker she seemed!* Soul led them in "Amazing Grace" and several spirituals, then "Battle Hymn." They all sang the chorus—even the French family knew the chorus. Her second verse was so right for the soldiers:

> I have seen Him in the watch-fires of a hundred cir-
> cling camps;
> They have builded Him and alter in the evening dews
> and damps:
> I can read His righteous sentence by the dim and flar-
> ing lamps;
> His day is marching on.

Jean began to hum "The Marseillaise," and Sofia, Amanda, and Frenchy picked up on it. Amanda had a nice voice. Soul was able to strum a few chords, as they sang, *"Allons enfants de la Patrie. Le jour de gloire est arrivé!"*

The song restored Amanda's spirits but also broke up the party. For the five young soldiers, perhaps, *le jour de gloire est arrivé*. Maury explained that he had decided to go to Bowling Green with Soul. They would return by 1000 hours next morning.

The other soldiers took their dates to the picnic area. They were admonished that the girls had to drive home and should watch the booze intake. Grace then set the tone: "That's no problem if we just stay here and support our troops." Mike grinned like the Cheshire Cat. Miss Maxie left after hugs all around and a special *merci beaucoup* from Amanda.

Sofia urged Amanda to go to bed early; she nodded—no promise. It was not lost on Frenchy and Amanda that Maury, his roommate, was gone till morning. They hung out with the others for a while; then Amanda whispered, "leave your door unlocked." She arose, and went inside.

I wonder what her timeframe is, thought Frenchy, after he headed for his room, buying a can of ginger ale along the way and thinking, *Young champagne.* He undressed, put on pajamas—a very civilized status for a GI who was used to sleeping in boxer shorts. He lay down and stared at a stain in the ceiling. *No doubt a water leak,* he thought. *Give it twenty or thirty years and a nice stalactite might form.* He dozed till startled by the click of the door.

She stood before him in a blue nightgown—lovely in the soft light of a single lamp. She sat on the edge of the bed; he waited, not reaching out for her, as she took a hairbrush from a little bag and lightly brushed her long hair so it cascaded forward over her face, covering one eye. Her lips pouted. He thought, *God, how perfectly lovely.* She just stared at him; maybe a minute passed, seeming much longer, then a soft voice and a smile: "*Tu as pyjama; quelque chose nouveau.* I have never seen you in pajamas."

She threw back her hair—that defiant gesture—seeming to be quite different from the fading *fleurette* of earlier in the day.

"Next Friday your school program will end; you'll get orders; then—we French use the same word—a furlough. You must leave me and return to your home in the great farming country near your beloved North Woods. I have never before admitted this to myself or to you, but in truth, you will go to Korea. I recognize that it is your destiny . . . you do not want to get out of it. How I pray they settle the truce talks."

"Yes, yes; you are correct. It is my destiny."

He covered his eyes with his arms and lay on his back, as if lost in thought. He had just made a complete admission: he did not want out of it. It was his destiny.

"And I shall return to Paris and study music. Perhaps some handsome *galant homme* will, as you say, sweep me off my feet."

"Amanda, I know I must say I hope so. Hard though it is, I do hope so. You know, I will always say God bless you, using my special prayer, *Eternal Father, strong to save, oh hear us when we pray to Thee.* That's my prayer. God knows what I want; and one thing I want is for Him to bless you."

"So, after tomorrow, Arnaud, I will never see you again."

"Is that a question or a declaration? Whichever, never is a long time. You know my rough plans: after Korea, I will have the GI Bill and will go to college, which will guide me to a profession of some sort; at this point, all I know is I will surely leave the sugar beet country. Never see you again? Well, not as your young lover. I will never again be your young Romeo nor you my sweet Juliet. We will remember,

> She was a child and I was a child,
> In this kingdom by the sea,
> But we loved with a love that was more than love—

I and my Annabel Lee."

She said, "How sweet—to think of a love that was more than love! But now, it is all agreed; we see life as it is."

He made room, as she smiled and lay beside him, whispering, "We must make the most of this night, *mon amour*." He took her in his arms—so gently. Later, musing . . .

> And neither the angels in Heaven above
> Nor the demons down under the sea,
> Can ever dissever my soul from the soul
> Of the beautiful Annabel Lee.

Then he fell into a deep sleep, again having the giant black creature attack him in the Boundary Forest. Sitting up with a start . . . he was alone.

Chapter Twenty
Chosen for Chosin

Early Monday morning of the final week, Frenchy's class fell out for the morning run and then hit the mess hall. Word reached him to report to the first sergeant. At headquarters, he was told, "I don't know what you're up to, Desprez, but we had a call from a Lt. Spiro at the Range Office requesting us to have you assist him this week. Surprising thing is the colonel said to let you go through Wednesday. You'll need to be here Thursday and Friday to receive orders and clear the barracks for a new class. By the way, I checked your file and saw that you're near top of the class: congratulations."

Frenchy thanked him, wondering all the time what Spiro was up to and how he would get to wherever he was supposed to go.

"Hang on," the sergeant said as he dialed the range office. After a brief exchange, he handed over the phone. "Desprez? Yes, yes: Lt. Spiro here, about to run out the door. My demonstrator is on emergency leave. The sergeant says he can get you a ride to the firing range; be there ASAP. We'll have a Garand for you—zeroed in. Bye."

The sergeant, whose name was Stiles, had meanwhile called the motor pool. A Jeep was on the way, be there in a few minutes. Stiles motioned for him to sit down. "Trying for OCS, Desprez?"

Frenchy explained, no, he was advised to wait and see on that. The colonel had even discussed OCS with him; he was only eighteen. He felt ill at ease talking to a sergeant who looked to be about forty on the subject that he might someday be the sergeant's boss. Perhaps Sgt. Stiles sensed this, explaining, "I've got eighteen years in, reached the rank of major, then was passed over due to an obsolete MOS. They let me back as a sergeant, so I could get my pension, and then I'm going fishing. Do all you can with your army life—for that matter, with your whole life."

A PFC came in and waved at him. The sergeant shook Frenchy's hand, wishing him luck as he hurried out, the newcomer asking, "Can you drive a Jeep?" Frenchy nodded. "Okay, I'm supposed to be at the Tank Park; let's get you a trip ticket so we can both be where we belong." Not wanting to strip the gears, Frenchy eyed the shift positions as they drove back to the Motor Pool. *Of course, I've never actually driven a Jeep but—what the hell—it's sort of like a car, and the four-wheel-drive part can be picked up later; it's like a day off!*

And so it proved to be: three days of shooting a Garand with no extra duty. During some of the ten-minute breaks, he had one of the range assistants explain how to get the Jeep into four-wheel drive and into the extra low gear, which farm boys called "compound drive." He thought, *This is an extra arrow in my quiver; I'm a communications expert, a map expert, sort of a tank commander, an expert rifleman, a graduate of Infantry Basic and Armored Leadership School, a recent-but-awkward backseat lover, and now a Jeep driver!*

He was able to scrounge the Jeep for two more days. His range scores improved—*never shot better.* He attributed part of his success to the M-1; it was new and seemed a little truer. The lieutenant gave him a last-chance proposal to be on the rifle team. Again he surprised himself: "Sir, I may be crazy, but I truly think it's my destiny to keep going—you know—not stop along the way."

The lieutenant put his arm on Frenchy's shoulder.

"Yes, Desprez, I know exactly what you mean . . . I made choices like that, too. Good luck."

Thursday, orders were passed out. Frenchy and only a few others were directed to proceed to the Oakland Army Terminal, Oakland, California, on route to Camp Drake, Japan, AFFE (Armed Forces Far East), EDCSA: 18 May 1952. That was in three weeks. There was considerable processing. Like everyone, he followed the army pay system of going to a desk, saluting a pay officer and saying, "Sir, Pvt. Desprez reporting for pay."

On that Friday, the pay routine was followed by a more informal system of going to a desk, showing his orders, and receiving a number of vouchers. Soldiers in the Fort Knox Zone were given railroad vouchers good for passage from the Fort to Oakland Terminal via Chicago and Denver. Since he wanted to go to Minnesota, he was advised that Minneapolis and points west were in the same zone, and his vouchers would cover the comparable Minnesota trip. He would have to make his own reservations. Of course, the trip north was his responsibility, just as any Pullman car bookings would be. Per diem would be paid at Oakland on a very Spartan basis. He was admonished, "For God's sake, don't lose any of this stuff!"

Again, Frenchy endured sad farewells. Maury was off to Fort Belvoire, Maryland, for training to become an officer in the Corps of Engineers. Others went into Armor there at Fort Knox or Infantry at Fort Benning, Georgia.

All the boys on the Mammoth Cave trip seemed pleased with that excursion. Some spoke of how they scored with their dates; some were more gallant and kept silent. Maury and Hal—the more introspective of the friends—came up to Frenchy and acknowledged it been a far different experience for both him and his Amanda, a much deeper relationship with certain almost tragic elements—a veritable love story!

And so he started for home by way of breakfast in Louisville. The Fontenots had insisted he stop by, though all recognized that the storybook romance was over and that a back-bedroom finale or other gushy meeting was not to be. Still, he knew it made sense to stop and see them; there was no use running off like the whole thing had been a tragic opera.

They greeted him at the door. There were kisses with the women and a hearty hug from Jean. Sofia fixed hot cereal. As Frenchy pitched in, he treated the French to a final Americanism when he mumbled, mouth full, "We say this hot stuff sticks to the ribs."

Jean, as father of the girl in the heated affair, wanted to have him leave with full understanding and no regrets. "Arnaud, Amanda has told us about your *amour*—very frankly and in detail. In affairs of *amour*, we French are much like Americans; talk of liaisons with secreted mistresses and French *roués* with the finesse of a Charles Boyer are greatly exaggerated. However, if I may put this delicately, Sofia and I personally associate with you two and hold you both in our hearts."

That left poor Arnaud too choked to answer until Amanda grasped his arm, threw back her long tresses, and, for them both, said, "*Merci, Pére et Mére.*"

Before long, Jean said, "I know you must be off, Arnaud; remember, we will always think of you as our American cousin."

Frenchy almost choked with laughter, "An unfortunate choice *mon ami*! Our Great Emancipator, Abraham Lincoln, was assassinated while watching the play, "Our American Cousin;" try '*notre ami Américain.*'"

"*Meilleur; beaucoup meilleur; très bien.*" Thus, the final meeting ended on a nice happy note, and he was out the door.

The trip north was nine hundred miles—a ball-buster for one driver. He made it to Rockford, Illinois, crapped out in a cheap hotel, and was in his mother's arms by 1400 hours the next day— Sunday, 27 April 1952.

That same day, at Panmunjom, Vice Adm. Turner Joy, head in hands, bemoaned, "We are losing men at the front every day because I can't negotiate this damned truce."

Chapter Twenty-one
The Furlough

Monday morning Frenchy looked at the Harvey Brothers storefront. Dust swirled round the dirty windows and hand-painted sign reading, "CLOSED."

Pierre said, "We couldn't keep it going for you, son."

The younger man was annoyed, and, even at the risk of being rude and out-of-line, responded, "Damn it, dad, forget such a notion; that's not the point; it never was the point; I never wanted the place, never would have stayed here! Oh, I'm sorry to snap at you so, but the real question is what are you, mom, and Lucey gonna do? You're only fifty-seven, you goin' out to pasture?"

Somewhat surprised and taken aback, and perhaps sensing a sharing of family leadership with a new generation, Pierre said, "We'll have a council of war at dinner tonight, son, like old times; Marie and I have some ideas. Until recently, we were lulled to sleep by sixty years of success in an old-style place about one step up from young Abe Lincoln's general store at New Salem."

That brought a little chuckle from them both.

They walked around back and checked out a storage shed where they planned to store the red Chevy. Neither being sure what to do with it, for lack of a better idea, Frenchy decided to sign the title in blank and give it to Pierre—*certainly best if I catch a Chinese mortar round.*

Their next stop proved to be providential: the office of Mayor Finkle—one of Pierre's best friends. After some pleasantries, the mayor tilted back his swivel chair so his belly could clear his desk drawer. From there, he drew a holstered revolver and plunked it on his desk.

"We no longer issue firearms to our police-fire units. When old Marty retired, he turned this in. It must be twentyyears old and long ago written off on the town books; if you want it, it's yours."

As he spoke, the Mayor drew out the weapon. "This is a Smith & Wesson Model 10—the classic Police Special. The general type was first issued in 1905, little changed since except for the coil spring and plunger. This particular model has a two-inch barrel and only five cylinders. Look how short and thin it is."

He spun the cylinders to show it was empty, and then handed it across to his enraptured young friend who did the same, then pulled the trigger, cocked the hammer, and pulled again. "Gosh, Mr. F., a real beauty, I'm so grateful."

The mayor said, "It seems meant for concealed use—by a detective or undercover operator. For you, that's probably a good idea, since I don't think they want enlisted men swaggering around looking like George S. Patton or Wyatt Earp. The weapon also comes in a military model—just the same except for a lanyard swivel and a plain grip."

There were two possible ways he could carry and conceal the Model 10: in a shoulder holster or with the present holster in some garter arrangement attached to his calf above the boot and under the bloused trousers. *I'll see. After all, I'd never carry it except in dangerous territory; for now it'll be in the bottom of my duffel—my own little secret.* They thanked the Mayor, and, as they left, Pierre said they need not discuss the gift with the rest of the family.

Frenchy would not forget the so-called council of war at dinnertime. It started with a leave time review: he was taking the

Empire Builder, Great Northern Line, out of Grand Forks, North Dakota, on the afternoon of May 15. Marie had purchased a Pullman berth—a comforting arrangement and a new experience for him. He would change to the Union Pacific in Portland, Oregon, and then ride reserved coach to Oakland. Pierre planned to drive him to Grand Forks, a mere fifty miles.

Marie raised a finger, "Not without me."

Now that departure plans were settled, they would plan back from the 15th.

Norma was now in the College of Scholastica School of Nursing, and Raul was at the Duluth Campus of the University of Minnesota. That made it an easy decision to go to Duluth and to do so when Lucey would not miss much school. The trip was set for the first weekend in May; any later than that, and Lucey would be cramming for finals. After Duluth, Pierre and his son planned to go fishing in Lake of the Woods, with final days close to home and mother.

After the Christmas at the Star Hotel, Marie had received both a call and a thank you letter from May Cerutti—Big Joe's mother in Superior, Wisconsin. They decided to see if it would be possible to visit the Ceruttis as part of the Duluth trip. And, yes, Norma and Joe had gotten together back in February when Joe was on leave.

Son Arnold then turned the conversation to his concern over the store closing.

"My dear son," Marie began. "Have you heard the expression, *a cash cow?*"

He only smiled.

"Well, Arnold, that store was famous in this part of the beet patch for a long time, something like sixty years. My father or my uncle would sit up there on that platform and collect money; some for the big NCR and some for a cigar box. On Sundays, people came to church and then the store from all over the county. In the early days, there was no income tax. As you know, Harvey Brothers was a partnership, so even after the 1913 Income Tax

Amendment profits flowed through to my father and my uncle. At first, individual rates were low, and you can bet Uncle Sam didn't know the whole story.

"What happened to the profits? Well, I suppose some was frittered away. Sometimes they banked their customers, took mortgages, and were not above foreclosing, and . . ."

She looked at her son, smiled, and went on . . ."They bought stocks. What did they buy? Well, things they understood, such as automobiles and tractors leading to General Motors and John Deere. One day my uncle returned from a trip to St. Paul and reported an interesting meeting with a local businessman."

Of course, Frenchy knew about some of this. He piped up: "Enter Minnesota Mining and Manufacturing Company."

"Right!" She replied.

"They didn't need to invest much, it proving a phenomenal success—Scotch Tape: what a winner! Minnesota Mining was listed on the New York Stock Exchange in 1946. I read just this week that international sales were twenty million dollars. It's one of the biggest companies in the world. The point is, Arnold, the wolf is not and never will be at our door."

Clearly, the money was on Marie's side of the family. By way of endorsing what had been said, Pierre now spoke up: "When Lucey is through high school, we may find a winter home down south. At present we're enjoying Lucey and you both being here, anticipating Nancy's marriage, seeing Norma appearing to be content, as she would say, 'Norma being normal.'"

"All right, all right; I'll stop worrying."

Simply trying to change to a literary subject, he said, "Did I tell you I'm reading *The Three Musketeers* in French?"

"Whatever for?"

He gulped. Unintentionally he had opened up the most private part of his life—his love affair—as yet, so unhealed. The Amanda story, complete with tears came pouring out. Lucey blushed; Marie listened with rapt attention and then said, "First things first, could she be pregnant?" With Lucey blushing, Frenchy looked around the room, "Mom, is this the place? . . ."

"It sure is the place. It's obvious from the way you're acting that you two did have sex relations, *both only eighteen years old!*"

He just hung his head, and moaned, "It was not wrong."

"Look son, I'm not trying to be an inquisitor, but we all have responsibilities; so, let's get back to my question: could she be pregnant?"

"No mother, no, she is not pregnant."

"How do you know?"

"Look everyone; I was raised in a house with a bunch of women. I know the rudiments of the human body—male and female. I repeat: I know she's not pregnant, and I wish to avoid the details of how I know!"

He bowed his head for a minute; then, with an inner smile he thought, *I could always quote Amanda saying in French, "Mother will be glad to know I'm not pregnant."* The room remained quiet—Lucey, her prominent Desprez chin thrust forward, not blushing, trusting her brother and thinking her mother had gone far enough.

Then he said, "Thanks; you have a right, maybe a duty, to ask. I would never want to harm those people."

Marie spread out her arms at the foot of the table, as though delivering a benediction: "Well, we got that concluded. Now, let's plan a little procedure and keep it in place for at least six months. I will write Mrs. Fontenot and thank her for being so nice to you. Then you will write your Amanda soon, then once a month or until, as will probably happen, she does find her *galant homme*. Then we can reassess the situation. Give me their Louisville address and their Paris address. I believe nice people don't just walk away from such important relationships."

She turned to Pierre, "You may, if you wish, Signore Montague, write to Signore Capulet; that would be nice."

169

Frenchy was mighty glad that crisis was past. Yet in retrospect, he was glad his Romeo story had been told, was out and now a part of the family history, for him it was an unforgettable and cherished part.

The Duluth trip turned into a substantial family reunion at Uncle Guy and Aunt Ruth's house. Not only were Raul and Norma there, Nancy showed up with fiancé Roy Powers, and the Ceruttis, Joe Senior and May, came up from Superior. Norma gave them both a hug—so did Frenchy.

Raul Desprez was always something to look at—so damn handsome! Frenchy noticed he had filled out, lost some baby fat and thought he looked like a young Tyrone Power with his dark eyes, perfect long nose, and rugged chin. He was not jealous of Raul; actually he quite resembled him except for Raul's dark hair and striking dark eyes.

Raul was studying drama and was scheduled to attend Naval ROTC summer camp at Great Lakes Naval Training Center, North Chicago, Illinois. Frenchy said, "It would be a privilege to salute someone so pretty." That led to a boyish scuffle—like old times!

When Pierre saw the size of Joe Cerutti Senior, he said, "Boy, I'm glad you're my friend!"

Showing he was in on the joke, Joe replied, "Well, I can't speak for Joe Junior, but I'll sure tell you one thing: I've never done a pig-garbage detail, and I never will!"

Marie turned to May and asked, "Our children have known each other just a few days; can there be anything serious?"

May smiled, "You don't really think that big lout would tell me what's going on. Seriously though, I've admonished him; a lot of mistakes have been made by impetuous couples in wartime."

Frenchy winced at that remark, as he caught Marie's eye.

"Ladies!" shouted Norma from across the room, "Whoa, whoa; we've just reached the good-night-kiss stage."

I'll bet, thought Frenchy.

Joe Senior said, "The big news is Dago has his Wings—made the required five jumps, and graduated. We have a picture of the ceremony—a captain pinning them on. He seems to eat it up; they're keeping him on at the Parachute Training School, at least for a while."

Quiet Lucey spoke up, "What are wings?"

Her brother explained that it was a grey metal pin, showing a parachute with a wing on each side, highly coveted, so a soldier would wear his wings at all times for the rest of his career. Most RA soldiers hoped to fit jump school into their army careers; it looked good in the file, showed guts—plenty of guts!

"I may go see him," said Norma. "Fort Bragg is just outside Fayetteville, North Carolina."

A long way for a good-night-kiss, thought her brother.

Of course, being a presidential election year, the senior generation had to discuss politics. Everyone seemed to be for Bob Taft except Guy who said he liked Ike—typical of the brothers to be on opposite sides. Eisenhower had just submitted his report as Supreme Allied Commander in Europe and was now actively running for President. People were still not sure where he stood on the issues, but they felt he was electable.

The fishing trip was certainly a success, at least from the fishing viewpoint. They planned to catch Walleye, and they were jumping. Marie preferred Walleye to Northern—both good eating, but with Northern you were always fighting the bones.

Both Pierre and Frenchy realized it was an outing of two men—no longer a father and a boy. The only drawback was their anxiety: Frenchy was quiet during the day and suffered his bad dreams at night. They stopped and bought thirty-eight shells and, back in the woods, shot at tin cans with the Police Special.

At trip's end, back in North River, Frenchy found himself anxious to be off. They treated Marie like a queen on Mothers' Day. He tried to be extra attentive, but she found him gazing out the window, gave him a hug and said, "Poor boy, so fidgety, you'll soon be off—chasing your destiny."

171

Chapter Twenty-two
The Great Northern

There was more quiet time as Pierre and Marie drove him to Grand Forks, which lay on the confluence of the Red River of the North and the Red Lake River. The Empire Builder would pull into this small city around 1700 hours and would soon be gone. Frenchy insisted his parents leave him off and not wait, so they could be most of the way home before dark.

He had never ridden in a Pullman car, so Pierre and Marie passed the time by explaining what to expect. Pierre said, "Seems crazy, but the Pullman porter job is the only one exclusively open to colored men. I've always found 'em first rate; so give a good tip."

The train was actually a little early. The porter helped him aboard with his baggage, leaving the duffel on the car platform, Frenchy explaining that it held all his army gear so he dared not check it in some baggage car. "Without that duffel, Mr. Porter, I'd probably end in the stockade."

The porter tagged it and said, "It'll be fine right here, where I'll guard it like it was my own, and, by the way, my name is Louis, as in Joe Louis."

Louis carried the other bag to berth 6. As they walked past berth 9, a pretty woman looked up from her magazine and smiled.

He smiled back, giving her a quick salute. He sat down and stowed his bag just when the couplings clicked and squeaked and the car repeatedly shuddered as they got underway.

After a trip to the gentlemen's end of the car, he settled back, all alone in the Berth 6 seats, with the nice feeling of being organized and relaxed. In no time, they were in open country, Grand Forks left behind, leading him to shake his head, as he recalled that this small town in the heart of the wheat country—population 27,000—was the second largest city in North Dakota. He saw other crops as well and fields dotted with cow-calf units, the calves newborn and staying close to their mamas.

He looked up and standing there was the girl with the magazine. "Welcome to the Empire Builder, soldier, how far you goin'?"

When he rose and stood beside her, the object before him seemed more spectacular than when he had walked past—medium height, blond, pretty, well built, and a heavy scent of perfume—*wow a heavy scent!* He motioned for her to join him, saying he was headed for Oakland and would change trains Friday afternoon in Portland. She crossed her legs just opposite him and adjusted her pleated skirt with some care, rendering an enticing view of legs—nicely encased in nylon hose, and providing a striking sheen to knees and calves.

She was going to Seattle to see family and friends, maybe find a new job. Her name was Alice Perrers; she was working at the Mayo Clinic, in Rochester, and had boarded in Minneapolis that morning.

They talked, he saying his name was Arnold—a one-day escape from his nickname—and pushing his bashful self to keep up his end of the conversation, confessing he didn't know much about the famous Clinic except that his grandfather made several trips to Mayos and eventually died there, but thinking, even as he spoke, *I'm boring—she doesn't give a damn about my grandfather!*

He thought about comparing the electric diesels of the Empire Builder to the twin turbines of an ore boat but decided it would be better to appear shy than even more boring. She didn't seem to mind; she jabbered on and at least acted interested in his hunting and fishing experiences and his skill with the Garand. Squirming in her seat and shifting her position, she rather deliberately crossed over to the other leg, giving only a momentary view of bare inner thigh just above the stocking, quickly closed, as she again adjusted the hem of her pleated skirt. *Damn good legs; but she sure squirms a lot; maybe she's constipated. Wow, what an outrageously personal thought!*

She felt him out about his thoughts on going to Korea. With all this activity and talk, he loosened up a bit. "You know, Alice, I feel scared about going to a combat zone and maybe a little numb, but I also feel well prepared, well trained, that is. People say to me, 'Oh don't worry, something will come along for you to do behind a desk,' but I just keep goin' along. A war takes fighters, so that may be my destiny."

Just then a servant came through the car, playing four-note chimes and announcing, "First call to dinner."

"Come on, Arnold, let's be early customers."

He followed her to the forward door, taking the lead when he saw that getting through the two connecting doors was heavy work—hard to turn the lever, hard to pull a door open, hard to hold a door open. Everything on a train seemed to be super strong and durable and so not lightweight and not necessarily user-friendly. Between the cars, the clickety-clack was loud—much louder than in the sealed cars, and the overlapping floor plates where the cars joined would shift and slide, making stance uncertain. The two grabbed the handrails at each door and passed through two sleeping cars before reaching the diner, it seeming natural when she grabbed hold of his hand each time they passed between cars.

Reaching the diner, they were escorted to a small table—*just for two!* As soon as they had ordered, she was back to the former subject: "So, you're a sharpshooter, what if the thing on the other end is a human head, not a paper target?"

"You can bet I've thought about that a lot. You know, there are studies showing only a minority of soldiers are willing to shoot and have the flash reveal their position; others won't shoot to kill under any conditions. There must be lots of reasons for this: fear, worry about identity of the target, most likely religious convictions starting with The Sixth Commandment. In a World War II survey, it was found that only 25 percent would shoot to kill, which I consider an amazingly low number.

"Obviously, if I'm alone somewhere and twenty Chinese are stalking by on patrol, I shut up and stay hidden. In those conditions, self-preservation is a strong compulsion, but, in other situations, in attack or in defense, or if I thought I were in danger or my buddies were in danger, the answer is find and hit a target, whatever it is."

She thought his little speech left little doubt: *a long euphemistic way to say, "Damn right, I'd shoot!"*

She stared at him with a wan smile, a smile that was hard for him to read: *Was she merely admiring my soldierly attitude or was she thinking of the two of us and what we should do here and now? Is she glad we met up or do I now seem boyish to her, disappointing, perhaps immature and just trying to act tough? There she is squirming again. Where do I stand with this good-looking creature? For that matter, where do I want to stand with her?*

After dinner, she bought a bourbon on the rocks; he declined, thinking *it's strange to order a cocktail after rather than before dinner.* She took a long gulp and again was silent, eyeing him, apparently thinking. Another gulp, another squirm. She stared out the window, then just a sip. He looked her right in the eye with a sympathetic smile. *I wonder if I screwed up, if she's sort of dismissed me, would rather be alone; perhaps she doesn't feel well—couldn't be a bad stomach the way she ate. Maybe monthly problems?*

175

Then, mind made up, she very frankly laid out her position, "Christ! What am I involved with? You're 18, a handsome, attractive guy; I'm 25. How wet behind the ears are you?"

He almost choked, as he realized, *She's not disappointed in me; she's hot to trot! That's gotta be what I think is called "a proposition." What'll I say?* He weighed his answer carefully, eyeing her, smirking just a little, resisting the urge to reach across and take a gulp of the bourbon. The smell of the drink mingled with the omnipresent aroma of her perfume. He mused, *Amanda didn't use a fragrance, just had a clean soapy smell. This is new, different—kind'a exciting! Perfume and that glimpse of thigh!* It was his turn to pause. Then he sort of surprised himself: "I've done it in tighter quarters than a Pullman lower berth. You're lovely; I'm honored."

She reached over and shook his hand, then held it in both of hers. She cocked her head, beamed, and—down to business— asked if he had birth-control gear. He reassured her, and then, as if it had all been his idea, she shook his hand once more, and, to sort of seal a contract, concluded, "You sweet talker; how can I resist?"

He looked out: *The fields are dark now; we're headed into the western sunset.*

When they got back, their car was as they left it—not yet made up by his friend, Louis, who smiled at them and said he was about to start the nighttime preparation. She urged her soldier friend on to the Club Car, as she followed, holding his hand, finally pulling him back before the last door and saying,

"No need to hurry, no need at all . . ."

They kissed, not at all tentatively; then another kiss, as she groped his front and he responded by grasping her butt through that delicious pleated skirt—no fancy garment underneath, only flesh, feeling soft—just right, as he held her against him. They both thrust and pushed with their middles, he feeling the beginnings of a turgid state. *No, it was more than the beginnings!*

But then, they heard the door behind them start to open and just went on, as if nothing had happened, Frenchy pushing her ahead to hide the bulge in his trousers. She got the picture.

They found two seats together amid a number of people already in the Club Car. He was obliged to answer the usual questions put to a man in uniform: where are you from; where are you going; thanks for serving. She ordered another bourbon; this time he joined her. A nice passenger flagged down the waiter and paid for the drinks. A lady in slacks with blue-gray hair asked if they were married. Having just taken a slug of the whiskey, he smiled, gulped, and was able to reply, "Not yet, ma'am."

Alice pretended to cough, as they both fought off laughter. She crossed her legs, letting that pleated skirt rise above the knees but quickly adjusting it by just an inch or so.

She dotes on displaying her legs; that view of white thigh back before dinner was a deliberate, seductive ploy. Now she's displaying before these middle-aged folks. Actually, we're both on display before these nice people. Though I feel a decided urge to get on with it, sitting here with them and being the center of attention kills the time Louis needs back in the sleeping car.

The wait to have the berths made up provided time to conspire: both of them trying to act casually, prolonging things and adding suspense and fun to the whole scheme. As team manager, she whispered the ground rules: both would get ready for bed, use the facilities and return to their berths, then she would peek out, and, when there were no people in the aisle, she would casually arise in her robe and, if the coast were still clear, she would dart into his berth. She had been leaning over toward him, giving an excuse to put his arm on her opposite shoulder, feeling her shudder when he first touched her; showing she was keyed up, ready, anxious—time to end the prelude and head back.

On return, they saw that the metamorphosis of their sleeping car was complete—now they saw just a narrow aisle between curtains.

In she burst! Of course, there was no room except to fall on top of him. He chuckled, realizing that one didn't have to be a hound dog to trace her perfume trail from berth 9 to berth 6. Louis or any observant passenger would know what was going on. There were giggles, followed by admonishments to be silent throughout. For a while, he stayed under her while she untied the sash and pulled off the robe—her only garment. He had the foresight before she arrived to take off everything, plus, in his aroused state, to don a little raincoat.

They got up steam plenty fast with a non-stop kiss, her small body thrusting down on him, then halting, causing him to release her so she could move up, aligning her chest with his head and leaving her head nudging the aft bulkhead. He kissed wildly at her breasts until she again halted, drawing back, *just in time*, he bit his lip, and whispered he wanted to be topside.

Easier said than done, but the clumsy adjustment calmed them enough to keep either from going over the speed limit. However, once she spread her legs, raised her knees, reached out, groped in the dark, found him, and helped him enter, they were compatibly rapid. He pushed down, not tenderly; she wrapped her legs around his; he pushed once more; and down the tracks they flew at flank speed, as the whistle blew and they passed by Minot in a shot.

They remained coupled until they got their breath, and then began untangling.

"Wha'da ya call that perfume?"

"*Most Precious;* like it?"

"Well, it's sure something else; what's the word—enticing, alluring?"

They couldn't possibly sleep together in an area barely holding one person and so agreed she would be back for an encore at 0500 hours; he peeked out after she had retrieved the robe and told her the coast was clear; she left; and he fell into a deep sleep until there was a tug on the sheets at about five in the morning.

He headed for the gentlemen's end and found her in berth 6 when he returned, thus causing the initial positions to be reversed. He needed to see what he was doing and turned on the reading light, then squirmed out of his pajamas, crouched between her legs and rolled on a rubber. She stared at the process, really eyeing all of his body for the first time.

She leaned forward and whispered, "Great body and a perfect size for me, but a little moistening might help; lean back."

Soon she pulled him forward and whispered, "Now my turn."

He obliged, and moved up her body, pausing at the breasts. With those preliminaries aiding his entry, their encore mileage increased, going down the tracks, but this time without a train whistle!

At breakfast, they were in Montana's mountains: beautiful forests, sometimes patches of snow and far-off glimpses of tall, snow-capped peaks. He looked at her and smiled, "Well, Most Precious, you had that pretty well scripted last night, didn't you?"

"Oh, Arnold, what fun it was, how wonderful you are! On the first go around, I was so excited! You took over just in time, and how about the timing of the train whistle! As for having it planned, someone had to speak up. I got us started, knowing that sex with strangers is so exciting, with all those other people around, people a few feet away, behind us, in front of us, across from us—like we're extra naughty and getting away with something. Wha'd you think?"

"For a man, it's sort of a fantasy, an absolute dream, you performing great both in leading at first and then responding—perfect, no complaints. However, I scratch my head at the thought of what kind of wife you'd make. I'm told they don't use chastity belts anymore, and a husband isn't going to wait until you're both under a table at a cocktail party, in a telephone booth, or in the public library stacks."

She laughed, "Say, those are great ideas, but I could settle down, and I will some day. Today our relationship will be over officially when you get off in Portland, and, between then and now, I don't feel like pulling up my dress on one of the platforms."

He pretended to be disappointed, saying, "Why, I was planning to take you up front and ask the engineer and fireman to move out; that way we could blow the whistle again—just right!"

She raised a finger, "Think about that. Which one of us would pull the whistle—how do you come and pull at the same time? That would take practice."

They giggled some more, both finding the postmortem lots of fun. He didn't think her answer about promiscuity was responsive, but decided to move on. . . .

"You remember when you propositioned me at dinner? What if I'd said, 'Golly, gee, ma'am; all I know is what the big boys tell me?'"

She renewed her laughter, somewhat louder than before. "What're the odds on drawing a virgin boy, age 18? Pretty good, I suppose, and that's what I was pondering before, as you put it, I propositioned you. However, your talk about shooting to kill made me think you'd been around the block, but if you had come out with that golly-gee stuff, I would have backed off . . . a Pullman berth is just for fun, not for something important like a first romantic encounter, which should be done to 'Ravel's Bolero.'"

"Not a bad philosophy," he said, "Though I'm not sure I accept it. Your fun could go wrong: remember the sob song, 'But it was no joke when the rubber broke.'"

"Yea, yea, but that's not likely to happen, and life goes on, playing the odds and making choices. In our case, we both wanted—now let me think—we both wanted two things: berth sex and no birth. My first boyfriend and I used the rhythm method and got away with it; I keep track monthly, and last night, for example, I knew I was midway, in a probable fertile time, feeling raunchy, not in my safe time, so I asked questions, checked on you, and we were careful."

"So, Alice, what were some of your 'extra naughty' places?"

"Let's see: for sure the fitting room at Crayton's Department Store—twice there over lunch breaks; and, the second time, we were more or less caught by a sales lady when we opened the door to leave; however, what could she say: we were skirt-lifting, not shop-lifting?

All bashfulness now overcome, there was another round of uncontrolled giggling until he finally managed to suggest, "The sales lady could say, 'did it fit?'"

"Then we used to go to terrace dances at the country club. After a particularly slow, neck-to-neck dance, we would stroll away while the music played on and have a go on the practice putting green. We called making out our hole-in-one."

What fun! I never talked like this with my sisters, but then I'm sure they never acted like this. Or am I sure; you never know.

He asked, "Is this your first Pullman conquest?"

She pondered for a moment: "Yes, yes; I had one other opportunity, tempting, but for me the wrong time of the month—too many logistics; if I knew for sure I could find another Arnold, I'd plan trips accordingly, like a bride plans the honeymoon."

She paused, then had a thought, "By the way, what was the place smaller than a Pullman berth?"

He had joined in laughing at her jokes about a berth and a birth and about her trysts in bizarre locations, and then pondered her question about love in small places. He wanted to be polite, but the fumbling match in the rear seat of the Chevy with his bare-assed exit ironically seemed too sacrosanct to discuss, even after her descriptions and even without mentioning names and places. He laughed, cogitated for a moment, pointed his finger at her, then he paraphrased "Father William," an *Alice in Wonderland* poem:

"I've answered three questions, and that is enough;
don't give yourself airs; be off or I'll kick you
downstairs."

She at least smiled, probably knowing in advance he wouldn't tell her. She bowed her head in thought, and then looked him straight in the eye: "I know, I know, I've sensed for some time that you have had a deep, very moving experience."

He now regretted his flippant reply and answered, "Yes, you're right . . . I think about her, but just can't share my thoughts. You deserved a decent reply; I'm sorry."

That ended the discussion. They were soon busy gazing out the windows on both sides and pointing out landmarks. The Cascade Mountains were spectacular—all those volcanoes! There were Mount Adams, Mount Hood, Mount St. Helens, and, on the port side, Mount Jefferson. Finally, far off was the greatest of them all, Mount Rainier—second highest point in the lower forty-eight states. Frenchy knew that several of these volcanic peaks were still active, including Hood, St. Helens, and Rainier. He was fascinated by volcanoes. Lassen Peak, down in California, had blown its top in 1915. He thought, *There must still be huge cauldrons of lava in the bowels of the northwest landmass, all probably activated by earthquakes.*

At Portland, the memorable part of the odyssey ended. He threw a kiss to Alice, gave Louis a nice tip—to which the porter responded with a knowing smile and pat on the back. Then he dragged his bags to the Southern Pacific train and found his reserved coach seat.

"Hey, GI," a voice rang out, "Where you headed?"

An army corporal came through from the next car. He was short with red hair in a crew cut, Second Division patch on his shoulder, one row of three ribbons, low quarters, not boots. "I'm up front one car, saw you board, so I'm looking you up."

Frenchy stood and replied, "Oakland Army Terminal."

"Me, too; I was on emergency leave and am now headed back to Frozen Chosin. I'm gonna check out the diner; join me if you want. We should definitely share a taxi to the Terminal tomorrow. I'm Dave Davis."

"Arnold Desprez: army friends to call me 'Frenchy.' If you like, let's chow down now."

At dinner, and later in the Club Car, Dave explained that he was from Tacoma, had one year at Lewis & Clark College, got restless, signed up, and went through basic at Fort Lewis. He arrived in Korea in January 1952, and was held as a clerk typist in 2nd Division Headquarters where the brass liked him and promoted him, so he got himself a nice little niche. He explained that anyone with a high school diploma, much less one year of college, was looked upon as extra valuable property in the upper echelon headquarters.

Frenchy countered with tales of hunting, ore boats, infantry and armor, but soon they decided to crap out. Frenchy slept more soundly leaning back in the coach seat than the day before in the double-occupancy Pullman berth.

Chapter Twenty-three
Stalemate Explained

The Oakland Army Base was a huge facility, consisting of the Port and General Depot, Oakland Sub-Port of San Francisco Port of Embarkation, and the Oakland Army Terminal. Built in 1941, it lay just south of the San Francisco–Oakland Bay Bridge. During the Korean War, millions of tons of cargo passed through the Terminal.

The cab halted at a building titled "Fort Mason—Headquarters U.S. Army Transportation Command Pacific." The cab waited while Frenchy and Dave made for the main entrance, along the way encountering navy and army brass and proffering the necessary salutes. Inside, they were courteously directed to North Barracks, where enlisted personnel were housed and processed. The cab got them there, and they were duly checked in, assigned quarters, and given a map showing locations of the PX, theater, laundry, churches, infirmary, enlisted club, mess hall, cab and bus stands, etc. They were handed expense report forms and advised to handle travel expenses ASAP. Both were to attend a briefing at 1000 hours Monday—the next day. They were also told no vessel was leaving until Thursday.

Luckily, Frenchy and Dave were given the comfort and privacy of a two-bed room with latrine right next door. They decided to hang out together and headed for the laundry and then the Enlisted Men's Club for drinks and dinner.

They had heard the basic facts about each other the night before. Dave's emergency leave was due to his mother's death. He felt comfortable reminiscing about her. She had been a school teacher, had a radical mastectomy five years before, did well until the last three months, and then went downhill. He was lucky to get the leave, made possible because of his family situation and because he was a clerk in 2nd Division Headquarters. His company commander heard about his problems and made arrangements through the Red Cross.

Dave knew the war history from Pusan to the current prisoner struggle at Koje-do. On 7 May, while Frenchy and Pierre were fishing, the Communist prisoners on Koje-do Island seized prison commander, Brig. Gen. Francis T. Dodd, and held him as their prisoner. Dodd was released in three days but only after Brig. Gen. Charles F. Colson, the acting commander—fearing for Dodd's life—admitted to false charges of U.N. atrocities. It was all a horrible snafu, leading to criticism throughout the world and vitriolic acrimony from the Reds at the truce talks. It wrenched the stomach to even talk about it! Both generals were demoted and relieved.

Frenchy shook his head. *Somewhere men are laughing, and little children shout, but there is no joy in Koje-do—a real tragedy, so unexpected and so avoidable! It's awful to see your country screw up like that.*

Koje-do held some 150,000 POWs; it was overcrowded, and the prisoners were controlled from within by a vicious core group who were engaged in ferreting out and killing those fellow captives who were, in their judgment, not dedicated enough to the North Korean-style party line. In a new and sinister twist to the prisoner problem, some of the ringleaders had actually allowed themselves to be captured so they could cause this turmoil.

Brig. Gen. "Bull" Boatner, Assistant Commander, 2ⁿᵈ Division, was sent to clean up the prison. He called in the 187ᵗʰ Airborne Regimental Combat Team. As Dave and Frenchy sat together that evening, the situation was still chaotic, the outcome still uncertain—a tragic mess piled on a tragic war!

The issue of repatriating POWs had become the final point of contention at the truce talks. The U.N. side was determined not to force repatriation on those prisoners not wanting to return to the enslaved communist countries. The other side claimed these people were being coerced, which was probably true in some cases. The Koje-do prison crisis, being closely tied to the repatriation problem, fouled up the never-ending truce talks all the more.

Although it happened one and a half years ago and long before he reached the Division, Dave knew full well about the tragedy suffered by his 2ⁿᵈ Division on the six-mile stretch of the Kunuri-Sunchan road known as the Gauntlet. They discussed it, Dave explaining, "By now, we know so much more about fighting the CCF. Back then, my Division had two better choices: to retreat sooner was best—after all, they'd had ample warnings—otherwise to stay there and form a perimeter. The Division, intact at Kunuri, could have held out for weeks, resupplied by air, with the hope of being reached by a counterthrust. Instead of being abandoned or even run over by our own troops, the wounded could have been systematically evacuated by air. Remember, the 1ˢᵗ Marines, under O.P. Smith, were surrounded at the Chosin Reservoir and managed to escape. Gen. Keiser—a nice man, I'm told—might have been a hero instead of a scapegoat.

"I hate to make the comparison, but those 'don't retreat' orders out of Tokyo Headquarters do sound like Hitler's obdurate stay-and-die policy leading to 850,000 Axis casualties at Stalingrad—the turning point of the Second War and I think the greatest battle of all time. Just like Inchon was a turning point for us, the Gauntlet and destruction of my Division was a turning point for them."

As they lingered over dinner, Frenchy said, "So, tell me more."

"Well, you know they are through arguing about a truce line and all the other issues except repatriation, and it is said that only 70,000 of the 170,000 prisoners from North Korea and China are willing to go home."

"So I've heard," said Frenchy, cocking his head and pointing his finger. "Let me get this straight, Dave. We've saved South Korea at a terrible price all around. How many killed and wounded have we Americans suffered? I think the number is well over a hundred thousand. Now some of these guys who fought against us—until captured—don't wanna go home. To end the killing, I'd be tempted—very tempted—to say 'So sorry, off you go. I—the American savior of South Korea—I do wanna go home.'"

"I hear you, Frenchy. To state the other side, it's pretty certain that the communists would hold trials and have them executed. It's sad, but that's their past behavior pattern—well documented; Stalin did the same thing after the Second War. Many of these men were impressed into service, and we find that among the Chinese, some had fought on the other side in their recent civil war.

"But—and this is a big 'but'—at Panmunjom the communist negotiators correctly point out that the Geneva Conventions simply provide that, upon conclusion of hostilities, both sides are to immediately exchange prisoners. Truman made the decision not to interpret the rule tightly, based on concepts of liberty and justice—what we're beginning to call 'human rights.'"

Raising a finger, Frenchy asked, "Why don't they ship 'em off to some third-world country and let it be unsnarled there?"

Dave laughed, "Why not? They should send you to Panmunjom." He went on, "For a year now, we've been in a stalemate with our force strung out in what is called the Kansas Line, located just above the 38th Parallel and opposite their forces. On the east, it starts a little way north of Kansong and runs to the mouth of the Imjin River in the west. The line is about 155 miles long. Between the two MLRs is a no-man's land, varying in width from a few hundred yards to a few miles, depending on the terrain and how the forces happened to end up. It is to be called the 'De-Militarized Zone,' or 'DMZ.' This has already been fully negotiated at Panmunjom, which, by the way, is a little village in the DMZ.

"Neither side has mounted an all-out offensive since last year. There have been efforts to, as they say, 'straighten out the line' and to protect the rail and road system to Seoul as well as to secure the Hwach'on Reservoir furnishing electric power—that sort of thing.

"U.N. Forces have contested and retaken ground in the Punchbowl, which is a dead volcano crater, located east of the Iron Triangle—a communications hub around P'yonggang, Kumhwa, and Ch'orwon—and they have fought over other areas west of Ch'orwon.

"For example, last August, there were savage struggles on the west side of the Punchbowl at Bloody Ridge. U.N. forces suffered 2,700 killed, wounded, or captured; the North Koreans, about 15,000. Finally, 23rd Infantry, part of my Division, took Bloody Ridge on 5 September. We then tried for Heartbreak Ridge—just 1,500 yards to the north. There were a whole series of successful and unsuccessful attacks, followed by counterattacks and so on. Whoever had Heartbreak Ridge would be shot up—exhausted, short of ammo, and, so, subject to counterattack."

Frenchy rested his head in his hands, and then shook his head, remembering the training at Fort Knox and the time he came within a few feet of aggressor Maury Burley before he saw him. He remained silent, as Dave went on.

"In one of these attacks, we were being forced off once again when a Hawaiian, Pfc. Herbert K. Pililaau, agreed to stay and cover the retreat. He shot his BAR until his ammo was gone, then threw grenades till they were gone, then used his trench knife until shot and bayoneted. From a safe position, his buddies could see all this. They later found over forty bodies scattered around Pililaau's remains. He received the Medal of Honor posthumously. Later, by changing tactics and clearing the way for Easy Eights, Heartbreak Ridge was finally taken by French soldiers last October."

Frenchy interrupted, "That incident I knew about from my French girlfriend's father. They were led by an incredible three-star general, fighting as a lieutenant colonel under the *nom de guerre* of Raoul Monclar. What a guy! But go on, Dave."

Dave shook his head, "You're right—a legend of the War—an amazing soldier. Anyway, the enemy has this massive cave system, and, as we speak, I'm sure there are thousands of Chinese and North Korean gnomes digging 'em deeper. Sometimes the caves run through a mountain to a camouflaged window facing us. Actually that window thing is something we also use but far less elaborately than the Red cave system, which houses sleeping quarters, hospitals, arsenals, ordnance works . . . all sorts of facilities. Some cave areas are big enough to hold battalions. Their guns, vehicles, mortars, and other materiel are underground or camouflaged. Our observers fly over and see nothing. We bomb suspected entrances; we scatter napalm.

"Now, the hell of it is, in the next row of mountains—to the north—they have another set of these damn trenches and caves, then another. So they have a defense in depth, not strictly a main line of resistance like ours. Our Chinese prisoners tell us these fortifications sometimes go back twenty miles."

Frenchy gasped: "So if we go for Hill XYZ, we lose 2,000 soldiers and gain a useless mountain, probably in an exposed salient making it subject to recapture."

"You got it! We would get a rocky mountaintop, blackened by napalm, denuded of trees and brush, complete with fecal matter, dried blood, bones, and other human body parts. Some trenches and bunkers might still be there, some flattened, most oriented in the wrong direction. To resupply our new acquisition, we would face mortars, artillery, and direct flanking fire from unseen locations. Of course, the same would be true if they came after us."

Frenchy, asked, "How many enemy soldiers are there? I suppose millions."

"Well, anyway, 900,000. But it gets worse: these guys are there until they die. There's no thirty-six points and you're gone; no Chinese Marshal is going to say, 'So solly, boy-san, go home to your mama-san's funeral.' No, they have no rotation system that I've heard about, and many of them are veterans of the Japanese war or their civil war against the Kuomingtang. A thirty-year-old Chinese soldier may have been fighting his entire adult life and know nothing else!"

"Pros versus amateurs like me!"

"Exactly, Frenchy, and me, too. The communist leaders can send the same men out on fifty patrols, send 'em out every night, till they don't come back. We're sending an experienced sergeant, or maybe an inexperienced second lieutenant, and a bunch of kids like you and me. By the way, the word 'second' in second lieutenant is a euphemism for 'inexperienced.' Which patrol is going to know the pathways, the danger points, the ambush points? To put it crudely, who is apt to get garroted?"

Frenchy shook his head, "Ye gods, you're describing my friend and supporter Lt. Milton Mason four square. His MOS is infantry platoon leader, but what chance would he have on a point in no-man's-land!"

Dave continued, "I've been up to the 2nd Division's MLR: no fancy caves; the men live and work in shantytowns of reinforced bunkers on the back slopes, living quarters called 'hoochies'—a Japanese word. There are no trees or even bushes—all plowed up by bombs, howitzers, and mortars. The hoochies are made of logs and sandbags—hand carried up rear slopes by Korean porters—called 'Yobos.'

"In some areas there are shoulder-high connecting trenches, staggered to minimize enfilade fire. You know those words?"

"Yes, 'enfilade' is fire down the length of the enemy trench line—favorable to the attacker; 'defilade' is the opposite—where the defending fortifications furnish protection and the attack is vertical to the trench line."

"Right, Frenchy. That's why trenches zigzag—to limit enfilade exposure. Anyway, back to our MLR and the everyday problems a soldier faces: slit trenches to crap in are down drainage, below the bunkers, probably in an offshoot of a connecting trench. The men throw garbage, like C-Ration cans, off the forward slopes. The rationale is that infiltrating enemies may rattle the junk and alert our troops. When the garbage does rattle, it's more apt to be a pack of foraging rats, which, by the way, carry the viral hemorrhagic fever—another horror of war: bleeding discharges . . . fever . . . death.

"We now have a system where a GI can go back a few miles, maybe every two weeks, and have a shower. Back in '50 and '51, sometimes those poor bastards might wear the same underwear—all the same clothes—for two months and, like everyone, be fighting diarrhea at least part of the time."

Dave took out a pencil and started writing on his paper table mat.

"What are the main obstacles—the main worries—for our guys on the MLR? Let me try and list them; let' see . . .

Patrol duty? Sure, *dai ichi*, meaning 'number one;'

lousy food and lack of water?—sure;

incoming artillery and mortars?—sure;

all-out attack by the enemy?—rated unlikely; and

terrible cold?—and how, another *dai ichi*.

"You know another? Last on my list, but not least, is bowel problems; call it intestinal disorders. They don't want to get up at night, especially when it's cold, so they get constipated, cramping. Then they get the opposite—everyone from generals on down get 'the GIs.' All it takes is a dirty mess kit. You know what dingle berries are? Nothing to laugh at! Yeh, gut problems are right up there with the enemy and the weather; the gut and the cold were the big casualty makers on the road back from the Reservoir.

"Finally, we don't have anywhere near the defense-in-depth deployed by the enemy. Our MLR is more of a thin, olive drab line. So, how do we manage? First, the enemy has an extended and difficult supply line, which they can best utilize only at night or in bad weather, because our air superiority prevents most daytime moves. Also, while we continue to help the South build a modern highway and rail system, the North Korean roads are poor; so is their trucking system."

"In contrast, we're the world's mightiest power. Goods, weapons, ammunition, and men come streaming into Pusan and Inchon from all over the free world—from places like this Terminal. Once in Korea, we have highways and railroads up at least as far as Uijongbu—one of our supply centers—located pretty close to the MLR. As I indicated, we even have local porters to carry our gear and local helpers to pull KP. Boys on the hilltops generally get one hot meal a day, while gas stoves are replacing the charcoal and wood hibachis they recently used.

"An American division has ten times the firepower of a Chinese or North Korean division. We have placed some of our artillery battalions in direct support of ROK divisions, so their fire power is about like ours. Gen. Van Fleet has been big on this integration-of-forces program. Incidentally, ROK leadership and training are much improved; they no longer run away. You will hear about Paik Sun Yup—a respected General. He's been serving as Korean representative at the truce talks.

"As far as tactics are concerned, we use the triangular system: two up, one back, as you were taught at Fort Knox. It's the same system all the way up: companies, battalions, regiments, and divisions. Those reserve components can be quickly inserted to close a breakthrough or a seam between units. Then, too, we have special independent units that can hayaku to anywhere, like the 187th Airborne Regimental Combat Team sent to Koje-do. You know, the Koreans all speak Japanese, and we pick up some expressions:

hayaku slipped out; we use it to mean 'hurry;' you'll encounter lots of expressions like that.

"Anyway, to go on, we just outgun them so much: a Divarty—that's Division Artillery, if you don' know the expression—may provide unified fire from 105 howitzers, 155 howitzers, Long Toms, and eight-inch howitzers. Would you believe they are bringing in 240 howitzers?

Take just the 105s, there is a 6-howitzer battery for every infantry battalion, hence a battalion of eighteen howitzers for every infantry regiment. That's all backed up by the heavy artillery, and also 80mm and 60mm mortars, Quad-50s, Twin 40mm guns, Bazooka rocket launchers, recoilless rifles, and 90mm tank guns.

"I haven't mentioned strikes from the air. We can use bombers, especially along supply routes; and our old prop planes, like the Corsair and the AD Skyraider, have the real advantage of flying slower, staying over target longer, and carrying a bigger payload than the jets. We also have great support from artillery observers in those little L-19s."

Dave held up a finger and smiled, "One more weapon and it's a biggie. For units on the east end of the MLR—I think that would be marine and ROK units—we have cruisers in the Sea of Japan ready to fire their eight-inch guns in direct support. The navy has observers from the ships working with our land troops in the Taebaek Mountains. When we evacuated from Hungnam, the marines adjusted fire from the *Missouri*—sixteen-inch guns."

Dave paused to take a breath and consider what else to say. He got a kick out of finding a willing listener and a guy so bright and able.

"Well, Frenchy, this war will not be remembered for the stalemate. No, it will be remembered for the villainous invasion, the Pusan Perimeter, MacArthur's last moment of glory at Inchon, the CCF entry, the resulting disasters like the Gauntlet and the Reservoir, and the firing of MacArthur. But I'll tell you this: they got us at Kunuri, at the Chosin Reservoir, and last year at Wonju by luring us in. Now in this World War I–style trench warfare, that's no longer possible, at least on a large unit basis. Some Chinese platoon might still sucker a U.N. platoon. Seems strange to put it this way, but the point is *they can't outsmart us any longer.*"

Frenchy shook his head at this bizarre admission.

"So, Dave, why all the casualties? We read about appalling numbers, still thousands a month, when they're down to one issue at Panmunjom?"

"Boy, that is puzzling, isn't it? The generals regularly say 'sit tight and don't get killed.' I've told you what I hear around Division Headquarters and what you can read in *Stars and Stripes* and other standard sources. I guess people get killed several ways:

"First, with all the exchange of artillery, scattered land mines, attacks from the air, thirty-below temperatures, intestinal disorders, and Walker-type accidents, there are lots of mundane ways to go.

"Second, let's talk about Lt. Gen. Mathew Ridgway. He commanded the 82nd Airborne in the last war. He replaced Walker as 8th Army Commander in December 1950. He replaced MacArthur in April 1951. Wonder of wonders, he recently replaced Eisenhower in Europe. Ridgway was always out for intelligence. Of course, he and his successors are right-thinking to be centered that way.

"In the old days, a general might eye a senior-ranking replacement and, without much thought to qualifications, say, 'Need a job? Okey, you're the new G-2.'

"But now the G-2—meaning division-level intelligence officer—is apt to be the smartest guy around; he grabs on to some Ivy League kids as they reach AFFE, he has some interpreters, and he is linked upstream in Army Intelligence, Naval Intelligence, National Security Agency intercepts, and also, I suppose, CIA findings. At all levels, *they want to interrogate prisoners.* Patrols are sent into no-man's land to snatch 'em from gook patrols out to do the same thing. In such a fix, people are going to die for sure.

"Finally, it is doctrine, probably from the military academies, or maybe from Caesar's Wars, that troops cannot be allowed to sit and do nothing. That includes sitting in those pathetic hoochies. So, there's another reason we send out patrols. Let's face it: we enlisted men and the company-grade officers are expendable; don't forget it!"

"My God, Dave, you're a whiz; I couldn't have gotten a better briefing from Gen. Ridgway himself; thanks so much."

"No more of a whiz than you, young woodsman. You had most of this stuff figured out. I must admit, it helps to be in a headquarters unit—an elite outfit; everyone there is capable. We overhear talk of these things."

Dave pushed back his chair, stood, and stretched. "I'm ready to hit the sack."

They started back to the barracks building. Frenchy said, "My father was in the First War, but where he was, St. Mihiel and the Argonne, it wasn't near the stalemate we're talking about. His regiment moved pretty steadily against the Germans."

"Yes; but remember that was a breakthrough at one spot; and it led to the Armistice. Basically, there were trenches stretching from the Channel to Switzerland. Don't ask me how far that is, but it's a lot more than 155 miles."

They walked on. "Sorry about your mom."

"Thanks."

Chapter Twenty-four
The Hungary i

The assembly room was far from full, maybe one hundred men for the briefing. Seeing a gray-haired sergeant on the stage reminded Frenchy of the Isle of Guam codger, winding up his career back at Camp McCoy. This old fellow had the vigor to stand and holler "Atten-hut" as a Navy Lieutenant Commander entered from back stage and signaled a very fast, "As you were . . . seats."

Frenchy figured: *the navy officer was worried that some members of the audience who were forced to stand might outrank him—amounting to a small discourtesy.*

"You men did not luck out; nor did I for that matter. I'm Lt. Com. Knowles. We leave on SS *James Murtaugh*, Thursday at one bell, afternoon watch.

He paused and smiled. "Well, if you want to learn, we'll teach you; that's 0900, army time. No matter, you shouldn't care because you're due on board the day before, as I shall explain. The *Murtaugh* is a cargo ship from the Second War—called a Liberty Ship—14,000 tons, 440 feet in length, 56 feet abeam. We built thousands of 'em for ourselves and for the Brits; we built 'em faster than the U-Boats could sink 'em!"

As the Commander continued, Frenchy recalled those days two years ago: *the ore boat crewmen would impress Raul and me with stories of the run to Murmansk, of Liberty Ships, and U-Boats.*

"*Murtaugh* was built in separate pieces at different locations and then assembled at Kaiser-Vancouver. She's been modified to hold five hundred troops; bear in mind, she was built for cargo—not troops. Except for the Conflict, she'd be scrap.

"We'll ship with you men here and about two hundred more who'll report in tomorrow, taking the Great Circle Route, by way of Adak, Alaska. Yes, I said Alaska. Adak is over a thousand miles out in the Aleutians, nothing there but a naval base and airstrip, which we make runs to resupply, this time carrying a new generator you'll see strapped down amidships. You may be surprised to know that if you run a string on a globe between here and Yokohama, it'll miss Adak by less than four hundred nautical miles—hardly out of our way.

"The bad news is the ship is old, and seas will be high in those northern latitudes. Most of you will feel seasick. It's no disgrace; I'm a Naval Officer and have been at sea for six years; but, on a voyage like this, it's hard for me to face a square meal the first few days out. Your duties will be to keep all troop areas clean; seasickness is no excuse from duty. We had an army doctor on the last voyage, and he would advise his sick call patients, 'I'll relieve anyone from duty who can prove he's sicker than I am.' Anyway, after a week or so you'll all be salty old dogs. Now, do we have a Maj. Hughes here?"

A tired looking army major stood.

"Good morning, major. I'm used to being outranked by the passengers; this time we have the same rank. No matter, Nels Jensen is Ship Captain—an old seafaring Norwegian, working for the Military Sea Transport Service, called MSTS. I'm Military Commander, and you, Maj. Hughes, are Troop Commander. Ah ha! I see by your brass you're a Chaplain; this may be your largest troop command; you can tell your children about when you ruled the waves."

197

The major raised both hands and said, "Unlikely with the vows I took."

"What's that? . . . Ah ha! You're a Catholic priest?"

There was laughter as Com. Knowles continued, "Well, I'll back up; you can weave your travels into a homily."

The major appeared to be a good sport; he laughed with everyone and said, "God willing, we'll get on fine."

"I'm sure we will, Father. Your duties will be to form up the passengers so there are junior officers and senior NCOs in charge of cleaning bunk areas, heads, lavatories, and common areas, with the rest of you assigned to work in these areas. It's all laid out: you'll have a roster, a list of your leaders, and a list of these areas. You and I will hold a joint meeting with those selected leaders and be shipshape before we weigh anchor.

"Your special additional duties will be to pray for good weather and a safe trip, and, on the Sabbath, to hold whatever services you wish. Your sermons have to be better than the captain's.

"Now, I have a special chore for everyone. The Terminal Commandant is tired of getting calls from trooper families asking how they can reach thoughtless sons who haven't given them an address. They say 'Where's my boy? How can I write him?' Of course, in an emergency the Red Cross will help them; for ordinary mail, the sergeant will pass out penny post cards. On the back it says 'Dear blank, I have shipped out to Armed Forces Far East. You may write me care of A.P.O. 201, San Francisco, California.'

"Everyone get it? These cards will be collected as you board. You may give us a personal letter instead; we will trust you to send the indicated message. If needed, take more than one.

"The next subject is money. We change U.S. currency into Military Payment Certificates, called MPC, either at dockside or at the Fort Mason Building. On board ship, in Adak, in Japan, and in Korea, only MPC is used at military installations. At Camp Drake, you may purchase yen; the rate is 360 yen to the dollar. By the way, the South Korean won continues to undergo devaluations;

so you should stick to using our post exchanges and MPC; also stick to abstinence, especially in Korea.

"Now, one little hint in advance of night forays to Tokyo: Yen is necessary; your *musume* most likely will not take MPC; she can't spend it or swap it, and every year or so, we call in the outstanding MPC and issue a new batch. It's easy for you to keep on top of these MPC changes, but your *musume* cannot. Don't start out trying to take advantage of these girls; their life is hard enough; with them, use yen. You'll receive a more expert lecture on VD and Tokyo nightlife later on."

The commander took questions. Frenchy remembered some answers:

"Yes, wait until you're in Japan to buy cameras. There are great buys of both Japanese and German 35mm cameras at the Camp Drake PX and of Canons and Nikons at quality Japanese stores. Our former enemies make the best lenses, so they also make the best binoculars—another great buy to send home.

"You'll get a physical and health lecture at Drake, and, as I already said, listen up before you hit the houses in Tokyo.

"If you want to go to San Francisco, we will be issuing passes here. See me or the sergeant for non-expert advice.

"Buses leave for the *Murtaugh* 1500 hours Wednesday. Be there!"

Frenchy and Dave were first in line to question the Commander about a San Francisco outing.

"Going today? Can you spend, say, twenty-five dollars? Well, take the army shuttle bus—leaves every hour—to Market and Powell. Then take a Cable Car to Chinatown where you change cars to Fisherman's Wharf. Once there, eat at Alioto's."

He smiled and looked them over—*two clean-cut young men.* "Catch the early show at The Hungary i. That's spelled with a little 'i.' It's at 599 Jackson in the North Beach District. They have young entertainers. Last time I was there, they had a sensational singer named Barbra Streisand. Show starts at 8:00—2000 hours that is. Go to the front desk for maps and maybe better advice."

That was about the way it happened: the bus got them to the cable car turntable from where the Nob Hill ride defied gravity. Swinging off at Chinatown, Frenchy said it was like riding the boom at the Soo Locks! Back on the Mason Street car, they went down to Columbus Street, over to Taylor Street and right down to the famous Fisherman's Wharf.

There was Alioto's—a three-story restaurant overlooking a maze of piers and boats.

Old sailor Frenchy stood there fascinated: a few vessels looked sharp, but most were simple, utilitarian commercial fishing craft, showing the ocean-going ravages of saltwater, dirt, barnacles, gull droppings, and plain hard use. They were surprisingly small—a tiny cabin just behind a sharply curved bow, an open hold from there aft—not half the size of a bumboat or a victualer.

Still, there was a familiar atmosphere to the harbor with the purr of motors, the lapping water, and the slapping lines—all the vessels bobbing on the small waves, while overhead the gulls soared back and forth, keeping up an overriding cacophony of squawking.

Frenchy thought: ***Dago Cerutti would love it here in this traditional Italian–American, fishermen community—folks like the DiMaggio family; what a chunk of honest American history!***

Alioto's was big and informal. Frenchy asked for a local specialty, not too expensive. The waiter steered him to Cioppino, a fish stew derived from the catch-of-the-day—with Dungeness crab, clams, shrimps, scallops, and a tomato and wine sauce, all served over spaghetti with a toasted baguette. Frenchy figured it was the American equivalent of Bouillabaisse—standard, everyday French cuisine. He quoted the waiter: *"Delizioso!"*

Dave was more daring and much more extravagant: he ordered abalone and was served a delightful piece of broiled seafood. The waiter explained, "The meat is derived from a mollusk found in the Pacific, all of the creature savored on the Japanese market. Along the California coast in fine restaurants, a part called the 'foot' is separated, rested, sliced, and pounded with wooden mallets. After all of these tenderizing processes, we serve abalone in a butter sauce. You will find it, too, is *delizioso*."

Frenchy struggled with his special utensils: a crab fork and a shell cracker; laughing and slurping, careful not to spill on his GI shirt. Alioto's was a big success.

When the waiter brought the bill, Dave grabbed it. Frenchy frowned at him—"What's up?" Dave exhibited his first show of emotion: "After mother died, we had a family meeting: the probate judge had approved a plan to advance me twenty-five thousand dollars. I left Tacoma with a checkbook and the admonition to live as comfortably as possible. What am I to do—get wallpaper for my hut? You're the nicest guy I've met in the army, Frenchy; evening's on me."

Equally choked, Frenchy bowed his head and whispered, "Thanks, I understand . . . I understand."

They asked directions to The Hungary i and were sent back up the Taylor Street Car to Jackson Street, thence a short walk to the nightclub. They arrived by 1900 hours and decided to case the place before committing. Frenchy had little idea what to expect, his nightclub experiences limited to those skin joints in Calumet City when going uptown with the boat crew. When they opened the door, a greeter asked, "Here for the early show?"

Sensing their hesitation, he led them back to a surprisingly small room with tables and a stage. "You can have a front-row seat, have a couple of beers and you've spent your minimum. The show's a riot, an absolute riot!"

Soon the owner came by, and on learning they were Korea-bound, said the first round was on him. He also took their names.

Promptly at 2000 hours the curtain drew back and they were introduced as guests of honor. An attractive black fellow named

Bill Cosby came on stage and sat down in a plain chair by a microphone. He told the most hilarious stories about when he was a kid. There were the problems of getting his tonsils out, a story of sleeping with his brother, Russell, who wet the bed. There were friends Fat Albert, Rudy, and Old Weird Harold. Frenchy and Dave laughed till they choked—a great show—*nothing like watching a stripper in Cal City.*

The Hungary i was an incredible place, instrumental in launching the careers of Barbra Streisand and The Kingston Trio as well as about every comedian of the mid century: Lenny Bruce, Mort Sahl, Jonathan Winters, Woody Allen, Dick Cavett, Phyllis Diller, the Smothers Brothers, Joan Rivers, and, of course, Bill Cosby.

They took a taxi all the way back to the Terminal.

Chapter Twenty-five
Target Practice

Dave was so excited with the Monday trip, he asked Frenchy to join in a bus tour the next day, but Frenchy shook his head, "You can tell I'm a moody guy—my sisters call me Arnold the Moper—I'm going to write some letters, maybe see a movie, and read."

At breakfast, Tuesday, he saw a Marine Shore Patrol Sergeant. On a lark, he asked if there were a post rifle range, explaining he was a sharpshooter headed for Korea. The sergeant looked him over in a fairly snooty manner, which, after all, was what Frenchy expected. Then, to his surprise, the marine said, "No range, but a handgun area for S.P. and M.P. use. You got a handgun?"

"A 38 Smith & Wesson Model 10."

"Well, sit down a minute and tell me your story."

Another marine brought up a food tray, sat down and both listened as Frenchy described the gift from the mayor and answered other questions about his life, covering Fort Knox, ore boats, moose hunting, and family life as a boy in the farmlands and in the North Woods. The marines conferred; then the fellow he had first met said, "Well, Pvt. Desprez, get your 38 and be in Building 460 on Nimitz Road, about a quarter mile south of here, at, let's see, 1100 hours this morning; Gunnery Sgt. Moore, here, will show you some pistol basics. Don't bring shells."

Frenchy hurried to the PX and bought two pairs of elastic bands for blousing trousers, then went to his barracks room. He rigged the holster to his right calf, adjusted the trousers and walked about—it felt Okay and seemed to be perfectly hidden. He finished writing letters to his folks and, as promised, to Amanda, then hiked to Building 460, which proved to be a sort of police headquarters.

A formidable looking woman looked up from her desk, "So, here's Gunny Moore's young warrior—and a handsome one at that." The gunny sergeant, who had been around the corner, hollered at her, "Leave him alone, Midge; he's too young for you; and he's off to FECOM tomorrow. This way, Desprez."

He was steered to a small room lined with cabinets, desk, chairs, files, and photos of what appeared to be military pistol teams. However, his attention quickly shifted to the window and door on the opposite side, through which he saw a long room of about one hundred feet and a target clipped to a pulley-retrieval system. The gunny looked over the Model 10 with some indifference and said, "Perfectly adequate short-range weapon."

He took ear-protectors and a box of 38s and escorted Frenchy to the next room. After loading, the gunny said, "Squeeze off five."

"Low, but a very decent spread for a two-inch barrel. Let's talk a few basics: place feet apart facing the target; crouch with knees flexed; put the left hand palm under the gun-butt and right hand heel. You know the sight picture; you have been taught the military system breath-aim-slack-squeeze. The problem with a revolver is the squeeze: it has to move the hammer back and rotate the cylinders—a lot of mechanics all flowing from your right forefinger. As you know, the recoil-operated 45 Automatic has much more of a hair trigger—like the Garand. The trigger pull on a Garand is about five pounds; the pull here is more, making the squeeze the real trick. By the way, don't let anyone try to adjust the trigger pull—Smith and Wesson knew what they were doing.

"Although the 38 kick is not bad, of course you gotta let it fall back or you'll be shootin' at the sky.

"Keep the top of your hand at the top of the grip; keep your forefinger out of the trigger guard until you are ready to fire. For short range, we recommend what is called 'point shooting.' Keep your arm straight and extended, down about 45 degrees. The wrist is always locked.

"Now I wouldn't be here with you if I thought you were into target work; you're going to where the lead and steel are flying in anger. Don't fuss around too much with the hammer cocked; when would you ever have a chance to pull it back and cause the tell tale clicking sound? You don't ambush someone with this thing; it's for defense; you use it after your Garand or carbine is spent and your grenades gone, maybe just before your bayonet. Aim for the rib cage. In police work, the average range is seven feet. Yes, just seven feet!

"You remember Jimmy Stewart in "Destry Rides Again?" . . . No? . . . Well, Destry is this mild-mannered guy no one is afraid of until he starts shooting. He shoots the finials off the hotel façade and then shoots bottles and coins—all sorts of stuff! Now, Destry never sights down the barrel; it's from the hip or shoulder-high— like skeet shootin.' Let's try some shoulder shots from halfway down the range. As before: stiff wrist and finger outside the trigger guard."

Afterwards, they lunched together. Gunnery Sgt. Moore explained that he had been with the 1st Marines directing traffic on the road down to Hungnam. His best advice—"Dress warmly! I've never been so fucking cold. I lost some toes, now am only fit for limited duty, and am wondering where I go from here; I suspect into corporate security work."

He shook Frenchy's hand and said, "May God hold you in the palm of His hand."

That evening at the post theater, he saw "The Quiet Man" with John Wayne and Maureen O'Hara—a lesson from those two leading characters that life is tough, and both men and women have to defend themselves.

Chapter Twenty-six
Goodbye Mama, I'm off to Yokohama

They were all aboard the SS *James Murtaugh* late Wednesday afternoon—about 500 troopers in all. Bunks were four high; Frenchy turned down Dave's offer to flip for the bottom bunk, saying, "Rank has its privileges—the corporal gets his choice. Besides, how do you flip an MPC Note?"

Dave's E-4 rank also exempted him from the clean-up crews. Frenchy was assigned lavatory duties—keeping the washbasins clean. There were one hundred basins on one deck, fifty to port and fifty to starboard. They were cleaned twice a day. A sergeant named Milspaugh was in charge of the detail. He was, of course, dubbed "Milspaugh of the Murtaugh." Frenchy wondered, *What would Dago Cerutti make of those names—probably Irish, sound like Gaelic heritage. Oh, Dago, I miss your silly ways!*

Regardless of these special assignments, all aboard were permitted on deck as the Liberty Ship weighed anchor and passed under the two great bridges—the Bay and the Golden Gate. On that beautiful day, 22 May 1952, they viewed Treasure Island and Fisherman's Wharf on their port side, Alcatraz Island to starboard. The skyscrapers of San Francisco and the beautiful Golden Gate caught the imagination of even the dullest soldier.

They were reminded of their great circle route by the length of time the shoreline northwest of the Bay remained in view, but by late morning, after Point Arena, there was nothing but ocean. The boys caught Lt. Com. Knowles in an idle moment and thanked him for the suggestion of the Alioto's-Hungary i outing. They learned that it would be seven to nine days to Adak and six to seven more to Yokohama *if* the Pacific stayed pacific. The Commander eyed Frenchy and asked him if he had ever been to sea. Frenchy responded, "Three summers on a Great Lakes ore boat, Sir."

No, he had not been seasick. Yes, they had encountered gale-force winds and been forced to Thunder Bay in Canada, an emergency harbor. The Commander said he had trained at Great Lakes Naval Base and knew about the rough weather and deadly lake storms. He explained that he needed a volunteer to take notes and fill out a checklist during the morning inspections. On his last cruise, the appointed scribe kept getting sick and, reluctantly, had to be replaced. It seemed to be good duty, and he would be off the lavatory detail.

"Sir, it would be a privilege."

Dave Davis had another idea. He had found two troopers who played bridge, but they desperately needed a fourth, and drafted Frenchy. Dave would give him a crash course, and they would all help him some by bending the rules during play. Bridge was a unique game because it had two utterly different phases called bidding and playing. The bidding part was arcane but had fairly recently been reduced to various formulas invented by a guy named Goren. To help Frenchy learn, the other players allowed him to look at an outline of these formulas during the bidding phase. Playing was something else; it took longer to learn but was mostly common sense. After each hand he would be told how he screwed up, but the big screw-ups would usually only come when he was 'declarer' and that would likely be only one-fourth of the time. Frenchy fancied he could be good at all card games and readily agreed to play and learn; after all, it was adding another arrow to his quiver!

And so, a routine set in: breakfast, cleanup, inspection, chow, bridge, walks on the deck, exercise, chow, a movie, the sack—not exactly a cruise ship to the Greek Isles, but not bad duty. The inspection now was fun because he was in contact with the ship's military leaders. The commander led the group, followed by the padre major, three junior officers (all there were on board), a master sergeant, and Frenchy. At each stop, the NCO in charge would report to both the major and the commander and would then accompany the team through his area.

The heads (toilets) were impossible in the early days. In addition to morning calls of nature, there were men feeling nauseous, men leaning over the bowls, and others tarrying, not daring to stray after an opening round of retching. The whole cleanup experience had to be handled on a pragmatic, do-your-best basis. Everyone knew the situation and also knew the work was necessary and in keeping with military traditions of clean quarters.

Seasickness is a form of motion sickness, tied to the body's sense of spatial orientation. The sick bay offered Dramamine and ginger capsules and advice that it was better to stay topsides and keep busy.

Since Frenchy was part of the inspection team, it was inevitable that Maj. Hughes—who liked to be called "Father Mal"—discovered he was a Catholic boy and asked him to serve as acolyte for the services on Sunday—the fourth day out. There were two services: one ecumenical, with the MSTS Captain participating, and a separate Catholic service. Frenchy held the cup, reciting "The blood of Christ;" he felt good about the whole thing.

Yes, the sea got rough, and people got seasick. Three days out, one of the bridge players showed up late carrying a paper bag—another victim of the rolling sea! And during their game, Frenchy pulled off a four-spades contract via a successful finesse, modestly explaining, "How could I miss, is not *finesse* a French word?"

Even the sick boy laughed, as he found the joking and the diversion of cards at least a somewhat helpful way to fight *mal de mer.*

They learned a few facts about Adak: a small volcanic island in the Andreanof group of Aleutian Islands, 1,200 miles south-west of Anchorage, and the southernmost community in Alaska. It was long occupied by Aleuts, but abandoned by them years ago, as those native people moved eastward following the Russian fur trade. The skies were almost always overcast, the weather fairly moderate, but with terrible winter storms.

Little Adak played a major role in World War II. The Japanese held the western Aleutian Islands—most notably Attu and their major base at Kiska. U.S. Forces in Alaska were a fairly equal balance of air corps, army, and navy. The common word was they had two dangerous enemies: the Japanese and, probably foremost, the weather. The air corps had been forced to make the long run from a landing strip on Umnak (just west of Dutch Harbor) to Kiska, flying mostly B-24s at very low altitudes with a mission taking eight to twelve hours—incredibly hard on men and equipment.

Adak was selected as an advanced air base far out in the Aleutians and much closer to Kiska. On 30 August 1942, army and navy forces arrived at unoccupied Adak in the middle of a fierce storm. The flat bottom of a dammed and drained lagoon was made into an airfield by ingenious Army Engineers and Navy Seabees. Headquarters units were moved there, as Seabees hurried to erect all needed facilities; thus jumping U.S. Forces 1,000 miles nearer the enemy at Kiska. Adak was a prize, indeed.

A city was built in Kuluk Bay, population at its peak reaching 90,000. From Adak, U.S. 7th Division attacked Attu at the western end of the Aleutians in May 1943. The cold was frightful and the death toll staggering: the Japanese were annihilated—many ending life under the Bushido Code, only twenty-eight captured out of a complement of 2,900; the U.S. Army suffered 3,829 casualties—more from weather-related injuries than enemy fire. In terms of number of troops engaged, casualties were second only to Iwo Jima.

Lessons learned about cold-weather fighting were forgotten in the next seven years, as evidenced by the poorly equipped marines at the Reservoir and all other U.N. Forces throughout Korea during that first horrible winter of 1950–51.

Then, a complete surprise: in July 1943, the same type of U.S. invasion took place at Kiska—*but the island was empty.* Just days before, 5,183 Japanese had been evacuated—a troop-saving coup by the Imperial Navy!

The story of the War in Alaska—the only part of World War II fought on American soil—was tragic, especially the battle for Attu; but the whole struggle was, all too soon, almost forgotten.

Frenchy and the other troopers gazed northward as Adak came into view; the usual haze yielded glimpses of green mountains and snow. Later, old SS *James Murtaugh* weighed anchor at the only wharf. Then everyone was allowed ashore, where they found it took a few minutes on dry land to walk a straight line. Frenchy used the mail drop. He had written his folks and the three Fontenots, mostly to tell them he had found a new meaning for the word *finesse*. They were encouraged to take a walk and stretch their legs, but there wasn't much to do except go to a game room or watch the unloading of the generator and the drop-off and receipt of cargo.

The terrain was mountainous with patches of snow and lush green undergrowth, *but nowhere on the island was there a single tree!*

That evening, with everyone back on board, they headed southwest for Japan.

The next morning, back on the morning inspection grind, Frenchy overheard Com. Knowles say, "Father Mal, that doesn't look like a bible under your arm."

"Right Knowles, this little tome is a translation of *The I Ching or Book of Changes*—Chinese wisdom, conceived maybe 2000 B.C. and now called a book of divination."

Frenchy inched forward as much as he dared and listened, as the priest, now facing them both, continued, "As long as I was headed east, I thought I should get a pinch of oriental mysticism and religious history; it's always good to learn about other traditions. You know, there were a number of wise Chinese sages hundreds of years before our Lord walked the Holy Land. The Koreans also know and use these symbols: their flag contains four basic trigrams, standing for heaven, water, earth, and fire, and in the flag's center is a red and blue circle of yin and yang—standing for the dual cosmic forces and showing universal harmony."

Frenchy thought, *Wow, Father Mal isn't afraid to learn about other religions; I wouldn't get this stuff from the nuns at St. Pat's; they wouldn't stand for what they'd consider blasphemous respect for alien cultures—it's all kinda neat!* The priest admonished the two: "Confucius said it's not enough to just say the ancient rites; he said what counts is the spirit in which they are performed. Doesn't that sound like our Lord saying 'do not heap up empty phrases; honor with your hearts, not just with your lips?'"

Father Mal watched the commander and the private standing there mute and pondering. Then—struck with a new thought— he said, "My friends, come to my cabin about 1300 hours—after chow—no more sermons, we three will dig into the *I Ching* together.

In the tiny cabin and after an introduction, Father Mal said, "Okay, Frenchy, what can the *I Ching* help you with?"

Always intrigued by matters symbolic and mathematical, Frenchy had a ready answer: "I'm always pondering whether I'm asserting myself enough: should I passively go with the flow or speak up, volunteer or complain; should I somehow try to climb off the front-line pipe line?"

"Okay. Far as I know, 'Should I speak up more' is a fair question; throw the three coins.

"A head and two tails—a young yin line," Mal said as he drew two short lines. Next, three tails were thrown, and Mal said this was an old yin line and drew the same two lines separated by an X. Frenchy threw six times and a hexagram of short lines (yin) and long lines (yang) was constructed. Old yin and old yang lines were then changed to their opposites, resulting in the following two hexagrams·

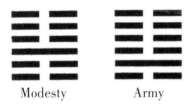

Modesty   Army

"My goodness," said the priest. "That's a lot of yin lines and only two yang lines; let's look them up."

The first was Number 15—*Modesty,* the basic trigram symbols being earth above a mountain. Frenchy read the text, noting and jotting down various references, such as:

> *A superior man of modesty and merit carries things to conclusion. Good fortune.*

> *It is favorable to attack with force.*

> *A truly modest man must proceed with great energy. He must discipline his own ego.*

> *Modesty is the way of heaven. It is the way of the earth to be lowly and to go upward.*

The change produced a startling hexagram: Number 7, *Army.* First readings of the text were challenging—not very helpful:

The army needs perseverance and a strong man.

The army must set forth in proper order.

In the midst of the army, good fortune. No blame. The king bestows a triple decoration.

Authority is not being executed by the proper leaders.

Sometimes the army must retreat. No blame.

Frenchy was aghast: "Sixty-four hexagrams and I had to pick one named 'army.' Then, too, I've been bashful all my life, and I pick 'Modesty.' All well and good, but it hardly answers my request for guidance, though I like the 'good fortune' and I'm intrigued by the 'three decorations.'"

Knowles also looked puzzled, but Mal raised his hands in protest, "You've got to spend more time with it; what struck me was that modesty is the way to heaven and that the way of earth is to be lowly. Remember when I said that we Christians don't have a sole claim on all great ideas; notice the parallel: Jesus said in *The Sermon on the Mount,* "Blessed are the meek, for they shall inherit the earth."

"Now, sit and take more notes if you like or borrow the *I Ching* and read Numbers 15 and 7 over and over; there are pages and pages of text—not just the lines you hastily picked. Remember, these words are a guide, not an answer, they're supposed to get you thinking, pondering; and I might add—praying."

Frenchy thought: *Well, I'm not quite ready to call this a new arrow in my quiver. Time will tell.*

On deck, Thursday morning, 5 June, the Honshu shoreline was visible off the starboard bow, and, by 1300 hours, the old ship had turned west, yielding spectacular views of Mount Fuji—highest mountain in Japan and its greatest landmark—a national logo.

From there, it steamed north into the great Tokyo Bay with Boso Peninsula to the east, Miura Peninsula to the west. Frenchy and Dave leaned against the rail and contemplated one of the world's most famous harbors: Commodore Mathew Perry had anchored there in the 1850s, and the instrument of surrender had been signed there aboard the *Missouri* on 2 September 1945. The latter event so touched the minds of the Japanese that, at least in conversation with Americans, they would not use the word "surrender" but spoke instead euphemistically of "*the Missouri.*"

Disembarkation, bus travel to Camp Drake, and assignment to barracks took the rest of the day.

Chapter Twenty-seven
Sukiyaki and the Sermon

Camp Drake was northwest of Tokyo, rather like a suburb. It escaped bombing even though it had been a Japanese Army base. The barracks were in better shape than old Able Battery back at Knox, and there were attractive pine trees and pathways, giving the look of a planned Japanese landscape.

Since it was Friday, it appeared that not much processing would be done until Monday; however, in anticipation of issuing passes, there was an orientation to explain that the so-called "geisha girls" they were apt to meet in town were not the traditional geisha entertainers who were highly trained in music, dance, and light conversation, but only prostitutes dressed in fancy kimonos.

It must be assumed that the women available to the GIs were apt to have one or more of the three venereal diseases: syphilis, gonorrhea, or cancroids. Contracting VD was a courts-martial offense, but, in accordance with the sound principle of not belaboring an unenforceable order, the message was not, "don't do it," but rather an admonishment to use a condom and afterward use a prophylactic kit. Suffice to explain that the pro kit contained inter-alia, a tube of antiseptic goo with a thin, pointed area at the open end. As it said on numerous bulletin boards, "Play it cool; do it right; take a pro every night!"

After the sex lecture, Frenchy found Dave standing outside waiting for him. It was another of those sad army farewells. The Division regretted that Dave had been processed by surface transportation and had arranged to fly him that afternoon from Tachikawa AFB directly to Kimpo—just outside Seoul. The two friends hugged and vowed to get together—God willing. *Alas, first I left Dago, then the Mammoth Cave guys, now Dave.*

Frenchy had fallen in with two men he sat next to on the bus: Rich Morrison and Harold "Soddy" Mecham from, of all places, Soddy-Daisy, Tennessee. If nothing else, that hometown explained the nickname. Short and freckled, Soddy was unabashedly a gregarious, country boy with buckteeth and curly red hair. Frenchy sometimes called him Mortimer Snerd, as in Edgar Bergen's lesser-known dummy. Those were just first impressions: in time he would learn that behind the country boy façade was a disciplined, well-organized person, gifted singer, and a loyal friend.

Rich was quite the opposite—tall, broad-shouldered, thin-waisted, and shy like Frenchy. He came from Matfield Green, a tiny community in the Flint Hills of Kansas, and had spent one year at Kansas State University, located in Manhattan, Kansas—right next to Fort Riley, where he took basic training. Rich wanted to eventually study engineering and so had taken the basic courses—lots of math. He sometimes described with longing the limestone formations of the beautiful Flint Hills, which grew native bluestem grasses perfect for cattle grazing. When not in school, Rich rode the rangeland, herding cattle and tending to other cowboy chores.

The three banded together and decided to hit Tokyo, but for something milder than a bordello destination; so they settled for the well-known Tokyo Onsen, which was a five-story bathhouse in the famous street and shopping area known as the Ginza.

Tokyo was amazing for a place that had been fire-bombed and mostly destroyed just seven years before. Sure, there were few fancy buildings, but there were cars on the road—thousands of taxis—and construction was everywhere. Even large buildings were put up with rickety-looking, bamboo-and-rope scaffolding, with construction around-the-clock: three eight-hour shifts, seven days a week! To provide work, there was plenty of featherbedding, with taxis often having two drivers.

Onsen technically meant "hot springs," but the Tokyo Onsen used tap water. The baths were fun, the massages given by cute girls—he knew they were called **musumes**—their services included walking up and down the customers' backs. With a toothy grin, redheaded Soddy jokingly said, "Ah wanna come back t'morrow for more of these here massages!"

They promenaded up the famous Ginza Street until Rich spotted a restaurant serving sukiyaki. GIs did not go for all Asian foods, especially things like raw fish, but sukiyaki was a big favorite. In the windows were mock-ups of all the entrees—known as plastic food displays and always very professionally sculpted so the customer could duly expect his meal to look exactly as shown in the window's never-spoiling plastic artwork.

Once inside and seated on floor cushions, they watched with anticipation as the very expert waiter brought them the raw ingredients—thinly sliced prime beef and vegetables. He cooked them in a wok over a small grill. Soy sauce, sugar, and mirin were added. Finally, the waiter showed them how each bite was gathered with chopsticks and dipped in a bowl of raw eggs. They were delighted but realized that the success of the meal was largely due to the delicious Japanese prime beef.

Soddy laughed, "Ah could also come back for some more of this here stuff!"

However, they decided the best idea was to take the Sunday afternoon tour of the city, but first they would all go to the early service at the post chapel.

The next day, when Frenchy was one of the first worshipers to arrive, an army captain confronted him, complete with nicely-trimmed beard and Yarmulke, his brass the shape of the Commandment Stones—obviously a Rabbi.

"Hello young warrior, I'm Rabbi Goodman, doing the ecumenical service; are you a Christian?"

Frenchy stammered, "Yes, Rabbi."

His host went on, "Then I hope you'll assist me. I need help passing out the programs, and then I need a New Testament reader. I could do it, but lay readers are best."

Frenchy reckoned he had never met a rabbi. *What the heck, another new experience.* He had a chance to read over his part and was told where to sit. A little Japanese lady played a prelude on the Chapel piano, and a good forty people entered. They sang "Joyful, Joyful, We Adore Thee," which he knew was great Beethoven music. The Rabbi offered a prayer and then read the Old Testament Lesson: Exodus 32, about how the people in the desert became restless after Moses went up on the mountain and gathered around Moses' brother, Aaron, who made for them a golden calf and built an altar before it.

Next, Frenchy stood and read the New Testament Lesson from Ephesians 6:13,

> *Therefore take the whole armor of God,*
> *That you may be able to withstand the*
> *evil day, and having done all, to stand.*
> *Stand therefore, having girded your loins*
> *with truth and having put on the breastplate*
> *of righteousness, and having shod your*
> *feet with the equipment of the gospel*
> *of peace; above all taking the shield of*
> *faith, with which you can quench all the*
> *flaming darts of the evil one. And take*
> *the helmet of salvation and the sword of*
> *the Spirit which is the word of God.*

He had read it over enough to be able to really hit them with that last line! *With my work as acolyte on the Murtaugh and now as pulpit assistant, maybe I'm developing a new skill—no, not likely!* No time to ponder, the Rabbi rose and delivered his sermon.

"Folks, I don't know exactly how Aaron fashioned that golden calf. Sure wasn't a good idea, was it? Makes you sore when you read about it. Earlier in the Torah, in Exodus, we found out all about Moses—you know the bulrushes story, a terrific guy, raised like a prince, performed miracles—then these people, *including his own brother,* all supposedly his followers, they all join in screwing things up.

"Yes, the ornery people couldn't keep the faith once their great leader went up the mountain! The text says the wrath of the Lord burned hot against the Israelites. The Lord said the Israelites were a stiff-necked people—and we all agree with that, for so they were—but Moses intercedes with the Lord who sort of calms down, and, therefore, does not destroy the people. That's a harsh, harsh story and would make a fine sermon; yes, indeed.

"But that's not what I'm aiming at, because I'm just focusing on one part—and it may surprise you: I'm zeroing in on that golden calf. I wonder how Brother Aaron made the ugly idolatrous thing.

"Out there in the desert, could they have a big furnace? Notice the text says a *molten calf.* That sounds like it was melted down, doesn't it? You know in those ancient days they knew about casting copper, bronze, and gold. Have you seen pictures of the gold mask found in the tomb of Pharaoh Tutankhamen? The workmanship is as fine as if made in modern times. No, no, I'm wrong; let's face it, it's *finer*—totally beyond our grasp, a unique thing, never to be duplicated in any age, never to be matched! But I stray. . . .

"Back to Aaron's golden calf . . . somehow, he made a mold, perhaps made in parts by the lost wax method . . . anyway, a mold started the process.

"Then what? He had to have the stuff to melt; sometimes it's purer than at other times. Twelve-carat gold is about half copper;

even twenty-two-carat gold has copper in it. Remember what the text says: 'Aaron said to them, take off the gold rings that are on the ears of your wives, your sons, and your daughters and bring them to me.'

"Let's call this donated jewelry the 'ingredients' or the 'body.' So we have the ingredients and the mold we talked about before. What else do we need?"

The Rabbi looked around the room; someone said, "Fire."

"That's it! The mold and the ingredients are nothing without the heat necessary to melt the ingredients. For gold, that's over 1,000 degrees centigrade. You see, I've done my homework with respect to these technical aspects!

"Folks, *we are sort of like that calf.* At birth, we are given a mold by our parents, and we also are given certain basic ingredients. We grow and our ingredients are tested, more or less discovered, by us and those around us. We're also affected by outside things—from microbes on up. Some of us find that we can sing; some are tone deaf and discouraged from singing; some are tall; and some are short. These ingredients are God-given qualities. Which of us will be the opera singers, the basketball players, the jockeys, and which of us will be perfectly happy with some simple job, while a very few will be famous scientists? Think about the rest of us—the great mass in between.

"I'm sure you're way ahead of me now. We get where we are going by the heat of life. *I say again, the heat of life!* Yes, the heat of life can be the terrible cold of a Korean winter. All those bad breaks and good breaks shape us; so does all our training. You hit the target by practicing.

"In my case, I learned the hard way that you close the bolt on an M-1 rifle by sticking your thumb into the breach, then getting it out of the way. To use a Yiddish expression, I was what you call 'a klutz' with the M-1, and I had an M-1 thumb to prove it!

"We need God's help to see us through. I don't think there's a person here who has not been praying in his own way: perhaps for his safety, for strength to do his duty, for his buddies, certainly to give those at Panmunjom on the north and the south sides of the table the wisdom to settle this awful, awful war.

"Remember Jesse Owens? A good Old Testament name—Jesse was the father of David, tribe of Judah. Jesse Owens received a good mold, a healthy body, and a strong will to win; he made the most of it—won four gold medals at the 1936 Olympics in Berlin, Germany—near the height of Nazi power! If Jesse had not trained in the fire of the cinder track, he would have been just another guy!

"You know, athletes have an expression: 'no pain, no gain.' It fits, doesn't it? How many men, black or white, had the opportunity to thumb their noses at concepts of the master race! Did you know that after Jesse won, Adolf Hitler left the stadium and did not return? He had planned to have the Games promote concepts of Aryan racial superiority and depiction of other races as inferior. As you know, he had some screwy ideas about a master race.

"I pray that your Korean experiences will give you hope, a hope which I fervently have, that we can create a better world. You will encounter the most ravaging fires of your young lives; you will come out sorely tested; it will be the makings of you; it will take you to your destiny. That destiny may take you beyond this life, or perhaps home with new problems, new wounds, and new anxieties. Turn bravely to the heat . . . know about it . . . expect it . . . handle it . . . grit your teeth . . . pray to God!

"I met with a marine lieutenant at the Yokosuka Naval Hospital. His platoon was ordered to attack Hill 908. In retrospect, the problems of the attack were underestimated; it was a near suicidal mission. A bullet struck him in the spine just as they reached the hilltop. He continued to fight but was losing so much blood he soon collapsed and was triaged in the beyond-hope category.

"However, at the foot of the hill a Jeep was able to ford a river and carry him to a MASH unit, thence to a hospital ship, then by airplane to Japan, finally to Yokosuka. He had a body cast, with openings for his two open wounds: one where the slug went in and one where they dug it out. Sensation was beginning to return in his paralyzed legs. He had a very strong religious experience—new to him. He felt serene; God was with him.

"The ancient Israelites faced this in their many battles for the Promised Land. Think of the time, his kingdom established, at the height of his powers, a golden crown on his head, King David heard of the death of his rebellious son and, in one of the most poignant passages ever written, David lamented, 'O my son Absalom, my son, my son Absalom! Would God I had died for thee. O Absalom, my son, my son!'

"Oh what heat there is in the Bible; what heat there has always been for mankind; what heat there is with us still. Take our parents' generation, suffering the Great Wars and the Great Depression! Perhaps the heat turned up when you, as a little child saw your mother crying after your father lost his job.

"This has not been an easy sermon to give; we've got to call it like it is. At heart, we are peacemakers. We worship the God of peace. When the heat increases, we are all the more aware that we need God's help, that we are children of a loving God. Like the golden calf, we came from a mold, inherited certain ingredients, grew in wisdom and stature, and endured life's fires. We confidently pray that we may find comfort, peace, and favor with God and with all mankind.

"Paul sums it up in such wonderful martial words: 'Take the whole armor of God, gird your loins with truth, put on the breastplate of righteousness, take the shield of faith, take the helmet of salvation, take up the sword of the spirit, which is the word of God!'"

The Rabbi closed with the familiar benediction: "May the Lord bless you and keep you . . ."

Afterward, Frenchy felt tears welling as he shook the Rabbi's hand. *Would my father ever be forced to say, O my son Arnold, my son, my son Arnold! Would God I had died for thee? Oh Arnold, my son, my son. . . .*

Chapter Twenty-eight
The Dream and the General

The tour of Tokyo that afternoon was also memorable. They went to some temples and gardens, the harbor, the famous five-story pagoda, the Imperial Palace, and a place right next to the Palace, a place he had never heard of—the Dai Ichi Insurance Building—headquarters of The Supreme Allied Commander, Pacific. There was now a brand new top dog. With Eisenhower's resignation in Europe, Gen. Ridgway took the SACEUR job, and Gen. Mark W. Clark took SACPAC. Back in February, Gen. Maxwell D. Taylor had replaced Gen. Van Fleet as 8th Army Commander.

Monday morning, 9 June, Frenchy, his new friends, and about one hundred other replacement troops underwent the usual sort of physical exam. It was routine, so he hardly paid attention until the "short-arm inspection," another new experience.

Five or six at a time were lined up before a medical assistant, who, holding a flashlight, demonstrated how each was to grasp his penis, rotate it, and, as the medic walked past, "milk it down." It was a test for gonorrhea; if pus came out, the soldier would be sent to the hospital, given an antibiotic, and sent on his way in a few days.

One wise guy piped up, "I wish mine was as big as your flashlight!"

The final interview was before a young-looking first lieutenant who introduced himself as Dr. Beck. He reported that Frenchy was one of the healthiest-looking men he'd seen that morning. The doctor asked him if he had any anxieties, special fears, or personal problems. Frenchy answered in the negative. The doctor had one last question:

"Do you have any special dreams?"

"Oh, yes Sir; I sure do!"

Frenchy then described the giant black moose that repeatedly attacked him out of the brush in the Boundary Area. He did not fail to mention the actual moose hunt and the fact that he had been a hunter since childhood. He said the moose head was now in his uncle's den. The effect on the doctor was unexpected: his eyes lit up; any late-morning ennui was gone.

"Pvt. Desprez, I don't want to in any way alarm you—you have nothing to worry about—but if you would wait a few minutes for me to complete two more interviews, I would like to buy you a cup of coffee or maybe a lunch."

Frenchy could tell that those last two interviewees got fairly short shrift; then the doctor escorted him to the Officer's Club—another new experience. They made small talk for a few minutes. Dr. Beck had been in the army a shorter time than Frenchy, having also been drafted, right out of internship, then given a commission as a first lieutenant and an army short course, as he put it, "So I'd learn how to put on and shine my brass, salute, and blouse my boots."

Then he got to the point. In med school he had taken a seminar in Jungian Psychology, been fascinated, and now was interested in further studies in psychiatry after his army days. He explained that Jung and Freud were considered the founders of modern studies in the science of the mind. The two had been friends but had parted years ago.

Carl Gustav Jung was in his late seventies and lived and practiced in Zurich. One of Beck's great ambitions was to go through psychoanalysis at the Jung Institute, a process he felt confident would guide him in the right direction. The doctor then frankly admitted, "I'm like the guy who wants to be a chess master but has just learned how the pawns move."

God! Thought Frenchy, *this fascinating, learned man is treating me like an equal, telling me his inner thoughts and using apt scientific expressions, which I hope I'm following fairly well.*

The doctor continued, "Jung stresses that dreams can have quite different roots, depending on the dreamer. Jung would not hazard a dream's meaning without evidence based on other dreams and repeated interviews. There are several universal dream subjects, which he calls 'archetypal.' Jung has traveled the world, studying primitive societies, also studying behavior, fairy tales, myths, art, writings, alchemy—all sorts of things, parts of man's evolutionary nature.

"These archetypes include such subjects as men dreaming of the female 'anima' figure and women dreaming of the male 'animus' figure, and other subjects, including the 'shadow,' the 'trickster,' the 'earth mother,' the 'wise old man,' and so on.

"He also sees dreams as revealing our unconscious. Dreams are always mystifying to us when we awake, because they bring to us pictures of something we are not including in our view of ourselves."

The doctor asked, "How do you feel about the dream?"

"How do I feel? Well, I shoot and shoot at this creature; he keeps coming; then I'm enveloped by it. How do I feel? Let's see, I guess, when still asleep, I'm *disappointed* that my bullets have no effect, maybe the more apt word is *frustrated*. Bang, bang, bang . . . but nothing happens; finally, when it's on me, *scared, shocked, shaken* all seem to apply. Then, a moment later and fully awake, I curse the thing, saying to myself, another time I have to see that damn black thing, like a black cloud, my dark enemy, another nightmare involving that damn creature!"

"Your dream about a giant moose clicked with me, as what Jung calls 'a shadow figure.' The shadow is the part of our unconscious in closest proximity to our conscious awareness. Sometimes in dreams we struggle with a dark stranger; that is our shadow; it is *the dreamer himself.* I repeat, that creature or person may be you. When a dream is repeated, it may be a knocking at the door of our conscious self.

"Jung reports dreams about giant wolves, huge black spiders, and other animals. People who have lived all their lives in cities and never even seen such creatures have these dreams—a sign of the dream's evolutionary aspects—dreaming about things they never experienced in their lifetimes. Our predominantly rationalistic culture condemns our primitive parts to a more or less underground experience."

Frenchy didn't interrupt, but his mind snapped at the doctor's last words. He recalled a line from "The Raven"—"Long I stood there, wondering, fearing, doubting, dreaming dreams no mortal ever dared to dream before. . . ."

Then, like a revelation, he saw, *Surely the black bird was something from Poe's unconscious and from our collective unconscious—a shadow figure! That's why the screwy poem was so real, so enchanting to Amanda—to all of us!* But Dr. Beck was going on:

"Jung feels that modern man has lost contact with the natural world—a time when we were surrounded by animals—and modern man makes up for this in the more primitive aspects of his dreams. Remember, just thirty generations ago, people like us were living in caves; for other races the period varies from somewhat longer to much shorter, so it's, indeed, likely we still dream like stone-age people with whom we're genetically unchanged. Anyway, we frequently dream about animals and should just accept them and not worry about them, treating them as part of being human.

"Jung himself reported dreaming about being attacked by a giant wolfhound. Sound familiar? He interpreted the animal as what he called 'the Wild Huntsman' who had come to carry someone away. The next day he received word of his mother's passing.

227

"Do you recall the Bible story of Jacob wrestling in the night with a strange man? Presumably, this was a supernatural being, maybe an angel or God himself, who changed Jacob's name to Israel and changed Jacob's personality from a crafty rogue to a patient old man—a patriarch. This angel confrontation can be interpreted as a shadow figure reasserting in Jacob's dream what Jacob already knew—that he was unworthy to lead his tribe. After that encounter, he would never again be the arrogant schemer! Never fear, Desprez, I'm not trying to put you in Jacob's shoes. . . .

"Look, it's 11:30—oops, we army people should say '1130 hours'—let's order lunch; I've been talking my head off!"

And so it was that Frenchy had a hamburger at the Officers' Club, Camp Drake, Japan. The doctor went on to say that, since they had so little time, he would dare to state an opinion about the moose dream. "It seems likely that your unconscious was preoccupied with feelings of death. Perhaps you had mixed feelings about killing so noble an animal and later seeing its head on the wall of your uncle's den.

"After that, you had spent six months in the army, learning to kill, all the time knowing that you're good at killing, also knowing very well there would still be death for many GIs in Korea, just across the Sea of Japan. Finally, you may have been disturbed by being in a country where, just seven years ago, your fellow Americans killed millions of people—millions!"

"The whole point, Desprez, is that all this dream material is perfectly normal. You would be a little bit nuts if you didn't feel this way! That is, if you didn't think about these unpleasant things and if you didn't have fears. I know I have squirmy thoughts when I'm in Tokyo—especially when I see scarred and maimed people. When you're sitting around having bull sessions, let your conscious express your feelings; you don't need to be morbid, but let your thoughts come out, encourage others to do the same. If you are alone, tell God your feelings. Don't repress your dreams or fear them. Don't lose your spiritual side; develop it. You are, of course, an introvert."

"Yes, Sir, though I think I'm climbing out of it a little."

"No, no! I must insist; do not—as you wrongly put it—'try to climb out of it;' just *be yourself!* Carl Gustav Jung, by the way, is an introvert . . . so am I . . . I rather suspect so is our President, along with Gen. Bradley and Secretary Marshall."

"Well, Sir, I'm going to disagree with you on one thing: I think you are way past just knowing where the pawns go. On the other hand, I suspect that you have correctly understood my personal situation. As for you, I hope and pray that you are able to get back to school and study to become a psychiatrist; that is your destiny."

They wove their way through various tables toward the door when, to his amazement, he heard a voice shout, "Frenchy!" He looked around and waving and coming toward him was his *ami*, Lt. Mason!

They shook hands—what a coincidence! He introduced the two lieutenants and noticed that Mason now wore the brass of a general's aide—an eagle over a shield. The doctor paid the tab and would have backed away had Frenchy not taken extra time to thank him for the lunch and the talk. They shook hands and wished each other best of luck. He turned back to his friend, who explained, "I'm working for Brig. Gen. Webber, due to an incredible piece of luck. He was just promoted from O-6, knew my family, knew I spoke French, so he looked me up and hired me. Part of his command is a French Brigade. Most of their officers speak some English, but, as you know, the French can be a little insular. The general wanted to please them by having someone fluent at headquarters. We just flew to Tachikawa from Kimpo. We'll have four days of meetings on various subjects I can't talk about."

The lieutenant pondered for a moment . . . "Let me see, do this, have on clean Class As at 1730 hours. What barracks you in?"

Frenchy gave him the barracks number, and was instructed, "Okay, be out front; *tu comprenez?* I'm not keeping you from *un bordel*—some den of iniquity—am I? Well, frankly, the general has hogged my time and probably kept me out of trouble. Officers, at least junior officers, have the same hormones as a rooky in the rear ranks. See you at 1730."

The PX at Camp Drake was a wonder. He stopped there and zeroed in on cameras. Lined up right there were two of the most famous cameras in the world, the German Leica and Contax, and alongside the Japanese copies Canon and Nikon, so he could compare shutter speeds, lens openings, and prices. Canon appeared to be the best buy. Uncle Guy had given him some money, but he couldn't bring himself to spend it, so, empty handed, he walked back to the barracks.

Soddy and Rich gave him mock salutes when he said he ate at the O Club. The two were unabashedly off to a bordello, a place they said was highly recommended. Frenchy wondered—*What can the features of a whorehouse be to highly recommend it: good music? Well-oiled bedsprings? Acrobatic damsels? Fair prices? Warranties? Free antibiotics?*

He wished them well, with a reminder—"play it cool; do it right; take a pro every night."

At 1730 hours, a jeep appeared, and he was waved in by a sergeant who said, "You seem to have friends in high places." He let Frenchy off in front of a new-looking BOQ, with the instruction, "Ring suite 1-A."

Lt. Mason answered the door. It seemed to be cocktail hour, the only other person present was obviously Gen. Webber, highball in hand. Something told Frenchy that he was *not* to salute in this social indoor situation. The general looked remarkably youthful, probably early forties, in great shape, airborne, ranger, combat infantry badge, wearing a perfectly fitting, pinks-and-greens dress uniform.

"General, this is Frenchy Desprez, whom I've told you about."

"How do you do, Sir."

"Welcome, young man; how about a drink?" He looked at the sergeant who had apparently parked the jeep and entered just after him. Frenchy said he would like a beer. For a moment he regretted it, since Marie had taught him not to ask for something the host didn't have and he saw no beers out with the whiskey bottles; but the quarters seemed to be like a studio apartment, and the sergeant promptly pulled two beers from a small refrigerator, opened both, handed one to Frenchy and kept the other for himself. The general motioned him to a seat, as he pointed at the beer.

"I get a kick out of this! I'm from Wisconsin; look at the label—*Sapporo Beer, the Beer that Made Sapporo Famous.* I presume this is one of Japan's flagrant trade name infringements, but it happens to be really good-tasting beer. Sapporo is the largest city in Hokkaido—Japan's Northern Island. That good taste may be because Sapporo and Milwaukee are both on the same latitude— both good for growing and brewing hops. Cheers, everyone."

As Mason touched Frenchy's bottle, he added, "*Santé.*"

Frenchy responded, "*Santé.*"

"Well, I hear you recovered an entrenching tool for the barracks wimp; you refereed a black-and-white fight; you have a nice family; you're a sharpshooter; now you're a graduate of Infantry Basic and Armored Leadership School. What else?"

Frenchy looked questioningly at Lt. Mason.

"Remember Sgt. McNulty, the old sailor? He kept me very well informed. I'm sure he never let on to you, but he thought you were a wonder. You know, the army is built around senior troops at all levels who, like McNulty, have an interest in helping younger troops; go on, what else do you do? The general forgot to mention you speak French and you're ornery as hell."

Frenchy almost choked on his beer, and then realized it was his turn to speak.

"Well, Sirs, I worked three summers on a Great Lakes ore boat. I can sure hose the decks; I worked up to communications assistant and know basic radio procedures using an RCA Marine Radio, but have no experience with army equipment. I taught and enjoyed map reading; I just plain enjoy teaching; and, believe it or not, I like poetry. I don't like tanks; and, let me see, I can drive a jeep. My best subjects in prep school were math, English, and history. Sports are hockey, hunting, and fishing."

Mason threw in, "Ever spend time in the penalty box?"

"Ye Gads, Sir; you couldn't have gotten that from McNulty!"

"No, from your dad."

Mason turned to the others and added, "Incidentally, his father was a sergeant in the First War, fought at St. Mihiel and the Meuse-Argonne—those were legendary battles and legendary times."

The general then spoke, "Well Desprez, or I guess I'll say 'Frenchy,' in the pipeline we get, maybe, one soldier in two hundred with your skill levels. I would say especially the math, maybe, too, the orneriness. Our rotation policies mean we get a fellow trained in a technical job just in time to have him move out. This is especially true in the artillery where there are all kinds of skill jobs featuring math, such as battery and target area survey, fire direction center, even adjusting on the OP.

"There's another discouraging factor. The Chinese don't rotate their men—Asians tending to be good in these technical subjects anyway. They are catching up in artillery, at least gaining, and they aren't suffering as severe a brain drain as we are."

The general turned to his aide, "Milt, let's see if we can flag him at both Inchon and Uijongbu as well as his 201 File in this regard. All right with you, Frenchy?"

"Yes, indeed, Sir. May I mention that the two guys I've been hanging out with have one year at the University of Tennessee and one year at Kansas State University."

When asked for their names, he got Richard Morrison right, but it was a little embarrassing that all Frenchy could think of was "Soddy" Mecham. They said that was good enough.

Frenchy realized that he had never heard Lt. Mason's first name before; so it was Milt, of course short for Milton. He couldn't help remembering how quiet, almost bashful Mason had been back at Fort Knox. A stint following the general around might be the best possible assignment for now; for at least a year, it would keep him from trying to lead a platoon of infantrymen up in the MLR. By then his active duty time would run out and he could get back to teaching French or whatever he had in mind. Following up on these thoughts, perhaps not very subtly, he said, "I'm so happy for you, Lieutenant, happy that you hooked up with the general."

Mason smiled, "You read me like a book, Frenchy. Back there in Fort Knox, I didn't know my ass from my elbow. I was right out of ROTC Basic Officers' Course, no experience working with or leading enlisted troops. The general understands this: second lieutenants out of OCS have more experience leading troops, inspecting, asserting themselves. . . ."

The general interrupted, "Yes, that's the stereotype, subject to many exceptions, and those comparisons exemplify the advantages I had by going to the military academy: four years to learn the trade and plenty of time to pick on underclassmen and develop leadership skills. All the chicken-shit serves both sides: the receiver is duly cowed and learns respect and discipline, the giver develops leadership skills. The flip side is that the ROTC men had time in school to learn the technical aspects at which they usually outshine the OCS officers. In eighteen months, both groups make first lieutenant and by then, these differences are past, and it's survival of the fittest. From your standpoint, Frenchy, remember we all put on our trousers the same way."

Frenchy smiled in wonder—*It does all make sense when explained this way.* He asked for the lieutenant's card with an AFFE address included, knowing that all army officers carried calling cards—a custom of the service. Then he thanked everyone, actually got a little hug from Mason, and said his farewells.

The sergeant drove him back to his barracks, wished him luck, and sped away. One day later, Tuesday 10 June, a bus drove the troops back to Yokohama—next stop: Inchon.

Chapter Twenty-nine
An APA to Inchon

The *USS William Conrad (APA-96)*, having been redesigned in the early 1940s for amphibious assault operations and later retired, had been taken out of mothballs and recalled to its duty as an attack transport. It was a sturdy vessel of 9,500 tons, 491 feet. Any voyage to Inchon had the amphibious element because shallow water and extreme tides prevented ocean-going vessels like *Conrad* from coming close to, much less reaching, a dockside.

Japanese tugs, contracted by the navy, backed the ship out into the Yokohama harbor, and then saw it steam south. Rich, Soddy, and Frenchy leaned on a starboard rail and admired the great view of Mount Fuji. At 12,388 feet, the sacred mountain's perfectly formed summit was still snow-covered—even in mid June. Past Tokyo Bay, in the Sagami Sea, Fuji was only about forty-five miles away and even more spectacular. Frenchy now wished he had bought that Canon camera and a telescopic lens as well. To assuage his dismay, he told himself, *What the hell—maybe I'll be back here.*

A half hour later, his friends caught Frenchy mumbling—apparently cursing to himself. Talking to old Arnold the Moper, Soddy asked, "What's up, old boy?"

The ornery one pointed: "See those islands off to port, the first and largest one not more than a mile away? I've checked it out:

there are five little volcanic islands in a string as we go south, the first and largest one called O-Shima, with a little town plus a lighthouse. It's just one mountain: thirty-five square miles, 2,500 feet high. I think some of the other islands are barren."

His friends grunted, wondering where he was going.

"Well, here's the point: it's August 1945, the Pacific War still boiling. Suppose we call the Swiss Embassy and have them deliver a message to their Japanese Embassy to the effect, ah, let me see, reading something like this: 'In the interest of humanity, the Forces of the United States and its allied powers have something to show you.' I see you guys get my drift: we drop Little Boy smack-dab on O-Shima or any one of 'em. Instead of exploding it up in the air at 2,000 feet like we did at Hiroshima and Nagasaki, we might let it hit the ground or something like that, leaving details to the experts.

"Of course, everyone there is toast—well, worse than toast, sort of vaporized along with Old Mr. O-Shima-san or, at least, a part of him. The Japanese get the message, as they did at Hiroshima, but the high command probably hangs in there, after all, with those damn atrocities, Premier Tojo and his inner circle know they're as good as dead anyway. All they can plan on is a knife in the gut— *hara-kiri*, the bushudo code of the samurai—or perhaps a bullet in the head, though Tojo did survive a bungled suicide attempt and was later hung for war crimes.

"So, we wait one or two weeks, probably try to deploy the Swiss again. Perhaps we add a subtle admonishment that O-Shima-san will be radioactive for the next umpteen years. No waving a white flag yet? So then we send Fat Man to Hiroshima or Nagasaki. I think we end up in the same place; we're hailed as great humanitarians; we save at least 100,000 lives. Remember, the bomb killed 200,000 innocent, ordinary people at Hiroshima alone. That's a lotta people!"

"Sounds great to me, Frenchy, but I wonder if a B-29 can hit a target the size of this O-Shima place."

"I wondered about that, too, so I sort of checked it out: Nagasaki is on a finger of land down on Kyushu that looks about the same size as O-Shima. By the way, we'll go by it tomorrow."

Frenchy raised his arm: "However, there's at least one other way to do it: we could take two submarines—one with Little Boy and a skeleton crew. They set a switch, leave the Little Boy sub, and bug-ass on the other sub. If some natives get too close, there's a proximity device. Whammo—the big mushroom! In that case, how far away did the retreating sub get? The submariners are definitely volunteers—a highly dangerous mission, but what a great way to go! Either way, get this boys . . ..

> Emperor Hirohito
> Looks out the palace window,
> Over the moat and through the trees,
> What do you think he sees?
> The cloud of doom . . .
> The big mushroom!
> He wants no more
> And ends the War."

Rich figured Frenchy had been working on the idea and the doggerel since they were driven past the palace last Sunday. Frenchy went on, "The point is, guys, apparently nobody thought of this demo idea—not Truman, not his staff, not the air corps, not anyone working the Manhattan Project. You remember that Truman had never even heard about the bomb until he was sworn in as President just four months before. Truman had only met FDR twice; he stated he never considered not, I say again, never considered *not* using the bomb. Anyway, guys, I got that off my chest. I think we can scrounge some coffee below decks."

Once settled in the food service area, with a twinkle in his eye, Soddy turned to Rich, "Well howdy there new President Truman, a'm yer Chief-a-Staff, Five Star General of the Army, George Catlett

Marshall. Ya see, it seems, Sir, we got this here new doomsday device. It blows things beyond smithereens, Sir, I repeat beyond smithereens. Ya see, Sir, smithereens is little bits, but our new doomsday device, it don't leave little bits. We can do in if we push it, say, a quarter of a million at a time."

Rich caught on: "Well hello, George. I hadn't heard a peep about this device; what do ya call it?"

"Well ya see, behind your back, we had this here 'Manhattan Project,' named for the drink ah believe—bourbon and vermouth—those boys call it the 'Atomic Bomb.'"

"Kind of a corny name—think of something catchier, like 'The Gilead Bomb.' What'cha got in mind for it?"

"Well, Sir, we figure it will cost us a cool million casualties to invade Japan, so we thought up this here now demonstration project so as to be polite . . ."

"Wait a sec; how many of these Atomic Bombs have we got?"

"Actually, right now, we got two, Sir; we call 'em 'Little Boy' and 'Fat Man.'"

"Well, Five Star George, I don't know what you learned at the Virginia Military Institute, but I learned as a captain in the Great War that a bomb is a weapon of destruction, so that's what I suggest you do with your Little Boy. Now, damn-it, George, Gen. Harry Vaughan and I along with some of the boys are playing poker tonight—want to join us?"

Frenchy laughed, "Damned if you two don't beat Hope and Crosby off on a new hit movie—'The Road to Inchon.'"

Frenchy had already told Rich and Soddy he had dropped their names to Gen. Webber and Lt. Mason, explaining that his back was to the wall; it was then or never, so he went ahead and spoke out, hoping they approved. Both assured Frenchy they did, indeed, approve and appreciated his volunteering their names for possible artillery service.

While they were seated with their coffee, Rich produced a sort of guide pamphlet, a special edition of **Stars and Stripes**, entitled

Land of the Morning Calm? He stabbed at the paper with his hand.

"Well boys, I've been reading up on this place, Korea, where we are headed—sort of from the non-military, historical viewpoint. It is quiet a place; look at this map: a peninsula separated from China and the Soviet Union for the most part by the Tumen and the now-famous Yalu Rivers, an 890-mile border. The peninsula extends south some 680 miles and is about 125 miles wide at its narrowest point, mountainous on the east and throughout the north."

Frenchy added, "There's very little room for farming, especially in the north. The mountain chains up and down the east seem to have fingers extending west. Rivers tend to flow southwesterly out of the mountains."

"That's right," responded Rich, "Only about one-fifth of the land is arable. Farming is in the west and in the river valleys. Two crops a year can be grown in the south. The staple crop, north and south, is rice. In the south, the weather is much milder, and the population is dense. North Korea is less populous and is more industrialized by use of hydroelectric power. Its winters are cold—especially in the mountains, where it's extremely cold."

"This is interesting," Frenchy added, as he thumbed through the pamphlet. "It says here that Koreans are descended from Tungusic tribesmen and are ethnically distinct from the Chinese and Japanese. I wondered about that because these so-called Asians do come in all shapes, sizes, skin tones, and so on. Of course, they all have dark hair and brown eyes. We'll soon get a good look at the South Koreans but hopefully not a look at too many Chinese and North Koreans."

Rich turned a page. "This, to me, is the most fascinating aspect. The guide makes geopolitical comparisons with Poland and the area once called Palestine, which includes Israel, Jordan, and Syria. Those countries and Korea have been bounded by larger powers, which ravaged them for millennia. For example, in Poland, it has been Russia, Sweden, and the Germanic countries. In Palestine, we go way back to the Babylonians, Assyrians, Ottomans, and Crusaders.

"In Korea, it has probably been even more constant and tragic. Going back a thousand years, it has faced China, Mongolia, Russia, and Japan. A Korean proverb describes the country as 'a shrimp between whales.' The country longed to be left alone and was sometimes called 'the Hermit Kingdom.' Its true beauty inspired the name, 'Land of the Morning Calm;' tragically, it's now 'the Land that God Forgot.' The article says they've been invaded eight hundred times."

They also read that, like many Asian countries, Korea had historic periods of being divided into separate warring states and periods of unity and comparative strength. Over many centuries, Korea's culture had been more closely tied to China, but for the past fifty years, Japan had been the big bully.

Talkative Soddy hadn't offered a comment to that point. He finally said, "Like the puny little kid on the block—picked on by everyone—all he kin do was go home and kick the dawg!"

With that, they laughed, sipped coffee, and Rich asked, "Tell me, Soddy, when you were a kid, were you the *picker* or the *pickee?*"

"Some a both, Rich, but, since ah put on this here uniform, ah've definitely been the pickee—the shrimp among whales!"

The conversation ended, as both Frenchy and Rich laughed and then added an "Amen! Me, too" to Soddy's telling remark. Before they hit their bunks, Soddy remembered the "Gilead Bomb" dialogue and sang:

There is a balm in Gilead
To make the wounded whole,
There is a balm in Gilead
To heal the sin-sick soul.

Frenchy earnestly turned to him, "Soddy, you've got a real good voice. I know you carry a harmonica, but till now we haven't heard a musical peep out'a ya. Why so?"

"All us Mechams are musical; mom's a choir director; ah sing and play at the Chicamauga National Military Park in the summertime, all duded up in Civil War uniforms. Trouble is ah play banjo and sing, an' banjo playin's hardly possible for us now, so ah bought the harmonica an' ah'm-a struggelin' with it—jus' can't sing and play at the same time."

"Well, sing or play something for us."

"Yeah, Soddy," added Rich.

"Civil War songs are beyond comparison; ah know dozens. Here's a great one 'bout a prisoner:

In the prison cell I sit, thinking mother dear of you,
And our bright and happy home so far away,
And the tears, they fill my eyes 'spite of all that I can do,
Tho' I try to cheer my comrades and be gay.

Tramp, tramp, tramp, the boys are marching,
Cheer up comrades they will come.
And beneath the starry flag we will breathe the air again,
Of the free land in our own beloved home."

Frenchy noticed that Soddy's drawl left him when he sang the sad war song in a light but rich baritone. Other soldiers had gathered round, and before he could hit the sack, he sang "Yellow Rose of Texas" and "Battle Cry of Freedom."

Frenchy thought, *What a surprise and what a treat!*

The second night out, in torrential rains, *Conrad* turned north into the Yellow Sea, finally dropping anchor in Flying Fish Channel off Inchon at 0500 hours, 12 June 1952.

They were met by a school of LCVPs: Landing Craft Vehicle Personnel. These famous little guys, also known as Higgins Boats, were said to be "the boats that won World War II." Just over thirty-six feet long, with a beam of ten feet, their draft was only three feet. Of course, the voyage of the **Conrad** was planned to hit Inchon at high tide, but, even so, only a vessel like a Higgins Boat could cross the mud flats holding thirty-six troops and get them ashore dry and ready to move out.

The men tossed their duffels to the crew or to a comrade, climbed down the netting, and sprawled into the bobbing boats, which would then head for shore at their top speed of nine knots. Frenchy told his buddies that, in civilian service, comparable little boats were called lighters.

He eyed the inner harbor. There were several cranes, Quonset huts, tents, and larger prefabs alongside roofless walls, debris, and other remains of gutted buildings. He could see a motor pool and military vehicles parked there, with other vehicles on the move— quite a bit of hustle for so early in the day. Docksides looked new. His boat veered to port just inside a causeway leading due north to Wolmi-Do Island—the first point seized by the marines prior to the landing on 15 September 1950. Another causeway connected that little island to Inchon on the mainland.

The boat turned back east and soon hit land, its hinged bow falling forward and allowing the troops to scamper ashore, all safe and sound with no bullets flying around. Frenchy thought of the famous role of the little boats throughout the last war—from Omaha Beach to Iwo Jima.

A sergeant who had been put in charge back on the APA formed them up, checked them off, and reported to a warrant officer: "All present and accounted for, Sir."

Sure enough, certain names were then read off, including Pvts. Desprez, Mecham, and Morrison, the three reporting to the warrant officer, who gave them orders to Uijongbu and thence to the 62nd Field Artillery Battalion. A train was scheduled to leave at 1000 hours; they had time to eat at the mess hut, then to struggle aboard with their duffels. It started raining again—all-in-all, thought Frenchy, *a gloomy but fitting entry to this war-torn land.*

Chapter Thirty
Finally, Part of a Team

The train rumbled out of Inchon forty-five minutes late. They rode in an ancient passenger car with dirty canvas seats, cracked windows, and a few bullet holes. However, the diesel engine looked new and was probably sent from Japan to the Port of Pusan, from where it could come north on South Korea's restored main line. Railroads were the dominant transport for the U.N. Forces. The boys viewed a countryside much more forlorn than postwar Japan. Under devastating combat, the Seoul-Inchon area had changed hands four times in less than a year; but as the three friends headed northeast, they could see that bridges, rails, telephone lines—the basic services—had been restored, that the first rice crop was near harvest, and that along the rutted and dusty roads were dilapidated trucks, a few cars, plodding ox carts, and many, many bicycles.

They passed over the Han River where, on 28 June 1950, the original railroad bridge had probably been destroyed too soon by the fleeing South Koreans. After the demolition, General Paik Sun Yup managed to get about 10,000 soldiers of his 1st ROK Division across on ferries and other boats even after the NKPA had seized Seoul.

Frenchy chuckled quietly, as he thought about his last train ride. He couldn't bring himself to share the Alice Perrers affair with his buddies. *I guess that's called "kiss and tell" . . . whatever you call it, I'm no good at saying I did this or I did that.*

Uijongbu was only about fifteen miles northeast of Seoul; they were there by 1330 hours.

Uijongbu was known as a satellite city of Seoul; however, when the boys arrived, the part of the city they could see was primarily an army camp, comparable in many ways to Fort McCoy. It was a supply and replacement depot with a Mobile Army Surgical Hospital—known as a MASH unit—and a small airport. The incoming troops were assigned to a barracks and a mess and given extra bags to store their Class A uniforms for which they would have no immediate use. From warehouses they were issued summer field gear: helmet liners, steel pots, bayonets, entrenching tools, ponchos, sleeping bags, shelter halves, webbing, more fatigues, underwear, and gloves. Remembering the Bingo Heusting lesson, Frenchy marked each item and urged his friends to do the same.

They had a really good meal that evening. It was a relief to see that KP was performed by the natives who, Frenchy noticed, were increasingly called "gooks," whether they were the South Koreans or the enemies. The derisive word seemed to come from *Han-guk*, meaning "Korean." He decided it was a poor expression, which he would try not to use. *These people are no more gooks than the Fontenots are frogs.*

That evening, he wrote letters to everyone, starting them all with "Greetings from the Land of the Morning Calm." On an impulse, he also wrote Anne Robards; what the hell, she seemed to linger in his thoughts, so why not! He was told not to expect mail until about two weeks after he was duly ensconced in his new unit.

Next morning, 13 June, he was sent to the Ordnance Tent. With his new Military Occupation Specialty as an artillery crewman, the Table of Organization and Equipment called for him to carry an M-1 rifle. He stood in line; and when he reached the counter, he gritted his teeth and spoke up: "With respect, Sergeant, and if at all possible, I'm requesting a new M-1. You see, I'm a qualified sharpshooter and expert rifleman, a former hunter, and, recently, a demonstrator and instructor in the Combat Command, 3rd Armored, Fort Knox."

He tried to make it sound like some important person had told him to make this request. The sergeant, who was called the armorer, glared at him, leaned forward on the counter, so as to be face-to-face, and said, "On top of all that stuff, you're also a pain in the ass!"

But as the armorer turned toward the back of the warehouse, Frenchy thought he detected a smile. *This guy's hard time is all a tease!* The armorer returned with a Garand wrapped and taped in amber-colored paper; the fellow was definitely unthawing. "You know how to get the Cosmoline off? Use hot water and detergent."

He threw some cleaning patches, larger rags, and a cleaning rod on the counter but had second thoughts: "Wait, wait, there's a bucket back here; if you have time, try to get the worst of it before you leave."

Cosmoline was an icky dark gel resembling Vaseline that is swabbed on new weapons by ordnance and could prevent rust for years; gasoline would dissolve it; but hot water and soap were safer and easier on the weapon's wooden parts. Either way, it was a messy, gooey process. Frenchy worked on it a good half-hour, even disassembling the trigger housing. The Garand was a real beauty: no bluing scraped or rubbed off and the walnut seemed to him to have an extra nice grain. He tossed it in the air, caught it, cocked and released the bolt, looked at it and thought, *What will our future together be?* He then went back to the armorer, thanked him, shook his hand, looked at his nametag, and said, "I think I'll call this beauty 'Murphy.'"

Armory Sgt. Murphy laughed and said, "Put some notches in it; No, no, more important, you just take care of yourself!"

They talked for a while. Murphy had been shot in the leg and butt, choppered out to the MASH unit at Uijongbu, fixed up, put on rehab duty, but kept at Uijongbu because he already had thirty-two points of the thirty-six needed for rotation. A soldier got four points a month on the front lines, two points anywhere else in Korea. As he walked away with his new weapon, Frenchy smiled and shook his head, as he thought about his old fear of sergeants: *Most are decent men, just doing their job.*

Later, Frenchy got the word: he was headed for the 62nd field, now in a rest area located south of the ROK 12th Division. It would be a long, all-day truck ride starting next morning. The 12th was somewhere east of the Punchbowl, almost over to the Sea of Japan. It sounded like their new unit was in direct support of the South Koreans; Dave Davis had talked about that—how the army, under Van Fleet, was feeding artillery support into the ROK Divisions.

That afternoon, he finished cleaning, waxing, and oiling Murphy while listening to Armed Forces Far East Radio. He heard Pfc. Eddie Fisher singing "Wish You Were Here," Kay Starr singing "Wheel of Fortune," Jo Stafford singing "You Belong to Me," and The Four Aces singing "Tell Me Why." He learned that his favorite ballplayer, Hank Sauer, was leading the National League in home runs.

In the evening, the boys saw the movie "High Noon" with Gary Cooper and Grace Kelly. Rich had seen it before but felt it was worthy of seeing several times. Frenchy watched Cooper's action with the colt and rated it darn realistic. They thought that Grace Kelly seemed too down-east and prissy with her Philadelphia-patrician accent to possibly be a frontier wife and that Gary Cooper was old enough to be her father, but, what the hell, the damn music, sung by Frankie Laine, was what made the movie a real winner. All the next day, Frenchy found himself humming, *Do not forsake me, Oh, my darling, on this our wedding day.*

The sentimental song reminded him of Amanda; this made him stop and think, realizing that in the last few days, she had sort of popped out of his head, but those words, "Oh, my darling," brought her back and made his head spin; *never again, never again, could I have, nor could I endure such a physical and emotional experience, especially the cave trip. I may fall in love again but never with such dizzy feelings and that crazy poem—I could not love thee dear so much loved I not honor more.*

They were joined for the trip to the 62nd by two other bright prospects—John Purvis and Chick Walsh—so they all piled in the back of a six-by-six amid supplies and ammunition. Rain poured down. They were issued clips and told to load their weapons, as there were sometimes guerillas in the hills along the east-west road, even though they were some twenty miles south of the MLR.

The aroma of night soil was now upon them, as they crossed the lowlands with paddies on each side—impossible tank country. Going up the valley toward Ch'orwon, they were only some two hundred meters above sea level, but they could see hills on each side.

The "night soil" was human waste, carefully collected and brought to the fields in what were called "honey buckets," which were tied to each end of bamboo poles and balanced on the shoulders of humble porters. They saw women in conical straw hats, stooping knee-deep in the soupy brown stuff and transplanting each rice plant seedling. *What a job—stone-age agriculture!*

They left the paved road after about thirty miles, went over a pass, down to more paddies, then up again, passing just south of the Hwach'on Reservoir, then over two more passes for another twenty miles. The rain had stopped; the quietness allowed Frenchy to hear rumbling sounds to the north—from many miles away, he was hearing his first artillery rounds shot in anger! *God be my helper . . . this is it . . . I'll soon be up there!*

There were checkpoints and ROK MPs to guide the driver. Frenchy had learned the polite way to saw hello—a startling complex *annyong-hashim-nikka*, which he tried out with fairly good success. He learned that *annyong* alone was sort of like saying hi and would usually do just fine. Finally, they reached the Kangyung Road intersection and took it, heading south into a valley where they saw a sign, "62nd F.A. Bn. Hq." Under the letters, the Battalion logo was a crest showing a round bursting in air and, under that, the words, *Fuego de Acero*—meaning "Steel Fire" in Spanish.

Two hundred yards down the road was a fence and gate. The guard waved them through; right inside they came upon a large tent—Battalion Headquarters . . . wherever they were, Frenchy had found his unit, his new home. The dripping flap of Headquarters tent was pulled back, and a sergeant major appeared and directed them to get all their gear and simply stand by—no need for a lot of formalities at this end-of-the-line location.

"Evening, men, we've been waiting for you; I'm Sgt. Maj. Flowers; welcome to the 62nd Field, known as Steel Fire. Tonight, you will chow and sack out here in Headquarters Battery; tomorrow the colonel will welcome you and send you off to the firing batteries. All of you, grab a piece of the floor for your fart sacks right here in this tent. Then take your kit; mess is in another tent, just behind this one; Headquarters' enlisted latrine is the hex tent in that little dip; if you see a yellow flag out front, take it and enter, if no flag, it's polite to wait; it's just a one-holer.

"A final thought: for safety, empty your weapon, but keep it and a clip with you; we're right on the edge of the combat zone. Any questions? Fall out, and get going."

The same day, 14 June 1952, other events occurred in Korea: The 187th Airborne and the 338th Infantry put down the riots in Koje-do Prison by moving prisoners from Compound 76—the hotbed of the troublemakers. This sorry episode spoke both for the fanaticism of the enemy and the manifest incompetence of the U.N. Command and its forces assigned to run the prison program.

That night Frenchy heard the sound of the guns and was re-minded that, in general, U.N. Forces dominated the battlefield by day, and the enemy dominated by night.

He later learned that, as he was lying there, trying to sleep, a medical aid man from the 40th Infantry Division, named Sgt. David B. Bleak, volunteered to go on one of those typical patrols sent out to capture enemy soldiers for interrogation.

Bleak was not carrying a weapon when the patrol came under fire; he tended to the wounded, then went on up a hill, came under fire again, leaped into an enemy trench, killed two of the enemy with his bare hands and a third with a knife. He then threw his body over a comrade to protect him from a concussion grenade. Bleak was struck by a bullet, but was still able to pick up another wounded man and was carrying him off the hill when attacked by two soldiers armed with bayonets; he disabled both and brought his man back to safety. Because of these incredible feats, Sgt. Bleak was awarded the Congressional Medal of Honor for heroism performed on the night Frenchy joined the 62nd Field Artillery Battalion.

He fidgeted and slept poorly. The Duty Officer was in and out, as the guard changed, and as the DO saw fit to inspect the guard. The telephone rang every hour, requiring the DO or the night clerk to give it a crank to ring back, then pick it up and say "sinew"—the routine password to signal all is well and the line is open.

Just after 0800 the next morning, Lt. Col. Roger Podolsky—a tall, lanky, grey-haired man—welcomed the five recruits, ex-plaining that the Battalion was in direct support of ROK 134th Regiment. The new men would each be immediately assigned to one of the firing batteries, but the assignment was subject to change, depending on how they all worked out during the ad hoc school he had organized—the school to be held in Charlie Battery and supervised by its Executive Officer, 1st Lt. Oliver Riggs, and its Chief of Firing Battery, M. Sgt. George Brownell.

As to the Battalion, it was a National Guard outfit, which arrived in March 1951, just after two Guard divisions replaced two divisions that had suffered through the War's horrible first nine months. The Battalion was a proud unit, formed back in the days of busting one's butt riding horse-drawn ammunition and supply wagons, known as "caissons." The name Fuego de Acero came from its service on the border during the Mexican War when Black Jack Pershing was chasing the elusive Pancho Villa.

Podolsky himself was regular army and had been Battalion Executive Officer in one of the 1st Cavalry artillery units. He was commonly and respectfully known as Col. Pods.

Finally, the colonel made a special point: "Frankly, I don't usually orient enlisted replacements, but we've been here just long enough to lose most of our original contingent. I'll level with you: by and large, Guard troops tend to be better-educated than the GIs in other units or their conscripted replacements. What I'm getting at is we have suffered a pretty thorough brain drain in survey crews and in fire direction centers at both battalion and battery levels. We're working hard to get new leaders, and we plan to apprentice you five in some key spots. The TO&E for these jobs calls for corporals and sergeants. I pledge to act promptly on any promotion recommendations I receive from the battery commanders; however, there will be no special breaks; you five simply appear to have more schooling than we find among run-of-the-mill replacements. Don't let me down! Any questions?"

Of course the five newcomers were more than sufficiently cowed by the silver oak leaf to remain silent.

Facing north and assuming Headquarters Battery was located at twelve o'clock, Able would be at three o'clock, Baker at six o'clock, and Charlie at nine o'clock, with Service Battery in the middle. These units were only about a quarter mile apart. If they had been at the front, on line, Headquarters and Service would more likely be in the rear with the three firing batteries in line to their front. Frenchy and Soddy were assigned to Baker Battery;

a truck delivered them, going clockwise, so Rich got off at Able, Frenchy and Soddy at Baker, and the last two, Hiram and Chick at Charlie.

Frenchy and Soddy stood there rather forlornly, next to six howitzers, three large tents and about fifty hex tents. The first big tent said Baker HQ, so they walked to it and entered. 1st Sgt. Powell Hinkley greeted them and directed Supply Sgt. Hirsh to show them around and get them organized. They were directed to an empty hex tent where they stashed most of their gear, located the latrine, which was another hex tent, and were shown the mess tent and Fire Direction Center tent. The hex tent was a six-sided, soft-walled olive drab pyramidal tent, supported by a telescopic tent pole. It could hold up to five men and weighed fifty-six pounds.

Back at Headquarters tent, the Battery Commander brushed back the tent flap—a sharp-looking soldier, carrying his carbine, a man of average height but chunky, frowning and gritting his teeth, looking like he surely played football somewhere along the line. Capt. Jake Anthony had apparently heard of their arrival and greeted them with another pep talk: they would not be permanently assigned until after the ad hoc howitzer class was completed; they both had encouraging records so he was confident they would fit in well. His firing battery had a proud and successful past going back over forty years. The newcomers were to be at Charlie Battery by 1400 hours; his driver would buzz them around. Responding to the usual, "any questions?" Frenchy got up his nerve and said, "Yes, Sir. I'm anxious to sight in my Garand. Is there a time and a place provided for that?"

"Ah-ha, I looked at your files. You must be sharpshooter Desprez? Frankly, I don't think most of our cannoneers could hit a Red soldier at ten yards with a shotgun, but you have a good point. We have targets, and First Sergeant Hinkley can arrange a shoot for after chow tonight. You can plan to shoot due east at our perimeter's edge; tell the other new men we'll be hosts; and they're welcome to come along. One of our gunners will be in charge, but, Desprez, I'll expect you to straighten out anyone who can't hit the target; we may even assign you extra duty as rifle instructor. That will be all; carry on."

He said "carry on" so fast they didn't have time to salute before he saluted them! His show of respect—where the officer salutes first—was a nice opening touch on Jake Anthony's part. Frenchy muttered, *good leader, good man.* How right he was!

Chapter Thirty-one
The 105

The five neophytes assembled at Charlie Battery at 1400, as required. 1st Lt. Oliver Riggs questioned them, determining that none of his pupils had any training in artillery. Frenchy could see right off that the tall, thin, pale-faced officer with receding hair and eyeglasses had a natural gift for teaching—clear enough why the colonel had selected him for this extra duty.

"Well, lucky soldiers let's get right at it: Artillery, the King of Battle, is our number-one killer here in Korea; for our enemies, I'm sorry to say we fall victim most often to their mortars. Commentators and experts have already dubbed this the 'Artillery War.' These weapons add what we call 'depth to combat.' Our mission is *to move, shoot, and communicate*; we must excel at all three. Think about it: a weakness in one of these three areas would shut down the other two, erase that combat depth, and thus limit all our forces. Rest assured, you will have essential roles, most likely in the shoot and communicate functions.

"Our firing batteries are normally a mile or so behind the MLR. This means shooting over friendly troops, over hills, rivers, roads, forests. We hit the enemy out of nowhere by *indirect fire*. I'm sure you all get it and could have given this talk so far: howitzers, guns, and mortars deliver indirect fire; whereas machine guns, small arms, recoilless rifles, and bazookas furnish direct fire; tanks can function either way. Now that I think about it, a grenade can furnish mini versions of both direct and indirect fire. Indirect fire at twenty yards . . . now that's something to ponder, but true enough!

"Howitzers and guns are different creatures: howitzers fire a larger payload a shorter distance with less velocity than guns, such as used on ships and tanks and with field artillery's own 155 gun. As I said, I assume every one of you knows all this; let's move on."

The boys learned about the 105 howitzer in detail. The weapon was designed in 1919 but not produced until 1940. By the end of the War, 8,536 had been built at the Rock Island, Illinois, Arsenal. It is the smallest piece in service; the others currently used in Korea were the 155 howitzer, the 155 gun—called the Long Tom—and the 8-inch howitzer.

There was also a 75-pack howitzer, toted by mules, which U.S. troops had used in the last war's mountainous Italian fighting. Interestingly, when they overran a Chinese position, U.S. Marines came upon a batch of these 75-pack howitzers in perfect condition, complete with ammunition. Apparently they had been sent to Chang's Forces by the U.S., then seized by the Reds, and then retaken by the marines.

Riggs walked around to the howitzer's front—the business end. "Well, you all know the tube opening is 105 millimeters. Anyone know how much in inches?"

After some hesitation, Rich speculated, "Well, I can slip my hand in, but if I make a fist, it won't quite fit. I guess better than four inches."

"You wouldn't be sharpshooting me would you, cowboy? It is actually 4.14 inches—about the same size as our 4.2 mortar."

Rich raised his hands in joking protest; he had just guessed. The lieutenant went on: "While we're standing here, look at the lands and grooves. These spiraling ridges catch the rotating band of the shell to give it a stabilizing spin. As you know, they are now found in most all weapons, large and small, and their development in the last century revolutionized warfare. By the way, the spin does impart a slight curve to the trajectory, as it cuts through the air—just like throwing a curve ball. However, if you want an athletic analogy, it's a lot like throwing a football. When you stand behind a 155, you can watch the projectile flying away."

They circled the piece, Riggs noting the rubber tires, the small shields, and the spread trails.

"You three men, grab the right trail and draw it in toward the left."

They managed to comply fairly easily.

"That's the thing about the 105: it weighs just over 4,400 pounds, but it's sufficiently well-balanced on the tires for the crew to manhandle it into position and then easily hook it up to the deuce-and-a-half prime mover for quick transport. Two key aspects are to have part of the crew moving and lifting the trails while others give a heave-ho to the wheels—thus satisfying mission one: *to move*. Sometimes it helps for one or two men to hang from the tube, helping lift the trails like a teeter-totter."

"Pvt. Mecham, how do I control the range of this thing?"

"Well, Sir, if ya wanna go farther, you raise the tube." Soddy paused and smiled. "But, Sir, there's a sorta magic point where raising the tube shortens the range, like a mortar."

"Perfect answer—we call that high-angle fire. It's good for lobbing over steep hills and hitting valleys and gullies. The trouble with high-angle is you have to lower the tube each time to reload."

"Now, Pvt. Desprez, what do you think is the number one problem with cannons on land and sea throughout the ages?"

"Recoil, Sir; for every action there is an opposite and equal reaction."

"Right on! Damn, you guys are smart! Military designers have been struggling with Newton's Third Law of Motion for centuries. The charge, which drives the projectile in one direction, push-es the tube in the other direction with equal linear force. With small arms this is called 'kick.' As you know we let kick serve to discharge the cartridge and reload some of our automatic and semi-automatic weapons."

Riggs went on, now more professorial and warming to his task, "In the old days, cannons were simply allowed to lunge backward from their place in fort, field, or ship. Woe to anyone standing behind such a thing! After firing, they would be repositioned by their crews, sometimes with the help of a block-and-tackle. Of course, it was darn hard to get it back exactly where it had been so that accurate adjustments could be made for firing the next ball, though elevation was pretty well controlled by use of a wedge, known as a 'quoin.'

"The 105 handles recoil with hydro-pneumatic tubes, one for recoil, located above the firing tube, and one for counter-recoil, located below the tube. Oil in the recoil tube stops the barrel and sends it back; then the counter-recoil tube stops it."

Riggs showed all this by pointing to the two cylinders. He then turned and pointed, "In addition, some of the recoil is taken up by the two trails, which are dug into the ground. If the ground is frozen, we must place logs behind the trails to cushion the recoil, otherwise these spade-like trail ends might actually crack. Another ancient problem was loading."

Riggs went back to the front of the howitzer and pretended to be going through old-time procedures. "For centuries, powder and ball had to be rammed down the front of the cannon. This required the cannoneers to go in front of the piece, thus completely exposing their bodies to enemy fire. After reloading, the weapon had to be re-aimed—an inexact procedure. Finally, if a spark had been left in the tube, a dangerous premature explosion could result. In 1640, King James II of Scotland was killed when one of his cannons exploded at the siege of Roxburgh.

"In the nineteenth century, breach mechanisms were developed, first for naval guns, then field artillery; however, as late as the Crimean War and the American Civil War, most cannons were still front-loading. Any sort of breach assembly had to perform two functions: permit rear-end loading and then provide some sort of sealing process so gasses would not escape to the rear."

Riggs then signaled for a ten-minute smoke break. The expression always annoyed Frenchy who didn't smoke, didn't particularly like to be around heavy smoke, and considered it a filthy habit.

Sgt. Brownell fetched a projectile and a shell casing. At the end of the break, the lieutenant announced that the upcoming ammunition talk would cover the subject on a more academic basis. He turned to the sergeant and said, "Right, Sgt. Brownell?"

"With respect, Sir, you're the professor—not me. As you well know, my usual method is repetition, constant practice, and maybe chewing a little ass."

"Yes, yes; that is exactly the problem. We don't have weeks to train these guys in something they'll probably never do, much less excel at, but still must understand."

Sgt. Brownell couldn't resist interrupting his boss, "There's a certain fascination for pulling the lanyard. I remember one of our cooks who would sneak down to the guns and beg for a chance to fire one; I'd say, 'Out, out, go make a cake!' Then I'd laugh and let him do it. He could tell his grandchildren, 'Yes, I fired at the enemy.'"

Frenchy figured the two leaders had worked this out in advance. He also said to himself, *fascinating, really fascinating.*

Riggs was back at it: "Okay, I guess it's Pvt. Purvis' turn. What do we mean by the propellant train and the explosive train?"

There was a pause before Purvis spoke, "First, I admit I am not familiar with these terms; but it is apparent that a howitzer goes boom when fired, and then there is a wham when the round lands. The propellant train must be the boom part, driving the projectile out of the tube, and the explosive train must be the wham part at the end of the projectile's flight when it explodes—hopefully on the enemy."

"Well done, Purvis. Of course the booms and the whams are related to the types of explosives used for the two trains. Ordnance chemists brew up a propellant that oozes thrust and power, whereas the target explosive cocktail is strident, quick, brittle. To tell you more than you need to know, the stuff is a mixture of trinitrotoluene, called TNT, and ammonium nitrate, called amatol. Sgt. Brownell has kindly brought us two of the key elements: a shell casing and a projectile. All explosives have been removed from both. Okay, Sergeant—the propellant train."

Master Sgt. Brownell picked up the brass shell casing. "There are three parts to this casing when it comes to us from Service Battery and before that from Ordnance. At the bottom, there is a highly volatile detonator, also called the "primer," which is triggered when a cannoneer pulls the lanyard. The canister is loosely stuffed with seven powder bags, called "charges," labeled one to seven and tied together, in order, with connecting string. The number of charges to be used depends mostly on the range; the FDC people will go into this with you."

"Let's say charge five is selected. One of my men removes charges six and seven by breaking the string between five and six over the sharp top edge of the canister, or "casing," as we sometimes call it."

Brownell paused, looked around, and then concluded, "The projectile is dropped in the casing, and a cannoneer may then thrust the combined parts in the breach. He holds the parts in his left hand and thrusts forward with his right fist—to avoid catching a finger in the machinery. The whole thing weighs thirty-seven pounds, so it's quite manageable."

Lt. Riggs stepped forward. "With respect to my able friend, I want to add something for everyone to remember from this time forward: there is nothing more dangerous than using the wrong charges—nothing! You remember that a cannoneer removed two charges in the example. Except in dire combat conditions, that man must show me or Master Sgt. Brownell those two bags before firing. Obviously, if three charges were removed by negligence, we'll land short and maybe hit our own troops. Carry on, Master Sergeant."

"Thanks, Lieutenant, I now turn to the explosive train, which also has three parts: this projectile, the black powder inside, and a fuse. There are other types of shells, such as the white phosphorous round, known as 'willy peter.' The fuse is a cone-shaped device that screws in the point of the projectile.

"There are many fuses; I'll tell you about two: the most common is fuse quick, which explodes on impact; however we're more and more using fuse VT, meaning 'variable time.' Like radar, it sends out pulses that bounce back as it nears the ground, causing an air explosion at a planned height of, let's say, twenty meters. None of the explosion is wasted plunging into the ground and just churning up dirt as will happen with fuse quick, making VT lethal against troops in the open and especially troops in trenches who would be spared absent a direct hit using fuse quick. Of course, fuse quick is less expensive, so we often adjust with quick and fire for effect with VT."

Brownell put his hands on hips, as if fully satisfied with his efforts. "Any questions?"

Frenchy was delighted with the whole training and eager to learn more. He addressed the lieutenant and the sergeant, and not knowing how to handle the military courtesy, he simply said, "I suppose that the canister seals any gasses surging to the rear?"

The lieutenant responded: "Exactly. We call the 105 ammo 'semi-fixed ammunition.' Bigger cannons, like the 155mm howitzer use 'separate loading ammunition.' We slide in the shell, or projectile, as we've been calling it, then we jam in the selected number of powder bags and close the breach. The breach block on the 155 looks sort of like a little bank vault door, with stepped-down screws so it can be opened or closed with a small turn. This round door seals the breach with the help of a padding called an "obterator;" no canister is needed.

"Okay, Pvt. Walsh, let's see what you know. Suppose there's an enemy survey crew working out in the DMZ. How do we hit 'em?"

Walsh was more than ready for the question. "I know this is a terribly deadly business, Lieutenant, but in the abstract, it is sort of like a game. We have forward observer teams in observation posts. We call them FOs in OPs. They see that enemy survey crew out there, decide they make a worthy target, and radio or telephone Fire Direction Center, giving the azimuth, location, and nature of the target—all in a precise, mandated way. Those FDC guys process the data and give commands to the guns with respect to charge, elevation, deflection, and fuse. The data is set and the guns are fired; the FO sees 'em land, gives corrections and so on till the enemy lies dead or has bug-assed—end of mission."

Riggs turned to the sergeant. "We ought to let them teach; that was one great answer.

"Now, Master Sgt. Brownell is Chief of Firing Battery. He has six sergeants under him, called 'Section Chiefs.' He is responsible for laying the battery—we'll get to that later—and for firing the howitzers. I'm his boss and know how to do those things but not with the overall skill he has acquired by years on the job. I usually hang out by the guns or in FDC and go where needed; I'm second in command of the battery, which means I might have to take over the whole thing; God knows in some cases Sgt. Brownell might have to take over the whole thing."

Another ten minute break followed. Then Master Sgt. Brownell called for order.

"I want to thank the Executive Officer for the nice words. I have served in the artillery since the last war and have held most every enlisted job at the battery level. With the integration of the services, as a colored soldier I am proud to command some ninety men of all colors and sizes. Lt. Riggs was picked to teach this class because of his leadership, professional skills, and attention to detail. Before long, God willing, he will have his own battalion—not just his own battery."

Riggs waved and nodded, saying, "I'll settle first for railroad tracks and my own battery, but if you want to lighten the discussion, give 'em your Lady Howitzer story."

The master sergeant laughed, "Okay, you suggested it, Lieutenant; so I can't be blamed for obeying a direct order. I see the howitzer as a woman; I don't know about the lady part."

He fondly patted the breech block and held its handle.

"Forward in an engagement we may have the breastworks, but you can stay below them. To commence, we spread the trails and line her up, sometimes repositioning her; then, one hand grasping here, we open the breech; with care, we insert the projectile, grab and use the lanyard; if everything was done right, she recoils back, then forward; off she goes, leaving a little gas and powder smell behind!"

Sgt. Brownell paused—the men started to applaud—but he raised his arms signaling for quiet. "There's more: you don't want to overuse her or put extra, unnecessary charges in her, but that tube can take lots of use and some abuse. Periodically, she must be shut down, the breech opened and the piece swabbed clean."

As Brownell bowed, they laughed and applauded, Soddy saying, "Ya sure made an impact on me."

Riggs added, "That story is as old as the army, but I'd never heard the part about gas and powder smell. Now, I'm afraid we've got to get serious again."

"All right, Sir." The sergeant said, and continued. "If the proper settings have been made on the howitzer, it is ready to fire. A crewman pulls the lanyard, which drives a pin into the primer, igniting the charges. Boom; the round is gone, the tube has recoiled and is back in battery. A crewman now reopens the breach; the empty canister is automatically ejected—just like the cartridge is removed from a bolt-action rifle when the bolt is pulled back.

"The Table of Organization and Equipment for a 105 howitzer calls for eight men on each piece; however, five can fire it well enough. The Chief of Section is in charge of the howitzer and its crew. The Gunner sets the deflection, pulls the lanyard, and opens and closes the breach. Number One sets elevation. Number Two loads the shell. Others prepare the fuse, cut the charges, unload the ammunition, drive the prime mover, and handle other details. All jobs are critical, and cannoneers take turns doing 'em all. Practice is called 'cannoneers' hop' and is conducted most every day, just like ball players take batting and fielding practice."

The problem for Frenchy and his friends was that they couldn't fire the weapons in their present rear area nor could they prepare the ammunition. What they could do was simulate all of those steps. They could also practice setting deflection and elevation on the howitzer as if the information had come from FDC. The Exec and Chief Brownell were clever at combining lectures with practice, and the afternoon was soon over. Frenchy advised that they planned to zero their M-1s that evening, and they adjourned until the next day.

Chapter Thirty-two
Fire Direction Center and Otto

Next morning in Fire Direction Center, Lt. Riggs was sounding more and more professorial: "We have here a topo of the Black Tooth Sector of the Kansas Line. We're pretty sure that's where we will be headed next week. This eight-mile segment is roughly the line of ROK 134th Regiment. Last I heard it was 1st and 2nd Battalions on line, 3rd back here somewhere in reserve. That's Black Tooth back up here, also known as Hill 870—around 2,800 feet high. It's held by the North Koreans. When you see it, you'll know why we call it 'Black Tooth.'

"To the west of Black Tooth, there's a road and a river, called the Yeppun Kang, then there's this significant ridgeline averaging about five hundred meters high, which we call 'Black Ridge.' We figure there are many, many caves and mortar emplacements on the north slopes of Black Ridge. As you can see, Black Tooth and Black Ridge constitute the North Korean Main Line of Resistance.

"To its south, between the lines, we have the no-man's-land or DMZ—being about two miles in width on the west and east extremities of our sector and at the midpoint, a good three miles from our Hill 710 to Black Tooth. Our MLR runs pretty much straight east to west with Hill 710 being the highest point and with its east ridge sloping gently down and only slightly lower, averaging, say, some five hundred meters.

"This area in between—the DMZ—consists of a flat valley plus a river, Yeppun Kang, with three connecting streams, all flowing intermittently. I've been told it's an old crater area like the Punchbowl. There were rice paddies out there till we started fighting over it. Drainage here is to the east, to the Sea of Japan. There are intersecting dirt roads and also two small hills, which— in honor of Black Tooth—we've dubbed 'Cuspid' and 'Bicuspid.'

"Note that our main supply route is the Kangyung Road, which we are now fronting; all we have to do is drive north. The road enters no-man's-land—now called the Demilitarized Zone or DMZ—through this low point in our MLR, at a spot called the 'Kangyung Gap,' which lies west of Hill 710. Then, running due west from the gap is a ridgeline sort of matching Black Ridge, which we, of course, call 'White Ridge.' The trouble is White Ridge averages only about 450 meters high and furnishes limited shelter against counter-battery fire. In summary, our MLR from west-to-east will be White Ridge, the gap, and Hill 710 and its easterly slopes.

"Our field of operation will probably be this eight-mile, east– west strip and north as far as the guns will shoot. We will have up to nine forward observer observation posts spread evenly along our MLR.

"The ROK 134th is already in this area, east of the MSR by this stream bed south of Hill 490. The 2nd ROK Battalion will be west of the gap; the 1st ROK Battalion will be east of the gap. I haven't heard which companies will be where. As I already said, 3rd ROK Battalion will be in reserve.

"You may well ask, 'where will we be?' The positioning is a bit unusual; we will all be in this area west of the gap and south of White Ridge, spread out Able, Baker, Charlie, from east to west. In other words, the Infantry Regiment is on one side of the road; the Artillery Battalion is on the other. This is not standard, and

I'd say the position is awkward—barely satisfactory. We will have good fields of fire but will be subject to counter-battery fire and also direct NK infantry attack. Any questions so far?"

The lieutenant looked around—all were silent, so he shrugged his shoulders and continued, "What are our goals? Where do we go next? Frankly, I would be very surprised, very surprised, if we were ordered to take Black Tooth, in this stalemated war; it would be like the Heartbreak Ridge Bloody-Ridge Campaigns, fought last October in the Punchbowl area—bloody, way, way beyond reason." More silence . . . he shrugged again, "Maybe I'm indiscrete, talkin' tactics with new replacements, but—what the hell—that's how I feel."

Frenchy remembered Dave Davis talking about his 2nd Division fighting at Heartbreak, which was seized by a task force of the 23rd Infantry plus a bayonet-charging French Battalion. Jean Fontenot would be proud. Riggs went on, suggesting future problems.

"However, I'm sure we will be contesting the two little tits out in the valley—Cuspid and Bicuspid, but whoever tries to take and hold them will have a very nasty time. There will at least be listening posts and nightly ROK patrols out in their area with similar moves by the North Koreans."

Frenchy shuddered: after Dave Davis' vivid descriptions, night patrols held no appeal. He listened on.

"Anyway, this is the area where we are apt to throw hot steel. There are checkpoints, designated CP-1 and so on. These include a road intersection, an old culvert, a destroyed tank, a black napalm smear, a rock covered with green lichen, some old ammo boxes, and other pieces of materiel. The FOs and the men in the FDC tents will surely designate and register on more checkpoints; we want to get it so we can hit any point in the valley in a minute or two. We have other checkpoints that can only be seen from the air in an L-19; these are designated LCP-1 and so on; they are located over the Black Ridge, along the Yeppun Kang, and behind Black Tooth.

"Why am I telling you five newcomers all this? Two reasons: first, there is talk that at least one of you will be selected as radioman for one of our FO teams. That person must be prepared to replace the FO, which, as I think you all know, is a second lieutenant's job. I must say, I well remember FO duties from the dark days of 1951. The battalion's young lieutenant FOs and their two-man crews are key players behind millions of dollars of materiel, dozens of higher-ranking personnel, and hundreds of crewmen. Second reason, some of you will be selected for FDC operations. Each firing battery and headquarters battery operates an FDC—four duplicative teams—so we're talking important jobs for at least ten enlisted men—key jobs for sergeants, led by the battery execs and by the battalion S-3—a major's job, filled by our Major Middleton Willis, a good guy.

"So, here we are in FDC. We pin this chart where the battery is; we pin where the FO is—if we have an idea where he is. We don't have to know where he is, but if he stays put at his OP, we will know by survey exactly where he is.

"Then we put a pin where the FO says the target is. The FO gives us an azimuth; we plot a back azimuth. He gives corrections based on his FO target line, which we convert to data based on the gun target line. We use this plastic deflection fan that gives us both the range and the deflection. If there is a difference between the height of the guns and the height of the target, we adjust what we call 'the angle of site,' which is set off by a separate dial on the howitzers. Here in the Black Tooth Sector we won't mess much with height differences.

We select a charge, based on the range; then we pick up one of these slip-sticks—we have one for each charge. We line up the range on the applicable slip stick and it gives us the elevation of the howitzer tube; we get the deflection from the fan. Word is passed by mouth, radio, or phone to the Chief of Firing Battery and thence to the Section Chiefs, telling them in this order: deflection, elevation, fuse, and charge. The cannoneers place the data on the guns, prepare the designated charge, ready the projectile, load—fire!

"All this happens about as fast, or faster, than I just described it. When the rounds are fired, the FO is told, 'on the way;' he says, 'on the way, wait;' when the FO sees that he is within fifty yards, he calls 'fire for effect.'"

Master Sgt. Brownell interjected. "Once we're up and running, each step takes around fifteen seconds—first: FO to FDC; second: FDC to the guns; third: guns to 'on the way.' It's my duty to see that any holdup is not at the guns but not at the risk of neglecting safety. No matter where you participate, you guys'll adopt the same prideful attitude to your part'a the process."

It all seemed clear to Frenchy, who nodded, *I think I understand perfectly—good stuff.* Riggs continued, "There's just one more piece to our mathematics: we have to know where our battery is. In these stalemate conditions, we must have battery-area survey, and it's important to have OP and target-area survey, as well. We use the aiming circle, which performs like a little transit; anyone have survey experience?"

Frenchy thought of his days computing latitude on the ore boat and studying trigonometry at St. Pats. Both he and Rich raised their hands. The lieutenant smiled and nodded, obviously making a mental note; meanwhile, Frenchy looked at Rich and pondered, *Where the hell does a cowboy learn survey?*

Riggs went on with his new topic, "It'll suffice for now if I simply say that we use trigonometric functions for battery-area survey and target-area survey. You'll understand, Rich and Frenchy, that we compute target area survey the same way we compute distances to the planets and stars—the law of tangents. In both cases we're gaining information about a point we can't just go to. There you have it: math on the OP; math at FDC; and math in survey. That's why you five were taken out of pipeline and sent here. We need able help and right away!"

They were taught to lay the battery, using the aiming circle. The desired direction of fire is set on the aiming circle, using its compass; next an angle is measured in mils from the direction of fire to an instrument on the first howitzer; and finally, the howitzer's gun tube is cranked to form the opposite angle between gun tube and aiming circle. In this way, the direction on the gun tube is then the same as the direction of fire on the aiming circle—by the laws of plane geometry: when two lines are cut by a transversal so that the opposite angles are equal, the lines are parallel.

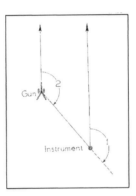

The Chief of Firing Battery or other leader at the aiming circle would then announce "Number One is laid," and he would do the same procedure with the next howitzer until all six are pointed in the selected direction.

For four days, they worked on cannoneers' hop, laying the battery, and FDC procedures. Riggs or Brownell would send a mock fire mission, and the boys would process it and send it to the guns. Other times they laid the guns on a new azimuth, taking turns at the guns, aiming circle, and FDC. Members of the regular crews at those places checked their work and demanded perfection—good training for everyone.

All five spent one day with the battalion's survey crew. They chained the distance from a bench mark at Battalion, down the winding road to a visible range pole, thence to the next visible range pole, and, eventually to a bench mark at Baker battery. A 'chain' was a unit of measurement—in the artillery, one hundred feet. Years ago, it actually was a chain—sort of a much longer version of the ten-yard football chain—but Frenchy was taught with a graduated steel tape on a spool.

Markers called 'chaining pins' were pushed into the ground at the end of each unit of chain. The rear chainman started with no pins and would pick up pins as the team moved on, and by counting his pins upon completion and by checking with the lead chainman, they had a good double check on how many chain-units were measured.

The five recruits measured on-the-double, pausing as they moved down the road to sketch and jot down the raw data on specially prepared worksheets.

They then sat around a camp table and, using the helpful worksheets, calculated distances east–west and north–south using the angles and distances calculated at each turning point along the way. They used trig tables and multiplied long series of numbers by using logarithms. In the process, it was necessary to interpolate odd fractions into decimals; Frenchy did the interpolations in his head. It took five separate calculations to reach the battery. They came within ten inches of the result previously determined by the battalion survey crew using a transit; they had used an aiming circle—standard equipment for a firing battery but not as accurate as a regular surveyors' transit.

Frenchy and Rich were the only ones to get the correct answer at all five points. The system was always to have at least two men do the calculations and compare each result. The computations were complex enough that if two people got the same answer, they could be assured it was correct. They worked quickly, and, it was not embarrassing as beginners to be wrong once or twice. With all the troops coming through the pipeline without much education, it was easy to see why their leaders were having problems at all levels finding young draftees capable of this work.

There was no time to rest. That evening, they met with the battalion communications officer and two NCOs. None of the five had been to one of the army's Signal Corps schools. They were introduced to the SCR-619 vehicular radio, the SCR-300 portable unit used by FO teams, and the AN/PRC-6, called the 'prick six' but officially the 'Army-Navy, Portable Radio, Carrying, Model Six.' The AN/PRC-6 was an updated version of the old walkie-talkie. All were compatible FM transmitter-receivers. As might be anticipated, the range of the radios increased with their size and weight.

There were separate bands of frequencies available for armor, artillery, and infantry. Artillery was 27-38.9 MCs. Frenchy understood all this before he reached the 62nd, and when shown the dials, he understood how to change frequencies. The others stood and watched.

"So, Desprez, tell me about your radio experience."

"Well, Sir, I was working the radio on the ore boat, *Hawkeye*, when she was caught in a gale off Keweenaw Peninsula on Lake Superior. We had to put into Thunder Bay and successfully bypass Isle Royale. It was ten hours of knee-knocking work—total concentration with calls back and forth to those and other locations."

"What type of radio?"

"We had two radios: a very high frequency, FM radio for thirty miles and under, and a medium frequency, AM radio good for short, medium, or long, made by RCA Radio Marine. We could easily call Duluth–Superior from the Soo Locks; that would be close to four hundred miles, Sir."

They had him explain the whole procedure, down to the call to Isle Royale to rouse the radio man.

"Just how big are these boats, Desprez?"

"Big, Sir, though they come in many sizes; ours was close to seven hundred feet with a seventy-foot beam."

"My God, that's about the length of the *Missouri.*"

"Oh yes, Sir, some of the Lake boats are longer than a Battleship. They're narrower abeam; they're like a huge barge with boat essentials at each end."

"How long before you could operate this SCR-300?"

"I'm pretty sure I can operate it now, Sir, though I'd need the call signs and some protocol."

Meanwhile, the 2nd Division was fighting on Old Baldy—an outpost hill four miles west of Ch'orwon and about one mile south of Pork Chop Hill. It lay in the area between the two armies and was fought over throughout the summer of 1952 with great loss of life on both sides. Men in bunkers on Old Baldy called for VT fire on and around their own positions. Old Baldy again represented the irony of the Korean battlefield, since it was an outpost battle, sure to end up in the DMZ when and if a truce were ever signed. That part of the truce talks had been fully negotiated. Now, the 62nd Battalion was about to come forward to the MLR and render direct support in a sector with potentially similar outpost behavior.

After five days of study, Soddy and Frenchy trudged back to Baker Battery. It was Friday, 20 June, and they hoped to spend one quiet evening; however, soon after chow, the cry went out, "Pvt. Desprez to Headquarters tent."

He was greeted by a short, stocky second lieutenant who strode forward, hand extended, "I'm Otto Rentner."

Frenchy felt he should salute, but there was no time; he shook hands. He was motioned to a chair. The character before him certainly didn't look like a second john: he was slightly pudgy, he seemed to have a cleft lip—perhaps slightly repaired. There was also about a quarter-inch division between his front teeth; his receding brown hair was cut short. Frenchy thought, *He looks awful Prussian—a sort of Baron Otto Von Rentner . . . but, most noticeably, he looks about twent-eight or thirty years old, way too old to be a second john!* Actually, he was twenty-six. Another first impression was his warm, reassuring smile, and twinkling eyes.

"Well, take me all in; I'm the damnedest looking second lieutenant ya ever saw, right?"

"Well, Sir, if I had my wits about me, I'd make some non-committal answer. Right now, all I can think ta say is, you're right!"

"Oh, you've your wits about you all right; that's a good answer to an unfair question. What ya see is what ya get. Until recently, I was at the top of one greasy pole with the rank of master sergeant; now I'm at the bottom of another even-greasier pole. The reason ya haven't seen me around Baker Battery is that the FO crews have been up on the MLR, doin' some shooting, sizing up the DMZ, and sort'a acclimating. It's a lousy, bitter, stalemated war—hateful!"

Frenchy shuffled his feet. "So, what may I do for you, Sir."

"I hear they call ya 'Frenchy;' that's easy enough ta figure from your name. Your 201 File is excellent: artillery's your third combat branch; you're a sharpshooter and we just found out you're ready for FDC, survey, or communications NCO. Am I correct?"

Frenchy could see *the man's holding back—not ready to commit himself.*

"Well, Sir, I've not been enthralled with all the army work, but the FDC and survey have been interesting, and I had communications training in civilian life."

The lieutenant then drew out of him the whole story of the ore boat, the storm, the commo needs, and the calls to Isle Royale.

Then the old soldier described his Third Army days in World War II with the 949th Field, including the Bulge and the Saar River crossing. Then there was garrison duty as a supply sergeant at both battery and battalion levels. His bookkeeping skills, common sense, and manifest leadership ability led him to study and pass high school equivalency tests. He had taken some college correspondence courses. He was not married.

Frenchy thought, *He's been liked and respected all his army days.*

His former commanding officer and good buddy had filled out an application for Officer Candidate School and insisted that he sign it. Like many old sergeants, he had never aspired to be an officer, wasn't sure he wanted it or would fit in. Anyway, he did as he was told and signed up.

Artillery OCS had proven a bad choice. From the early days of the twenty-two-week course he was one of the most popular candidates, but when they got to gunnery—one of the last parts of the curriculum and after four months of eating humble pie—he was lost in the maze of math. As he put it, "My mind would sort of shut down; I couldn't add two and two." His classmates and the cadre tried to help, but he was about to wash out.

A class delegation went to the battery commander who counseled with the school commandant. They put him back not one or two but three classes so he could be put on TDY and tutored at length by volunteers—an unheard of procedure! Officers and men gave hours of time to helping him. He was inserted in a class just beginning the gunnery phase, had to endure six extra weeks of OCS chicken-shit, but finally, he learned to interpolate fractions to decimals, solve FDC problems, and—up to his ears in the stuff—he easily made it!

He was offered the executive officer position in a service battery and respectfully declined. He wanted to follow the pathway of a typical graduate; that meant on the line with Military Occupation Specialty Number 1189—forward observer. He had always been good at adjusting fire—that had not been his OCS problem, and by being set back, he had a double dose! More than that, he knew how to adjust from his enlisted days.

"Okay, Frenchy, what I'm telling you now is not an order; let's just say it's what I need. The TO&E for an FO team calls for a lieutenant commanding, a recon sergeant, and a radio operator. The sergeant drives the jeep, if a jeep is used. He also takes over if the FO buys the farm. We use an SCR-619. Regardless of what the TO&E says, in my team, we share the loads not necessarily by rank, or TO assignment, but in accordance with our God-given strengths and terrain conditions. We're able to carry the radio, but in the Stalemate, both sides are tied back by multiple telephone lines, which can get cut so we keep our radio on the ready.

"As you know, we are in direct support of ROK 134, in their 1st Battalion front; that means a language problem and draws a fourth man to our team, at present, we have a very good ROK soldier, a Sergeant named Lee-Mo. Naturally, we call him Le-Mon. He speaks Korean, fluent Japanese, and pretty good English; he seems to enjoy teaching us Japanese words and phrases, especially about what he calls *chiisai jo-sans*, meaning 'little girls.'

"Here's where I stand: I have no Radio Operator and my recon is a short-timer and very reluctant to stick his head out of the bunker. Due to, shall we say, his personal situation, in an emergency he is totally incapable of replacing me. You are the only guy in this so-called ad hoc group with communications experience. Off the cuff—don't repeat this—according to Riggs and Brownell, you are the highest rated man in the new group. Need I say more? I need you as a radio operator and heir-apparent recon sergeant. What do you think, Private First Class Desprez?"

"PFC?"

"I let that slip accidentally on purpose. You're to go ta Battalion tomorrow where all five of ya will receive assignments and a batch of chevrons. You haven't answered my question."

Frenchy got the picture: *Lt. Rentner wasn't authorized to say that this was a volunteer assignment, but if I balk, the lieutenant can say he wasn't satisfied with me, and they can come up with another solution.* Behind this friendly exchange, Frenchy's bottom line was, *We both know full well that the position of forward observer was one of the most dangerous jobs in the world!*

There was an old saying, "Put a gold star in your window, mother, because your son is an FO!" It wasn't just that the FO crew was on the infantry front line, they were in a recognizable bunker, a spot of high ground; sometimes they were in an OP forward of the MLR; sometimes they were on patrol; and the guy with the radio—recognizable by the aerial—was an extra-special target. The enemy knew: silence the radioman, you silence the FO team, and you silence the guns.

Frenchy paused; his head spun a little. *I've reached the end of that line I've been thinking about; this is it—no division clerk job, no teaching map reading, no sinecures on the MLR!* Gazing straight at the lieutenant, he answered, "Sir, I thank you for choosing me. I will be proud to serve with you and, God be my helper, I will serve you well!"

As if scripted, the stillness was then broken by the thunder of artillery in the distance.

Black Tooth Sector Map

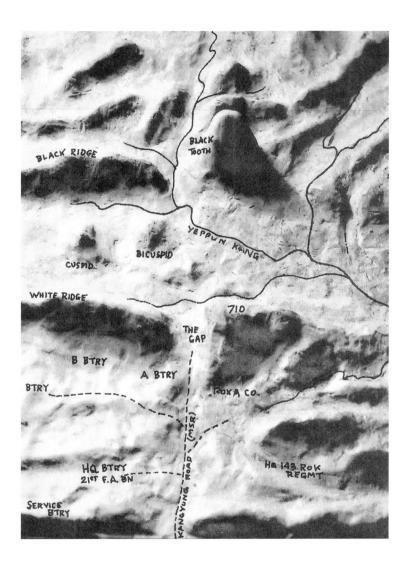

Chapter Thirty-three
March to the Sound of the Guns

That next morning, Saturday, 21 June, the five scholars met by the mess tent in Charlie Battery with Lt. Riggs, Lt. Rentner, Sgt. Brownell, and others responsible for their training. Boxes of PFC chevrons were on a camp table, in batches of eight—enough for the summer fatigues and field jacket, with some left over. The mess sergeant served coffee, and it was all treated like a little graduation celebration. Assignments were announced: Purvis and Walsh to Headquarters FDC, Mecham to Baker FDC, Morrison to Battalion Survey, and Desprez to the Baker FO team number one, Lt. Otto Rentner III, commanding.

Frenchy heard Riggs refer to Lt. Rentner as "Pop." He looked surprised. The two Lieutenants laughed and Riggs said, "You don't get it, do ya? How 'bout the rest of ya?"

There were blank looks until Rentner explained, "My folks really stuck me; I'm actually Otto the Third, but no kid of mine would have that name. It's a palindrome."

After a pause, Rich said, "Sure; Otto Rentner III with the letters reversed is still Otto Rentner III; same with the nickname: Pop is Pop."

"Well, yah," said Otto, "But my favorites are when the whole thing'll work backwards and forwards, like 'a man, a plan, a canal, Panama.'"

Sgt. Brownell, usually deferential with southern whites regardless of rank, nevertheless spoke up. "Speaking of names, I'd like to get to the bottom of something else: where did 'Soddy' come from?"

"Well, ah was stuck with it comin' in the army—jus' like Arnold here was stuck with 'Frenchy.' Ah come from a place called Soddy-Daisy, Tennessee, about fifteen miles north of Chattanooga—really now a suburb. They were separate towns along Walden's Ridge where separate hills were called Soddy, Daisy, Flattop, and so on. Soddy's origin's obscure: one theory's it comes from the Cherokee word, *tsati*, meanin' 'sweet water.'"

"I've been to Chattanooga—a great stop for a Civil War buff," added Riggs. "No wonder they fought so much there: four rail lines entered the city, plus the navigable Tennessee River. The terrible battle of Chickamauga, just south of Chattanooga, reflected the confederate's interest in preserving this gateway to their heartland."

"Yes, Sir, an' what really gets me is the similarity between these here mountains and those back home, especially the Blue Ridge."

"Right," added Riggs. "You find a mountain here we haven't ruined with trench diggin', artillery, and napalm—thank God, that's still most of 'em—and it'll remind me of Lookout Mountain right there at Chattanooga. You know, Hooker's men charged right up that mountain and took it from the Rebs. It's about 2,200 feet— somethin' like seven hundred meters—about the average height of a Korean mountain, like our Hill 710."

Soddy could not let that kind of talk pass. "Yes, Sir, but, with respect, Sir, and beggin' your pardon, the Confederates were outnumbered on Lookout six-to-one."

Riggs tried hard not to laugh. "Soddy, when you're talkin' about something that happened almost one hundred years ago, you can dispense with all that excessively flowery military courtesy."

Soddy blushed while everyone else laughed. They all knew that the battles at Chattanooga and just south at Chickamauga were turning points in that great struggle.

Then Rich piped up: "Sir, your courteous pupil, Soddy, used to be part of a chorale singing Civil War songs at those battlefield sites; perhaps we should hear one."

The lieutenant was up to the proposal at once, and Soddy said, "Ah'll give you my sentimental favorite, with a warning that it's sad; join me on the chorus." After playing the haunting melody on his harmonica and as other soldiers turned toward him, he launched into it:

> *Just before the battle, mother,*
> *I am thinking most of you,*
> *While upon the field we're watching*
> *With the enemy in view.*
>
> *Comrades brave are 'round me lying,*
> *Filled with thoughts of home and God*
> *For well they know that on the morrow,*
> *Some will sleep beneath the sod.*
>
> *Farewell, mother, you may never*
> *Press me to your breast again,*
> *But, oh, you'll not forget me, mother,*
> *If I'm numbered with the slain.*

Riggs knew the song, and pitched in on the chorus along with some of the other cannoneers, but Frenchy thought, *Too sad— saddest song I ever heard! What would my mother think if she were hit with that maudlin song—too sad!*

Word came down later in the day to start packing; the battalion was moving out Monday the 23rd; an advance party had already left.

With the traditional yells of "CSMO," meaning, "close station, march order," the 62nd Field Artillery Battalion moved up by batteries: Able, Baker, Charlie, Headquarters, finally Service. The Baker vehicles followed Able until the lead battery turned north and Baker was signaled to bear left. 1st Lt. Alfred Marcin, the Baker Executive Officer, had gone ahead and selected the complete battery layout: guns, headquarters, and supply tent, FDC tent, mess tent, and mess truck, latrines, and truck service, and parking area. The howitzers were forward, then the hex tents of the gun crews, then the other facilities.

Marcin stood there, shouting and pointing, holding a clipboard, looking like a soldier with too much on his mind. Al Marcin still looked like what he had recently been: an eager college boy— medium height, solidly built, perhaps too small for football but husky enough to be a tough soldier and make it through the past horrendous Korean winter. He had spent his rookie days with a stateside training unit, reached Korea in the fall of '51, served his time as an FO, been promoted and named Baker Exec. While a natural leader, his last assignment had tempered his eagerness to criticize and to expect too much.

Marcin repeatedly shouted and pointed out the direction of fire, which—as everyone knew in this case—was north to north-northeast. He was just doing his by-the-book duty, starting with the basics, because he was in charge of the guns, the gun crews, and their training. This traditional responsibility of showing the direction of fire really amounted to pointing where the enemy was located and probably went back to antiquity—perhaps Gideon pointed to the Midianite camp.

The guns were in a flat area behind White Ridge, which formed the MLR to their direct front. Charlie Battery trucks drove on by, passing over a little rise to the southwest, then down to another flat area before another rise on the westernmost end of the 62nd Battalion's sector.

Five of the nine 62nd Battalion OPs were to be established along White Ridge, Able Battery on their right, and Charlie on their left. To the east of the hills in front of Able Battery, was Kangyung Gap, then higher hills, first Hill 710 where the Battalion's dominant OP would be manned by Lt. Rentner and his crew.

Black Tooth and other mountains extended north to the horizon , but, from the gun positions, all these mountains were masked by White Ridge to the immediate front, part of the U.N. main line, known as the Kansas Line. The Truce negotiators had already determined that the area to its north, as far as Black Tooth and its adjacent east–west Black Ridge would be the Demilitarized Zone.

A ROK artillery battery had just moved out into reserve, but Capt. Anthony and Lt. Marcin decided to set up Baker Battery behind the former ROK area and clear of their slit trenches and buried garbage. Cleanliness was not as big a thing with Korean soldiers.

Telephone poles were already in place; FDC tied in to the battalion's PBX in Headquarters Battery—located one mile due south; and communication teams were busy installing lines to the OPs.

The potential weak spot in the U.N. Forces' MLR was Kangyung Gap, located between White Ridge to the west and Hill 710 to the east, thus forming a pass where the Kangyung Road— the main supply route—ran due north into the DMZ. At that point it ceased to be a useable road, since anyone foolish enough to be on it would, in a matter of minutes, come under fire from either the Reds or the U.N. Forces.

Because the Gap was not much higher than the river valley in the DMZ and about four hundred meters in width, very special defenses were required and duly furnished by ROK Able Company, 19th Tank Battalion, attached to ROK 134th Regiment. From north to south the defense included listening posts, a minefield, and concertina barbed wire. All these defenses ran up into White Ridge to the west and Hill 710 to the east. The listening posts were connected by zigzagging trenches, and there were guide wires from them back through the mine field.

Behind these obstacles were six tank pits protected overhead and on the sides with timbers and sandbags—known as revetments. The pits were three to four meters deep, enabling the tanks to remain in defilade and still have shooting room. Enemy indirect fire weapons lacked the muzzle velocity to take out the armored vehicles, while direct fire projectiles would zing right over the defiladed tanks. The ROK soldiers were upgrading the revetments by adding sand bags and concrete and digging connecting trenches.

81mm mortars and heavy machine guns on the adjoining hills were zeroed on approaches to the Gap, so final protective fires could be shot day or night. Ironically, the so called weak spot had been made into a strong, flexible, and useful area—the U.N. Forces' only vehicular gateway to the DMZ lying in the Black Tooth Sector.

The tanks could remain under cover or could roll forward to a slightly raised area for more offensive fire. Similarly, they could back out and take various routes, including northward pathways through the trenches and minefield.

They were M46 Pattons—an upgraded version of the M26 Pershing and the main battle tank of the U.N. Forces. It was superior to the dreaded Soviet T-34 of the early fighting and far superior to the Sherman Easy Eight, which Frenchy drove at Fort Knox. Primary armament was a 90mm gun. Also included were two 30-cal. machine guns and one 50-cal. machine gun. Four of these vehicles were regularly kept on the Kangyung Gap with four in reserve. Since the CCF and NK knew they were there, they served as a constant, northward attack threat in addition to their primary defensive role.

Upon arrival at the new position, Baker Battery deuce-and-a-half trucks circled right-to-left, enabling the guns to be unhooked in the correct alignment, with crew hex tents and duffel bags thrown from the trucks near their assigned howitzer. A battery was at its most vulnerable during this set-up stage, so extra ROK troops were on full alert on White Ridge to their front.

Frenchy had come forward by jeep with his new compatriots—Lt. Rentner and Recon Sgt. Mudge. The latter seemed to have a personality fitting his name. He was sullen and rude, as Frenchy expected, but he hadn't expected to see that Mudge was a handsome young soldier who kept himself as neat as possible, indeed, extra neat, and drove the jeep with care. Frenchy wondered about the guy: he seemed bitter—Mudge, Grudge, or Sludge—time would tell.

Frenchy found Soddy by their tent, which Soddy had already erected near Baker FDC. He stored the duffel after putting some gear in his rucksack, including the Police Special—no need to hide it any more, though he remembered the Mayor admonishing him not to look like Wyatt Earp. The Supply Sergeant had given him a second bandage packet for his web belt, where he crammed extra 38-caliber bullets. He then jogged over to the mess truck where they had been promised a hot meal. It was a good one—Salisbury steak, green beans, and mashed potatoes.

Frenchy and Soddy shook hands outside their tent. Some twenty yards away, they could hear Sgt. Ken Balsh, the Chief of Firing Battery, laying the guns on azimuth four hundred—north-northeast. Balsh shouted readings to each section leader who shouted back the same commands. Instead of using "nine," artillerymen used "niner" in order to avoid confusion with sound-alike "five."

Balsh's last instruction was to put aiming posts out to the left at deflection two . . . eight hundred. A crewman would then trot out from each howitzer and stick red and white poles in the ground, as specified by the gun chief. Frenchy returned to his jeep and found they had been joined by the Exec's jeep with Lt. Al Marcin in the passenger seat next to his driver, Cpl. Minsky, while, nearby, Lt.

Otto Rentner stood by his jeep. As Frenchy saluted both officers, Otto explained, "Lt. Marcin and Cpl. Minsky will come forward with us to get a look at the target area and help us move our gear and get settled in. We're waiting for our driver . . . ah, here comes Mudge now." Turning to Lt. Marcin in the lead jeep, he shouted, "All set, Sir."

They drove south, then east past Able Battery, then north up the Kangyung Road about three miles in all, to a turn-off about three hundred yards short of the elaborate block of revetments and Patton Tanks at the Kangyung Gap. Black Tooth could be clearly seen, which meant, of course, their vulnerable little FO party could be clearly seen from Black Tooth. They scooted off to the east side of the road along a poorly defined trail and halted in a sheltering ditch.

The Exec shouted, "Hurry; hurry!"

He waved at a group of six Yobos—Korean Service Corps Laborers—who obediently came trotting down the hill to unload the Jeep trailers. A Korean soldier was with them, their colleague on the OP—Sgt. Lee-Mo. Boxes of grenades, other ammunition, two radios, C-rations, water, and other supplies were tied to the Laborers' A-frames.

"We're exposed here! Bug-ass uphill," the Exec shouted.

As if in response, they heard the whistle of rounds followed immediately by loud explosions behind them.

"Those are 122mm howitzer rounds; this is big trouble; they'll drop two hundred and be on us! Head up and right!"

Hill 710—their destination—now separated them from sight of any North Korean observer on Black Tooth, but they were located, and the enemy observer could infer where they were headed. The next four rounds landed to Frenchy's left—the closest no more than thirty yards away—deafening whams, followed by the sensation of a strong wind. He felt himself lifted up, thrown sideways, and tossed hard on his right side amid loose boulders—leaving him feeling like he had been tripped up while skating all out and had slid into the boards head first. Dazed and deafened for a few seconds, he knelt on hands and knees, then arose, grabbed his Garand, and was up and running like a scared jackrabbit.

"Back left!" The Exec shouted. They ran back toward and above where the four rounds had landed. Good move: the howitzers shifted east where they had been. They had zigged when the guns had zagged. *Al Marcin knew what the hell he was doing.* That was the last salvo.

Frenchy looked back . . . the trailing yobo was down! He dropped his pack and rifle and ran back. Two other Korean workers, first hesitating, followed after him. They took off the poor fellow's A-frame and dragged him uphill; others ran back for the A-frame. The Korean soldier, Lee-Mo, was on his AN/PRC-6 calling ROK 2nd Battalion. The Koreans hovered over the stricken man. Amid the jabber Frenchy caught the word, "Medic."

Then, there were pitiful little screams and wailing from the laborers, and repeatedly, *chugun, chugun,* meaning "dead, dead."

Lt. Marcin turned to the Korean workers and muttered the well-known Japanese words of sorrow or regret, "*Gomen nasai, gomen nasai!*"

The fallen man was their leader and must have taken the full blast of a 122mm shell. Marcin turned to Minsky, "Get the jeeps out'a there; they may probe for them next. Take the FO Jeep to that last sheltered spot west of the MSR before we turned out of the hillcover; then come back and do the same with our jeep. Wait there for me; I'll be there probably before dark; stay on guard; but don't shoot me! You know today's password?"

"Jelly Roll, Sir."

"Roger, you got it; now run and good luck!"

The yobos, Marcin, Rentner, Frenchy, Mudge, and Lee-Mo all struggled up the hill. Frenchy felt dizzy, tired, and asked himself, *What's the matter with you; you should be the strongest one of the bunch; get your ass in gear!*

Lee-Mo guided them through concertina wire, past a surprising slit trench, into a shoulder-deep trench, which angled sharply into their hoochy. The yobos, now five in number, dropped their loads and prepared to hurry back to their fallen comrade. First, however, each came forward, bowed, and shook Frenchy's hand. They repeatedly said,

"*Domo arigato gozaimasu, domo arigato gozaimasu; kamsa, kamsa.*"

He knew they were thanking him; all GIs picked up the Japanese phrase, *arigato*, but at first he didn't know why they picked him for this courtesy; then he realized it was because he alone had returned to the impact area—in retrospect, perhaps foolishly—to aid the fallen man.

Lee-Mo confirmed that the laborers had thanked Frenchy first in Japanese, then in Korean; Lee-Mo then stood proudly by, showing how he had cleaned up the cave and dug it deeper into the back slope of the hill. It looked like an ungainly dormer window, facing south with sandbagged sides and a heavily timbered roof overlaid with many layers of sandbags and dirt.

Lee seemed to have a place for everything; he had dug little shelves into the walls and larger recesses for sleeping. There were cots made of wooden poles and woven scraps of telephone wire—always found in abundance along the MLR. Lt. Marcin, having probably spent months with the infantry on OPs, cared little for their luxuries and had passed on up the walking trench to the east of the hoochy and on to the business office—a hilltop bunker.

There was a slit opening in the bunker's front, about eight inches high and ten feet long—called an "embrasure." The outer side was covered with chicken wire to repel grenades. The roof timbers were sufficiently high to allow a soldier to stand once he ducked and entered, and, once inside, they could sit on a hand-carved bench, complete with the writing, Kilroy was here.

The bunker's crowning object was a   twenty-power BC scope—more powerful than the Zeiss 7 x 50 binoculars and more stable because it set on a tripod—an FO's dream, designed for use by the Battalion Commander. With the advent of the Stalemate, BC scopes should have been issued to artillery battalions by the dozen; but this was not the case; they had to be begged, stolen, or scrounged.

In spite of all the day's activities, it was only 1530. Lt. Marcin checked the valley below with the scope and turned it over to Lt. Rentner. Frenchy thoughtlessly hit his head entering and still seemed a little rocky after his fall. He felt banged-up all over but managed to help Mudge set up and test the SCR-619. Through the battalion switchboard, Frenchy then rang up Baker Battery on the phone. His left side hurt like hell, as it now appeared to be the center of his many aches—surprising since he had landed on his right side.

Otto Rentner took the phone and said "Fox Oboe Baker, fire mission, over. . . ."

Baker FDC could be heard responding, "Send your mission, over. . . ."

"Azimuth 6400, base point registration, CP seven, a culvert over. . . ."

"Azimuth 6400, base point registration, CP seven, wait . . ."

"On the way, over. . . ."

"On the way, wait . . ."

They could hear a low rumble, followed by a screeching sound as the rounds passed overhead and slightly left. All looked at the remains of a culvert to their direct front. Two puffs were visible beyond and to the right of the target, followed in a second or two by loud whams! Otto turned to the others,

"Definitely long, correct?" Everyone agreed. All FOs knew horror stories of sensing off-line shots for range and being wrong. For example, if you think it's over and it's really short, you will drop, get the rounds in line short, then add half of what you dropped to get a bracket, then maybe add again, and in desperation add again, and perhaps never hit the target. Otto called, "Left four zero, drop two hundred, over. . . ."

"Left four zero, drop two hundred, wait . . ."

Again, booms and a screech.

"On the way, over. . . ."

Again, Otto replied, "On the way, wait . . ."

Two puffs on line short and whams. Otto said,

"Add one hundred, over. . . ."

And so it went. FDC repeated his command, the guns fired, he got two rounds long and said "drop five zero." If there had been bad guys out there, he would have said, "fire for effect," but this shoot was to register the howitzers. Additional rounds were fired and Otto gave sensings after each, until he had shorts and longs and was generally right on. Then he said, "cease fire, end of mission."

The FO and FDC now had one target down pat, known as the base point. Through the combined efforts of the FDC and FO teams, the howitzers were now in synch with the target area. It was now possible to give base point shifts to hit other targets. Word would be sent to other FOs that the culvert was to be the registered base point. It had been selected by Lt. Marcin because it was in the center of the DMZ and could be seen from all OPs. Because of changes in weather or perhaps changes in ammunition lots, the base point would be registered regularly, sometimes every day.

Chapter Thirty-four
The Fragment

The whole base point registration took about ten minutes. Otto turned to Frenchy to have him call Able Battery but instead muttered, "What the hell!"

Then they all stared at Frenchy, whose left hand was covered with blood.

"You're hit!"

Frenchy was as surprised as the rest. He mumbled, "Not bad," but Marcin unhooked Frenchy's web belt, took his bandage from its belt pouch, and directed Frenchy to pull down his fatigue trousers.

Otto ignored this crisis and calmly told Mudge to call Able Battery. Since they were at the dominant OP and the first FO team up and running, it made sense for them to fire base point registrations for all three firing batteries. Meanwhile, Al Marcin tended to the wound.

"Yeh, that round that knocked ya down put a fragment in your left side at hip level. Lucky dog . . . look where it went through your webbing. Don't ever part with this web belt; it literally saved your ass! We've gotta get you back to the battalion medic. No, no, don't protest, Frenchy, you'll be back up here maybe in a day or two, but you've got yourself a Purple-Heart wound from a Soviet 122mm howitzer!"

Good God! First day on the line, and I'm wounded!

They got the bandage in place and secured it by re-clasping the web belt. Although hating to leave, Frenchy finally recognized that he needed help and was impressed by how Marcin had switched from able and aggressive commanding officer to sympathetic helper of an injured soldier. His head spun. Reaction was already setting in.

Lt. Marcin ordered him to stop at the hoochy and take all his gear, and to take, then and there, a big slug of water from his canteen. Over Frenchy's protest, the lieutenant took his rucksack, leaving Frenchy with just his M-1. They jogged down the hill and reached the road in twenty-five minutes. It was still light when they approached the jeeps and Marcin shouted, "Jelly."

A grateful Cpl. Minsky—alert and at his post—answered, "Roll."

Such words were picked as sign and countersign because of Asian problems differentiating and pronouncing Ls and Rs. Minsky was very relieved: the role of a jeep driver left alone with his vehicle in a combat zone was very daunting, since roving infiltrators liked to pounce on solitary vehicles.

Both jeeps shot down the Kangyung Road. Lt. Marcin in the OP jeep had not been to Battalion Headquarters and had to ask the way. He pulled up in a cloud of dust and shouted, "Medic!"

Evidently, the team at the OP had called ahead, for Col. Pods and the medic, Sgt. Gielow, promptly appeared from behind the tent flap. Marcin saluted and gave an account. The colonel put his hand on Frenchy's shoulder as Marcin explained that, although wounded, Frenchy had gone back into the impact area to assist the downed Service Corps Laborer. The colonel added, "My first Black Tooth Sector casualty."

They helped Frenchy, now pale and weak, out of the jeep and guided him toward the tent, but to their surprise and with some show of strength, he reared back and staggered away from the others and from the tent.

"Wait, Sirs; I'm gonna be sick," Frenchy gasped—courteous as always—just before losing the Salisbury steak and trimmings. He was much relieved as they got him to a cot, turned him on his starboard side, and bared the wound. Medic Gielow prodded and made Frenchy flinch. He then turned to the lieutenant colonel and first lieutenant:

"I would guess it's a small fragment, but it's still in there along with clothing bits and other debris—hence out of my league. The nearest MASH, as you know, gentlemen, is located just north of Division Headquarters—manned by a GI surgical team—we can get him there in our ambulance in about thirty minutes or five by chopper."

Marcin turned to the colonel, "Sir, regardless of what we do with Frenchy, let me say that the yobos were extremely upset with the death of their fellow; I'd guess he was the leader. Hence I would suggest a call to the 134th to express regrets."

"Right," the colonel replied. "Then we ask if MASH can send a chopper." He turned and shouted, "Get 134th Headquarters, ask for Col. Young-No, if possible, or the S-3, Major somebody; I can't remember his name . . . Yeh, yeh, Maj. Kim."

Meanwhile, Sgt. Gielow applied iodine and a fresh bandage, then gave Frenchy a penicillin shot and attached a label indicating how wounded and treatment thus far received. Frenchy declined morphine, then asked to send word for Minsky to take his gear back to Pfc. Soddy Mecham—especially the M-1 rifle, now christened with a dent in the walnut stock, as well as the cut-and-bloody web belt with the ammo pouch, Police Special, and holster attached. Lt. Marcin said, "Don't worry, it'll all be waiting for you"—a nice gesture of care and concern by the Exec.

Soon they heard the thup-thup of a descending helicopter. Frenchy thanked Sgt. Gielow, declined assistance, and walked to the copter. Before climbing aboard, he looked back; the colonel and others had reappeared; he saluted and waved. It was 1830.

Some fifteen miles southeast, the helicopter eased down on the MASH unit's landing pad, and lifted off on another mission as soon as Frenchy was clear. Aides ran to him, read his tag, and immediately led him to the Admissions Quonset to the left—about twenty yards left front. One of the aides held his arm and led him at double-time. He was given a bag for his boots and cruddy uniform, directed to put on a gown, robe, and paper slippers, and then he was sent through a partition to the end of a ten-man line in a waiting area. It was army hurry up and wait at its worst.

He later learned that the system was simple enough: there was a substantial building set back in the center that housed Surgery, Central Supply, and other services. To its front was an open area where an attempt was being made to grow grass. To the left and right were Quonset huts: the shorter one on the left for admissions and work-up, the longer one on the right for recovery and the usual hospital ward areas. Areas inside each building were partitioned with canvas drapes. The MASH staff lived in tents behind the unit, along with decent shower and toilet facilities, a mess tent, and happy-hour recreation tent.

In an hour, at 2000 hours, he was fifth seat, nauseated, in pain, scared, and having second thoughts about eschewing the morphine; then the world spun round and all went black, as he keeled over—softly falling to the tent floor. Someone must have hollered; he awoke to see a Korean nurse looking down at him and, with the help of another patient, lifting him back to his bench. She offered him a fruit drink, saying, "*Gomen nasai, soldier-san.*"

He perked up a little and was soon led behind another partition where a corpsman put him on a table and scrubbed him, scrubbed hard, with no compassion—especially in the wound area. His blood pressure and temperature were taken, an IV was started, and he was given plasma. He soon felt much better, probably due to the plasma and to the indications that he was finally being cared for.

At last, two hours after arrival, at 2100 hours, he was wheeled to the Surgery Building in the center. There were bright lights and people in masks. An orderly stood with him, and a masked woman appeared. She listened to the status report:

"Frag left hip, clothing in the wound, probably from his web belt and fatigues—undoubtedly filthy, considerable blood loss, no fever, low BP now stabilized, some nausea, fainted in the waiting area, pint-a-plasma, blood type O, not much pain at first, but now increased pain level."

The woman spoke in a firm, reassuring voice: "Hello, soldier. You heard the report; you agree with all that?"

Frenchy tried to sound cool, "Yes, ma'am; I guess so."

"Well I'm Capt. Snuffles, a surgical nurse. There's no guessing about the fact that you stopped a shell fragment today; I'll take it out and clean up the wound. I will probably insert what we call a 'Penrose Drain.' It's a flat, rubber tube, a half-inch wide and as long as necessary. If there is no infection, your medic can take it out in two or three days, and may add some stitches. If you develop an infection—evidenced by fever, pain, increased drainage, you come back here."

She stood looking at him, putting a hand on his forehead, then she went on, "Don't worry; this is very routine. That's why you had to wait; we triage the wounded and tackle the more critical ones first. We know it's hard to wait, but you're important to us—very important. Never forget that! You're in the Surgery Unit; I've done about five hundred of these procedures; they call me 'Snuff-frags.' You connected up with a real expert—none better! Now we're going to sedate you, just calm you down a little."

They put a hypo into his IV tube. Frenchy started to recite, *"Eternal Father strong to save . . ."* but then he drifted. He was vaguely aware they were hustling around him; then oblivion. They took him to a recovery hut at 2145 hours—completing the longest and most unforgettable day of his life. He slept.

He awoke the next morning with a powerful urge to urinate. He'd been transferred to a bed: all the IV gear gone, a new bandage in place. He shouted, "Gotta pee," drawing attention and help to the latrine in the back of the tent. Seeing him on the move, a new nurse checked his vital signs and gave him another shot. *Am I still under the influence or is she damn attractive?*

She said, "You are surviving, my man; Capt. Snuff-frags found your piece of steel about two inches deep—just missing the pelvic bone. More important, she's quite sure she got out all the stuff that went in with it. You could have lived for years with the metal, but all that other junk would cause infection and delay your recovery. She inserted a Penrose Drain; you probably won't notice it. Today is Tuesday, the 24th; if all goes well, you can leave here tomorrow afternoon. Your medic can take the drain out next Friday or Saturday. Try to stay in your company area—no extra duty, heavy lifting, that sort of thing. Sit around and be content to be the sick boy."

She put her hands on his shoulders and leaned over, her head just a foot from his—*a warm, sort of a motherly sensation. No, it wasn't exactly a motherly sensation.* The nurse was dressed in standard GI fatigues—probably men's size small—with a soft cap mounting a single silver bar, no makeup, blond hair in a careless bun with strands fallen out of place, maybe twenty-five years old, attractive with zero glitz. Still, you wouldn't say she was unkempt . . . in fact, *she has appropriate dress and bearing and looks damn perky.*

"This envelope we hung around your neck encloses the fragment as a keepsake, together with a report in duplicate on what we did and care instructions. Keep one copy—don't lose it! Give the other to your CO for your 201 file; you're entitled to a medal—a purple heart with a golden cameo of George Washington. It's your

CO's duty to follow up on this, but just in case, you'll have a copy, and this unit'll have a copy. Ya want a sponge bath?"

"Hell, yes." He didn't exactly know what a sponge bath was, but *it'll keep her here, and who wouldn't want the touch'a this pretty young woman?*

She then scrubbed him from bow to stern; and, when she approached certain points amidships, he first wondered if he would be aroused; then he wondered if she was wondering if he would be aroused; finally he wondered if she gave a damn.

In any case, no matter, whatever they had done to him the night before left him limp as a wet noodle throughout the whole sponge bath process.

It made him think back to when he was a little boy, when Marie would bathe two or three of the children together and when older sister Nancy would sometimes help with the process. Yes, there hadn't been a lot of privacy for the family's only boy in that little North River house.

The nurse seemed to enjoy the work and volunteered, "You have a good body—a pleasure to see and touch."

So maybe she did give a damn! In a rare gregarious moment, he replied, "Well, from what I can see, so do you."

"I guess I asked for that, Arnold. I get compliments and whistles and, off duty or on duty, about a proposition a day."

"How do you handle 'em?"

"Now there's a sparkling retort; I'll classify it as today's proposition. The answer, Arnold, is that I'm married and I'm playing it very cool."

"Well, you read my name on the tag; at least tell me your name."

"I'm 1ˢᵗ Lt. Sylvia O'Connor."

"Who is Silvia? What is she, that all the swains commend her?"

"Well, good for you, Arnold! You know your Shakespeare, and I presume you are one of those swains that commend me!"

While he tried to think of a snappy reply, she looked around and quickly bent down, kissed him on his lips and abruptly left the tent. *Would I ever see her again?*

A Korean orderly directed him to a partition at the other end of the Quonset where he was issued new fatigues and paratrooper suspenders instead of a belt to take pressure from the wounded area. His boots had been brought there; he dressed and ate like a horse. They took his vital signs again.

The other recovery patients in his area—all ROK soldiers—were up and around and jabbering. Most Koreans were reticent with foreigners—after years, indeed, centuries, of being kicked around they figured that no good was likely to come from such involvements. However, there in recovery, they were friendly enough and, with a bow, proffered the Japanese morning greeting, '*Ohayo gozaimasu*,' or the same in Korean '*Annyonghaseyo*,'" which he returned in kind with a smile and an awkward attempt at a bow. He was bored but knew he was stuck there for another day.

And that next day, his vital signs remaining steady, Capt. Snuffles visited him, repeated the basic instructions and said, "Good to go."

A Korean nurse and an orderly stopped at each bed; the Korean patients bowed respectfully so he did the same—again feeling a little awkward. Boxes of bandages and rolls of tape were passed out, and he managed to say, "*Arigato gozaimasu, kamsa.*" The nurse gave him a formal Korean goodbye—"*Annyung hee ga sip si yo.*"

An orderly led him to the MASH headquarters area. A Korean NCO and an army sergeant were loading ambulance trucks; Frenchy was directed to one. By 1800 on Wednesday, 25 June, he was back in Headquarters Battery, where Sgt. Gielow checked the wound and his vital signs.

"That drain needs to work for at least two more days before I release you for duty on the OP. Go back to Baker and cool it; check with me late Friday afternoon. If it looks good and you have no fever or other signs of infection, I'll pull out the drain, maybe add a stitch; let me assure you in advance, it will be unpleasant, and jerking the drain may cause a fever. I see you already have a supply of bandages and tape."

A jeep took him to Baker Battery where Soddy gave him a hug, then showed him their foxhole. "While you were screwin' off, ah had to dig this here thing. We git hit by gook counter-battery fire three ta four times a day, but, absent some direct hit, this here hole is pretty safe. Believe me, when them first rounds come in, we bug-ass for these holes. The old-timers say the enemy likes to be hittin' us at chow time, which seems ta be true. One of them prime movers took a direct hit and a tent went a-flyin', but no casualties so far—'cept you."

Frenchy retrieved his cut and bloody web belt with the ammo pouch, revolver, and holster still attached. With some adjustment to expand the belt's size, he saw that he could sling it around his neck very much like the bandolier of an old-time Mexican soldado.

He found Lt. Marcin in the FDC tent and reported in. He explained that he had been grounded from the OP for at least two more days and that he would like to spend time in FDC and at the guns. The Exec tersely acknowledged his return, readily agreed with his plans, but, at the same time, seemed to be a little distracted as he added, "Hit the sack early, Frenchy, but be alert; hell may be a-popping soon."

Frenchy formed an opinion: *The Exec is tryin' ta not get overly familiar. I hope someday we can have a few beers and talk man-to-man.*

Chapter Thirty-five
They Came Out of the West

About 0300, Frenchy awoke, startled by Soddy's urgent voice: "Foxhole on the double!"

Already fully dressed, they had only to grab their boots, put 'em on unlaced, and run for it. The North Korean counter-battery fire landed mostly to the north and was over in three minutes—sort of a wake-up call. Frenchy recalled that Lt. Marcin had put the battery about two hundred yards behind where the ROK battery had been in order to be clear of their trash and slit trenches so perhaps the enemy only knew about the old location and fired a little short.

Soddy went to FDC; Frenchy, his legs not yet steady, returned to the tent and dozed. Later, at chow, he heard that Capt. Anthony had called an all-alert meeting for 0730 hours.

With few formalities needed at the front, the captain simply stood about twenty yards behind and facing the howitzers, Lt. Marcin and Lt. Blake standing beside him, the men fanned out by the guns facing the three officers.

"Hear this! The North Koreans don't like us here: counter-battery fire's been stiff; we're planning some protective changes down the road with help from the combat engineers. Meantime, there's an urgent problem: Battalion tells us, and no doubt Division G-2 is telling Battalion, that there's an enemy build-up behind and west of Black Tooth—along Black Ridge.

"Now, if there's to be an NK attack in our sector, we figure no one's gonna climb Hill 710 or the other high hills to the east. The Kangyung Gap? Maybe, but that's becoming a virtual Maginot Line, with a mine field, armor on line and in reserve, revetments now being reinforced with concrete, and mortars registered from east and west. I'd like to see 'em try it.

"So where is the danger? I'm looking at it—direct front. Those low hills behind you men, called White Ridge, are guarded by 2nd Battalion of the ROK 134th Infantry. If we're attacked, expect it from direct front. ROK Easy and Fox Companies are on line with George Company in reserve and bivouacked just back of Hill 710. We've three FOs up there on White Ridge, and we've our own Otto Rentner on 710. You all know we've registered twenty check-points, today adding some high angle screens just in front of the ROK outposts to our north."

Capt. Anthony raised his arm and shook his fist for emphasis: "There's more—two Quad-50s from ROK How Company will be placed like bookends for our six howitzers. We've already added listening posts and improved our machine-gun emplacements. Service Battery is sending extra willy peter and illumination rounds.

"Everyone, listen up! Do your duty today, but cool it; remember, the enemy comes alive at night; so be ready! Now, Exec, give us your latest."

Lt. Marcin stepped forward. "Thank you, Sir; that was a great report. Our men at the guns will be ready; I say again, our men at the guns will be ready!"

At that point, M. Sgt. Balsh, Chief of Firing Battery, interrupted with the cry: "Yah, yah, here, here," then taken up by all the cannoneers. Marcin shook his fist, encouraging them, finally waving for silence, then going on, "You've heard Battery Clerk, Cpl. Crabtree, practicing with his bugle. U.N. troops find it practical ta copy the Chinese bugles. Neophyte Crabtree knows one call: *Attention*—just three different notes in a group of four, to be repeated indefinitely. It is a warning call. We think that's what Gunga Din used in the movie to warn the Brits of an ambush. Give us a toot, Crabtree."

The corporal stepped forward and sounded off, playing the same three notes until the lieutenant waved him to stop.

"Now when you hear this, take your night-emergency stations. If there's a question about your assignments, check with your section chiefs soon as we're done here! The battery officers and the Chief of Firing Battery will be checking on you; you must know your assignments. The bugle call's also the signal for listening posts to bug back to the Battery and take up secondary assignments. Those in machine-gun nests are to hold their positions at all costs—I say again, at all costs. Each Section Chief . . . you are further directed to send a man to supply for extra M-1 clips. Good luck; good shooting; God give us strength and bless us one and all!"

Frenchy hadn't received such an assignment since he'd been up Hill 710 or in the MASH facility from arrival on. He knew Jake Anthony and other leaders feared they'd be overrun by greatly superior numbers; artillery units always feared infantry attack. Soddy said, "Don't make waves; jus' stick with Ole Soddy, cuz you really belong up on the Hill."

"I'm with you, Soddy; let's get some more clips. I want lots of clips and a bag to put 'em in; you do the same—snitch all you can get! By the way, you remember Kipling's poem, "Gunga Din?" *Tho' I've belted you an' flayed you, by the livin' God that made you, you're a better man than I am, Gunga Din."*

Later, coming from inside the FDC tent they heard, "Fire Mission!" Soddy ran for the tent; Frenchy followed. They heard Otto's voice giving an azimuth, then an adjustment from Checkpoint Niner, followed by, "Enemy troops in the open; request VT; will adjust."

The enemy had been spotted just east of the Yeppun Kang, and Bicuspid—easternmost of the two little hills. FDC Sgt. Hudson shouted, "Prepare charge five, fuse quick, all guns prepare fuse VT; he'll be close with the first rounds, and they'll probably spook right away!"

Hudson was incredible: just a draftee, he stood six feet three, with the command presence of a captain. In fifteen seconds more, Sergeants Hudson and Oder had computed the elevation and deflection, which were shouted to the guns. About as fast, howitzers 3 and 4 fired fuse quick, and Hudson phoned Otto, "On the way, over."

Otto responded, "On the way, wait."

Frenchy heard distant rumbles, as the rounds landed; soon Otto called, "Add one hundred."

New commands were given to the guns. Pieces 3 and 4 fired again. All howitzers made the corrections; he could see the other pieces preparing fuse VT—the proximity fuse.

"On the way, over."

"On the way, wait . . ."

"Drop five zero, fire for effect."

Hudson had anticipated that command and gave the small correction to lower the tubes, followed closely by, "All guns; fuse VT; fire for effect!" There was a sputtering blast, as all six pieces fired at about half-second intervals, and more VT was prepared. With VT, they tried not to fire simultaneously so the travelling projectiles would not prematurely set off each other along the way.

To Frenchy's surprise, after the usual "on the way" exchanges, Otto said, "Left one zero, repeat range, repeat fire for effect; then give me another left one zero, repeat range, repeat fire for effect."

The guns adjusted and fired, then adjusted and fired.

"Cease fire, end of mission, but put Baker One on; let's talk about it, over."

Capt. Jake Anthony had been standing right there. "Fox Oboe Baker, this is Baker One; wait while I try to plug in Acero One on another line, over."

That was the Col. Pods' call sign. "This is Acero One; I'm with you; let me hear Fox Oboe Baker, over."

The captain was connected to the colonel and the FO on separate lines, but he could hold the phones so Otto could be heard. "Well, Sirs, that was the damnedest fire mission I ever shot; we have just nabbed about 140 gooks in the open mid morning! They must have rounded the west base of Black Tooth, crossed to the west bank of Yeppun Kang and headed for Bicuspid. They were carrying ammo cases and some light machine guns.

"When I first saw them come around Black Tooth, I wondered if this was some sort of sucker play, a feint, to test our diligence. As I'm sure you in FDC realize, they took off for Bicuspid and I anticipated this with the three different fire-for-effect orders—just staying with them, as they ran right into the VT. I never had a better mission—for the enemy, a bloodbath! Please tell the men in FDC and at the guns exactly what happened . . . their rapid response made all the difference. Even old Mudge up here gave a little cheer, over."

Capt. Anthony spoke, "This is Baker One; fabulous shooting, Otto. Now, Acero One, your advice, Sir, over."

"Well, Baker One, are you thinking what I'm thinking? Something big is up if they thought it was worth chancing the lives of 140 men to bring up more ammo, over."

"Roger, over."

"Well, I'm having our air observer take a peek, and then we'll have Skyraiders with some napalm shake 'em up on the north side of Bicuspid, as already planned. Pass all this on to Fox Oboe Baker with my best regards and advice to be ready to catch any gooks bugging out. Acknowledge, over."

"Roger, Acero One this is Baker One, out."

The captain called Otto back to pass on the continued diligence warning. Otto responded, "Roger Baker One, by the way, Capt. Jeung is in the bunker with me and extends *'dai-jobu* and good shooting' to the men of Baker Battery. Out."

Frenchy was very excited, having never been in the battery during a shoot. He figured there would now be a lull as the airborne friends got orders and got going, so he borrowed a jeep for his run back to battalion. Sgt. Gielow was there but dead pooped. There had been two casualties in Charlie Battery, and the medic had been up all night. Nevertheless, he looked at the wound and gave the drain a little tug. There was still a little reddish-yellow stuff seeping out.

"We can take it out tomorrow, Frenchy, keep cooling it."

By day's end, with some two hundred enemy dead on the north side of the little hill and with more dead strung out along the riverbank, the North Koreans learned once again that, by day, the U.N. Forces controlled the sky and were masters of heavy artillery.

Soddy hacked away at his harmonica by the tent that evening, as cannoneers gathered round, and he sang:

> *We're tenting tonight on the old campground,*
> *Give us a song to cheer*

Our weary hearts, a song of home
And friends we love so dear.

Many are the hearts that are weary tonight,
Wishing for the war to cease;
Many are the hearts looking for the right
To see the dawn of peace.

Tenting tonight, tenting tonight,
Tenting on the old campground.

The next day, 26 June, was quiet with the usual counter-battery fire. The medic inspected Frenchy's wound, pulled out the Penrose Drain, added a stitch, and gave him another penicillin shot. The leaders were tense; obviously there were more sightings of enemy troop movements—a lot of troop movements, but Otto saw nothing to report from the bunker on Hill 710. The weather clouded up and rain began—limiting air support.

It finally hit the fan two days later on Saturday, 28 June. Soddy and Frenchy awoke about 0330, alerted first by Crabtree's bugle, followed by small arms and mortar fire, and then, a minute later, howitzer fire. The boys secured their boots, grabbed their M-1s, plus the extra clips, and headed for the relative safety of the foxhole. The sky lit up to the left—to the west—not the north as planned! Great confusion followed as the men remained uncertain: were the instructions of two days ago on or off? Where should they go? No reports came down from either the ROK units or from battalion, forcing the Baker Battery men to stand and wait. They witnessed the old story: a good plan until the first shot was fired.

Then the bugle blew again, and word was passed—the attack was concentrated west of ROK Easy Company at the north–south line between Easy and the unit to its west—part of some other regiment. The enemy had followed centuries-old doctrine by attacking at what was called "a seam," often a tactical weak point between units under different commands.

Enemy in battalion-size force—more than 1,000 men—poured down in a virtual suicide mission, taking heavy losses until they broke through the front lines, and could ooze sideways east and west. Moving west meant hitting Charlie Battery's left flank—no doubt by now it was in extremis, fighting desperately, perhaps already overrun. It was always tough for artillery to defend against infantry on the attack but so much worse if by surprise, at 0400 hours, and with overwhelming numbers! Only disaster could result! Would they soon move on and engulf Baker Battery?

Again the bugle—Capt. Anthony yelled,

"Cannoneers, Section Chiefs, and four crew men . . . stay with each gun! Swing around . . . prepare for direct fire west . . . pile up the willy peter. All other crewmen, follow the Quad-50s to relieve Charlie Battery!"

Afterward, troops were interviewed as to exactly what Jake Anthony said and what then took place that morning. He repeated his orders several times, the intended gist: some men go west to save Charlie and fight as infantry; the other men stay to defend Baker in case Charlie is lost. He had no time to hand pick, no time to point and say, "You three go, you four stay." Anyway, Frenchy wasn't part of a crew; so it was clear, no specific orders needed—his duty was to go, and, as it turned out, he was the first to go!

Each Quad-50 vehicle carried four 50-caliber Browning machine guns, which could be fired one-at-a-time or in unison. The guns were mounted two-over-two on a half-track truck—a very formidable direct-fire unit, originally designed as an antiaircraft weapon but now called the number one demoralizer of enemy infantry. In a single day, one Quad-50 could fire 100,000 rounds. The two Quads assigned to Baker Battery turned on their lights and chugged west.

Frenchy ran after the Quads, bayonet fixed, with five extra clips; looking back, he saw Soddy running behind him in his usual ungainly manner, holding his M-1 and also carrying an extra bag of clips. There seemed to be very few others, although each section chief was required to send three men. There was more confusion or at least pretended confusion: the men were reluctant to leave their howitzers and their crew buddies, and resisted running helter-skelter to another unit and there be forced to fight in the open as infantrymen—the old saw: *an opportunity for somebody else, not me.* And so, for various reasons, Capt. Anthony's order was not promptly and enthusiastically carried out by the Baker cannoneers.

Frenchy found out later that Capt. Anthony was guiding the counterattack from the lead Quad-50. Their sister battery, Charlie, was only about a quarter mile over a rise to the west, then a little south.

Frenchy was the first to arrive on foot, just as the sun rose over the hills behind him, giving him the big tactical advantage of facing away from it, while it blinded the enemy when they turned his way. The panorama revealed chaos: noise, flashes, the booms of the howitzers, the steady blat-blat-blat of the Quad-50s, all against the background of small arms—tremendous noise! The four howitzers farthest away to the west were out of action, already captured by the enemy; the nearest two howitzers had been rotated due west and were firing white phosphorous shells at point-blank range into the other four and beyond them as well. The bulk of the soldiers he saw before him were North Koreans—easy to spot in the early dawn by their brown uniforms, not the olive drab of U.N. Forces, and by their cloth caps and gym shoes, not the U.N. steel pots and leather boots. There were hundreds, some running toward him, some milling about, probably uncertain of what to do next. The dominant impressions were the terrible noise, flashes, smoke, cordite smell—chaos!

He saw he need go no farther . . . he knelt in a clump of rocks and killed a North Korean with every shot! Eight and a new clip, then another; *I can't miss; I will not miss; how can I? It's like the fifty-yard range at the foot of Agony Hill!*

Soddy knelt to his left. Eight more rounds, and eight brown shirts fell. Neither Soddy nor Frenchy saw the four enemies with burp guns approaching from the left. Soddy struggled to get a clip in place while the two concentrated straight ahead to the west at the central melee and the Quads, which seemed to be firing at more distant targets. To protect the half-track vehicles, Frenchy selected targets close to the Quads.

Then he heard burp guns to his left. Dirt and rock chips flew up in his face; he heard a peculiar "thup" right next to him; it had to be Soddy getting hit—a sound he'd never forget! Another clip gone—he was on his last. He looked to the left. Soddy had fallen sideways toward him, allowing him to grab his friend's M-1, stand up, and, from the hip, blast away, killing the first burp gun guy and two of the three running close behind. But the last soldier was upon him with his gun raised like a hatchet, lurching forward and impaling himself on the thrust of Frenchy's bayonet. It was a struggle to draw back and extract the Garand, which was imbedded in the soldier's chest up to its front sight! *Control your madness; this is still a thinking-man's job; get on with it!*

He found Soddy's bag of extra clips—five more! He fired off a clip with Soddy's M-1, letting his rifle cool. He swung back to the Quads just as one vehicle exploded—probably under a suicidal grenade attack.

Then an unnoticed enemy stood—not more than twenty yards away—for a second, Frenchy held fire. This was a skinny boy, probably Lucey's age, mouth open with buckteeth, squinting into the sun, perhaps sensing that unseen death awaited him from that direction. Frenchy observed this and more in a flash: this was no Marxist, no Maoist—just a confused kid. No more delay: he fired—chest dead center. The kid's body flew backward like a grotesquely yanked puppet, arms raised, burp gun and hat left behind!

Less victims at point blank range now . . . he switched back to his weapon for more distant targets, killed maybe six more—all at a greater distance. Two victims wore service caps and pistols on Sam Browne Belts—officers! The North Koreans were scattering back to the west or lying dead. He kept picking them off, now at ranges of two hundred or three hundred yards, instinctively aiming a little higher to adjust for range; then he tried a shot at about seven hundred yards—way past the Garand's so-called effective range, but the soldier fell! He glanced to his right: ROK soldiers were streaming past him, on the run, *must be from ROK George Company—the 1ˢᵗ Battalion reserve.* He couldn't shoot through them, even if he had the ammo, so he crouched on his knees, exhausted. Frenchy knew when he heard that "thup" sound right next to him that dear Soddy took one in the head. His best friend had been killed instantly.

Chapter Thirty-six
New Plans

At full sunrise, they found him on top of Soddy with his arms locked so firmly to his friend's body that a puzzled ROK soldier had trouble separating them, called for help, and a sergeant from Baker Battery intervened.

"Okay, Frenchy, it's all right; the battle's over. Soddy's gone . . . come on boy . . . come on."

Frenchy looked up, then again hugged his friend's remains. They left him alone for a full five minutes; then Frenchy slowly arose and inquired, "What do we do with him?"

First Sgt. Hinkley had come up. "We got a mess on our hands, Frenchy. ROK Easy Company's probably wiped out: thirty-eight dead so far from Charlie, five from Baker, and ten from ROK George Company. Then there're twice that in wounded now evacuated, with ambulances coming from the 143rd and from Division. Other teams will come from Division ta take out the dead; ya know we've special units for that work."

He went on, talking as much to himself as to Frenchy. "The North Koreans lost maybe four hundred before they broke through ROK Easy Company; then they lost six hundred more. That's a batch ta handle. We released a prisoner with instructions that we will not fire on a recovery party in the DMZ for the rest of the day so they can remove their dead. How many did you hit?"

"More than sixty; I guess more than seventy."

The first sergeant, mouth agape, hands on hips, stood there. It was an incredible, impromptu statement and an incredible number—almost an unbelievable number! He pondered, *Frenchy is in deep mourning, thinking of his dead buddy . . . he would not lie . . . he hadn't time to dream up some wild story. Besides, everyone knows he's a hell-of-a-shot.* The sergeant's whole attitude changed from confused leader at battle's end to soldier with a new mission.

"Where'd you get the ammo?"

"Soddy and I each had five extra clips. I took his clips plus his fully loaded Garand. I knelt so far forward I couldn't miss—about fifty yards. I never missed . . . couldn't miss . . . kept shootin' . . . couldn't miss. I must have shot over ninety rounds, so I guess I got a lot more than sixty. I got one guy running away at about seven hundred yards—my best shot. Count those with 30-caliber slugs, not the 50s from the Brownings. They're mostly all mine; I got two officers by the burned Quad-50; then, just as I was out of ammunition, the G Company ROKs ran by and I had to stop anyway."

Frenchy looked down at the body at his feet, "Oh yah, I bayoneted this one."

Hinkley turned and pointed his finger at the other sergeant and in his command voice said, "Now, listen up! This is an important order and you must act at once, before the battlefield is more screwed up by medics and looters. Do what he suggested: make an inventory. Figure a way to mark each dead body so you account for them all, but be careful to count each body only once. The Quad-50s will make a hole at least the size of a fist, or a grapefruit, the Garand—smaller. Look at these bodies right here—three killed by Frenchy's 30-caliber bullets, the fourth a cleaner slice. One way to mark 'em is to cross one leg over the other. There's going to be an investigation here . . . this is Sergeant York stuff! Do the best you can, using your whole section to help. Again, check the four burp-gunners right here—the closest probably got Soddy. Get to those gook officers soon 'fore they're looted. This is god-damned important, sergeant; I'll get some more help for you; I'm counting on you; the colonel's counting on you! Eventually, some damn officer will take your sworn statement and Frenchy's and mine as well."

Hinkley slung his carbine and knelt with Frenchy. They took everything from Soddy's pockets. The sergeant took one of his dog tags. He counted twelve empty clips, each had held eight rounds, meaning—*just like Frenchy said, as many as ninety-six shots had been fired from this spot plus the bloody shiv!* Frenchy left-slung Soddy's red-stained M-1 after they had closed his eyes and covered the torn face with an empty ammo sack. Hinkley tugged at Frenchy's arm, pulling him away.

"Come with me Frenchy . . . hold your head high . . . stop the damned weeping or you'll have me doin' it!"

During the walk back, a rifle on each shoulder, he was in a daze. He seemed to float over the ragged ground. Hinkley made him stop and very deliberately unsnapped Frenchy's canteen and made him drink while the sergeant did the same. As soldiers ran by they patted him on the back. Word was already spreading.

At Baker, they were shooting a fire mission—ironical: all in a day's work. Hinkley steered him to Headquarters tent. Col. Podolsky was there with Lt. Marcin and also Maj. Middleton Willis, the Battalion Operations Officer, all very solemn. Capt. Anthony had been killed when the first Quad-50 exploded. The senior officers were working out the details: Marcin was named acting Battery Commander, Lt. Blake, the Recon Officer, replacing him as Executive Officer.

The Charlie Battery Commander was seriously wounded; Frenchy's friend Lt. Oliver Riggs had taken over. He heard later that Sgt. Brownell was also wounded. Sgt. Hinkley wanted to tell the officers in private about Frenchy's incredible shooting spree, so he told Frenchy to get something to eat—at least some coffee—then come right back. Frenchy meekly obeyed, simply walking away from his superiors, without comment—no courteous response.

As he ambled, body shaking, Frenchy thought, *Poor Capt. Anthony; he had it all planned out, except they attacked from the west instead of the north . . . Anthony is a hero—my martyred leader. Oh, God, what hell this is? I'm so sad, so screwed up, so sad. I'm not sorry about shooting those men . . . it was us or them . . . but I'm so sad.*

Things hit home. *I provided for Soddy to come with me when I met with Gen. Webber at Camp Drake, so I'm indirectly responsible. I altered Soddy's destiny.* Then he tried to shrug off such notions: with that kind of thinking, the world changed every time a big shot took any step.

In his confusion, a strange thought struck him: he remembered Alice Perrers' question, "What if the thing on the other end is a human head, not a paper target?" *I sure put that question to rest, but it's all so sad!* He remembered Bernie Weinman saying, "When do two enemies meet with empty rifles and fixed bayonets?"

As directed, he returned to the Headquarters tent. Lt. Marcin was there, head-in-hands, with the bugler, Cpl. Crabtree standing by. The colonel and the major had left.

"Christ, Frenchy, I never wanted the CO job. I'm just a college boy Rot-C officer doing my job, waiting to get out. Now the Colonel is giving me a battlefield promotion to captain, and there was nothing I could do but thank him for his confidence."

"Sir, I heard your inspirational talk, saw how you performed on Hill 710—how you dropped everything to save me. You're a fine officer. Without your zigzag yell, we wouldn't be here."

Marcin raised his hand in protest: "Enough about me and my self-pity. The colonel went back to Battalion; on his orders, Maj.

Willis and Sgt. Hinkley went to the remains of Charlie Battery. Do you know why?"

"No, Sir."

"To check on your bizarre shoot-out story, which, by the way, I don't doubt at all. Maj. Willis has been named to make an investigation. Field-grade officers are taught how to do this sort of work. Your deposition will be taken right away."

"It's not important, Sir."

"Well, I respect you for saying that, but you're very wrong; it'll prove to be mighty important. From where I sit, do you realize that in the last two days my FO team of Rentner and Desprez separately killed about three hundred enemies? And you did it a stab and one shot at a time! In your situation, they've already found a cannoneer from Baker who was hunkered down behind you and witnessed you blasting away—the whole thing! Incidentally, he's a Native American named Lance Hoosky; you should look him up. They'll get his deposition plus a body count and send you to Divarty for some sort of award. Not bad, Sergeant."

"Sergeant?"

"Yes; it's going to be Capt. Marcin and Sgt. Desprez whether we like it or not!"

"God, I'd like to go back to Fort Knox and kick some ass!" *I shouldn't have said that! What a dumb joke . . . I'm all screwed up!*

But the thoughtless remark broke the tension. Crabtree joined in, shaking Frenchy's hand and saying, "You can start by kicking me!"

Frenchy waved at him, "You're an unlikely target; of course, I was joking, but I did have in mind a certain mess hall corporal—name long forgotten."

That afternoon, Lt. Col. Podolsky and his staff met with Col. Young-No to make some basic decisions: first, remove Charlie Battery from the line, since it was over half gone, indeed, four of its six guns had been destroyed or badly damaged. Then, move

Baker forward and westward so that caves for all personnel could be built into the hillside in front of the guns and, at the same time, revetments could be built behind the guns for headquarters, FDC, and mess facilities. Division's combat engineers would be needed for such major projects.

In addition to the North Korean breakthrough and the subsequent Charlie Battery melee—which was now being called the Charlie Battery Shootout—there had been too much counter-battery danger where they were now positioned. The 62nd Field and the ROK Regiment had initially made bad battery and ROK company position choices. It had been ill advised to put all the U.S. artillery on the west side and all the ROK infantry on the east side of the MSR, all counter to Gen. Van Fleet's plan to more fully integrate the U.N. Forces.

Charlie would be reconstituted on the site of ROK George Company, George coming forward to replace shot-up Easy Company. How Company—the ROK Heavy Weapons Company—would strengthen George and Fox. Finally, and as soon as possible, Easy would be reconstituted with soldiers from George and Fox, and all three companies would be assigned fresh replacements. In that complex way, all three companies would have an equal blend of veteran and new troops.

Coupling all these needs with the increased rigidity of the stalemate positions, Col. Pods and the Divarty staff concluded that the time, effort, and expense of the fortified construction was necessary. Able Battery would also move forward and have caves and revetments constructed.

All this would take weeks to complete, with the guns moving after the new locations were in place. Any awards ceremony would also be weeks off. The medics had no time for his wound, now almost closed, so Frenchy and Marcin agreed that the new sergeant should get cleaned up and go back up the hill.

Chapter Thirty-seven
FO Frenchy

Frenchy packed Soddy's duffel. Considering the contents mostly useless stuff to be boxed and shipped home to a grief-stricken family and perhaps pilfered along the way, he helped himself to some personal items. He was surprised to find a picture of a young girl whom his friend had never mentioned. *She looks kinda pretty, but a little toothy like Soddy. Maybe his sister, but I wanna think Ole Soddy had a girl and had some fulfillment with her. I was blessed to have Amanda, if only for a few weeks— so important—tres excité.*

Not sure what to do and feeling so moody, he just sat there for an hour, doing nothing but staring at the duffel contents, finally stuffing the picture in his duffel. *Maybe someday I can go to Soddy-Daisy and tell 'em what happened. What would I say?*

Somebody's darling, somebody's pride,
Who'll tell his mother how the boy died?

His mother wouldn't want to hear that Soddy's weapon and extra clips let me kill dozens more enemies—much less that I used it to bayonet a charging soldier. Boy, I'll have

314

to get ahold of myself before I try that pilgrimage! Then he remembered:

> *Farewell, mother, you may never*
> *Press me to your breast again,*
> *But, oh, you'll not forget me mother,*
> *If I'm numbered with the slain.*

He wondered if Soddy's mother had heard him sing "Just Before the Battle Mother," then thought, *Of course she has, along with* "Dying tonight, dying tonight, dying on the old campground" *and* "Somebody's Darling." He rose, shook his body like a wet dog as if he could shed his busted feelings, then took Soddy's stained M-1 and field gear to the Supply Sergeant and was solemnly given a supply of buck-sergeant chevrons and more M-1 ammo. The supply man honored the morose new Sgt. Desprez with silent respect. On his way back and forth, men lined up to shake his hand.

Rich had gotten word and came down to see Frenchy. They sat silently together to share their grief. Frenchy began to cry softly. For a while, Rich held him in his arms. They sat out the usual counter-battery fire, talking in the foxhole. Funny how soldiers got used to routine and unavoidable danger: a few weeks ago, the incoming fire would have had their full attention; now they just hunkered down and spoke over the noise, both realizing, *What the hell—if an enemy round lands in this hole, we'll never know it. The odds are maybe one-in-a-hundred—acceptable for a routine day of combat life, but if a soldier is under these conditions for, say, a year . . . odds catch up!*

By 2 July, the wound had closed, and Frenchy perked up when his first mail from the States arrived. There were letters from the whole family. Everyone was fine. Norma had gone to Fort Bragg to see Joe, apparently playing it cool and normal. Marie sent cookies, Pierre a shoulder holster—a big improvement. He could now wear the cut-and-stained web belt, but he kept the suspenders, planning to hook on a Ridgway-style hand grenade.

Amanda wrote—from Paris! Sofia and Jean sent their *amour*; she would be looking for that *gallant homme*; her music school would start soon, closing *avec amour*. He thought, *It's kind of a nice, polite letter but perhaps just a little cool.*

Then the big surprise: the letter from Anne Robards.

> *Dear Arnold,*
> *How sweet of you to write, how unexpected, but how welcome.*
> *I no sooner turned you over to Amanda last winter than I thought*
> *What a fool I was to let you go. You are always in my thoughts,*
> *in my heart. Am I a fool or is there hope for us?*
> *Fondly, Anne*

He dropped everything and wrote back. Yes, there was hope, but they must face the problems. They both now realized—through the letters—that there was affection between them, but they had no one-on-one time together. That must wait. He just had two close calls, probably more to come, plus another year in Korea. He wanted her to write often but always level with him. She had no rival, but he had no right to expect any "I'll wait for you" promises. He closed by asking her to read Longfellow's "The Courtship of Miles Standish."

He didn't want to frighten Marie, but, what the hell! He wrote that he was now a sergeant and that he was "an observer." Marie wouldn't catch on, but Pierre would understand full well, knowing the dubious life expectancy of an FO. Pierre could explain things to the family, as he thought best.

He got out Lt. Mason's calling card, and wrote him, explaining that there was talk of a ceremony back at some higher headquarters. Of course, he signed *Sgt.* ***Desprez***—a chance to show off a bit and then see what happens.

There was now a new and much safer route up to the OP on Hill 710. With no need for firecrackers, on Friday, 4 July, he loaded the jeep and trailer with supplies and drove back through Battalion Headquarters, then straight across Kangyung Road at a point two-and-a-half miles south of his former, dangerous route, the new approach being beyond the sight of the enemy on Black Tooth. The ROK combat engineers had bulldozed this new entry leading to their First Battalion. This area had been spared impact of artillery and aerial bombardment. The rolling hills were green with pines, and what Frenchy took to be maples and oaks. He found himself thinking *It really is a pretty country; I wish I knew what these wild flowers are.*

He saw that he was approaching some unit and stopped at a guard post.

"*Annyong.*"

"Good morning to you, sergeant.

Of course, the ROKs had no serious security problem when they saw a uniformed Caucasian—it had to be an American or another U.N. ally. He asked for Able Company, as he was instructed by Lt. Rentner. The guard directed him to the next guard post, and so on, until he reached Able Headquarters at the south foot of Hill 710. He asked for Sergeant Lee-Mo.

"*Ohayo gozaimasu*, new Sergeant Frenchy-san. How you feel this day? You better now from last time I know, *hai*, yes?"

"Oh yes, *hai, hai*," Frenchy replied when he was sure Lee-Mo finished his little half-English, half-Japanese greeting. They shook hands. In all the time he had been in Korea, he had seldom spoken with a ROK soldier.

"Captain-san now drink tea. Come."

Frenchy knew that *san* was a Japanese term of respect stuck on the end of a name, even a first name, so he was Frenchy-san. He also knew that *hai* meant yes, *ohayo* meant good morning, and *gozaimasu* was sort of a polite expression, like "please, pardon me for speaking." All Koreans knew Japanese, since it had been the language of business, commerce, and government during the long and hated colonial period.

He followed Lee-Mo into a large hillside bunker. "Capt. Jeung, here famous new Sergeant Frenchy-san to say hello."

Frenchy saluted. The captain bade him sit and have tea, as a servant bowed and hastened to serve tea and a cookie. The two Koreans jabbered for a moment. Both used the words *Paek song-jang* several times, followed by an almost childish giggle, a giggle he found common with those people.

"You are welcome to Able Company as an FO, sergeant. We like your Lt. Rentner very much. I see the fire missions last week. Very successful, *dai jobu!*"

"Yes, Sir. I was in FDC and heard the report."

"But you, sergeant, also have great work. We know of your wound and how you kill one hundred enemy!"

Sergeant Lee-Mo said, *"Paek songjang, Paek songjang!"*

Frenchy held out his hand to protest, but then backed off. *What the hell difference did it make if they thought I killed paek songjang—one hundred enemy!*

Capt. Jeung stood and dismissed them, as he said, "Eat here, then to hill. Good shooting!"

The tough part of the Korean mess was the lingering odor of *gimchi*—the all-purpose concoction of fermented cabbage the natives used daily in salads and soups. Frenchy only knew he didn't like the smell, not really knowing anything at all about Korean food and little more about Asian food, in general, having been exposed only to American-style Chinese food and Japanese suki-yaki, as served on the Ginza in Tokyo. Lee-Mo solved the problem: with a quick instruction to the cook, Frenchy was given fried eggs and toast plus a drink made with Korean red ginseng—said to be beneficial after all the troubles Frenchy recently faced. As Lee-Mo said, "ginseng keep Frenchy-san's yin and yang in balance."

Frenchy thought, *Damn, how I'd like to study those ancient mystic teachings like Confucianism, Taoism, the I Ching. The South Korean flag depicts four basic trigrams plus the yin-yang circle—all fascinating!* He tasted the ginseng—*tastes kind of blah.* He looked at the Korean, "So this drink is supposed to rev up my sex drive? That's not what we need on this mountainside."

"No sweat, Frenchy-san; ginseng no make Lee-Mo *sekkusu hancho.*"

So, the ginseng root would not make him a "sex boss" either. *What the hell, another famous Asian food and a new experience for me.*

Then they were off up the hill, this time on a flight of stairs with several switchbacks, newly made from stone, sandbags, and logs. Alongside, a cable-and-pulley trolley system hauled supplies to troops on the hilltop. He was instructed where to leave the jeep and trailer and told his supplies would be sent aloft. And so, ten days after his injury, Frenchy returned to the OP.

Otto gave him a hug, then patted the new sergeant chevrons to indicate his approval; even Mudge smiled and shook his hand. They looked none the worse for their time in the bunker and the hoochy. Since at least one member of the FO crew stayed in the bunker at all times, they were glad to see Frenchy and Lee-Mo back on line and ready to spell them off.

Old-time observers from the days of fighting up and down the peninsula in 1950 and 1951 would scratch their heads if they saw the static arrangement of a back slope hoochy and hilltop bunker. The whole south-facing side and the ridge line were pocked with caves and bunkers—a shanty town. The north-facing side of the hill mass sloped sharply from the rise of Hill 710 at the Kangyung Gap easterly for the next five miles. In the DMZ below lay mines and concertina barbed wire, with listening posts set at 250-yard intervals, connected to the hilltop with walkie-talkies. Down there and along the two main lines, much of the greenery was gone, since there was hardly a spot that hadn't been hit with some destructive force—artillery, mortars, bombs, napalm. Still, evergreens and scrub oak were fighting back together with those marvelous wild flowers. To the north were rows of mountains, the more distant the lighter gray color as they faded into mist—all looking so deceptively peaceful. Yet ROK and enemy patrols were out there in the DMZ every night in a life-and-death struggle. Machine guns and mortars were placed on the line in a manner to provide crossfire and forward firing lanes, the mortars covering gullies not reachable by the direct-fire weapons. This was a stale-mate situation for sure.

Backing up all this was the air support and the artillery—King of Battle. Still, as Dave Davis had so well explained, higher headquarters were thinking up actions and counteractions—like those patrols—for the men on the line, and the enemy command was doing the same. Troops on the line were expendable.

The first evening back, Frenchy was forced to explain his role in the Charlie Battery Shootout and the deaths of Soddy and Capt. Anthony.

Lee-Mo muttered *"Paek songjang!"* Frenchy had enough of that. "No, no, Lee-Mo, that's not the number. Look, we had twelve clips—that's ninety-six rounds. You can't get to one hundred out of that. Cut the bullcrap!"

Otto held out his hands and closed the subject, "Okay, Okay, you two, cut your quibbling; so you only killed sixty or seventy of our enemies; let it go at that."

The next week, Otto let Frenchy shoot all the routine fire mis-sions. These included registering additional checkpoints and one mission at NK soldiers, laying barbed wire. They were pretty sure there were artillery pieces and mortars behind Black Ridge, so they fired interdictory fire there at irregular intervals.

The 750 binoculars had a horizontal line imprinted on the optics with vertical reticles at five-mil intervals. The rule was: *one mil subtends one yard at 1,000 yards*. Thus, if the binoculars indicated that the round landed twenty mils left of the target and the range was 2,000 yards, the correct command to get on line would be "right four–zero, repeat range." The BC scope had a similar but more complicated grid.

Otto taught Frenchy to judge deflection by extending his hand, palm out, and counting how many fingers left or right the round landed. One finger was worth, maybe, forty mils. The distance factor—normally a guess for the observer—was pretty easy in their static condition: the slope of Black Tooth was some three miles away, and the base point and numerous checkpoints were figured either by the survey teams or by accurate guesses.

One day, when Frenchy and Mudge were alone in the bunker, Mudge described some of the wild flowers, including spirea, viburnums, holy, and hydrangeas. They conversed back and forth pleasantly enough until Mudge suddenly changed the subject: "How could you?"

"How could I what?"

"Run down into the impact area after that dead Korean service worker!"

Frenchy paused, not really knowing himself. "Well, first I guess we should remember that we didn't know he was dead."

"True, but there was a damn good chance another salvo would land in or overlap that same spot. You had just been hit and yet you risked your life on a dangerous and probably futile venture."

Frenchy pondered his reply. "I hear ya . . . I hear ya, but none of that rational thinking went through my head. I jus' saw he was down and ran to him—no way heroic. There was a difference between us: you up here for months, compared to my first day on the line. I should'a said to myself, 'think twice, baby, don't rush into anything.' Tell me, are you annoyed or pissed off at what I did?"

"No, no. It was a brave thing. If I'm lying on the hillside, I want you to come get me."

"Well, Mudge, does it make a difference to ya' that he was a civilian Korean, what some people unfortunately call a gook?"

"I'm forced to say, yes—a difference. You think about it for, let's say, five seconds, and then, if you see Col. Podolsky down there, you say to yourself, 'He's important, worth the risk of my life to save him.' Off you go, figuring he's worth a thousand native workmen. Heck, thousand's not a high enough number, but you see my point."

"I see and I get your point. Thanks. Maybe it's like playing hockey—sometimes sheer instinct or being just plain mad—plain mad—takes over, and you suddenly get involved in something you just gotta do, like seeing a rival wingman coming toward me, so I just gotta check him into the boards."

"I know, Frenchy, I know; you've done two brave things this week; I'm jus' saying, count ta five before ya go; to paraphrase the adage about pilots,

There are old soldiers and bold soldiers,
But there are no old, bold soldiers."

"Well, now you're into my milieu, Mudge—poetry and history. You know, I was raised in Minnesota, which has been a sort of New Scandinavia. In the schools they teach about the great King of Sweden, Charles XII—the conquering hero and for a while the most powerful man in Europe. After fighting Peter the Great and others year after year, always successfully, never wounded, he took a peep out of a bunker and was killed by a single Norwegian bullet."

"Fate is weird," Mudge replied. "Contrary to what I said about old soldiers, remember Chesty Puller—the most decorated marine? He fought in World War I, then some banana wars, then World War II, then Korea. He led the 1st Marine Regiment at Inchon. What happened ta him? Nothing. I guess he was the perfect old, bold soldier, but I'm saying, don't try it!"

"Tell me about yourself, Mudge; I can tell you're not typical and you're certainly not a happy camper."

The story unfolded.

"I was a school teacher, teaching and at the same time working on a masters degree. My friends were joining the National Guard, and I thought, why not? It gave us some extra pay, we avoided the draft, and we made important friends in the State—good political contacts, especially for someone like me, someone on the public payroll. Our artillery unit was particularly prestigious, tracing its history back ta the Mexican border war and using the fighting words, *Fuego de Acero*. The field artillery reputation in the Guard, I might modestly say, called for a higher IQ and meant riding in a truck, not slogging along on twenty-mile marches. No sooner was I committed than along came the North Korean invasion, and the next year the Guard was called up, including this unit—the 62nd Field.

"The low point for me should'a been the winter of 1951–1952; the cold and the fighting were awful, but not the worst of it; for me, no not nearly the worst of it. The worst was that my wife wrote, simply saying she had found someone else and wanted a divorce, even sending consent papers—all done up by some divorce lawyer who said he would handle both sides.

"That was in February. Strange how you can endure cold, pain, danger, incompetent leaders, stuff like that, but that letter simply shattered me, leaving me in a daze for weeks on end, shunned by comrades, transferred to a different unit, as they frequently do with misfits. I jus' crawled into a shell, a cuckold, blaming everything on the National Guard, the Korean War and some real-life Jody who had done me in. Me—Mudge—who had always succeeded at everything he tackled, was now Mudge the cuckold!"

Mudge gritted his teeth as he spoke. Frenchy recalled the infamous Jody cadence when they headed for Agony Hill back at Fort Knox:

> *You had a good home but you left. . . .*
> *Your gal was there when you left. . . .*

Jody was there when you left. . . .
You're right!

"Mudge, I think the Guard, the War, and that Jody fellow are incidental. What happened is you made an unlucky choice for a wife. What did you do with the papers?"

"I signed 'em. Why make trouble. Neither of us had an estate worth fighting over, and no kids."

"That's what I probably would have done. Have you talked to anyone?

"Just a few. I had to say something when people are shouting, 'What the hell's the matter with ya!' But mostly just to you and Otto. He's such a good man, like an uncle to me, but sometimes I let him down. The story about how I stick to the bunker because I'm a short-timer is sort of a cover we use so people won't expect a lot out of me. Actually, I didn't give a damn about the danger. Like I said, at first I felt like I'd been violated—a Dear John from my perfect partner! I thought about the other guy—now climbing around on her, she holding him—groaning. I wanted to rip his balls off! For a long time, those kinda thoughts made me shudder, made my head spin. Bad thoughts linger."

Frenchy thought, *How different; I was madly in love with Amanda, but that night at Mammoth Cave I told her we must part and she should find some gallant homme. Of course, we'd made no commitment.*

"Mudge, I don't need to tell you that the words are 'move on.' I had to leave a girl behind, and we agreed it was all over. She was a French girl, her folks on sabbaticals. There was no future for her and a North Woods country boy; I even told her to find someone else, someone we called her *gallant homme*. Consider yourself lucky—no kids and you got rid of a lemon. She reeks of lemon; get that through your head, and you didn't even pay the attorney's fees!"

Mudge laughed. He actually laughed. Frenchy saw his perfect teeth.

"You're a handsome guy, I'll bet better looking than this Mr. Jody—a guy who probably happened to be there when she got horny. When you get back stateside, complete your masters on the GI Bill, move away, maybe out of state, have fun chasing the broads. I should turn you over to my last date, except all I know is her name. You see, back in May, I took the train from Grand Forks . . ."

Frenchy proceeded to tell the Pullman car story for the first time. He dwelt on the post-sex discussion the next morning, about taking on strangers in strange places, even making love in a department store dressing room and on a putting green. Mudge laughed again.

"Well, I think you've helped me. Another thing that helped me was Otto's incredible fire mission when he kept throwing that VT and letting those poor bastards run into the moving fire, like the guy in *Li'l Abner*—Joe somebody-or-other, the world's worst jinx who always had a rain cloud over his head. The difference is those guys had a cloud of steel—every drop a killer! Afterwards, in his rehash, Otto said, 'Even Mudge cheered.' I sure did! I'll never forget that fire mission!"

Chapter Thirty-eight
The Window and Long Tom

"There's a nice twist here," Frenchy said. "On this hill, we're snug in our little house; they bring us one hot meal a day, and the position seems impregnable. With all that, we're on the front line. Meanwhile, back in the so called "safety" of the firing battery, they're getting counter-battery fire, and we had a battle royal last week—which is going down in history as the Charlie Battery Shootout.

"Ya know, Otto, as a kid I loved a book called *Animal Heroes*, written back in 1905 by Ernest Thompson Seton. One of the stories, "Badlands Billy," is about a huge wolf that lived on a butte and would descend each night to the surrounding plains where he'd hunt and kill cattle, then scoot back up to safety on the butte. They chased him with packs of dogs and a team of riflemen but never caught him. Well, that's about what both sides are tryin' ta do when they come off the ridges and down to the DMZ . . . course, Billy was much better at it than we humans."

Otto laughed. "Maybe what we need is Billy to smell out the enemy, though I think it takes a mighty fancy nose to detect differences between North Korean and South Korean *gimchi*. As far as life up here, from my standpoint, I'm the boss of an important unit, can have a real effect, can play a real tune in this sector. I must cooperate with Capt. Jeung and his ROK platoon leaders and, of course, Col. Pods, Maj. Willis, new Capt. Marcin, and Lt. Blake at Baker Battery, but it's sure great having your own fiefdom as a lowly second lieutenant. Forward Observer is an important god-damned job. Speaking of fiefdoms, what da ya make of my old World War II boss, Gen. Ike, being nominated for President?"

"Sounds Okay to me; course, I'm not old enough to vote. I know my father is in mourning; he's a big fan of Senator Bob Taft—Mr. Republican."

Otto scratched his head and thought for a moment, knowing that politics always seemed to stretch his brain. "Well, I voted for Truman four years ago, and, to everyone's surprise, he won. I guess people figure Ike can win, whereas they see Taft as real smart but sorta colorless. Both those guys are good men, and I suppose it's probably time for a change, but Lord knows the Rentner family suffered during the depression and thought of Roosevelt as their savior, making the notion of voting for a Republican seem almost a betrayal."

Frenchy's thoughts moved on, as he saw ravens circling over the valley below, soaring, then diving, seeming to be at play. If the war ever ended, and if the area below remained a part of the DMZ, and therefore unoccupied and forbidden territory, then it would become a sanctuary for native plants and wildlife—nurtured by the blood of thousands and an ironical disposition of troubled land between troubled countries.

Each week, the three GIs—Frenchy, Otto, and Mudge—were able to go back, one at a time, to the reserve area and enjoy a shower and clean fatigues. Late afternoon when he returned from his first trip, Frenchy exclaimed, "I'll be darned! Those guys have a window near the top of Black Tooth. It's been cleverly disguised, but they opened something like a venetian blind just before it got dark tonight. Look, Otto."

"Yah—I see it now; it's like any big regular window. Of course, for them it's a great OP; maybe they could also have a gun or a howitzer in there, maybe a mortar, no not a mortar, definitely a gun port. Hey Le-Mon, take a look."

Lee-Mo peeked, then said, "Oh yes Otto-san. Have seen that hole . . . must go from north side."

Hearing Lee-Mo say he knew about the window, Otto rolled his eyes, "Damn it . . . we can do something about it!"

"For 105, take super lucky hit."

"Yah, yah, but it's very possible with a 90mm tank gun like we've got in the gap or maybe a Long Tom from Divarty. Thinking extra big, I guess there's no chance with naval guns, since Black Tooth's south face is in defilade to anything in the Sea of Japan. Let's think of heavy artillery at Division level. Frenchy, call Battalion, ask for the S-3, Maj. Willis; his call sign would be 'Acero 3.'"

He got right through to the major, who in a friendly breach of security and protocol said, "This sounds like Frenchy, over."

With a quick acknowledgement, the phone was handed to Otto who explained the situation.

"Yes, Sir; yes Sir, over. . . . Oh, the sooner the better; they don't know we're on to them, over. . . . Yes, sir, we'll await your call, out."

Otto turned to the others. "The major is calling Divarty. He sounds sold on the idea of using 155mm guns, called 'Long Toms.' Perhaps they aren't as accurate as the 90mm tank guns, but, good God, what a load they could deliver—four times the size of a tank projectile!"

Otto held out his fists and opened his fingers to indicate a big explosion. "The rest of you get some chow while I await the call-back."

Frenchy returned with some cocoa and biscuits—his favorite C-Ration snacks. "Otto, I don't think I've even seen a Long Tom."

"Well, let's advance your artillery training. As you know, a gun has higher muzzle velocity and delivers a smaller round than a howitzer. Guns have longer ranges with greater penetration force.

Practically speaking, they're more accurate for deflection than a howitzer and less accurate for range. Against a cliff-side fortress, range is almost immaterial and our howitzers might just give away that we spotted them. The ROK tanks would maybe suffice, but before resorting to them, why not keep it in the artillery family and try the Long Toms?"

Otto went on, "To get the gun's additional muzzle velocity, a bigger firing tube is needed. All artillery pieces consist of a tube and a carriage, sometimes called the chassis. From World War II days, our howitzers have come in four sizes: 105mm, 155mm, eight-inch, and 240mm. As you know, the 105 can be self-propelled or can be drawn by a deuce-and-a-half truck; the bigger guns need to be self-propelled on a tank chassis or need a tractor prime mover. The clever ordnance people over the past three wars came up with the concept of putting smaller bore guns on the carriages of larger bore howitzers. Thus, the 155mm gun, which we call the 'Long Tom,' is on the same carriage as the eight-inch howitzer, and the eight-inch gun is on the same carriage as the 240 howitzer. You get it?"

Frenchy nodded.

"There are bigger guns, but remember the mission of the field artillery: move, shoot, and communicate."

"Yes, Sir; bigger guns have to be in a fort or on a ship."

"Yes, or perhaps on a railroad. Now, 155mm is just over six inches, and the Long Tom armor-piercing projectile weighs almost one hundred pounds. As I recall, the weapon takes a crew of fourteen with four pieces in a battery."

Otto smiled and paused as he put his hands on his hips, and continued, "Here's the big news: Maj. Willis called back. A self-propelled Long Tom and crew will soon leave their present position about five miles south and five miles west of here. They will set it up down on the west side of the Kangyung Road. It needs to be just barely hidden by the mask of White Ridge to our west. You see, with the Gun's level trajectory, it couldn't lob a round over our Hill 710 without having it also go over Black Tooth.

"Our battalion recon crew is bringing survey over to a tentative gun location, so we will have coordinates of the Long Tom site—as you know, that's an easy job. The big gun's battery commander may change the location . . . that'll be his call. We've the coordinates to the base of Black Tooth. I assume personnel from our 62nd Battalion FDC will be assigned to the new Long Tom gun site and will work with their FDC people to aim the gun. To achieve complete surprise, there can be no base-point registration."

Frenchy pondered, gestured with his arm, then spoke: "The Long Tom fires at least fifteen miles; I assume they're bringing it over here so it has a direct, south-to-north shot at a south-facing target, rather than an angle shot from long range out of the southwest."

"Yes, the straight-in, enfilade shot has a better chance of raising all hell inside that mountain. Then, too, the accuracy of the Long Tom may be exaggerated; you could put one right in the hole and think you have it all figured out and then have the next one miss."

Frenchy snapped his fingers. "Sir, if there is a tunnel going right through Black Tooth, and if we do cause havoc in there, fire or smoke may come out the north side revealing the hidden entrance. How about deploying a Corsair or AD Skyraider on a bombing run?"

"Great idea! If we could just mark that spot, we could keep picking on it! I'll call Willis again. Now, you hit the sack; Mudge'll relieve me soon. Tomorrow may be a big day!"

Soon after sunrise the next day, 12 July, Col. Kim appeared, striding toward their bunker along the trench line and shouting orders. As senior occupant, Otto stepped forward and saluted on behalf of himself and his men.

"You start the big flap, Lieutenant. Now is coming your Divarty Commander, Brig. Gen. Hines, so also comes my Taicho-san, Col.

Young-No of the Regiment. Each has his aide, maybe more. We bring coffee, other drinks, extra binocs. How many fit in bunker? You think maybe six, seven?"

"Sir, I imagine you have an expression like we have—*too many cooks spoil the soup*. There will be a captain from the Long Tom Battery—essential for adjusting its fire. I'll be there with the general, and since the general is coming, Col. Podolsky will surely come. . . ."

Col. Kim interrupted. Four ROK soldiers had arrived with tent poles, canvas, and shovels. Rapid instructions in Korean followed. Otto and Frenchy wondered what the hell was happening.

"*Gomen nasai* to interrupt, but we make a tent for your fancy toilet. Generals and bird colonels deserve private *hwajangshil*."

Frenchy squelched a laugh. They did, indeed, have a famous crapper; even back in his wounded condition, he had noticed it when he first came up the hill. Usually, the soldier had to squat with a leg on each side of a narrow trench; however, in their plush facility, atop a wooden box, someone had set a real toilet seat! Was it stolen from a barracks building, troop ship, or sent from home? So far, it had survived all the enemyfire the nearby hilltop OP had attracted. It could be nasty when a slit trench took a direct hit! As a final touch, someone had written on the side of the box the famous words, *Kilroy was here*.

The hoochy was also equipped with urinals, made from cut-up brass shell casings sunk, one on top of another, at an angle into the hillside trench with the lowest casing running out the southern downslope.

For the Koreans, as well as the Chinese and Japanese, a toilet seat was an alien device—unwanted. They had always used a simple hole in the floor. The story goes that Chairman Mao saw his first toilet seat when he visited Moscow. He was annoyed and tried to have it removed from his dacha. Both east and west could argue from a hygienic standpoint as to which system was best. Frenchy already knew the oriental system was smellier.

Otto gritted his teeth. *Here I am—still in charge—and trying to pull off an attack developed by Frenchy and me; meanwhile the colonel is fussing around like he's planning a Sunday picnic.*

"So, colonel, with respect, if I may continue, I also want Sgt. Desprez in the bunker. If you come, that's more than enough. If we draw fire, the others can duck in the trench line or go to the hoochy. Of course, this is just my notion . . . I guess the general can decide to kick us all out; however, I believe that the men in the bunker should be the artillerymen responsible for the mission."

Col. Kim thanked Otto, apparently not objecting to, or perhaps not fully understanding the manifest put-down Otto had just handed him. The colonel then inspected the fancy latrine and the path just below the ridgeline leading back east to the stairway.

To Otto's relief, Col. Pods arrived next. The colonel could now be responsible for entertaining and ushering about the more senior officers. With the colonel was the big gun commander, Capt. "Doc" Blanchard, who was introduced to Otto and Frenchy. Everyone realized that any army officer who chanced to be named Blanchard would be stuck with the nickname "Doc," after the famous West Point fullback and Heisman Trophy winner.

Doc got right to the point, "Okay, Otto and Frenchy, I see Black Tooth; now show me the window."

Otto nodded at Frenchy, who explained, "It's in the center of the BC scope circle, Sir."

"I don't see much, but that's not surprising. I hear some of the ROKs knew it was there and you guys just found it."

Otto answered with a wan grimace. "Yes, Captain; they just didn't bother to tell us."

"Well, it'll be fun to play dentist and try to poke a hole in the tooth, get some of the poison out, and maybe show our ROK friends some fine oral surgery! Now show me the applicable surveyed checkpoint."

Wondering if the captain had rehearsed the tooth metaphor while climbing up the hill, Frenchy turned the scope down to focus on some rubble in the middle of the mountain base. He then said, "The biggest of those rocks has some lichen or moss shading it green. We call it 'CP BT Base.'"

"Got it! Almost directly below and maybe five mils right of target."

"Exactly, Sir."

"Okay, do you have your FDC line and my FDC line hooked together at gun site?"

"Yes, Sir. By the way, I was asked to tell you that the brass have arrived."

"Let them wait one minute more—call our combined FDC lines; ask for my Exec, Tom Thumb three."

Frenchy made contact and handed the phone to Capt. Blanchard.

"Hi Tom, the expected VIPs are here. And to speed the process, I'll give you some raw data to analyze so you can set the Gun for the first round. Are you ready? Over."

"Roger, Tom Thumb One, what'a ya got? Over."

"Calculate the angle of site from your position to CP BT Base. The window is left about thirty yards and at least three hundred yards above the checkpoint, over."

"Roger; the target is thirty left and three hundred higher, over."

"Roger; that's conservative; we don't want to lob the first one over the mountain into some noncombatants; call when you have it figured. Out."

Col. Pods had already backed out of the bunker and stood with Brig. Gen. Hines and Col. Young-No. The two senior officers were an odd couple. Hines was little and pudgy with a warm smile on his jowly face; the Korean was tall and handsome with high cheekbones and strong Mongolian features. Frenchy looked at him and smiled—*No question where Native Americans came from.*

Young-No sported an elegant gray mustache, and was crowned by a gold-braided, French Army style kepi, rather than the steel pot worn by everyone else—*Not as protective, but super stylish. I guess a ROK bird colonel can wear whatever he chooses.*

Behind the two leaders were Lt. Col. Kim, Capt. Jeung, and Hines's aide, 1st Lt. Mike Wonder. Lt. Col. Podolsky introduced the OP crew to the general one at a time. They came forward, saluted, and shook hands like a receiving line. Frenchy held back at first, but was waved along. Meanwhile, the general held onto Otto's arm.

"We met when you passed through Divarty Headquarters. I thought at the time, 'there's a maverick if I ever saw one.' You were in the European Theater, right?"

"3rd Army, Sir, August '44 till the end."

"Your unit?"

"949th Artillery, Sir. Usually with the 90th Division, later the 87th."

"Oh, you saw plenty of it—Metz, the Bulge, crossing the Saar—and now, at your advanced age, they've kicked you upstairs and made a gentleman out of you!"

He took Frenchy's arm and turned to Col. Pods. "And, Roger, there's a story to tell about this trooper as well?"

"Yes, General, a month ago I welcomed Frenchy, here. He was a buck private with great credentials, an honor graduate of Gordon Murch's Armored Leadership School. Remember Col. Murch at the Bowling Alley and, after the breakout, supporting Task Force Dolvin? We fitted Frenchy into this FO crew; he got shot up his first day on the hill. About a week later, he and the late Jake Anthony led the Charlie Battery Shootout, as I'm sure you know. What could I do but make him a sergeant?"

The general's aide, Lt. Wonder, raised his eyebrows, showing a new interest in the handsome young sergeant. Capt. Doc Blanchard, who had gone back to the bunker phone, now reemerged.

"With respect, gentlemen, FDC called . . . Long Tom is ready to fire a ranging round."

The general responded and solved the problem of bunker status. "Have at it. We will have only Capt. Blanchard and the regular FO team in the bunker. The rest of us will stand back here on the leeward slope and look over the hilltop only as the rounds land. There will be one or two minutes between rounds. I'm told the first round is predicted to land low on the mountain to assure we can see it."

Frenchy thought, *What a sharp guy; I'll bet he's seen plenty in his day!*

Blanchard, Rentner, Mudge, and Desprez were now in the bunker. At a nod from Blanchard, Frenchy said, "Tom Thumb Three, this is Fox Oboe Baker and also Tom Thumb One, fire when ready, will adjust, over."

After a very short pause, they heard, "On the way, over."

Frenchy's "On the way, wait," was drowned by a loud boom and a loud whistling sound to the left of the OP.

The round hit the hill, low and left of the window.

Blanchard turned to Frenchy and calmly said, "Right four zero; you are a good 150 yards low."

Frenchy repeated the instructions, which were again repeated by FDC. The adjustment technique was different in this situation. The range did not need to be extended, since the south face of Black Tooth was practically straight up and down—a precipitous cliff. The correction was, therefore, one of altitude. On the Long Tom, they chose to correct the angle of site, much like a golfer would need to swing no harder but would use a longer club when hitting up hill. At the gun, all this meant was the need to adjust the reading on the angle of site dial, rather than change the elevation dial. The gun would then be cranked up until the dial bubble was again level. It could have been done using elevation, since both systems would raise the tube. As instructed, they also turned the gun slightly to the right.

Col. Pods shouted, "I want everyone down in the trenches. They now know what we're up to and are likely to figure we are adjusting from this OP! I don't want to lose full-birds and one-stars on my watch!"

There were a few chuckles at this slightly audacious statement. The general said, "Oh, I don't know; think of the news report: 'Front-line-Hines shot on OP!'" Frenchy thought, *He's served his time on plenty of OPs!*

Back at the gun, while FDC calculated the new angle of site and deflection, the gun crew—using four men—placed the projectile on a tray behind the breech. Then other crewmen employed a ramrod to push the one-hundred-pound projectile into the breech. Separate powder bags were inserted, again with the ramrod. The breech, known as an Asbury breech, consisted of a block with a number of stepped-down, interrupted screws with matching parts in the breech. In the block's center was a disc-shaped obturator, which expanded when the gun was fired, stopping the gas from escaping rearward until the propellant train was complete.

The crew had to stay well clear and cover their ears, all this was to be done in just over a minute, then, "On the way, over."

The second round was heard; Frenchy responded, "On the way, wait . . ."

They saw the round hit. Otto shouted, "Just left and above it! Their camouflage fell away!" More calmly, Blanchard looked at Frenchy and said, "Down one click, right same. Tell 'em we're there!"

Doc Blanchard wanted the Gun moved right and down as little as the dials would permit.

"On the way, over."

"On the way, wait . . ."

They looked at a black square on a gray mountain. They heard a wham . . . a pause: then the hole exploded in a yellow ball. Another series of explosions and the fireball grew. They had hit a North Korean magazine! The South Korean Allies along the hill's western slope joined in a mighty cheer, while the colonels and the general shook hands. Blanchard, Rentner, Mudge, and Desprez hugged and jumped up and down like they had just scored the winning touchdown. Blanchard sensibly grabbed the telephone: "Cease fire; end of mission; complete success. Close station, march order . . . I'll catch up. How able—out."

The Long Tom was exposed to counter-battery fire; the sooner they bugged, the better.

As another series of congratulations began, Col. Pods insisted that they retire to the comparative safety of the hoochy area. Col. Kim produced bottles of champagne, saying, "Courtesy ROK Army."

Feeling obliged to make a little speech, the general said, "Shortly after Victory-Europe Day, Gen. Patton was watching an artillery fire demonstration. It was massive—a big success. Patton turned to the artillery officer and said, 'it would be a privilege to be killed in that barrage!' No one but Patton would say something like that; he was trying to show his approval, but at the same time, he half meant it. I can't go quite that far, but this was no demonstration, being the real thing, this was even better!"

Soon, the general was frowning and asked the three colonels to join him in the bunker. Everyone heard bombing and saw an AD Skyraider pass overhead and waggle its wings. They were later buzzed by their own L-19.

The general's aide, Lt. Wonder, made a special point of tipping canteen champagne cups with Frenchy while the two had a little time to become acquainted. Mike Wonder was from Indiana and had received his commission through the ROTC program at—of all places—Yale University. It might seem strange to some that an Ivy League boy—sans white shoes—would find himself in North Korea in a hilltop hoochy, but in fact, Yale sent many students to the Basic Officers' Course at Fort Sill and thence into firing batteries. Indeed, some Whiffenpoofs elected to make a career as field artillery army officers.

Frenchy told him that, to everyone's amusement, Col. Kim had provided privacy for the toilet and suggested he christen the new feature. He also asked if the aides ever got together and if Wonder knew Lt. Mason, but there didn't seem to be a connection. In parting, his new friend said, "Remember, Frenchy, you can share my BOQ tent when you get to Divarty Headquarters."

Col. Pods lingered after the others had departed.

"Well, men, I'm proud of each and every one of you. Today's mission was a real tour de force. It got the general up here, and, another thing, I'm thankful Maj. Willis called for the Long Tom instead of calling for the Patton Tank guns, thus keeping the successful mission in Divarty hands. A couple of things are up. I want Frenchy to come back to Battalion and ride out to our airstrip. He needs to see the other side of Black Tooth from the L-19, especially now that the pilot will know the tunnel location. You can come tomorrow."

"Yes, Sir."

"I'm sure you are curious about the general's talk with the three colonels. This may surprise you, but the general is interested in using both Cuspid and Bicuspid as sound posts. You guys understand sound and flash?"

Otto spoke up: "Counter-battery techniques deployed by special units. They can triangulate the enemy battery location from observed flashes, as seen from surveyed OPs. The sound part uses the same idea from surveyed microphones in forward areas."

"That's it. We'll help the ROKs set up and maintain microphones on Cuspid and Bicuspid. Gen. Hines says his staff has already established two or three mike locations west of here. Once installed and working, the heavy artillery would respond to missions sent to them from the Sound and Flash Company."

The colonel further explained that the ROK colonels, especially the Bird Col. Young-No, had already advised that he would have no part in trying to man OPs on the two hills, bluntly telling the general that the men wouldn't last one night. Pods concluded,

"I understand their positions; it would be touch-and-go out there. There's almost an understanding that those two hills are not worth fighting over, just spots in the DMZ—there forever and forever unoccupied. That means stealth. Patrols will have to go out there while technicians place the microphones. It has to be done using some subterfuge so the gooks won't think to go looking for microphones. This could mean you guys will be asked to join patrols in the DMZ."

"What else, Sir?"

"At least one happy note, the big Mongolian, Col. Young-No, is very impressed with you guys and is planning some award for all of you. I think it will be his personal commendation for your file—not exactly a campaign ribbon, but unique and different."

"Good timing," said Otto. "Mudge is due out of here this week, Sir. I'm glad he is included. I can only say that he has done well in spite of extreme personal problems and resulting emotional stress. Now that I think of it, Frenchy could take Mudge along and come back from his fly-boy outing with our new radio operator. Frenchy'll then officially move to Recon Sergeant, and Mudge'll be off the hill and on his way."

They all looked at Mudge who responded, "Thanks to all—all who deserved better. Time heals, with help from these great fire missions, some needed kicks in the butt, and good advice from Otto and Frenchy."

Chapter Thirty-nine
Over Enemy Lines

The brass had left, and, though Korea's monsoon season should have ended, heavy rain began. The dreary light was fading when an incoming round hit Hill 710 just below the bunker. In the past, they had endured NK artillery and mortar fire on a fairly regular basis, but just harassing fire—no one totally exposed, except if they happened to be using the fancy slit trench on the rear slope. Now, in came heavy artillery—two or three rounds a minute. At that rate, the bombardment would eventually destroy the bunker, the connecting trenches, and the hoochy.

"They're really pissed," said Otto, as he hunkered in the bunker corner. "They probably saw the AD Skyraider pass over and waggle its wings. Maybe some commie field marshal is shaking his baton at the North Korean colonel responsible for this sector and saying, 'I want vengeance!' They can see the bunker. To them, the embrasure looks like a little dark slit; they figure every close round will shake us up, and a lucky hit—whammo! Such a hit would be one-in-a-thousand. I remember in training we shot at a fuel barrel—a target for at least six months. Then one day when the smoke cleared—no barrel. At a range of, say, five miles, we had finally landed one in an eighteen-inch circle, a veritable hole-in-one. Well, this embrasure would be even harder to hit, and, if hit, folks in it would never know."

Otto was trying to reassure his young comrades. "The gooks must also know there are trenches and hoochies all along this back slope. We'll get a nice spread of NK 82mm mortar fire, maybe 120s. High angle mortar fire can hit these rear slopes—fire spread along our ridge line for three hundred or four hundred yards east to west, maybe more."

It was decided that Frenchy would take the first watch, then Lee-Mo, then Otto. They wanted to spare Mudge, since it was his last night on the MLR, however Mudge insisted on taking a turn and was given the last watch.

The pounding went on throughout the night. Frenchy saw that the hoochy roof had taken direct hits and was shaken and weakened even though sandbags were piled six rows high over rows of timbers.

Just at dawn, Mudge called a fire mission. The bastards had come down well in front of Bicuspid with a mortar squad. Baker Battery was on them with two adjustments.

Frenchy and Mudge left at 0700 hours. Since Mudge was gone for good, Frenchy helped him carry some accumulated possessions—mostly books. Frenchy looked disappointed, "Hey you're making off with two Spillanes I haven't read."

Mickey Spillane pocket books were about private eye Mike Hammer—ruthless hunter of bad people, especially communists. The books were fast reads, full of sex, mayhem, and one-man justice. Mudge asked, "Which ones you got?"

"Let's see, *My Gun is Quick* and *Vengence is Mine.*"

"Leave 'em both here—good reads if you like plenty of sex and violence!"

They hit the trail and were soon at the jeep, parked at 1st Battalion, 143rd ROK Regiment. They grabbed coffee and cereal.

Frenchy saw Col. Kim who said, "Extra noise up top. NK very mad about Long Tom shoot."

"Yes, Sir. I hope you can send a construction party. The hoochy was hit, and I'm worried about your *hwajangshil.*"

Frenchy was jokingly referring to the tent-covered toilet. Kim laughed, "We send crew soon."

Mudge drove slowly, anxious to talk; Frenchy gave him the Desprez family address so they could keep in touch.

"You know, Frenchy, your first talk with me about my Dear John letter and all those legal papers did more for me than a week with an analyst or a chaplain. I loved your Pullman car story. My course is clear: live a little. I won't even wait until I'm home; if I have a few days at Camp Drake, I'll try to hit every bawdy house in Tokyo."

"Good, Mudge, but remember: play it cool; do it right; take a pro every night."

Mudge joined in on the last line. Frenchy thought: *Although he outdid me as a moper, he turned out to be a really good man. There's good in most people.* Then he had an inward chuckle when he thought about one of Dago's aphorisms: *Anyone who thinks there's good in everyone hasn't met everyone.*

They wheeled up at Headquarters Battalion. Mudge learned he could get a ride to Uijongbu that day. They said their farewells, and Frenchy looked for Rich, learning his friend was off with a survey crew. He left word.

Frenchy asked Sgt. Maj. Flowers for directions to the airstrip. Flowers so advised, but told Frenchy to wait for the colonel who wanted to talk to him. The Battalion Commander soon emerged, saluting even before Frenchy could lift his arm.

"Morning, Frenchy. I hear you're taking a beating on 710."

"Yes, Sir. I fear our impregnable hoochy might cave in. We had close to a thousand rounds last night. They took offense at the Long Tom shoot and probably saw the Skyraider waggling its wings over us. I talked to Col. Kim this morning, and he's sending work crews up to check on the whole hilltop."

"All the more reason to get going with the L-19. With luck, their guns and mortars may still be exposed."

The colonel went on. "By the way, the 62nd is going to receive a Department of the Army citation in connection with the Charlie Battery Shootout. You will be in the ceremony, probably at Divarty Headquarters in two weeks."

Sgt. Maj. Flowers added, "Mudge's replacement is Cpl. Hiram Spachek from Headquarters Battery. He's a Signal Corps-trained communications NCO and will be standing by when you return."

The colonel asked, "Isn't he the fellow who seems to get lost only to show up with a pretty good excuse, like claiming he took a run to Divarty for more wire or batteries?"

"Yes, yes Sir," Flowers replied. "He's a competent young man, so we put up with some nonsense, Sir. His libido is a little stronger than most of ours."

"Certainly mine," Col. Pods said with a chuckle. "Get going now, Frenchy, and check out the back side of Black Tooth."

There was a round of saluting, as Frenchy wondered what his two superiors were talking about: *What's a libido?*

The airstrip lay three miles down Kangyung Road and off to the west. The sergeant major had said, "Follow the Kangyung Road." He arrived fifteen minutes before the planned 1000 hours rendezvous and stood there alone.

Meanwhile, Capt. Jim Forest took off from the airfield at Uijongbu. The day was overcast but clearing—no rain now. He flew due west, just south of the DMZ, then angled northward. On the east side of the peninsula, the DMZ actually ran quite a distance above the 38th Parallel.

Forest had been selected for Army Flight School out of college and basic training. They sent him to Field Artillery Officer Candidate School, Fort Sill, Oklahoma. He endured eighteen weeks of solid, everyday chicken-shit: everything on the double, punishment pushups, two or three people yelling at the same time, little sleep. Those eighteen weeks were followed by four weeks as an upper classman, known as a Red Bird. In that phase, he strutted around Robinson Barracks in a flashy uniform complete with red epaulets and a pith helmet. It was almost a comedown to take his commission after being a Red Bird.

He then went to flight school followed by a stateside training unit. A year later he was sent to Korea—his time now almost up. They had recently given him a new L-19 and sent him to work for the 62nd Field.

Back in 1950, the army needed a light military airplane to replace a collection from World War II. Cessna won the contract with a modification of its civilian Model-170: an all-metal aircraft with a souped-up engine, newly designed spring-steel landing gear, and an extended-vision cabin for the pilot and one observer.

Forest was a good pilot—very helpful and courteous to his observers. After six months in combat, he received a battlefield promotion to Captain—the standard rank for a pilot.

The fly-boys were recognized by other artillery officers as a different breed—not part of the day-to-day team. They didn't get to know the other officers and seemed to quickly forget their mundane artillery training. The next rank was major—a staff rank—out of company grade, into field grade. What could they do? In their company grade careers, all they had done was fly a little airplane. They had limited career opportunities compared to a captain who had served as forward observer, executive officer, and battery commander—a leader ready to jump to Battalion S-3 or the equivalent.

But there was an admitted glamour to it—being a fly-boy, buzzing the DMZ, engaging in extra-dangerous work. Forest's plane had been repeatedly riddled and patched. He had crash-landed twice.

The little Cessnas were called L-19 Bird Dogs. They were reliable, easy to fly, could take off and land in tight places with very low maintenance requirements. With few changes, they could deliver cargo, lay wire, and evacuate wounded. Gen. Ridgway was famous for flying all over the southern end of the Peninsula in a Bird Dog.

The drawbacks: no armor to ward off ground fire and a six-cylinder motor unable to out-maneuver other aircraft.

Ahead, Forest saw Strip C-10—the unpretentious dirt field of the 62nd Field Artillery. The layout consisted of a north–south dirt runway, a windsock, a shed with a lean-to porch, and a soldier standing by a jeep.

He made a beautiful bank, landed, and chugged and gurgled up to the soldier. Most observers were second lieutenants, so he was surprised to see a teenage sergeant. The fellow seemed to be a handsome young man, well built, middle sized, with a long, straight nose and a strong chin. He wore a steel pot, carried binoculars, an M-1 with extra clips, a small revolver in a shoulder holster, and two grenades. The captain thought, *There's got to be a story behind this guy!*

As Forest unlatched his door and unbuckled his seat belt, the soldier trotted forward and saluted.

"Good morning, Sir. I'm Sgt. Desprez reporting as your Observer."

The captain casually returned the salute, as he climbed down. He extended his hand and said, "That's all the military courtesy for the day. When we are flying, I'm Jim, and you are? . . ."

"Frenchy, Sir—I mean, Jim."

"Frenchy, eh? That must be the Charlie Battery Shootout Frenchy?"

"Yes. I'm an FO but was in Baker Battery at the time, recovering from a fragment wound. I'm an expert marksman."

Frenchy's standard reply to such praise was to say he was an expert marksman, as if that explained away his heroics—sort of made killing sixty-five people all in a day's work.

Forest smiled and nodded. "Yah, I guess you are, and with plenty of cojones—that means 'balls.' So what have Pods and Willis dreamed up for today?"

"Well, the Long Tom mission yesterday was sort of my idea, and the colonel wanted me to follow up." Frenchy then started to describe the blasting of the Black Tooth window, but Forest held up his hand, explaining that he was the observer and had seen things then and there. Frenchy added that the North Koreans had responded with a tremendous bombardment of Hill 710, and perhaps their artillery was still exposed.

"Okay, now tell me, Frenchy, have you ever been in an L-19?"

Frenchy couldn't help smiling, as he remembered the crashed L-19 and the Tank Leaders' Reaction Course at Leadership School.

"No, Jim, I have not." Unless asked, he figured he need not add he had never been in *any* airplane, except his ride in the MASH Unit chopper.

"I assume, Frenchy, you want to see the north side of Black Tooth and the east–west valley running west from there—called Black Ridge?"

"Yes, Sir."

Forest nodded again and then continued, "We think those areas fester with caves, allowing them to run their howitzers and mortars in and out, perhaps on camouflaged rails. Divarty Commander, Gen. Hines, is anxious to cut their recent counter-battery successes.

"Anyway, Frenchy, I've had considerable success with first-time air observers, so let's go over some basics. You adjust using the gun-target line, as you must know pretty cold. We have a gyroscope, and the Black Tooth targets are all about due north. We'll fly over Baker of the 62nd so you can get your bearings."

"I'll help you with ground distances by estimating my altitude over the target. If I say, 'three thousand OT,' what does that tell you?"

"You're talking feet, so, dividing by three, that's one thousand yards over target. One mil subtends one yard at one thousand yards; so I'm playing with a simple factor of one times my separation from the target in mils. I can use my binoculars or, more likely, just eyeball it."

"Good answer! Now, when you call a mission, it's my job to get you in position to observe. I do that by listening to Fire Direction Center. When I hear 'On the way,' I estimate the projectile's flight time of, let's say, twenty-five seconds. I then put the Bird Dog in a bank and dip the starboard wing so you are looking right down on the target area. You'll find it's the easiest shooting you've ever done. Just remember, adjust on the gun-target line. Got it?"

"Hope so!"

"Okay, while I rev up the Bird Dog, call and alert Baker Battery. Frequency's set." As Jim taxied to the leeward end of the dirt strip, Frenchy called: "This is Air Fox Oboe Baker, alert call, over."

"This is Baker Sugar Three, reading you and standing by. Good luck, over."

"Roger, Baker Sugar Three, out."

In seconds they were airborne. The little ship's rapid, ungainly rise thrilled Frenchy. In a minute, they were over Baker Battery, where he saw Sgt. Hudson—obviously Baker Sugar Three—waving from just outside the FDC tent. Jim banked so Frenchy could wave back. They rose over the guarding White Hills and flew north across the DMZ, heading for the pass west of Black Tooth.

Wow, unbelievable! Behind the west shoulder of Black Tooth were four howitzers—undoubtedly the chief tormentors of Hill 710. These Soviet-designed, 122mm weapons looked remarkably similar to our 105mm howitzers, though larger, with a bigger shield, a screw-type breech, and the same over-and-under recoil devices. But he spent no time dwelling on sizes and shapes!

"Air Fox Oboe Baker, fire mission, over."

"Send your mission, over."

"From Baker Tear Niner, right four hundred, repeat range, howitzer battery in the open. Request all available fire. Over."

347

Baker Tear Niner meant Black Tooth Checkpoint Nine. The FOs had registered on dozens of checkpoints in and around Black Tooth and its valley.

"From Baker Tear Niner, right four hundred, repeat range, howitzer battery in the open, all available fire; wait. . . ."

Frenchy saw the North Korean cannoneers struggling around the big howitzers. *They wanna bug out . . . must'a spotted us.*

"On the way, over."

"On the way, wait. . . ."

Jim put Bird Dog into the promised bank. It was like sitting in a chair, looking down, and playing chess! As hoped, both rounds were long and just to the right. On high, there was no problem of sensing over-target rounds.

"Left five zero, drop one hundred. They are trying to CSMO; fire for effect now, now, over."

Frenchy had deliberately violated protocol by not splitting a one-hundred-yard bracket. He could see the prime movers backing up as the crews hooked up the trails. He couldn't wait—it was then or never.

FDC repeated, "Left five zero, drop one hundred; fire for effect, wait. . . ."

FDC then called, "105s on the way; 155s to follow in thirty seconds, wait. . . ."

The first barrage was on target with destruction aplenty. The second barrage from the 155 howitzer battalion was long.

Frenchy enthusiastically called, "First barrage, repeat range, repeat fire for effect. Second barrage, split the adjustment; drop fifty and drop one hundred; fire for effect; request all available fire; got 'em by the cojones, over."

"First barrage, repeat range; second barrage, drop fifty and drop one hundred; getting their cojones, wait. . . ."

Jim gained altitude to get out of small-arms range.

"On the way, over."

"On the way, wait. . . ."

Frenchy looked down, as before. He heard rumblings and saw red flashes; but the explosions obscured the target in a blanket of fire, smoke, and debris.

Captain Jim finally spoke, "Have 'em repeat FFE two or three more times; we're bugging out! By his response, I don't think Baker Sugar Three knows what cojones are!"

And so the scene ended. Some NK colonel got too mad and tried for a revenge that did not come off. Frenchy's first day as an air observer was, indeed, memorable.

Jim called Col. Pods, "Acero One, I'd like one more day with your remarkable FO sergeant. As you know we're directing fire tomorrow for the Corsairs. With your permission, Sir, I'll put him up tonight in my BOQ, and we'll be back tomorrow, over."

"This is Acero One. Permission to steal my FO reluctantly granted, out."

Chapter Forty
The Corsairs

They cleared the DMZ. Frenchy reported the entire North Korean firing battery destroyed, probably with a loss of all hands—about one hundred men.

As Capt. Forest turned west, he explained his position.

"Frenchy, that was fine shooting. For both of us it was a great day's work—one of my finest missions. What I can't believe is you never hesitated, never flinched, never asked my advice. Dropping one hundred and going into fire for effect and spreading out the 155 howitzer rounds were both decisive and daring.

"You may not have noticed the flashes of groundfire from the woods at the foot of Black Tooth. We might not have lasted one more banking turn. I'm a short-timer and wanna live to fight another day, soon to leave this land of the morning calm."

"So what's up for us, Jim?"

"Well, tomorrow I'm scheduled to guide a squadron of Corsairs, where I serve as the FAC—Forward Air Controller—for those carrier-based, fighter-bombers. We'll go back to the same area and put down some marker rockets. This afternoon, we'll plan the sortie with the help of the navy land commander who serves as liaison between the Corsairs and the FACs. While my Bird Dog gets fueled and ready to go, my houseboy will wash your uniform and you can have a hot shower, which, incidentally, you need. By cleaning you up, we can later have some beers and a steak dinner at the Officers' Club."

"Sounds great, Jim, but I'm interested in one boondoggle: my uncle gave me a role of twenties to purchase a really good 35mm camera. I priced 'em at Camp Drake and just couldn't bring myself to cough up the money, but now, with my stupendous sergeant's pay, I think I'm ready and want to scout out the Uijongbu PX. Is it far from your neck of the woods?

"No, you can get there, but let's try something else first. We have a warrant officer who runs our ground operations. He's a camera nut. I'll get him to take you and help you pick something. I'll try to find him."

Jim called the airport and explained the camera mission to someone named Gabby, who gave a "roger" to the plan. They flew through a mountain pass just south of Hwaaksan Mountain—4,817 feet—and soon circled over Uijongbu, as Frenchy looked down on the full might of a United States repo-depot. There were rows of Quonset huts, truck parks, rail sidings, and a MASH unit. In addition, there were the tattered remains of Seoul's old satellite city and beautiful hill country to the south.

It was only 1130 hours when the Bird Dog slowly landed. The whole business of flying over no man's land, destroying a howitzer battery, killing about one hundred enemy soldiers, and flying back to Uijongbu had taken little more than an hour.

Frenchy followed Jim Forest to the tiny airport office where he was introduced to a venerable, grey-haired, Chief Warrant Officer, known as Chief Gabby Hartnett—no doubt after the Hall of Fame catcher of the Chicago Cubs.

The office was lined with spectacular pictures of L-19s in all sorts of poses: flying over mountains, parked with pilots along side, and one where the L-19 was upside down, with the pilot alongside standing on his head. Jim described their successful mission, and Gabby gave Frenchy a fatherly pat on the back.

"So you're interested in a 35mm camera with a good lens and adequate shutter speed. I'll be glad to run you to the PX and help you select."

Jim added, "Good, good. First we'll grab a lunch here in the mess; then we'll get this grubby front-line boy cleaned up and in civilian clothes so later on we can get him some beers and dinner. After lunch, we can go to the PX and then meet with navy ground command. Gabby, make a date with Com. Hypes for 1500 or thereabouts. Come on, Frenchy."

After a fast lunch in the local mess hall where Frenchy's soiled combat uniform stood out alongside the starched look of the off-line, supporting soldiers, they walked to Jim's BOQ—part of a series of Quonsets arranged in sets of two joined like the bar of an H by shower, toilet, and lavatory facilities. There were eight rooms in each hut with lieutenants sharing rooms and captains having private rooms. Jim shared his houseboy with several other junior officers. Frenchy was unceremoniously stripped of his soiled uniform and sent to the showers.

He thought, *How pleasant right here, but every day Jim Forest has to go out with the sands of time running—never sure he'll return in that unarmored piece of tin.*

He was loaned a pair of Levi's and a polo shirt with an "Army Flyers" logo. Gabby picked up Jim and Frenchy, and they were first off to the PX.

They saw the same array of Contax, Leica, Nikon, and Canon cameras. Frenchy zeroed in on the less expensive Canons, so Gabby steered him to an F-2, 1/500 and to a separate light meter and helped him buy film and load the Canon—a very simple operation.

Next stop was the Navy Office, manned by Lt. Com. Thomas Hypes who served as liaison between the carrier planes and the little Army L-19s in their role as Forward Air Controllers. Tall, thin, and almost bald, Hypes looked to be in his late thirties. Captain Forest and CWO Hartnett saluted, so Frenchy, although dressed in mufti, joined in. Forest introduced Frenchy and explained the clothing situation.

The Commander began, "So you want to get back to the Black Tooth area. I understand you had a good fire mission today."

"Yes, Sir. It was a great shoot, thanks to this young man. Needing no advice from me, he destroyed a battery of four howitzers and wiped out the crews. As you know, I was also over there last week along with one of your Skyraiders. Today, I formed a definite two-part opinion."

"Let's have it."

"First, as prevails all along the north side of the DMZ, all enemy equipment and soldiers are hidden in caves. We usually fly over and find nothing. Today, probably their fouteenth or fifteenth hour of shooting that 122mm howitzer battery at us, they risked leaving the guns out in daytime—fully exposed on the northwest side of Black Tooth. Frenchy figures it's the same battery that put a fragment in him a couple of weeks ago and killed one of the Korean Service Corps laborers."

Gabby turned to Frenchy and muttered, "Sweet revenge!" Frenchy eyed the older man and, with marked sincerity, smiled and nodded firmly.

Not minding the interruption, the pilot continued, "Second, we figure the no-man's-land valley south of Black Tooth is the remains of an ancient crater floor, sort of like the more famous Punchbowl to the west, where Bloody Ridge and Heartbreak Ridge proved a source of misery to both sides. Now these hills—including U.N. Hill 710 and the enemy's Black Tooth—are the remains of a much higher volcanic peak or peaks.

"The series of ridges held by the enemy, which face south, show outcroppings of volcanic rocks: granites and basalts—all hard igneous and metamorphic structures, looking a lot like Hwaaksan, 25km east of here. They constitute the inner rims of one or more craters and now constitute the enemy's MLR. I'm no expert, but you can see as you fly by that it is hard rock. On the other hand, the land on the north side of these enemy ridgelines may be loose debris with gentler slopes, probably washed down from the ancient days when the volcano's sides were much higher than the remaining low hills.

"So my second conclusion is they cored into the softer northern sides of all these ridges—not into the steep south sides of any of them. I figure the same is true of the next row of ridges behind Black Ridge and behind Black Tooth. A final argument is that these north-side slopes are more in defilade to us, thus requiring high angle howitzer, mortar fire, or air strikes to have any hope of hitting them. This cuts our potential bombing targets in half."

The commander smiled at Forest. "Thanks for the geology lesson, Jim. To sum it up in one sentence, let's bomb the base of the north slopes of the first row of east–west ridges—known as Black Ridge.

"Exactly. I was more long-winded because I thought you would like to know why."

Frenchy squelched a smile at the captain's sarcastic retort of his superior officer, but he sensed the two were good friends and probably drinking buddies. It might be lonely being a navy officer at a rank equivalent to major there at an army post amid younger army men.

Not to be outdone, the Commander replied, "Okay, wise guy; what about using eight Corsairs, maybe three behind Black Tooth and five in the west hills?"

"Sounds good. What do you think, Frenchy?"

Frenchy paused—it was quite a long pause. His three superiors stared at him.

"With respect, captain, I have a different hunch behind Black Tooth. When we destroyed the south-facing window with our Long Tom, there was evidence that behind the window was a storage area. As you know, there was a second explosion when some stored ammo blew. I think a good part of the north side is tunnels and trails zigzagging to the window and not a main cave site.

Regardless of the terrain, I feel that the caves we're lookin' for are on the south side of the hill behind Black Tooth or . . . maybe behind that hill. I further sensed this when we fired at the 122mm battery."

This argument drew another pause, Com. Hypes left the room and returned with aerial photos.

"We have photos of the entire DMZ. Unfortunately, our Black Tooth pictures are none too good, but let's have a look."

Using magnifying lenses on little legs and passing the photos back and forth, they all eyed the valleys behind Black Tooth, Black Ridge, and adjacent areas. Lt. Com. Hypes broke their concentration, exclaiming, "I'll be damned! You two are both on the right track! Check this: first, the hill behind Black Tooth—let's call it 'Sore Tooth.' It's not very high or very long east–west. There's no sign of tracks going into its south side, contrary to Frenchy's suggestion, but go north on the west side of this river . . ."

"Yes, yes, the Yeppun Kang!" Frenchy interjected enthusiastically.

"Yes, my boy. Of course, there are tracks along the river, as there must have been in all probability for hundreds of years when this was farmland, but just behind this little Sore Tooth is what appears to be an intermittent stream. The little stream is a phony—a dirt road meandering to look like a stream. There's a little ridge, then more fake stream just where it abuts our little Sore Tooth. That tangent point, boys, I'll bet ya, is a cave entrance—probably the biggest cave in this sector!"

Gabby said, "Ah-ha, they're trying to convince us of the impossible—that an intermittent stream can flow in both directions from the little ridge, which forms a pass just north of the Sore Tooth hillside."

"Yes, and, as I said, Jim is correct—all caves are on the north side of the east–west chain of hills. Also, Frenchy is very correct—he pegged this Sore Tooth location—one side or the other as a one-cave location. Wow, now for a change of plans!"

The Commander twisted in his swivel chair, stared out the window, waited, turned back, and scribbled some notes—very worked up. He turned to Gabby and Jim. "What other L-19 pilot can we pre-empt for tomorrow?

Gabby spoke up. "Any of 'em, Sir, just call the Officers' Club, and get the most sober. One of your yeomen can pick up the lucky choice and bring 'em here.

Jim phoned the Club, asking for one of the army pilots. "Wiggins? How long you been there?"

After some discussion, Lt. Johnny Wiggins was ordered out the Club door to be driven to the navy office.

"What ya got in mind?" Jim asked the Commander.

"I'm going as observer and taking on our new discovery. It'll be safer with two aircraft, and Frenchy can take the area west of Black Tooth."

"That's bullcrap, Tommy, you have no business doing this. You shot down three Zeros in the Pacific War, were called back in this war, then shot down, severely wounded, grounded, and given this important job. I feel like protesting!"

Frenchy thought, *So the commander's name is Tommy Hypes—a guy with a fabulous record!*

The commander raised and pointed a finger at the captain, "We'll have no more of that kind of talk. I flew L-19 observer missions when they first gave me this job till I was confident I knew the ropes. This will be routine; I figured it out, and I'm seeing it through! We're good friends, but remember: you're an O-3, and I'm an O-4. Regardless of rank, I'm also the linchpin of this combined arms air team. You got that through your head?"

That ended all talk—a calm standoff followed until 1st Lt. Johnny Wiggins arrived. As he was introduced to the short, blond-haired, young officer, Frenchy thought, *Hotshot Charlie from Terry and the Pirates!* The fellow wore a scratched-up leather jacket, emblazoned on the back with a Chinese tiger, and a peaked cap with visor, the cap bent on the sides to fit under his earphones and also soiled—probably deliberately—so it would have a so-called "fifty-mission crush."

Capt. Forest inquired, "You're sure you only had half a Heineken?"

"Yes, Sir . . . just enough to cure a hangover from last night's big tilt."

Frenchy could tell this was all a tease. Flyboys probably drank too much but knew how to handle it on a short-term basis anyhow.

The plans were quickly explained to the newcomer, while the commander made a call in to the *U.S.S. Joshua Tree (CVS 51)*, an *Essex* class, long-hull carrier, cruising to the west in the Yellow Sea off the coast of North Korea.

He followed a routine checklist: the enemy, the mission, the armament, the time and place of rendezvous with the FACs, and the frequencies and call signs. Since the commander made this sort of call every day when there was fair weather, it quickly fell into place. There was no talk about the fact that one observer would be a navy lieutenant commander with eight years of service in two wars, and the other would be an army draftee who had recently been a buck private!

In one surprising result of the planning, Gabby returned to the airstrip and supervised painting the rudder of Forest's L-19 a bright red.

They arrived at the Officers' Club at 1700 hours. It was another unspectacular building—two overlapping Quonsets fronted by a wood-frame structure and, by the entrance, a wrecked T-34 Red Army Tank. Army bases liked to scatter around obsolete weaponry—tanks, guns, even trucks. Jim cornered the club officer—a pudgy captain, who then sped away and returned with the loan of a sport coat to make Frenchy more presentable in the dining room. Civilian clothes were usually made in Hong Kong after being fitted by Korean salesmen right there at the club. The nice camelhair coat probably belonged to some guy who had bought the farm and never claimed his purchase—a sad wartime business risk.

The club officer helped him on with it and said, "Congratulations." Frenchy said, "Thanks," then turned to Jim and asked, "What was that all about?"

"I told 'em you'd just came off the line, and we're having a party in honor of you being recommended for a battlefield commission. I didn't bother to say that I was the recommender and that such promotions are a general's job."

The club was divided by the Quonsets with a bar and pooltables on one side and a dining room on the other. They turned left into the bar. CWO Gabby Hartnett soon joined the varied group of Lt. Com. Thomas Hypes, Capt. Jim Forest, Lt. Johnny Wiggins, and Sgt. Frenchy Desprez.

Some of the usual gang began to approach Jim and Johnny, but they saw something special was going on. The dour navy officer and the young kid in the fancy sport coat indicated a special meeting—not just the usual happy hour.

They had one beer and went to dinner. Jim bought Frenchy a filet mignon—a fine steak, well worth $1.35—so tender it could be ordered extra rare. He learned that the beef came from Japanese Wagyu cattle, nourished with sake, beer, and grain fodder and also massaged and brushed.

To the surprise of all, the club officer produced a bottle of Korbel California champagne in honor of Frenchy's unlikely promotion. Very straight-faced, Jim accepted the gift, directed Frenchy to thank him, and in an aside to Hypes said, "We'll have to try this stunt again!" Hypes smiled and shook his head in feigned disapproval.

They talked mostly about the upcoming mission, but he also learned that Gabby had a Japanese wife back in Japan. When stationed at Drake, he found her at the PX photo counter, the widow of a GI lost in the terrible early days of the War, which gave her a ten thousand dollar nest egg. She spoke adequate English and, as a war bride, waited to join Gabby when he rotated back to America. Many Japanese women proved to be devoted wives who fitted in well when the family returned to the soldier's home. Everyone wished him good fortune. The couple planned to open a photography shop in Fayetteville, North Carolina—near Fort Bragg, to be called "Gabby and Kimiko's Photos."

As they left the club, Frenchy prepared to return the elegant sport coat; instead the club officer waved at him and said, "You keep it. It's a perfect fit. I knew the guy who ordered it, and I think he would have liked you to wear it in good health."

On return to the BOQ, Frenchy found his fatigues cleaned, starched, pressed, and placed on Jim's extra bed. He was soon asleep—ending a memorable day at an early hour and with the next day promising more adventures.

Frenchy knew some facts about the Corsair. It was developed as a carrier-based, fighter-bomber during World War II, combining the beauty of its gull-shaped wings with incredible speed. It was used throughout the Pacific, most notoriously by the Black Sheep Squadron of Marine Maj. Gregory "Pappy" Boyington in the Solomon Islands. Boyington was credited with twenty-eight total kills, twenty-two in Corsairs.

Outmatched in Korea by the jet fighters, the AU-1 Corsair still proved excellent at close-air support. It worked well with Forward Air Controllers, such as the L-19 pilots but could not carry as heavy a bomb load as the AD Skyraider. Back on 4 December 1950, Lt. J.G. Thomas J. Hudner crash-landed his Corsair in an attempt to rescue a comrade shot down near the Chosin Reservoir. The President presented him with the Medal of Honor.

On Monday, 14 July 1952, Frenchy took off with Lt. Johnny Wiggins. They followed the red-tailed Bird Dog of Capt. Jim Forest and Com. Thomas Hypes. Initially, they used two frequencies: four Corsairs and Forest on "Red Tail," the others and Wiggins on "Wiggy." The L-19s had three smoke rockets on each wing and were equipped with all-terrain wheels.

The Corsairs had left the *Joshua Tree* and were soon, in navy jargon, "feet dry"—over land north of Seoul. The eight gull-wing aircraft flew in two formations of four until they met the L-19s just south of Hill 710, where each group connected with its observer.

Wiggins flew dead north and banked sharply left near the west slope of Black Tooth. Heading due west, it descended rapidly to the north slope of the hill line. Frenchy helped guide him: "Good heading, good, good. . . .Mark it just beyond those dark rocks."

The little rocket whistled off and landed in a puff of orange smoke. The lead Corsair called: "Wiggy Observer, this is Wiggy One. We see it. Is it on target, over?"

"Roger, Wiggy one; draw it out from there; will observe, over."

Frenchy wanted the bombs dropped in a line gradually shifting due west along the base of the hills. Wiggins put the L-19 in maximum climb and a right bank so Frenchy could observe; however, with this set-up the Corsairs needed no more guidance . . . they could hardly miss.

The first Corsair came on a forty-degree dive and dropped a 250-pound bomb just where the smoke had been. It banked to starboard, as Frenchy called, "This is Wiggy Observer; right on, Wiggy One, over."

"This is Wiggy One. Thanks, we got it from here. All on Wiggy channel switch to Red Tail. Acknowledge on Red Tail, over."

Then followed a rain of destruction: on separate runs, each Corsair dropping two 250-pound and one 1,000-pound bomb. The orange and black explosions were spread out westerly over a mile to destroy or at least expose cave targets.

Lt. Wiggins climbed higher. They could see flak from anti-aircraft guns. Looking northeast they saw the more concentrated fire of the other four Corsairs. Then there was a terrible sight! Due north and below them, they saw Red Tail spinning out-of-control, the tip of its left wing missing. They feared it would auger in, but it pulled up and glided due south into the DMZ. Frenchy gave a trembling call:

"Red Tails, Red Tails we have a May Day here. Stick around to give comfort, over." *Each Corsair carries six fifty-caliber machine guns. . . . God willing they can keep enemy ground forces at bay at least until dark!*

Wiggins banked right, followed Forest's L-19 down, and watched it bounce twice, spin to the left and tip over. He gave his plane a stiff starboard bank just before Hill 710 and glided back north along the pocked remains of the Kangyung Road in no man's land, coming to rest within fifty yards of Red Tail. Both Frenchy and Wiggins ran toward it.

The Commander was struggling to unbuckle Forest's seat belt and get him out. Frenchy opened the pilot's side and they got Forest out that way. He didn't appear injured—*He's just groggy . . . eyes open but glazed . . . probably hit his head.* Frenchy and Johnny half-guided, half-dragged Forest toward the other L-19; the Commander followed, carrying all maps and written material. Johnny took charge of everything. The Commander got in the observer's seat, and Frenchy and Johnny unceremoniously jammed Forest in on top of him.

Frenchy wondered, *Where the hell do I go?* But Wiggins quickly guided him to the pilot's side and shouted, "After I get in, jam one foot into the bottom of the wing strut; hold on to this handle on the underside of the wing, other hand on the strut . . . but wait, wait, first tell me—where's your damn airstrip?"

"Follow the Kangyung Road; follow the Kangyung Road . . . due south three miles, then right . . . I'll yell when!"

Johnny repeated "Follow the Kangyung Road . . . follow the Kangyung Road." He then taxied north about thirty yards, turned and revved the motor to an incredibly high pitch. The little airplane shook like a dog straining on its leash. The noise from the outside was deafening as they finally lurched forward, bouncing, bouncing—lucky to have the all-terrain tires.

But there was no sweat. Overloaded by three hundred pounds, the powerful little aircraft took off in some twenty seconds and inside one hundred yards.

Frenchy didn't have time to be terrified! By the time he realized he was not going to fall off and that he could look down, they were over the Kangyung Gap, and Johnny was singing "Follow the Kangyung Road" to the tune "Follow the Yellow-Brick Road" and trying to croak like a Munchkin. Frenchy soon yelled as they neared the 62nd Battalion's lonely little airstrip, and, in consideration of his outdoor passenger, Johnny did an extra slow bank and made a crosswind landing on the dirt field. Frenchy jumped down and helped open the hatch on the observer side.

Jim Forest more or less fell out, but immediately recovered and turned to Frenchy, "Get 62nd Headquarters on the line . . . I'll speak."

Frenchy got Sgt. Maj. Flowers and handed the mike to Jim. Obviously wanting his Bird Dog back, his orders were loud and clear: if they could recover Red Tail with an M-46 tank, they should then and there strip off both wings, since the good wing was also now useless and would be replaced by an all-new unit. The extra problem in this plan was that it was a ROK tank outfit, and a Korean interpreter would have to relay the instructions. It was surely worth a try and would spare enemy and friendly patrols from fighting over the pieces or, more likely, mortars from both sides simply turning the once-proud little ship into rubble.

Soon, an ambulance and two jeeps arrived. Lt. Col. Pods led the welcoming party. The newcomers found everyone looking healthy, though Jim Forest still seemed shaken. There was a brief summary.

The Wiggy east–west mission had shaken tons of rock and dirt from Black Ridge's North Slope, but results would await aerial photos. The so-called Sore Tooth mission by Red Tail had, indeed, hit pay dirt: a large cave was exposed and secondary explosions indicated substantial damage. The site of yesterday's fire mission revealed complete devastation of the enemy firing battery. Reports and fresh aerial photos needed to be prepared and a routine investigation held.

The commander anticipated that everyone would come out heroes except him—a senior officer who put himself in reckless danger while fulfilling a job adequately done in the other L-19 by a sergeant. Nevertheless, he would put Wiggins in for a commendation and urged Col. Pods to do the same.

Needing no persuasion, Pods took everyone's name and said that, through channels to the Fleet Admiral, he would write up the performance of the eight Corsairs and their Forward Air Controller. Uncovering the Sore Tooth cave had been a significant interservice achievement. He agreed with the commander to make special mention of Wiggins to Divarty Headquarters.

Sgt. Flowers called back, advising that the ROK Patton Tanks were chugging north into no man's land to recover Red Tail—sans Wings. The fuselage would be taken to Battalion Headquarters.

Frenchy laughed. His new camera was around his neck, and he hadn't taken a single picture! He also retrieved his M-1 from the L-19. Johnny Wiggins shook his head, saying, "You mean I lugged that thing out of the DMZ?"

"Good thing you did," replied the colonel, "That baby has already done in several dozen North Koreans."

Finally, Johnny and the commander decided to fly back to Uijongbu, leaving Jim Forest at 62nd Battalion to await the fate of his aircraft. The wingless hulk would probably be tied by its tail to a three-quarter-ton truck and easily hauled back to Uijongbu.

After a round of picture-taking with the new Canon camera, Frenchy found himself suddenly overwhelmed. He hugged all three of his new comrades and superior officers, at the same time wiping away tears. It was the same old army story—make new friends and leave 'em.

As they parted, Lt. Johnny Wiggins—the true hero of the day—turned to Frenchy with a loud parting cry, "Always remember—follow the Kangyung Road; follow the Kangyung Road; follow the, follow the, follow the Kangyung Road!"

Frenchy waved and hollered back, "To 'Somewhere Over the Rainbow!'"

Chapter Forty-one
Back to the OP

Frenchy's jeep faithfully stood by the airstrip shed. He loaded up his grenades, revolver, Garand, and camelhair coat and remembered he needed to pick up the new communications expert at headquarters, the guy with the big libido—whatever that meant.

At headquarters, he inquired for Rich and the new guy, Cpl. Hiram Spachek; he then went to the mess tent. Even though he had had more adventures that day than most people would have in a lifetime, it was just past 1300 hours. Rich was in garrison and soon joined him.

"Hey, fly boy, I hear you came in on a wing and a prayer; it's the talk of Headquarters, probably of the front lines on both sides! Don't you ever just have a normal day—maybe just two or three fire missions and some incoming mortar fire?"

"You're right, Cowboy. Ya know, I've flown on an airplane twice. I say *on* because the second time I couldn't get *in*. The first time was also a hell of a go: we destroyed a battery and may have killed fifty to one hundred North Koreans. By the way, I see you're now a corporal—congratulations."

"Yeh, they've got me in charge of a survey crew. We're working with the sound and flash people, doing target area work. Last night, we had a ToT in the next sector to the west."

"A ToT? We've never done a time on target from our OP. Tell me about it."

"Well, using an infrared sniper scope, our observers detected the enemy building a new OP—working, of course, entirely at night. We surveyed their position, and set our registered guns on the position. On the planned night, watches synchronized, we all fired at once. Baa-loom, boom, boom; wham, wham, wham! Our Battalion joined in with Division Artillery. We had 105s, 155s, eighyt-inch howitzers, and Long Toms. We fired fuse VT, fuse quick, and even fuse delay.

"Next morning, the area looked like a plowed field. Time on target is a great device, especially at night when the guns might otherwise be idle. Think of the horror of it: they have officers, perhaps specially trained engineers, up there supervising a gang, digging, building, installing, happily working away; then, all of a sudden, there is an overwhelming rain of steel and oblivion."

Frenchy ran his hands through his sandy-colored hair and then shook his head. "Lord, have mercy; it's all so horrible. . . . But that sort of thing, taken with actions like my mission against the 122mm howitzers yesterday and the Corsairs' attack today is what keeps our thin MLR competitive with their in-depth MLR and with their masses of troops. By the way, Rich, what's a libido?"

Rich laughed. "Well, I don't know if you've got one, but remember when Soddy and I went off to the sporting house in Tokyo? Our libidos sent us, in other words, our sex drive, plus, in that case, the sheer fun and novelty of the thing. What put that word in your head?"

Frenchy grinned and raised his hands as if in protest, "Well, I guess my libido is now in limbo . . . anyway, I'm directed to pick up our new communications NCO, and I overheard the sergeant major talking to the colonel about the guy's libido."

The conversation promptly ended when they heard a voice inquiring for Sgt. Desprez, and up came the subject himself—Cpl. Hiram Spachek—a nice looking, dark-haired fellow, standing about six feet, and sporting extra-long sideburns—hardly regulation. After introductions, Frenchy looked up at him and said, "Nice ta see you'll be able to carry your share of the gear and maybe then some. Our lieutenant's a great guy, but small and old."

Frenchy bade goodbye to Rich, and drove off with his new companion, first hitting Baker Battery to pick up mail. The supply sergeant was waiting for him. The 62nd was being issued a new type of body armor—known as the Model 1952A flak jacket. It weighed eight pounds and was made of twelve layers of laminated nylon. Frenchy and Hiram were fitted and also given vests for Otto and Lee-Mo.

Lastly, the sergeant presented a clipboard, said to be in response to repeated requests from Otto.

Frenchy ran into Capt. Marcin and inquired how he was doing as the new A Battery boss. Marcin's bad news answer was that Otto's FO crew would be going on patrols. In the past, it had been sufficiently difficult for them to get to an assembly area from Hill 710 that they were spared patrol responsibility, but now they were assigned to assist the Sound and Flash Unit and would be on patrol with them.

The new captain had changed in just two weeks: the man reluctant to take command of Baker Battery following the Charlie Battery Shootout and the death of the former commander now seemed hardened, assertive, and perhaps a little aloof. Frenchy sensed the strain inherent with the job; his friend was responsible for 125 men. Since he had taken command, he had written letters to each soldier's family, trying to say something different and personal in each letter, trying to say it like it is—all made extra difficult by Capt. Anthony's heroic death.

Frenchy took a chance. He held out his hand, grasped Marcin's arm and said, "We'll support you every step of the way, Sir."

Marcin thawed, shook Frenchy's hand, smiled, and said, "I know you will. Take care of yourself."

They left Baker and drove back across Kangyung Road, then east to 1st Battalion, ROK 143rd. He tried his hand at introducing Hiram to the ROK guards, using a Korean word he had picked up, which meant "new."

"*Saeroun* OP man."

To that, the guard would give a simple nod or, perhaps, *Ah so*, which was short for *Ah so desuka*—a Japanese phrase which had become universal in the Far East for "Is that so?" It seemed that the "ka" sound on the end of a word made it a question.

More language mysteries awaited them at 2nd Battalion. The Headquarters sergeant greeted him with *Nalgae Dallin*, which was followed by a big smile. A few weeks ago they had called him *Paek songjang*, meaning "one hundred enemies;" now it was *Nalgae Dallin*.

Frenchy bit: "What the hell does that mean?"

The sergeant replied with a grin, "Wing passenger."

Then he realized that hundreds, maybe thousands, of ROK troops—not to mention enemy troops—had watched him fly out of the DMZ on the wing of the L-19. Word was out that they made him fly on the wing because he had no ticket or seat assignment. He would have to play along.

Darkness fell as they reached the hilltop. Debris had been cleared from both the bunker and the hoochy, their rooftops strengthened, the slit trench repaired with fancy toilet seat back in place. Everyone and most everything had survived the rabid barrages of the North Korean artillery. Sadly, he learned that the shelling had uncovered gravesites on the rear slope just east of the bunker, revealing pieces of bodies. Dead soldiers could not rest in peace.

Of course Otto and Lee-Mo were there, Otto looking worn out. Weeks on the MLR under all that bombardment were tough on an ancient twenty-six-year-old.

Sergeant Lee-Mo extended a mock formal greeting to "Sergeant Nalgae Dallin." They were introduced to Cpl. Hiram Spachek—

the new communications NCO. Otto gruffly muttered, "You got the clipboard?"

When it was handed over, Otto looked at it, shook his head, and said, "You'd think I'd asked for gold bullion. Since Hiram, here, has no FO training, we're all going to write out a training memorandum. It'll do us all good. That's for tomorrow. Lee-Mo, you take Hiram to the Bunker; show him the target area; and let him take the first watch. Hiram, don't hesitate to come an' fetch us if you see anything, especially any gooks in the target area."

While it seemed strange to put a rookie out there alone, the others knew nothing much happened on the first watch, with the gooks probably just getting up. With his comrades still talking, Frenchy hit the sack, ending another melodramatic day of death and destruction.

Next day, Otto's FO crew held an extra fancy get-acquainted breakfast in the bunker. It was complete with canned fruit, tea, and powdered eggs sent up from ROK 1st Battalion.

Frenchy mentioned that he was a day late meeting Hiram at Headquarters. This brought a laugh from the newcomer.

"I thanks for that, Frenchy, I scrounged a jeep and went to see my girlfriend."

"Your what?" Otto rasped , as Lee-Mo laughed and Frenchy smirked knowingly.

"Her name is Hee-Won, I guess the polite thing to say is she's a camp follower. As you guys know, women have been part of armies since and before Qin Shihuangdi—China's First Emperor. In Korea, it's on a more modest scale. The troops who go back for supplies and others who can regularly get away from the front look in on the girls who set up shop in the huts along the main supply routes. With me, it's exciting and a chance to get my ashes hauled."

Trying not to act overly interested and wondering if Hiram knew the sergeant major and the colonel were on to him, Frenchy asked, "How's it work; I mean with VD risks and all?"

Hiram explained, "First, as you guys must know, everywhere is off limits. I suppose there are exceptions outside the combat zone, maybe like in Seoul or Pusan, but around here that's the rule. The Military Police know such rules are broken at every opportunity; so they established sort of a corps of licensed good-time girls.

"The girls are checked in clinics set up a mile or two behind our MLR and are issued health cards. They have to be checked once a week. Naturally, every *yoja*—girl—with any sense at all, is game for this, thinking cooperate and stay healthy. Now, let's say a girl gets the clap: she'll report the guy who gave it to her, and he'll be tracked down, disciplined, and cured."

Otto spoke up, "Come on; how many guys walk in a joint and say 'how do you do; I'm Pfc. Horney from Easy Peter Company?' Oh, I suppose the girl could say she knew what unit the guy came from; then the MPs could haul in a pack of medics to give surprise short-arms. However, even if you bring in a battalion of medics, line everyone up for penicillin shots, preach abstinence at troop infor-mation and education classes, it can never be a purifying system so long as you have newly infected players arriving all the time from Japan—currently probably the world's biggest hot-bed of infection. Those troops either returning from R and R or replacements are a pretty good-sized swarm—like infected Anopheles Mosquitoes."

Frenchy smirked: *Pfc. Horney from Easy Peter Company— not bad, old Otto!*

Hiram replied, "Yes, but, with respect, Sir, also remember, there's not that much going on here in Korea. From the buyers' standpoint, it's not like Tokyo where you simply ask a cab driver; here you gotta have the gumption, the transportation, the opportu-nity, and the know-how."

Otto grunted, "Know-how? Everyone *knows how!*"

The usually silent Lee-Mo entered the conversation, "We hear many GI big brass, colonels, and generals have girl-sans they call "moose"—back in Seoul. Sometime army business just monkey business."

The others laughed at the way Lee-Mo had come out with a pretty clever remark about moose and monkeys—species not even indigenous to the Peninsula. Then, thinking about the "big brass," Otto laughed and shook a finger in mock protest, "Now, now, don't you all know rank has its privileges!"

Getting ready to use his new vocabulary word, Frenchy added, "You gotta have a big something else, and that's the big libido. My sex drive went into low gear when I arrived in this country, though I gotta admit I sometimes lie in my fart sack, think of past encounters, and fantasize."

Otto added, "Sure, we all feel that way, even old Otto. This is my second war, and it's my observation that the men who go to all lengths to find poontang, acting like ardent dogs in the process and settling for some pretty scary stuff, are usually the married guys— men not used to celibacy. I'll bet you're hitched, Hiram."

Seeing the new man give a resigned nod, Otto backed off a little and closed the subject, "Well, Hiram, your days of running around are over for the duration of OP duty under my leadership. One thing you never considered is that some of these women are commie spies. They're caught fairly regularly. No hard feelings, but you are now a member of a very special and highly trained team. The three of us have destroyed dozens of trucks, guns, mortars, and caves. In one day, Frenchy and I killed about three hundred North Koreans in two separate engagements. We're now introducing you to the lore of the FOs at their best; grab this clipboard and start taking notes."

It was soon clear that Hiram already knew the basics: the sequence for sending a fire mission, uses of survey, FDC, adjustment commands, loading and firing of the howitzers, types of fuses, and— above all—communications. His Signal Corps training with radios and telephones had cross-over ties with artillery at every step. The four discussed improvement of their observation post, as well as the likelihood of attack on their position and on the adjacent positions.

They found that Cpl. Hiram Spachek understood the size and nature of their assigned sector. He knew where their 62nd Battalion positions were as well as those of the ROK 1st and 2nd Battalions and knew also the ridges, the mountains, and the river valley forming the enemy line. Lee-Mo took him down the slope to the east, where he met the ROK platoon leaders, platoon sergeants, and others. Finally he met Capt. Jeung, Commander of ROK Able Company. Jeung sent his regards to Sergeant Nalgae Dallin, showing how far and how high Frenchy's new moniker had spread.

With Lee-Mo's help, these friendly ROK neighbors pointed out the mine fields, barbed wire, and listening posts at the foot of Hill 710 as well as their machine gun and mortar emplacements. They also explained the crossfire procedures of these and other weapons and the way they covered the Kangyung Gap.

Frenchy was acknowledged to have more checkpoints memorized than even Otto, so he was appointed quizmaster in a name-the-target game. He would place the circle of the BC scope on a landmark and the others would name it if it were a checkpoint or give a shift from the nearest checkpoint for use in a fire mission.

Hiram was put to work memorizing the checkpoints. In their stalemate location there was no concern for azimuths or map coordinates, such as there had been back in wide-open 1950 and part of 1951, or in training back at Fort Sill. The next day, Hiram fired base-point registrations for both Baker and Able Batteries.

17 July was a sobering day for U.N. Forces. The Chinese renewed attacks on Old Baldy held by the 2nd Division. The battle was fought in the DMZ and showed an unexpected and unwanted determination by the enemy to step up the action like they had in the Charlie Battery Shootout.

Chapter Forty-two
Big Noise from Winnetka

On 18 July, Maj. Willis called and a three-way connection was made with Lt. Com. Hypes. Hiram put the call on a speaker so they could all hear. The commander advised that aerial photos of the Corsair raid showed destruction of one large cave caused by the Red Tail bombing and exposure and damage to three smaller caves along Black Ridge, as observed by Frenchy. Details and photos were being dispatched. There was already evidence of repair work, and the same eight Corsairs had been ordered back—this time without needing to use the fragile L-19s. It was shaping up to be a case of: destroy on Monday, repair by Thursday, destroy on Friday, and so on.

The commander had other plans as well. Heavy cruisers and a battleship were regularly steaming up and down the Sea of Japan to the east of the Korean peninsula. The Fleet Admiral directed that these caves be added to their harassment and interdiction fire. With the hills running east–west, the targets would be in enfilade fire for guns shooting from the east and would be in range of the eight-inch guns of the cruisers, not to mention the sixteen-inch guns of the battleship. The mission was being laid on, and a fire control officer from one of these ships would arrive by helicopter at Hill 710 ASAP. The commander added some praise, "No one as yet has said a word about my doing as good a job observing and directing fire as a certain nineteen-year-old buck sergeant, but, if I catch any flak, I'll say that being able to keep up with that certain buck sergeant manifests high efficiency, indeed!"

Frenchy simply said, "Not accurate, but thank you, Sir."

On 23 July, the International Amphitheater in Chicago again was the stage when Illinois Governor Adlai Stevenson was nominated for President at the Democratic National Convention. Frenchy and Otto had heard of him, but he was a new name to the rank-and-file soldier. Stevenson would now have to run against a soldier everyone knew.

On 25 July, in mid morning, word came that Lieutenant Senior Grade Horace "Ace" Whitaker would be arriving at Battalion from one of the cruisers—the USS *Winnetka (CA-141)*. His chopper would pick up Maj. Willis, proceed to the pad at ROK 1st Battalion, and then hike to the OP. Whitaker's helicopter planned to speed over the DMZ on the way in and would thus alert Otto's team.

Sure enough, at 1330 hours that day, a chopper could be seen along the U.N. front, hovering over Hill 710, spinning north, almost to Black Tooth, and finally heading southwest to 62nd Battalion Headquarters. Forty minutes later, Maj. Willis led Navy Lt. Ace Whitaker and Marine Warrant Officer Smithson along the trench line and to the Hill 710 bunker. Otto gave the usual ceremonial greeting and introduced his three-man team. Whitaker was the gunnery officer assigned to coordinate with land forces from the *Winnetka*, Smithson his pilot. The navy man got down to business: "Major, all you gentlemen; I'm glad to be here with you, especially since we think that, until now, the navy may have overlooked good harassment and interdiction targets in this so-called Black Tooth Sector. We know more about it since the Corsair raids exposed the caves.

"Now, as you all know, naval guns are extremely accurate for deflection compared to your howitzers but less accurate for range. Here along the ridgeline west of Black Tooth you have what we call enfilade targets in depth in the form of a series of caves. All this makes the range inaccuracy, an actual advantage. We have the aerial photos showing caves that you, Sgt. Desprez, helped uncover. These caves string out for at least a mile right along our ships' range lines. I'm sure you get it: it would hardly work to shoot some perfect range device and have it just dig a deeper and deeper hole.

"I said 'ships' because we have two heavy cruisers and *USS Texas,* an Iowa class battleship. I'll bet we'll be stuck in the Sea of Japan for the duration of this so-called conflict."

Maj. Willis responded, "What can the 62nd Field Artillery, and particularly this—our most successful FO team—do to assist?"

"We climbed up here to verify some assumptions about what you can do. I first wanted to test what you can see. Lt. Rentner, you were here when the Corsairs struck the ridge line; could you see the smoke over the Black Ridge hilltops?"

"First, Sir, with respect, I would like to say that on an army OP the man in charge can't have his crew always using military courtesy when they're together day and night for weeks on end. So here, I'm Otto, my crew is Lee-Mo, Frenchy, and our new Hiram. We're a little more formal with Maj. Willis, but he still calls us as indicated.

"In answer to your question, I clearly saw bellows of smoke above the hills. Of course, every third Corsair bomb was a thousand-pounder."

"That's as I figured. By the way, I thank you for the informal names. That's also how we operate on shipboard where our relationships last for the duration of the cruise, and informality is fine with me. I must say, I had heard of Frenchy before I got here; there's scuttlebutt up and down these hills.

"Back to our mission, the eight-inch guns could start with white phosphorous to make sure it's seen, then high explosive depending on whether the WP had to be adjusted in some major way. Our rounds weigh some 350 pounds. The battleship's sixteen-inch shells weigh one ton and they will sure as hell be seen.

"Now, radioman Hiram, I know you have nothing that can transmit to a ship at sea so you must tie into us via your Battalion Headquarters radio."

"By far our safest way, Sir, is by telephone line to 62nd Headquarters, then a relay to you."

The navy lieutenant—who had a rank equivalent to an army captain—advised that he wanted to land back at the *Winnetka* before dark. He could take two men with him, since they had a Sikorsky H-5, H035-1—a light four-passenger utility helicopter— a very popular, versatile machine, also used by the other services. They all knew it was a custom to take FOs back to the ship—sometimes called the ice cream run, easy enough to do and deemed a special way to integrate the services and show the navy's largess.

Maj. Willis said as operations officer for the battalion, it was his duty to go. Otto turned down the chance, and that left Frenchy as the fourth man in the four-man Sikorsky.

Frenchy argued with his boss, saying he should go, but old Otto seemed tired and had a *been there, done that* attitude. However, he shook his head, waved his hand, managed a smile, and said, "Now if anyone else wants to go, we can let Frenchy be the fifth man and he can hang from a strut."

Frenchy shook his head, pretended to be deathly afraid, and concluded the teasing by reciting lines from an old Bert Williams number—*Ziegfield Follies* vintage:

> *It's a wonderful opportunity for somebody;*
> *But it's gotta be somebody else, not me!*

Back down the hill, they found the Sikorsky—named *Mary's Folly*—under guard at 1st ROK. They flew over a part of the peninsula Frenchy had never seen. The Taebaek Mountains stretched away to the north and sloped abruptly down to the seashore, which angled northwest. The Sea of Japan, called the East Sea by the Koreans, was beautiful in the late afternoon sun; nevertheless, he shuddered when he thought of his marine brothers under winter siege back in 1950 at the Chosin Reservoir, some 160 miles north.

Small ships and their wakes could be seen coming and going, but the waters were dominated by two close-in warships, the nearest being *USS Winnetka*—their destination. She had a classic shape: long and thin and graceful, two triple turrets of eight-inch guns forward, one aft. The superstructure was amidships surrounded by six twin turrets of five-inch guns. The landing pad was aft, just forward of a set of cranes.

The ship's crewmen were old hands at receiving army and marine guests. On stepping down from the Sikorsky there were many salutes—most tendered as friendly greetings rather than strict protocol. The major and Frenchy were given a chance to shower and put on coveralls, afterwards led to a ward room where refreshments were served. Pictures on the wall told the ship's story: Winnetka, Illinois, was a suburb of Chicago and home of Harold Ickes—Roosevelt's long-time Secretary of the Interior. With a little inside push the small village got a cruiser named after it—the *U.S.S. Winnetka (CA-141)*.

She was built in 1944, a *Baltimore* class cruiser, displacing 17,000 tons fully loaded, speed 33 knots, length 673 feet, beam 70 feet. Frenchy smiled at the similarity in size to his old *Hawkeye*: length 768 feet, beam 70 feet; of course, there the similarity ended.

One of the junior navy officers pointed at Frenchy and, with a smirk, asked Maj. Willis, "You sure this guy is old enough to drink?"

"Probably not," Willis replied laconically, then, pausing for a moment to command more attention, he added, "But last month when one of our firing batteries was overrun by a battalion of North Koreans, though still recovering from a wound, he was old enough to kill sixty-five of them with his M-1 rifle plus a rifle he took from his partner and best friend who fell dead beside him."

That squelched the fellow's little joke and brought a series of questions Frenchy's way. One fellow got after him about his feelings on shooting all those enemies, "After shooting round after round at those enemy soldiers, what did you feel?"

Frenchy could not resist attempting a humorous reply to the unwanted and overly personal question: "What did I feel? Well, let me think, each time I pulled the trigger . . . I felt . . . a slight recoil."

That remark was overheard by Maj. Willis and added to the growing legend of Frenchy Desprez.

At supper, both the major and Frenchy managed to eat two helpings of chocolate ice cream. Just at sunset, they were given a tour of the bridge and then the gunnery operations room, whose computers were a far cry from field artillery procedures. Frenchy realized that the pitching, rolling, and yawing of the ship added bewildering dimensions to the task of delivering fire. Maj. Willis summed it up as a system designed by geniuses to be executed by ordinary people.

They met for breakfast with Lt. Ace Whitaker who entertained them with mountain climbing stories. He first told them there was a spectacular peak in Wyoming's Big Horn Mountains named Black Tooth—very steep and over 13,000 feet. He said it always appeared black because the black rock near its summit was too damn steep to hold snow. The Big Horns were remote; it would take a two-day pack trip just to reach the foot of the mountain. Black Tooth in the Big Horns had not been climbed until 1933—the year Frenchy was born. Frenchy thought, *Damn, someday I'd like to climb that Black Tooth!*

Ace had graduated from Williams College in 1948, had joined the navy and graduated from the Newport Line Officers' School. As a kid, he had climbed several of Colorado's Fourteeners and had worked on a dude ranch near Sheridan, Wyoming. Coming up in August, he planned to take a leave and climb Mount Fuji, or Fuji-san, as the Japanese called it. He would go by train to its foot and make the climb in two days. For a strong climber like Ace, it could all be done in eight hours up, three down; but he didn't plan to hurry; there were huts along the way and tradition was to be on the 12,388 foot summit at sunrise.

Maj. Willis asked if anyone did the climb on R & R.

The U.S. had taken over certain Japanese resort hotels where war-weary GIs could be sent. The troops called these vacations I & I for "intercourse and intoxication." Regardless of the name, they were sought-after trips for deserving service men and women. The Navy Lieutenant replied that Fuji was not an R & R stop—fairly obvious since the tough climb could wear you down with no rest or recuperation.

Before the breakfast meeting, Ace Whitaker had worked with the gunnery officers to focus on Black Tooth Sector targets; they planned to concentrate on the Black Ridge targets only. The first round would be white phosphorous, to be fired when the Sikorsky was in position.

It went as planned. While the *Mary's Folly* was over the Allied MLR east of Hill 710, the first eight-inch shell was seen landing near the stream bed north of the target line. The lieutenant brought it slightly south and added only one hundred yards to range. A three-gun salvo of high explosive shells were delivered to the north slope of Black Ridge, as desired. Then another salvo hit in the same area. Frenchy knew that the ship was facing shore and the two triple-gun bow turrets had fired.

The lieutenant seemed pleased and advised Maj. Willis that the attack they had witnessed would be repeated when the cruiser *Winnetka* and the battleship *Texas* were in position. Each time alerting the 62nd and Otto's OP in advance, he planned sporadic harassment and interdiction missions to commence with white phosphorous shells from the cruiser or high explosive shells from the battleship.

These plans were discussed as *Mary's Folly* circled southwest and landed at 62nd Headquarters. This ended the sea adventures of Maj. Middleton Willis and Sgt. Arnold "Frenchy" Desprez.

Chapter Forty-three
The Colonel Bogey

Back on the hill, Otto said they saw the navy show including the results of later cruiser fire, all feeling sure Frenchy's mission, the Corsair attacks, and the naval gunfire had, at least for a time, slowed the enemy's counter-battery capabilities.

Just two days later, Monday, 28 July, Frenchy was ordered to Battalion Headquarters for transport to Division Artillery, located with Division Headquarters north of Yongdae. Three army buses lined up, while Sgt. Maj. Flowers bustled around checking off and loading the troops. Frenchy was surprised to find his Class-A uniform retrieved and cleaned, needing only the sergeant stripes.

Ceremonies honoring a unit usually occurred when the honored group was transferred, but with no hope of that in the present stalemate days and with the battalion only back on line a few weeks, it was determined to go ahead with the ceremony but send only a small crew and thus not weaken the front line. That meant if Frenchy went, Otto could not, in spite of his many successful missions on the OP.

There were Oliver Riggs, now promoted to captain and commander of decimated Charlie Battery, and Master Sgt. Brownell, unfortunately now on crutches. The traveling party met for lunch at the mess tent, then loaded up. *Good to see these friends.*

380

In cooperation with the Republic of Korea, army units set up divisional headquarters a few miles behind the MLR in open country, rather than in cities or villages. Division Headquarters, including Divarty, consisted of the usual Quonset huts and tents set up around a jury-rigged parade ground and all fenced in—both to keep the soldiers in and infiltrators out—the latter including Hiram's lady friends. Just north of these facilities was a landing strip and Frenchy's MASH unit.

Since the ROK 134th Infantry Regiment was part of the division, the force was a combination of the two cultures. Most soldiers, no matter where they came from, gave little thought to the beauty of the country around them, known as Korea's Gangwon Province. Looking south, over pine forests and green mountains, they were within sight of Seoraksan, known as Snow Peak Mountain—one of a series of snow-capped peaks of great beauty.

These mountains had attracted Buddhist monks in the seventh century during Korea's strong Silla Dynasty. The ruins of temples from that time were still clinging to the bare rocks high on the mountainsides. Tragic and ironical that, some 1,300 years later, over a million men would assemble from all over the world to do battle just north of those areas of beauty and tranquility, so long ago dedicated to religious asceticism.

Soon after arrival, Frenchy found his friend from the Long Tom shoot, Lt. Mike Wonder—aide to Gen. Hines. Mike's houseboy undertook pressing the Class-A uniform and sewing on the sergeant stripes. As suggested, Frenchy stayed in Mike's BOQ tent. Mike Wonder—the Yale man—took the Canon camera and promised to memorialize the award ceremony. At Frenchy's request, Mike also invited Lt. O'Connor and Capt. Snuffles—the MASH unit nurses.

Tuesday morning, on the parade ground, a chaplain gave an invocation followed by the Division band playing the National Anthem and the South Korean patriotic song, "Aegukga." Frenchy and others received the Purple Heart Medals from the Deputy Division Commander, Brig. Gen. Fred Turman. The decoration was established by Gen. George Washington and was given as an entitlement, not as an award, to members of the Armed Forces wounded in action against an enemy of the United States. Most of the day's recipients had been wounded in the Charlie Battery Shootout. Master Sgt. Brownell had a flesh wound in his thigh—just missing bones or other even more vital areas. Soldiers who had been seriously wounded on that day had long since been evacuated. Frenchy and Brownell exchanged handshakes and hugs.

The next set of awards was the Bronze Star Medal. Three received it, including Frenchy and his recent partner, Johnny Wiggins, who was recognized for his heroic landing in the DMZ and rescue of the Red Tail crew. In Frenchy's case, a part of his citation read:

"Arnold Desprez's act of heroism took place on 23 June 1952, when he was under a barrage of 122mm artillery fire on the south slope of Hill 710, 134th ROK Infantry Sector, Republic of South Korea. Such fire emanated from the main line of the North Korean Peoples' Army. Although already wounded, dazed, and thrown to the ground, Desprez arose, saw that a Korean Service Corps Laborer had been downed, and ran back to the impact area, attempting to aid the fallen man. The laborer was the team foreman and had, in fact, been killed in the same barrage that injured Private First Class Desprez.

"The recipient having received this Bronze Star Medal during direct combat with an enemy force, there shall be appended thereto the Valor device to distinguish that it was given in such circumstances. This action was witnessed and attested by Captain Alfred Marcin and Second Lieutenant Otto Rentner III, both of Baker Battery, 62nd Field Artillery Battalion. It was also witnessed by Sergeant Lee-Mo, First Battalion, 134th Republic of Korea Infantry, then assigned to Baker Battery."

The general saluted Frenchy, then shook his hand. *I figured they'd make a fuss over the Charlie Battery Shootout . . . Wow, the yobo incident's sure a surprise!* As he stepped back into line with others there was a smattering of applause. He gritted his teeth and frowned, frowned hard to keep his chin from trembling.

Before the next event, Lt. Mason came running up, followed less exuberantly by Gen. Webber. Frenchy thought, *Regardless of the awards, this reunion makes my day!*

Although not connected to the division, Gen. Webber knew Divarty Commander Hines from past assignments, and the two general officers had arranged for Webber and Mason to fly in for the ceremony. The two generals had also made plans for a dinner party at the Officers' Club.

Next came a higher awards ceremony in which Frenchy found himself again front-and-center with Gen. Turman. A Deputy Adjutant commenced with the historic words, "Attention to Orders!"

This was followed by the same four-note bugle call—*Attention*—played back in Baker Battery on the fateful Shootout day.

"Sergeant Arnold Desprez (US 55294297) is hereby awarded the Silver Star Medal—205 ARSSM. The recipient's acts of heroism took place in the early morning of 12 July 1952 when he and his tent-mate, the late Private First Class Harold "Soddy" Mecham, were alerted of an attack by the North Korean Peoples' Army in battalion strength to the west of E Company, 2nd Battalion, 134th Republic of Korea Infantry.

"After a successful breakthrough, the North Koreans turned west and attacked C Battery, 62nd Field Artillery Battalion, which was in direct support of the 134th Infantry. Desprez was then assigned to a forward observer team of B Battery of the 62nd F. A. Bn.; he was, however, confined to the Battery area while recovering from surgery for the removal of a shell fragment suffered 23 June 1952, which is covered by Order of even date #14.

"Under orders of the late Captain Jacob Anthony, then Privates Desprez and Mecham with other cannoneers from B Battery ran toward C Battery. Being the first to arrive, Desprez halted in the limited coverage of scattered rocks and looked at the scene of intense combat spread out before him. Private First Class Mecham was killed by burp gun fire almost immediately, leaving Private First Class Desprez—an expert marksman and sharpshooter—with two M-1 rifles and ten additional clips of thirty-caliber ammunition. He was within a few yards of enemy soldiers. To Desprez' right, Captain Anthony advanced in a Quad-50 half-track vehicle from D Company, 2nd ROK Battalion. The vehicle was destroyed in a single enveloping explosion. Private First Class Desprez fired both rifles steadily at ranges of five feet to seven hundred yards. Among those he killed were a North Korean major and lieutenant. Firing halted when Republic of Korea G Company intervened from its reserve position.

"Eye-witness descriptions and body counts conducted after this so-called 'Charlie Battery Shootout,' indicate Private First Class Desprez killed at least sixty-five North Koreans, including the two officers. This figure was determined in part by counting the spent clips (ninety-six rounds) and examining and marking those dead appearing to be shot by thirty-caliber rounds. He also killed one soldier with his friend's bayonet.

"The action of Capt. Anthony and his Quad-50 crew, of the gun crews of the two howitzers remaining in friendly hands, and of Private First Class Desprez so decimated the attacking force that many survivors of C Battery gained respite and were saved, and the anticipated attack on B Battery and A Battery was abandoned by the enemy. Such action by Private First Class Desprez distinguishes him by extraordinary heroism, fully worthy of this Silver Star Medal.

"Investigation of this award was directed by Major Middleton Willis of Headquarters Battalion, with testimony by Master Sergeant Powell Hinkley, Sergeant Ramon Gomez, ROK Sergeant Lon Fin, Private First Class Lance Hoosky, and Sergeant Desprez himself. In particular, Private First Class Hoosky was approximately fifty yards behind Desprez and actually witnessed the firing and the bayoneting from start to finish. Hoosky characterized the action as 'resembling an expert in a county-fair shooting gallery.'"

As the general pinned on the Medal, he whispered to Frenchy, "This is the highest award we can offer at this time. On review by the Department of Army, I am confident it shall be raised to the Distinguished Service Cross. Frenchy, I know that on that crucial day you also lost your best friend. God bless you both."

Frenchy somehow managed a salute and a handshake, but it was all too much. His body shook with tears—Soddy's face appeared before him. The general gave him a long embrace until he collected himself and was able to stride back in line.

The Adjutant next announced that recommendation had been made for Capt. Jacob Anthony to receive posthumously either the Distinguished Service Cross or the Congressional Medal of Honor. An account was read of the captain's selfless bravery from the planning for the attack, which commenced two days before, then on until his death in the Quad-50 half-track.

There then followed a one-hour break while the men of the 62nd Field and other units of the division lined up for the pass in review. Maj. Gen. McWilliams and Brig. Generals Turman, Hines, and Webber lined up opposite the troops—McWilliams alone in the first row. The Adjutant then reached field center in a jeep equipped with a public address system.

Again the Division band played the "National Anthem" and "Aegukga" and the Adjutant commanded, "Attention to Orders!" Then the bugle call after which the Adjutant read the Distinguished Unit Citation awarded to the 62nd Field Artillery Battalion by the Department of the Army. The Award actually used the words "Charlie Battery Shootout," cited Capt. Anthony and Pfc. Desprez by name, and mentioned the praise given the unit by Lt. Col. Kim, Col. Young-no, the ROK Division Commander, Gen. McWilliams, Gen. Hines, and the Corps Commandant.

The Adjutant then commanded very slowly, with a pause between each word, "Pass . . . in . . . review!" and the jeep drove out of the way. The band played Frenchy's favorite march, "The Colonel Bogey," and the marchers circled the parade ground with the guidon bearer dipping the colors as Col. Podolsky saluted and those in the right-hand row turned their heads toward the generals. Frenchy marched separately behind the others and also saluted. Mike Wonder—running short of film—caught the moment on the Canon as did members of the press corps present and official army photographers.

A special mess for men of the honored battalion and other guests followed, after which two of the three buses returned to Battalion Headquarters. Frenchy was eager to take a break and return to Mike's tent, but he couldn't get away until interviewed and photographed by the press.

Then, Lt. Sylvia O'Connor ran to him, gave him a hug, and explained that Capt. Snuffles sent her best wishes and regrets; the captain was unable to break away from surgery and sent Sylvia to represent the MASH team. Frenchy asked her to stay for the dinner, but she waved away the invitation, saying a woman would likely cast a pall on the affair. Mike overheard, intervened, and seeing that both he and Sylvia wore silver bars, asked her date of rank.

"I see, ma'am, that I outrank you by a good three months and so order you to attend. Seriously, lieutenant, this will hardly be drinks and dirty jokes; we have a program planned; two generals will talk; and you are more than welcome."

Sylvia was up to the challenge: "Haven't I heard, Lieutenant, that rank among lieutenants is like chastity among whores? But if you really want me, I acquiesce; give me the time and place . . . *Sir.* The slight sarcasm in the word "Sir" was not lost on any of the three.

Mike had planned the dinner around Frenchy's friends, colleagues, and commanding officers. Attention centered on the two generals, Hines and Webber, who arrived with their aides, Wonder and Mason. Col. Podolsky escorted his Korean colleagues, Col. Young-No and Lt. Col. Kim, arriving about the time Frenchy and Rich came in locking arms with Sylvia. Sgt. Brownell hobbled in behind Capt. Riggs and Capt. Marcin. Finally Lt. Johnny Wiggins— hero of the Red Tail crash—entered from the club bar.

There was, in fact, a program designed by Mike Wonder. He wanted the generals to avoid the usual gung-ho pep talk, and the two agreed to come up with a subject they could share. The big Mongolian, Young-No, had already insisted that he had something important to say—in the form of a presentation. Sgt. Brownell said he would add a few words. That would leave the floor for the two rookies—Frenchy and Rich.

Cases of beer were brought in—to be drunk right from the bottle. A church key made the rounds, then salutations, with Frenchy and Milt Mason tipping bottles and saying *santé*. Mike Wonder called for attention and nodded to his general.

The general welcomed everyone, and then explained that he and Webber were at West Point at the same time. As an upperclassman he might very well have ridden Webber when the latter was a plebe, but neither could remember. He then explained that in spring of '51, Gen. Webber had been a colonel at the Pentagon and had followed the hearings of the Senate Armed Forces Committee regarding the dismissal of Gen. MacArthur with much care and had actually attended some of the hearings. Hines said he had also studied the career of the great soldier in a more general way. Eyeing some notes, he continued, "I want to emphasize that, though my friend and I may say things critical of the man, we both recognize his greatness. On 11 April 1951, President Truman issued a statement, which read in part, as follows:

With deep regret I have concluded that General of the Army Douglas MacArthur is unable to give his wholehearted support to the policies of the United States Government and the United Nations in matters pertaining to his official duties.

"Later on in his statement, however, the President added this paragraph with which General Webber and I heartily agree and which I hope you all put foremost when you think of the man:

Gen. MacArthur's place in history as one of our greatest commanders is fully established. The Nation owes him a debt of gratitude for the distinguished and exceptional service which he has rendered his country in posts of great responsibility.

"There are, I must say some startling episodes in his life. Douglas graduated from West Point in 1903 with every possible honor—he is a legend at the Academy. Wonder of wonders, his mother went to school with him, living just outside the gate.

"He was aide-de-camp to President Theodore Roosevelt in 1906, served with distinction in the Mexican War, already a general in the First War, he commanded the Rainbow Division, later led the Olympic Team, evicted the bonus marchers, was Chief of Staff, and—importantly—Military Advisor to the Philippines. You know that he shared Pacific Command with Adm. Chester Nimitz. In those days, we read about him daily, and folks felt warmly toward him. Who can forget his wading ashore at Lehte, his presiding on the deck of the *Missouri* with the Japanese foreign minister in top hat and tails hobbling across the deck? MacArthur stayed in Tokyo and steered that fallen country with compassion and great success.

"You all know we suffered a great loss in the Pearl Harbor surprise attack, but how many know what happened that day under MacArthur's command in the Philippines?"

The general looked around the tent room and, of course, received no answer to his question.

"Well, you're not alone. The record is murky and contradictory: reports lost, truth covered up. The point is, there was a war plan agreed upon by the High Command in advance, to be put in operation in the event of Japanese attack. Quite logically, most experts figured attack would come first in the Philippines—not Pearl Harbor—so planning centered there. We had a strong air component, based mostly at Clark Field on Luzon, which was to attack Japanese bases on Formosa.

"Get this straight: the plan was not to be a counterattack after Clark Field or some other target in the region was struck. No, once we were at war, it was rather to be a prompt strike by the thirty-five B-17s stationed at Clark. Maj. Gen. Lewis Brereton commanded the Army Air Corps, Far East, and fully expected to follow the war plan.

"Back in 1935, MacArthur accepted the appointment by President Manuel L. Quezon as Military Advisor to the Philippine Army. In 1937, Quezon made him Field Marshal, and he resigned from the U.S. Army. In July 1941, as war seemed more imminent with warlords in power in Japan, he was restored to active U.S. Army duty with the rank of major general. As a parting gift, and what we now see as a manifest conflict of interest, Quezon paid him $500,000—a huge sum for the time.

"Along came Pearl Harbor. It was soon revealed that we had several unheeded warnings of that attack. It was later learned we had broken the Japanese Code, but latest secret information was not to given Hawaiian Commanders Adm. Husband Kimmel and Lt. Gen. Walter Short, the two officers made the scapegoats for the disastrous attack.

"Of course, various high sources immediately wired and called Manila. MacArthur was awoken and advised by his Chief of Staff, Maj. Gen. Sutherland, at 0340 hours. Established directions were to carry out the war plan—meaning get the B-17s in the air and attack Formosa."

Gen. Hines paused. There was a grim half smile on his face; he looked around the room. There was the feeling among the listeners that he was carefully gauging his climactic remarks.

"Those airplanes never left Clark Field. At 1233 hours they were all destroyed on the ground—sitting ducks. This was over seven hours after the warning had been given!"

Again the general paused, shook his head, made the half smile, and ran his fingers through his disheveled hair, reminding Frenchy of a pudgy Will Rogers.

"Best evidence is that his Air Commander, Brereton, gave urgent requests to launch a preemptive strike. Apparently MacArthur said, 'No, only reconnaissance flights.' Why did this command failure occur? There are various theories.

"One possible answer is that he was dumbstruck—somehow suffered a mental aberration, which rendered him incapable of action. Another is that he did not connect the pieces, that Pearl Harbor was there and Clark Field is here—5,000 miles away. Related to that is the notion that the Japanese might not attack the Philippines. Quezon did have the strong wish and certainly the hope that his country could stay out of it. Wishful thinking, since his islands were on Japan's essential trade routes through the South China Sea.

"A more insidious reasoning is that MacArthur was at that time swallowed up by Quezon's attitude. Sympathy, love of the Philippine Islands, and half a million dollars may have overcome duty.

"*Time Magazine* interviewed Gen. Brereton but then killed any mention of Brereton's side of the episode. The Luce publication was, of course, in the conservative ranks, and MacArthur was a favorite of the far right, often discussed as a presidential possibility. President Roosevelt was well aware of the political implications. All the world knew of the Pearl Harbor disaster, but the Philippine military failure was to be covered up and MacArthur was to be raised to Lieutenant General—later Five-Star General—rescued from Corregidor, and given command of the Pacific Theater."

Hines paused and sipped his beer. Frenchy thought, *Of course my father and his friends were part of that crew supporting the far-off leader. Indeed,* Time Magazine *was an honored publication at the Desprez house.* The Divarty Commander then concluded, "Now I'm anxious to hear about the general before the Senate."

Gen. Webber arose and explained that he and Lt. Mason attended the ceremony because of interest in Sgt. Desprez, including Mason's Fort Knox French connection and the Camp Drake meeting. Then he pitched right in.

"In the last few minutes, I've gained a new insight into the thinking of this undeniably great man. In December 1941, Gen. MacArthur heard from the Pentagon, his Air Chief, and no doubt many others. Then he decided, 'I'll do it my way.' Does that sound familiar? Let's recall what happened nine years later in the fall and winter of 1950–1951.

"The general never moved from Tokyo, except to spend parts of a few days in Korea—never overnight. Folks came from around the world to see him in Tokyo—the Joint Chiefs, politicians, diplomats . . . even the President of the United States traveled half way around the world to see him. He listened, did not approve, and then sought to do his thing—just as he had back in Manila."

Frenchy nodded at Rich, thinking *That Wake Island junket was a real bad idea!*

"In this war, the differences between his position and the official Washington position are well known. He saw it this way: impose a naval blockade on Communist China, deploy Chiang's Army from Formosa, bomb air bases in Manchuria, create a nuclear waste zone along the China border, go all the way to the Yalu with U.N. troops, split the U.N. command, not heed the Joint Chiefs, and not worry about the Chinese.

"After the Chinese intervention he tended to despair, calling it 'an entirely new war.' However, with Walker's tragic accident and the appointment of Ridgway, things began to look up, and he tried to claim credit for Ridgway's successes. Truman dismissed him in April 1951, angrily saying he should have done so a year earlier. The general could see it coming."

Rich whispered, "Praise the Lord for Matt Ridgway!"

"He returned to the U.S. and was hailed a great hero and mobbed from coast to coast. No doubt people were interested in seeing this larger-than-life person. It was also big-time politics: conservatives in both parties were shocked, annoyed, or infuriated that their guy had been displaced by the Truman–Acheson–Marshall cabal. The general spoke to Congress and claimed there was no substitute for victory. He sounded very reasonable and made a strong impression.

"Now, the name 'limited war' may have been a little slow developing, but there is no doubt Truman, Acheson, Bradley, the Brits, and the U.N., in general, sought to have a contest that would not provoke the two great communist countries—Soviet Russia and China. In a limited, strategic war, the military actions can be part of a bargaining process, designed to bring about a termination of hostilities before the thing escalates into a major confrontation and perhaps a cataclysm. It was a new game, and Gen. MacArthur did not want to play.

"Thus, the Truman Administration's struggle with him was over the fundamentals of policy—matters of politics as well as strategy—not what you might call the battlefield management, such as the seemingly petty, but serious problems of splitting the command so Almond would report to MacArthur, not to Walker whom Almond disliked."

Frenchy gazed with wonder: he was in on a talk at the strategic level—concerning events that took place only one year ago—yet with the dispassionate attitude of the speakers, it might as well be a discussion of Lincoln's problems with Gen. George McClellan. At first he thought the two generals were being a little indiscrete; then he realized that the men being discussed—Five Star Generals and Admirals and two Presidents—were very remote to everyone in the tent room, including the two Brigadier Generals. He watched Milt open a second beer for the speaker who then continued.

"So, MacArthur returned to the States, was widely acclaimed, told Congress that old soldiers never die, and seemed ready to take on the Administration. The Senate Armed Services Committee called for hearings, which were held in May and June, last year.

"He testified for three days, defending his policies with respect to using the navy and using airpower. Adm. Forrest Sherman, Chief of Naval Operations tended to support the blockade use sometime in the future. There was also some support for bombing in Manchuria. The Bomber Command felt that there were no strategic targets left in devastated North Korea.

"MacArthur testified that he no longer saw a need for using Chiang Kai-shek's forces in Korea. His enemy was communism, in general, and, with this in mind, he looked at the war as a problem of timing. If we were to fight communism, we should fight the evil then, in 1951, not later when the communists had caught up in military strength—nuclear strength, in particular.

"His argument comes down to this: let us fight to win in Korea, and if it means a showdown with the Soviet Union—amen, so be it."

Rich eyed Frenchy at this point and gave a little shudder.

"The Air Force Chief of Staff, Gen. Hoyt Vandenberg, testified against bombing Manchuria. His bomber force was simply not big enough to do so and protect and advance other commitments. Vandenberg was backed by Secretary of Defense Marshall and Joint Chiefs Bradley and Collins. These moves were devastating to MacArthur's cause.

"Adm. Sherman came out against a naval blockade. The United States had stopped trade with China, and that was considered a sufficient step.

"In the end, the highly respected Secretary Marshall and all members of the Joint Chiefs of Staff testified against MacArthur. The potential for trouble coming in Europe was too grave for them to advocate making waves in the Pacific. It was repeatedly said that the Chiefs had the geographic advantage of global responsibilities. Their strategy was to be alert and ready in Europe and fight a limited war in Korea. Gen. Ridgway and Secretary of State Acheson also testified against the MacArthur position.

"I have just one final point: MacArthur's arguments at the hearing were often framed in global strategy, but when queried about

European plans, he would sarcastically say he only knew what he read in the papers. The side-show man was out of line! That is rather like my friend Divarty Commander Hines telling Gen. Mark Clark how to run FECOM."

As Gen. Webber sat down, Gen. Hines laughed and decided he could not let the illustration die just then, as he added, "Since you didn't use yourself in the example, I suppose you are leaving open the idea of *you* telling Mark Clark what to do?"

That broke the ice. As Webber jokingly answered, "Exactly," the subordinates around the room felt safe in having a good laugh. Young-No and Kim joined in, though the dialogue had probably been a little too swift for them to follow. There was a break as the waitresses put the turkey dinner on the table. There was little fanfare. Gen. Hines raised his glass and said, "To absent comrades."

In unison, the phrase was repeated: "To absent comrades." Frenchy again choked up.

Mike Wonder rose during the meal and said that Col. Young-No had something to say. The handsome Regimental Commander—now without his kepi—rose, took out a paper and a bag, and read a statement.

"Forgive me for reading. To make it easier for me and for all of you, my interpreter wrote this for me.

"As you all know, 28 June 1952 was a sad day for my Regiment. Easy Company was overrun and, along with Charlie Battery, suffered heavy casualties. Today we salute the entire 62nd Field Artillery Battalion and in particular two of its men. One is dead; the other is here—Sgt. Desprez.

A soldier in my George Company was the first to come upon the body of the North Korean major who was shot by Sgt. Desprez. He took this weapon from the body, and I am pleased to present it to Sgt. Desprez. Come forward, *dozo*."

Frenchy rose, completely surprised, and approached the towering Mongolian who continued.

"This is what we call a 'Baby Nambu' . . . the original Type-A Nambu was first designed and developed in 1902 by Kijiro Nambu, who was known as the John Browning of Japan. It looks much like the German Luger but was not based on that weapon. It is a semi-automatic device and was designed to fire 8mm ammunition. The Baby Nambu fires 7mm rounds. It lacks the killing power of the Grandpa Nambu, but was popular with Japanese Army Officers. In your country, you can purchase 7mm rounds and may be able to use it; however, it is primarily a war souvenir.

"As most of you know, I was in the Japanese Army, and I think the former owner of the handgun was as well. I make no apologies for serving your recent enemies. It was a good army, and I did my duty."

The colonel cocked the weapon and clicked the trigger—the customary courtesy to show it was empty. He then handed it to Frenchy together with its holster and a clip. Frenchy shook his hand and said, "Sir, I accept this with great humility and great respect; *domo arigato gozaimasu.*"

Next, Master Sgt. Brownell rose on crutches, Purple Heart on his chest, and spoke briefly of his gratitude, after years of service in a segregated force, for now having a position of leadership in the modern army and for being asked to attend the historic dinner. It was a touching moment when both generals shook his hand.

While they were eating, someone mentioned that they liked the march played during the pass in review. Lt. Wiggins spoke up, "That was 'The Colonel Bogey,' written in 1914 by an English bandmaster."

He paused and chuckled, then proceeded, "It's been parodied many times. The one that sticks in my head was used by the Brits while on training marches in World War II; it goes, *Hitler—he's only got one ball!*"

There was a general mutter around the room as people tried— with mixed success—to match the words to the tune.

Mike could bear it no longer; he wanted to get Sylvia in the mix. "I'm reminded that one person here has no balls at all, and we should hear from her—right, Sylvia?"

The MASH unit nurse rose—not at all intimidated by the brass, the occasion, or the manifestly crude introduction.

"Fortunately, I learned all about those technical anatomical terms you used in nursing school and gained practical under-standing when I got married. Thanks for the warm and appropriate introduction, Lieutenant, *Sir*. You see, folks, I'm obliged to speak because he has three months date-of-rank on me. What's more, I just learned he went to Yale . . . no wonder Mr. Wonder is so full of savoir-faire, or was that hot air?"

She had to pause . . . no one laughed harder than Mike Wonder! She continued, "As some of you know, I'm here because I gave Arnold a sponge bath while he propositioned me, and because of that process, I can attest that he has the usual number . . . two of them!"

That brought the house down, though with some blushing by Sgt. Desprez. She continued, "Actually, I'm very honored and thrilled to be here. I hope I don't see any of you ever again in our MASH unit; but I must say with pride that we do good work and save lives. Beyond the sheer horror of war, which we see every day, we also see little human dramas taking place, some being good fun like the repartee between Arnold and me, and some simply the friend-ships among staff members. Someone should write a book about a MASH unit in Korea, not a sad book full of suffering, but a book about the give and take among doctors, nurses, orderlies, different cultures, mix-ups, and affairs—those sorts of things. It could even tell about how we triaged Arnold until he collapsed on the tent floor, after which we finally thought we should get around to him. Thanks again, everyone."

The general response was eager applause, while Frenchy blushed.

They had just completed dessert—ice cream—and were settling for coffee and cigars when Mike rose.

"Well, we have heard from 'the brass;' and the general made me promise not to sing the "Whiffenpoof Song," so now let's hear from two guys who only recently escaped from the kitchen police. I'd call them 'young warriors,' except I think Rich, the cowboy, is about as old as I am, so I'll just say all right, men, you have something to say?"

Frenchy nodded at Rich who stood and with surprising poise got right into it.

"Frenchy and I could go on about how honored we are to be here, but you all must know that; so, we're going to talk about something we've discussed at length, called 'the minimax.' In bull sessions on the way over from Japan we discovered that we had both read about this concept; then we asked around today and found that no one here seemed to know about it.

"The minimax is a rule applicable to games, decision making, and statistics. In simplified form the rule says that in two-person, zero-sum games there is a value that is the best payoff for the opposing players. One player minimizes the maximum payoff for his opponent and also maximizes his own minimum payoff. Tic-tac-toe is such a game. Player A makes a move; player B sees that if he makes a certain move A will win, but another move will lead to a draw. He may see that he has no winning solution so he plays for a draw.

"I can make the game more complicated by drawing a matrix where A wants to achieve the largest positive number and B wants to achieve the largest negative number. Most likely, they will arrive at zero, in other words, a draw. Frenchy, take your turn!"

"Well, my uncle, an insurance agent, had a book on statistics and math games. It covered the minimax, and I recall studying it with my cousin. Some of you know that my cousin and I worked as deckhands on a Great Lakes ore boat; there was plenty of time for horsing around with things like this. The one I remember goes this way.

"Suppose that player A can choose any line of latitude and player B can choose any line of longitude covering any point in the forty-eight States. Also suppose that A wants the lines to cross on the highest possible point and B on the lowest possible point. They take turns. Don't ask me where, but ultimately they will agree on some one point, which is neither real high nor real low."

Frenchy then brought the question home to roost.

"I'm sure you are all anticipating that Rich and I are applying the minimax to the struggle in Korea with teams A and B being the U.N. Forces and the Communist Forces. So, Rich, my team A wants one Korea with your forces chased beyond the Yalu and the Tumen and the connecting land boundary."

Rich smiled and said, "Well, I won't say *my team B*, I'll just say, team B wants one Red Korea with your forces pushed into the sea. Team B knows that team A couldn't possibly defend the top of the peninsula where it broadens out to more than 890 miles and lies right across the boundary from the Soviet Union and mainland China, in many places amid high mountains in cold country."

Frenchy countered. "Team B completely lacks the logistical base for driving down into South Korea once again. They know that grand strategy must be based on logistics. We control the air and have them outgunned. Their supply support cannot take it."

"You forget that team B is a totalitarian state without Western notions of the sanctity of human life and with hundreds of millions of people available to throw into the battle."

"Big talk, but those millions have to be fed, clothed, supplied, and resupplied from primitive supply sources. Also, the size of the officer corps is a built-in limitation on the growth of Army B, and that officer force, consisting of a hodgepodge of former Nationalists and some poorly trained commie leaders, is already strained. You can't just add cannon fodder; you've got to lead them and not just with ex-farmers in epaulets. And, by the way, in spite of the current veneer of communism, currently led by a psychopath, China is a cultured nation; they do care about the sanctity of human life; Confucius taught the golden rule, the humane life, filial piety."

Rich now groped a little to follow up on this line. "Team A, you are forgetting Team B's infinitely powerful neighbor—the Soviets—who can supply these things."

"Supplies furnished by the Soviet Union mostly have to come by the Trans-Siberian Railway—a vulnerable and expensive way to deliver goods. On the current level of this foreign aid, I suspect the men in the Kremlin are already tired of the game, as indicated by the Soviet Ambassador first suggesting ceasefire talks."

Rich waved his hands to signal a time-out. "Surely in our game we are nearing a meeting of the plus and the minus or, we might say, of the high and the low, the yin and the yang. We could carry this on into the nitty-gritty of weapon systems, air and sea power, weather conditions—all kinds of things. We know we've been talking subjectively about an objective concept, but we hope this has been food for thought!"

Gen. Hines felt he should answer for the seniors. "Thanks men; it is good food for thought. Surely, the ultimate minimax experience is the game of chess. Should we shudder when we realize that the Russians are the best chess players in the world? No, I don't think so; chess players must be pragmatic; as you said, Frenchy, it was the Soviets who first suggested a ceasefire. Just like looking for the high ground, the player must think *If he gets my rook, I must be sure it costs him at least a bishop and a pawn.*"

Frenchy grimaced, *Wow, as I look around, it's obvious who the pawn is!*

Hines concluded, "For over a year, this war has been called a stalemate—a chess term meaning the player whose turn it is to move has no legal moves. A chess stalemate results in a draw and is why the term is applied to Korea. No soldier—no true competitor—wants to fight a draw!"

This ended a memorable evening. Frenchy gave Sylvia a hug and thanked his friends Webber and Mason for making a very special effort on his behalf, to which Mason responded that he and the general were off on another trip to AFFE Headquarters in Tokyo. He then admonished Frenchy to take care of himself, that the two were planning a new adventure for him.

Frenchy wondered, *What the heck's he talking about?*

Chapter Forty-four
On Patrol

It was Friday, 1 August, by the time Frenchy made it back to Hill 710 where he was warmly greeted and congratulated by all. However, he sensed more than the usual tension: Otto looked more tired, his normally round face more puffy, his shoulders more stooped.

A survey crew had chained a distance extending from Frenchy's bunker down the gently sloping ridgeline to the east a good three hundred yards, ending at the next OP. This was part of the plan first discussed the day of the Long Tom Shoot: to have Divarty's Sound and Flash Battalion add microphones in the Black Tooth Sector. The survey just completed had provided a known base for the target-area survey, the simple fact being that when you know the length of one side and the angles at each end of that given side, you can take bearings, compute the length of the other two sides, and find the coordinates of the point opposite the known side. Two new mikes would tie in to the microphone units already on line to the west and to the sound and flash base.

Gen. Hines had suggested putting the devices on Cuspid and Bicuspid; however, technicians had concluded that Cuspid could be used, but the other device should be farther away—farther east. There would be a meeting in the bunker to plan the mike placement, to be followed by final planning back in Baker Battery.

ROK Able Company sent out a patrol Friday night, a platoon starting by the tank revetments in the Kangyung Gap, then circling counterclockwise along the front of Hill 710, crossing the Yeppun Kang, then crossing its dry tributary, then back across Yeppun at a more north westerly point, thence returning to the entry portal. No enemy contact was made during this large sweep, at least not to the patrol's knowledge. The patrol system had improved, in part as the ROKs gained experience and confidence and also because the returning, dog-tired South Koreans could now be driven from the gap back to their companies in three-quarter-ton trucks—sort of a bus service.

Capt. Jeung strongly maintained that if patrols were now to increase, they should include a forward observer, and after Jeung voiced his position to Col. Kim, it was certain that Maj. Willis and Col. Pods were now in on Jeung's plan and would agree to it. It was, after all, the job of the 62nd Field to give direct support to the ROK Regiment. Patrol actions in sectors to the west had recently gained spectacular results by combining ambush tactics and groundfire with use of close-in artillery to knock out counter-attacking Communist patrols.

An Ethiopian patrol had become known as "The Incredible Patrol," famous for their night-fighting skills and clever use of shifting artillery barrages. For some inherent reason, the Ethiopians did not fear the night but instead instilled fear in the enemy. The ROK leaders hoped that they could latch on to these skills by deploying more integrated artillery and emulate the night-fighting Africans.

Since Otto and Frenchy knew the location of dozens of check points within the old crater valley, they saw forward observer action, including patrols, as their responsibility—not their flaming desire but, still, their duty. Frenchy realized that responsibility would, or should, come down to his going on two patrols to fix the microphones, better him alone, not Otto who had been stuck on the Hill while he ran off, got a bunch of medals, dined, and drank with those generals.

Frenchy thought, *Why am I now so nervous about this patrol crap; I was down there a few days ago in an L-19 and flew out hanging onto the wing and laughing? Screw it; it'll be another new experience.* He laughed, thinking about that L-19 episode. He thought about how much fun it must be to fly; he would have to learn, but for now, he had to clear his thoughts, be positive, and forget his instinctive dislike of patrols—*No, call it what it was: fear of patrols.* He thought about the confessions of Robert Burns.

> *But, och! I backward cast my e'e on prospects drear!*
> *An' forward, tho' I canna see, I guess an' fear.*

Next morning, they were joined in the bunker by Capt. Jeung and Capt. Norman Van Alter from the Sound and Flash Battalion; then, by Capt. Marcin and his Exec, Lt. Blake, from Baker Battery. Brimming with a confidence, which at first seemed like rudeness or arrogance, Van Alter led off with a full account of what had been accomplished and what needed doing.

"Since you people have different levels of understanding about sound and flash and what we've been up to, I'll start by describing our observation post and headquarters on Hill 690. You all know that's in the next sector to your west. It's south and west of here and overlooks the hills north of your battery and the hills on the North Korean MLR known as Black Ridge. I'm referring to those hills our forces have been attacking with Corsairs and now with naval gunfire.

"We think the enemy will find it efficacious to place more of its heavy artillery back of the next line of ridges—north of Black Ridge. Their 122mm and 152mm howitzers would have no trouble lobbing counter-battery fire from such farther-back positions.

"So, here's the problem: let's assume there are NK guns at un-known point X and we want to locate them using our microphones at points one through five, together with our OP on Hill 690. As you know, we have surveyed the two new microphone locations, just as we have the three locations to the west. That means, we have the coordinates of the six locations under our control, and thus we know all the bearings, angles, and distances between these points. We seek the coordinates of point X—the location of, let's say, a battery of enemy 122s. Remember: we know six loca-tions and now search for a seventh—enemy point X.

"Here's the whole thing: when the system is activated, a technician at our Hill 690 OP will control and process the six microphones, each of which can hear the distant boom of the en-emy gun emitting from point X. The microphones hear the sound at different times, depending on their distance from point X. The mikes are specially calibrated to pick up the fairly soft noise of the enemy's black powder propellant train and to ignore other noises. Sound travels about 330 meters per second. We thus gather six sound relationships from the five forward mikes and our OP mike. All measurements are based on the relationship of the sound to each mike. With these sound distances, we compute circles of sound distance, and, where those circles intersect—up north somewhere—we compute a new set of coordinates, which should constitute point X—the target area."

The captain exhaled then drew a breath, signaling he was glad that ended his little talk. He smiled, took off his helmet liner, ran his fingers through his hair, and said, "Any questions?" Then he went on.

"It seems like I give that little talk most every day. We feel the men on the line, including you guys, ought to know what's going on and why some of you will take needed hikes into harm's way. I'm afraid I sound like a recorded message or like someone giving a museum tour for the umpteenth time. Sorry about that."

Frenchy thought, *Now that he's thawed, this guy's all right.*

Captain Van Alter continued, "Okay, Lt. Rentner, let's find the exact locations for the two mikes."

Otto bent over the BC scope. "Just off the Cuspid hilltop, say at eight o'clock, there are three discarded ammo boxes, 30-cal. ammo boxes. They were there when I first arrived and are now shot up, covered with debris, and rendered useless and innocent looking. They were our survey point, and there we will place one mike."

Frenchy thought, *I don't like that "we will" talk. I've gotta do it, not Otto!*

Lt. Blake who was now the Baker Battery Exec but was formerly its Recon Officer added, "By the way, just to the right and exactly on the hilltop is a bunker, an enemy bunker with the embrasure facing toward us. If any gooks chance to be there, bets are off."

"For sure," Van Alter responded, continuing, "These will be clandestine operations; we can't have them see us carrying a black box, and, of course, six or eight men can't fight their way up to an occupied bunker anyway. That goes for the eastern mike and its patrol as well, and, since the eastern mike will give us broader sound dispersion east and west, it will be placed first. Now, lieutenant, let's find it."

Otto panned easterly, across the Yeppun Kang and the rough roadway by its side, then almost to the foot of Black Tooth, almost to CPBT Base—the check point used in the Long Tom Shoot. However the spot chosen was short of Black Tooth, so its slope would not interrupt gun sounds from the north and the northwest. There, the circle on the scope focused on the remains of a wheelbarrow—wheel missing—and, like the ammo boxes, now accepted as war-field trash.

Van Alter eyed the spot, and then explained, "The ROK patrol circled from east to west in this area last night and reported all quiet. The Wheelbarrow Patrol will go tomorrow night. There will be more planning today, then more planning tomorrow in Baker Battery. Capt. Marcin, I understand Sgt. Desprez is to go with the first patrol?"

"Yes we're putting youth with the longer hike and saving Lt. Rentner for the next one."

Frenchy felt like protesting but was afraid one of the captains would snap out an irrevocable order and screw up his plan to take both patrols; so he would bide his time. He slept until mid morning and was in Baker by noon.

Frenchy met with Sergeants Hudson and Oder and Lt. Blake in the FDC tent. The patrol would take the route of the Friday ROK patrol in reverse. It would head due north, just to the east of Bicuspid Hill where it would cross Yeppun Kang, continue north to the wheelbarrow, then southeast, across the tributary, back across the Yeppun, and homeward. Possible targets were selected at miles two through six, the targets really designed as checkpoints from where rounds could be adjusted.

They were joined by four ROK soldiers—veterans of the first patrol and actually veterans of many patrols in the valley. They were led by a sergeant, known as Jimmie, who could speak pretty fair English. The huskiest looking soldier, known as Jumbo, would carry the SCR-300 Radio Set. The complete set weighed thirty-eight pounds, but the battery could be carried by another person until time for use. Jumbo eschewed the opportunity to share the load. It was intended that the radio's range would carry to Baker Battery, but a station was set up at the gap in case relay were necessary. Radioman Jumbo was to stay close to Frenchy and to Sgt. Scala—the technician from the Sound and Flash Battalion who was a short, husky career soldier, appearing to be a confident and well-trained leader.

At first, Frenchy felt a little cowed by the older sergeant who was definitely the patrol leader and made that clear at first meeting. It was a curious relationship: a sergeant in a different army and two American sergeants from different units, both in direct support of the ROK unit but not attached to it. Frenchy remembered the old basic training motto: cooperate and graduate and vowed he would do just that. Sgt. Scala was accompanied by a corporal who explained that he was along in case his sergeant caught a round.

The seven-man patrol was driven to the Gap at 2200 hours. A member of the tank crew guided them through the minefield and a gate in the concertina, then on to the first listening post where passwords were exchanged. They moved out with Jimmie at the point.

Forty minutes later at the bank of the little Yeppun River, they hooked up the SCR-300 and reported all well in both Korean and English. The reply came back too loud and clear; they turned the receiver way down—way down—before crossing the little river. Scala joined Jimmie at the point with his corporal at the rear, and, in fifteen minutes, they were rummaging around looking for the wheelbarrow, feeling some frustration until it was found, and the mike was hidden right there, amidst the broken parts.

Jimmie again took the point, and the circle continued, turning southeast at the foot of Black Tooth, where they encountered slabs of hard igneous rock at the foot of the mountain face together with patches of loose talus, called *scree*, which could be slippery, sort of like walking on marbles.

They heard a small rattle of loose scree up ahead, froze in place and gazed forward into the gloom. Higher up among the rocks were voices, and they sure weren't from Brooklyn!

Pulling his bayonet, Frenchy winced at the clicking sound when he seated it on the underside of the Garand barrel. Scala crawled along side and whispered, "I don't think there are many of them, but they have the altitude advantage and will sure as hell hear us and then spot us if we move."

Frenchy gritted his teeth and muttered, "I can blow 'em to hell; where's the radioman?"

"Behind ya."

Frenchy grabbed the transmitter phone.

"Fox Oboe Baker, fire mission, over."

They were beyond the listed range limitations for an SCR-300, but luck held as they heard, "Send your mission, over."

"Azimuth 1600; from CPBT Base, left 100, add 200; Enemy patrol in open; we are about on CP Black Tooth; will adjust, over."

Sgt. Hudson's voice repeated the instruction and added, "Wait . . ."

The crew of the third and fourth guns were up and waiting, so within two minutes, "On the way, over." was heard and acknowledged.

The rounds landed well behind the enemy; Frenchy felt safe in directing, "Drop 100." The rounds hit amongst the enemy, some of whom could be seen silhouetted against the flashes. Frenchy ordered VT followed by enough salvos of willy peter and smoke to assure the escape of his patrol under its cover. Scala—ever cool, ever competent—signaled the other men, "On the first willy peter, bug ass down the hill toward base! Meet four hundred yards south. Stay together! Skidoo."

Jimmie repeated the order for his men.

The scree slope erupted in streams of phosphorous and smoke, which quite obscured the getaway. What a surprise it must have been to the enemy who had probably come from the east slope of Black Tooth and hardly expected big trouble right there in their own front yard at midnight.

Sgt. Scala signaled, "Assemble on me! On me!" Jimmie added, "*Moida! Moida!*"

Frenchy had lagged behind, hoping to fire another round or two, but he soon scampered up to the others. A head count revealed all present; they formed up and moved for home like horses headed for the barn.

A quick recap at Baker FDC summed up a successful mission. Ironically, Sergeant Mario Scala confessed that he had worried about Frenchy trying too hard to be a hero, maybe wanting to bring back prisoners, attack the gook patrol, toss grenades, or otherwise cause uncalled-for mischief.

"Where did you get such notions?" Frenchy asked with a cocked head and a grin. "Our mission was to place a mike; I've no interest in ordinary patrols. Most of these damn patrols are to keep the infantry on the MLR occupied—sort of keyed up, not relaxed like garrison soldiers. What it shows me is that, even in the stalemate, front-line troops are expendable in the eyes of the leaders. I don't give a damn for the whole patrol concept."

Capt. Marcin responded, "Hard to argue with that; patrols explain why we continue to suffer almost as many casualties each month as we did in the wild days of 1950 and 1951. Your trouble, Scala, is that you heard about Frenchy in connection with the Charlie Battery Shootout. That was a hell of a lot different than meeting gooks on a patrol. Back then, Frenchy was on orders to assist Charlie Battery, he happened to have super motor reflexes with a rifle, he got there and his best friend was immediately killed, he also saw our boss go up in flames and smoke—one crazy, tragic day, which gave us both battlefield promotions. Now, everyone, get some sleep as best you can. And you, Scala, learn to trust your buddies!"

Frenchy tried to approach Capt. Marcin about the next patrol and the idea that he should go, not Otto. Marcin put him off, "We'll see—no decisions at 0550 in the morning after being up all night; you won't go tonight anyway; folks need a day to recuperate and prepare."

Frenchy thought, *I could stay here and save the trip, but chances are it'd be better to get a big breakfast here, then sack out in the OP hoochy.*

Otto greeted him, "Glad you're back; we're in for a treat, a sixteen-inch show."

"Wow! We're going to hear from the battleship?"

409

"Due within the hour; Hiram has patched us through to the *U.S.S. Texas*. Meanwhile, tell me what happened."

Frenchy described the journey, planting the mike, and shooting at what he cleverly dubbed "The Scree Patrol."

Frenchy bit his lip, thinking, *Now's as good a time as any.*

"Otto, I want to take the next patrol, too."

"Bullshit! No way! There's one for each of us; Cuspid is mine; don't argue."

"Well, I'm going along tomorrow, just in case."

"No you're not, sergeant, this is the lieutenant speaking, and your job is here! Don't get too big for your britches."

"Hiram and Lee-Mo can hold this fort. I'm going; you can court-martial me later in the week."

Otto looked at him, smiled, and said, "You can sure be a pain in the ass."

Frenchy laughed, remembering arguments with his sisters and with the Uijongbu armory sergeant—Sgt. Murphy—and responded, "I've been called that before—and lots worse; it must be true: I can be a pain in the ass."

The bunker radio crackled with static and sprang to life. "Fox Oboe Baker, this is Acero three, stand by, will relay advice from Davy Crocket, over."

"Roger, over."

Although naval gunfire procedure was similar to field artillery procedure, since the guns would be firing due west, and as observers, they were facing due north, they had agreed with their navy friends that it would be simpler to give adjustments along the gun-target line, like they would in an L-19.

"On the way, over."

"On the way, wait. . . ."

They heard an enormous boom. But where?

Otto said, "I sensed it behind Black Tooth."

"Me, too," said Hiram.

"Fox Oboe Baker, have we lost you?"

Frenchy took the phone.

"No Acero Three; we're here, hoping to see smoke from behind BT, wait. . . ."

Sure enough, with wind out of the east, they saw smoke coming from the west side of Black Tooth.

"Smoke sighted, add five hundred, over."

"Add five hundred, wait. . . ."

The next round landed right on the Black Ridge ridgeline west of the river. The explosion was the largest Frenchy had ever seen—from a shell about as heavy as a Volkswagen! Otto adjusted right one hundred, drop two hundred, and saw the round actually hit the river. Ever after there would be a wide point in the Yeppun just west of the mountain! Then Otto made his final correction: "Davy created a pond in the Yeppun Kang and is now right on line. Recommend H and I fire in increasing increments of one hundred yards, over."

"Thanks much, Fox Oboe Baker, this is Acero three, out."

After a hot meal, Frenchy conked out for sixteen hours, rising only for calls of nature and C-Ration snacks. At sunrise, his concern for the Cuspid patrol mounted again. Then he whispered, *My Father, if this cup cannot pass unless I drink of it, Your will, not my will, be done.*

The walk down the hill and then the ride to the battery was solemn but not because of the squabble of the day before. Frenchy was quite overcome with a brotherly love for his friend. He thought of Soddy, his lost brother. He sensed Otto had the same feelings. As they pulled into Baker Battery, Otto grasped his arm.

"You don't have to do this, but, whatever happens, you're a great young soldier and a great friend."

Frenchy looked him in the eye, then had to cover his face. Again, it was too much, too much to bear. He struggled to recover, as they walked side-by-side to the FDC tent and the morning briefing.

They saluted Maj. Morris and Capt. Marcin, who both stood by the tent flap, most of the other patrol members from the wheelbarrow patrol being grouped nearby. Sgt. Jimmie waved, saying, *"Ohiyo gozaimasu, Ichi-ban FO."*

Ichi-ban meant "number one" but was used as a term of respect. Frenchy acknowledged with a little bow, *"Ohiyo gozaimasu."*

Maj. Morris, who had been the voice of Acero Three the day before, asked routine questions about the naval gunfire mission. Otto's comment was he wished they knew more about the results. Frenchy added that if the first round had been WP, they might have found it faster. The major said he would check out the idea but feared there wasn't such a thing as sixteen-inch willy peter and that, anyway, high explosive and white phosphorous rounds probably had different ballistic qualities, so the landing place of one might not work as a starting point for adjusting the other.

Capt. Van Alter, Sgt. Scala, and the sound and flash corporal were the last to arrive. Van Alter happily announced that the wheelbarrow mike was integrated and was functioning.

As the only newcomer, Otto was presented to the other patrol members, all noting he would be the only rookie and the only commissioned officer. However, patrols were often unique patch-together units, at times having specialists along from other units, other services or other countries, sometimes even civilians, such as embedded war correspondents. It was not taken as unusual or degrading when the two captains announced that the technician, Sgt. Scala, would lead the patrol with Lt. Rentner responsible for fire direction in emergencies.

Frenchy could come along under his actual new MOS as a recon sergeant in a forward observer team. Frenchy had worried that Otto might make one more attempt to remove him from the patrol; however, Otto remained silent, apparently at peace with the idea. Admittedly, it was advantageous for Frenchy to carry the radio with the big guy, Jumbo, carrying its battery; the problem was, both friends wished the other were not a part of this dangerous mission.

Inside the tent, Otto and Frenchy met with Sgts. Hudson and Oder and pondered special targets. Hudson suggested a treatment specially designed for small hills:

"Picture running a circle on a map of Cuspid Hill by using a drafting compass with its point placed dead center on the hill and with its radius at one hundred yards. Then label it like a clock with 1200 hours at due north. If a bigger circle is needed, use a radius of 150 or 200 yards and so on. From anywhere on the damn hill, you can simply direct something like, 'Radius one hundred at three.' Of course you would just eyeball these points—no map, binocs, or compass needed. That adjustment, 'Radius one hundred at three' would mean 'Shoot one hundred yards due east.' Does that help or only confuse things?"

Frenchy liked the idea, but waited for his boss to comment; he thought about playing bridge, where trying out a new bidding system could muddle things and lead to bad results.

Otto rubbed his chin. "Sounds good to me, so long as we can find north."

Sgt. Oder replied, "Good point, Sir; tonight will be clear with the moon in first quarter, Black Tooth visible in the north, northeast. Think of north as four hundred meters left of Black Tooth."

"Sold," said Otto, and they turned to selecting trail targets.

They again went off at 2200 hours, the same team except for the addition of Otto and with Frenchy toting the radio this time. They passed through the gap, the minefield, and the gate in the concertina wire, then on to the listening post at which point the radio battery was added and the device tested. The weather report was not totally accurate, as clouds rolled in creating a partially overcast, gloomy night.

Sgt. Jimmie took the point with other ROKs on the wings; Scala near Jimmie, his corporal as far away as possible. Otto, Frenchy, and Jumbo plodded in the middle, Frenchy bearing up well, though burdened with flak jacket, SCR-300, M-1, two grenades, and the 38 Police Special with its extra cartridge pouch. The route was direct, and inside thirty-five minutes they were climbing up the south and west slopes of Cuspid Hill.

According to plan, the two sound and flash men and two ROKs hooked left to the ammo cans' site while Otto, Frenchy, Jimmie, and Jumbo went on straight to the bunker, which was, as predicted, covered with a row of timbers and sandbags, then grass, with the so-called embrasure, a slit opening facing south. In size, it was about six feet wide, by four feet, and five and half feet high at the rooftop, with most of its north side gaping open. Frenchy thought, *They build 'em about like we do—pretty solid, but they build 'em smaller.*

A dark cloud obscured the young moon.

As Frenchy heaved the thirty-eight-pound radio off his back, he felt a cold chill, his body shuddering and snapping to full alert in some half-conscious reaction. He stood stark still. He thought there were noises to the east . . . and then he was sure of it! Next he heard the dread call of the bugle—very near at hand to the east—from the flats in front of the other hill. *Good God, they're on us—just a few yards away; we gotta fight, gotta fight!*

He saw flashes of gunfire from the northeast extending in a broad arc of at least two hundred yards to the southeast. The eight-man patrol was under siege by at least a platoon—forty or fifty North Koreans. What odds! He snapped on the bayonet.

The enemy may have sensed that they gave away their position and intentions sooner than necessary—perhaps born of high bravado and the confidence of facing only an eight-man patrol, an insignificant number who were now trapped on the hilltop. There was a hiatus in firing—a chilling silence—as the enemy circled the hill and closed in. The bugle signaled a soft, "ta-ta . . . ta"— whatever that meant.

In that calm before the storm, leadership clearly passed to Otto and to Frenchy. The microphone placement now forgotten,

Scala and the other four found temporary refuge on the north side of the hill, affording some shelter until the enemy encirclement was complete and trapped them all. Otto signaled them to enter the bunker and fire through the south opening. Frenchy figured the attack would not come from the steeper east side but mostly from the north—by far their most vulnerable attack point, the gentler slope, and the one leading to the exposed side of the bunker. He realized there could be an equally robust attack from the south and west but concerned himself only with enemy out of the north—*What the hell, do what you can do and hope for the best!*

Otto screamed, "Call Baker now, right now! Fire VT, all available VT on our command. Get to it; we can hold 'em just long enough. Get two ranging rounds first!"

Frenchy had at it, calling Baker, requesting one salvo of HE impact fuse on the Cuspid bunker, radius one hundred at twelve, to be followed by an adjustment, just time for one adjustment, then all available VT, including Able and Charlie Batteries and the neighboring 155s as well. The tension in the exchange was terrific, the FDC crew having never faced firing on their own men, including two men they knew well. Word spread: "Otto and Frenchy are out there!"

The salvo of impact fuse rounds landed just long, as planned. Of course, if they had been short rounds, they'd all have been toast. Frenchy called, "Drop five–zero, prepare to fire for effect, all available; wait for my order, then all at once; but wait, wait, wait, if you don't hear from us in three minutes, make it two minutes, two minutes, fire anyway, fire anyway—don't wait, 'cause we've probably had it!"

The enemy reached the hilltop first on the southwest side. Scala and two ROKs were hit. Big Jumbo dragged them to the bunker, then threw grenades and quieted the west side for the moment. Suddenly, Otto seemed to fly backward through the air toward Frenchy and the bunker. Fearing he'd waited too long,

Frenchy called, "Now, now, fire everything; we're done for, over-run, over!"

Loyal Hudson calmly acknowledged, "Roger—VT on the way, over."

He started to pull Otto into the bunker, but Jumbo took over the task; he then fired to the north, using the Garand from the hip until he heard the ping of its empty clip; he threw his two grenades. In succession, he felt a pain in his ear, then separate pains in his chest, finally a leg. Other enemies came right at him; he knew the 105 rounds were in the air; he had maybe twenty seconds before tons of steel would fall from the sky. An enemy ran into his Garand; he thrust, then back out. With lust, he thrust again. Out came the 38 Police Special.

He downed another attacker at a range of four feet, then two others. They fell almost on top of him. Inspired by their near-ness, he simply fell back against Otto, then, with Jumbo's help, he pulled those two plus the bayoneted enemy in on top of them to form an improvised plug, firing around them until the 38 was empty. He kept the weapon in his hand as he groped and found more shells in the little pouch, he stuffed a bunch in his mouth, spat five in his hand, pushed them into the little revolver and fired at shadowy figures on the open side. Extra 38 bullets taken from the pouch were again and again fed: mouth-hand-revolver. As he fired from northwest to northeast, one of the ROKs behind him was firing to the south out of the embrasure; there were other Korean voices—enemy voices—just feet away, more yelling, the noise of the burp guns going burr-rupp, burr-rupp, more yelling!

He shot at the sound of the voices and the burp guns; soldiers fell right in front of him, reinforcing the human block in the entry-way; the noise kept up—the ripping of the burp guns, the yelling!

Then everything changed: instead of the intermittent Asian yelling and screaming and the cracking, ripping, and burping sounds of small arms, there were uninterrupted, piercing whams—deafening noises—wham, wham, wham, wham, wham—no breaks!

Without letup as all three 62ⁿᵈ Field firing batteries responded with all eighteen 105 howitzers—truly *fuego de acero*! Soon, they were joined by the booms of the 155 howitzers—even louder noises. The variable time fuses gave the rounds their most deadly effects on troops in the open, but they also might, just might, spare troops under cover.

Frenchy found himself reloading the little revolver and arranging the three dead North Koreans in the bunker entrance, as other bodies toppled on them.

Back at each howitzer, cannoneers were rhythmically pulling the lanyard, opening the breech, jamming a round, pulling the lanyard, and at Service Battery, more ammo and VT fuses were being loaded. The men at the guns had heard that they were firing at their own troops and grit their teeth at the thought of it; what could have happened? Were the men alive? Cannoneers shuddered, sick at the thought of what the hell they were doing. Christ, how horrible!

Yet, firing at your own position was an old device, especially in static warfare, used recently on Old Baldy and repeatedly in the Second War, used in just this way when out-posts were overrun, when the main line was overrun, or sometimes when a command post was threatened, as employed by the legendary hero—Audie Murphy.

The howitzers ceased fire as they ran low on ammunition, Charlie Battery giving out first, probably since it was just back on line in its new location and not yet fully supplied. Fire was completely lifted, as two platoons from ROK George Company double-timed toward Cuspid.

It was overkill. The North Korean–reinforced platoon was annihilated, as sure as the Alamo! The bunker rooftop had collapsed beam by beam, sandbag by sandbag, section by section, and all was quiet.

One of the M-46 Pattons rolled out of the gap and toward the hill, Capt. Marcin sharing the turret. At the foot of Cuspid Hill, he saw ROK soldiers milling about and a GI walking toward him, helping another man. It was Frenchy walking and, with another soldier, supporting Otto; Frenchy soon handed over his friend to a tall ROK soldier in exchange for a rifle—no doubt it was the faithful and famous M-1, still with bayonet fixed. In the lead was Sgt. Jimmie. Five of eight walking out.

Marcin muttered to himself: *I may get busted for fighting it, but if I can help it, there will be no microphone on that damn useless hill, all a bad idea! Screw it—general officers getting too fancy, pushing the young soldiers to go out and die; the whole patrol system stank, stank; this senseless killing of young soldiers in the Demilitarized Zone was not the way to fight a stalemated war!*

Things were a little blurry for Frenchy that Wednesday morning. He knew there was a tank ride, then a jeep, finally a helicopter. Along the way, his old comrade Sgt. Gielow gave him a shot, and he found himself back at the MASH unit.

Chapter Forty-five
Where Do We Go From Here?

There he was in the general ward—no triage delay this time, although there wasn't a hell of a lot wrong with him: three burp gun slugs in the chest, all stopped by the flak jacket but one cracking a rib and all the hits damn sore, a flesh wound in the leg, a chunk of his ear shot off—a lifelong memento—and a concussion likely caused by a friendly-fire howitzer fragment penetrating the bunker roof, hitting his steel helmet and putting a souvenir dent in it.

By Friday, he was sitting up in bed and chatting with Lt. Sylvia O'Connor. What a good buddy she had been—like sister Norma. There had been serious moments when they talked about both his girlfriend Amanda and the possible new relationship with Anne, and also discussing Sylvia's husband—an army doctor, now back stateside. The quote stuck in his head—*Who is Silvia? What is she that all the swains commend her?*

Otto had also come to the MASH unit but had been transferred by air to a hospital ship in Pusan Harbor. He had been hit in the back by a burp gun, which knocked him forward and out of further line of fire. He also had multiple wounds from grenade fragments, one hitting an arm and another sticking in his skull—fortunately a small piece, but its removal was beyond the ken of the MASH doctors and equipment. The flak jackets had saved them both.

Frenchy was told the defense of Cuspid Hill would entitle him to another Purple Heart and at least another Silver Star. He thought of a moment far away off Adak, Alaska, now also seeming long ago, when the *I Ching* said,

In the midst of the army. Good fortune.
The king bestows a triple decoration.

He was interviewed by an army historian and was, in this way, prompted to write his own report about Jumbo, the tall ROK soldier—real name, Sun Ruh-Tra—who had acted promptly and heroically on both patrols, especially with respect to getting Otto to shelter and plugging the bunker's north side with the bodies of enemy soldiers. Frenchy asked about discharge from the MASH unit and was told they wanted to be careful with the head injury, and, in any case, he couldn't leave until seen by certain high-ranking visitors on Monday.

And it came to pass that they did arrive on Monday—a memorable day in his life. First to arrive were Lt. Col. Podolsky and Capt. Marcin, who reported that three members of the patrol had been killed, Sgt. Scala still alive but in critical condition, and the others were recovering. The survivors credited Otto and Frenchy for making the most of a terrible situation.

Capt. Marcin brought Frenchy's duffel bag and B-4 bag, all stuffed with his gear, including the sadly wrinkled, camelhair coat, the medals, and the Baby Nambu.

Frenchy replied, "What the heck's all that for, Sir? Where am I going? I'm not in bad shape."

"Wait and see," Col. Pods replied, as he pinned the second Purple Heart on Frenchy's robe.

To Frenchy's bewildered surprise, they were joined by Gen. Webber and Lt. Mason. After some small talk, silence fell in the ward, as the general spoke, "I'll just give this to you straight, no flowery speeches, no compliments, just let you have it. First, you're now too damn decorated to be kept on the front line. It's an old story from many wars: citizens will not stand to see their heroes exposed and exposed again and again, eventually to die. The colonel here or Gen. Hines could give you various choices of rear-area service. Unfortunately, that would be at two points a month, meaning you'll be here another year—stuck in tame duty, too tame for a guy like you—a year wasted in some unworthy job. However, we've been working on this for several weeks, and I am now officially authorized to give you two more complex choices."

Frenchy frowned, *Good Lord, what's happening, what could these choices be? This must be what Mason was hinting about at the ceremony.*

"The first choice is to return to the States, accept a good, healthy leave, and enroll in the next available company-grade Officers' Class at Fort Sill. This would not be the OCS program with the usual chicken-shit combined with a fail rate of 60 percent; no, it would be the class for proven leaders—already-commissioned soldiers. In other words, you would first be given what is called a battlefield commission to the rank of second lieutenant and sent there to round out your training. Get it?"

Frenchy nodded, thinking, *And if that happened, Midshipman Raul Desprez would have to salute me, instead of the other way around. What the hell is coming next?*

"The other choice is one I pray you'll accept." The general stopped and swallowed hard; the others saw that he was choked up and trying to get hold of himself. Lt. Mason offered to proceed, but the general, annoyed at his display of weakness, waved his aide away, "I'm fine . . . I'm fine. We've submitted your school transcript to the United States Military Academy, West Point on the Hudson—my alma mater. This is under the program established many years ago for appointment of outstanding enlisted personnel under a special Federal law. By this arrangement, you were actually nominated by your immediate commander, Capt. Marcin. In your case, there are endorsements by three Generals,

Col. Podolsky, and a very special recommendation—at least we think it's a recommendation—since it was written in Korean—by Col. Young-No.

"The point is you have been accepted, final action awaiting only your consent. You may, in fact, you would be required to join the fall class, scheduling your arrival for around 1 October, thus missing some of the plebe training but not missing any of the academic program."

Brimming with enthusiasm, Lt. Mason could not be still, "What do ya think, Frenchy?"

The bashful days were gone. He felt powerful—certain, but he was not going to be hurried, this constituting his big moment, he cherished it, remembering the Rabbi's exact words about the heat of life and the heat of war:

> *You will come out sorely tested; it will be the makings of you; it will take you to your destiny!*

His head swam with so many thoughts—his ore boat days:
> *Eternal Father, strong to save.*
> *The lake does not give up its dead.*
> *Set a course for Thunder Bay.*

There was Col. Murch:
> *I see the makings of a soldier in you.*

There was dear Amanda:
> *I could not love thee dear so much loved I not honor more.*
> *You don't want to get out of it.*

The pistol lesson:
> *The average range is just seven feet.*

Dr. Beck and the dream analysis:
> *Don't repress your dreams or fear them.*

The Rabbi and the sermon:
Take the sword of the spirit, which is the word of God.

Mostly, it was here in the Land of the Morning Calm:
Mecham was killed almost immediately.
Such action distinguishes Desprez by extraordinary heroism.
Fire everything—we're done for—overrun!

He cleared his head and addressed the general, "Tell me, Sir, may I major in literature?"

"Absolutely."

"And, Sir, is there a hockey team?"

"Of course."

"Is it a good team, Sir?"

"You got me there, but probably not. I suspect competing schools recruit Canadian players—hardly possible for us."

"Good; then I can make the team. I must also advise you that after my active duty commitment, I may very well seek to go on to graduate school to study literature, perhaps enter academia and join the army reserves. Based on these factors, Sir, where do I sign?"

They came up, one at a time—there in the ward of the MASH unit—to congratulate him and to say a few words. Sylvia also came forward, this time with a lingering kiss for all to see, while the officers, MASH staff members, and other patients gave them both an ovation.

Still eager, Lt. Mason asked, "What are your plans for when you first get stateside, Frenchy?"

"Well, Sir, let me think: I'll see my parents, probably teasing my mother that, in spite of her fears, I never got a certain *jolie fille* pregnant. I will tell the town mayor that his 38 Police Special saved my life and the lives of others. I will grease and oil my red Chevy, put on my sport coat, and take off for Louisville; from there, if all goes well, I will drive with a certain friend to Soddy-Daisy, Tennessee, to perform a sad responsibility."

Then he extended his arms as if to give a benediction, was silent for a moment, and proclaimed: "I shall abide by the oath: Duty, Honor, Country. God free us from this awful war. Thanks to all you wonderful people here beside me. God bless my absent comrades—both living and dead; and God bless America!"

EPILOGUE

And so Arnold "Frenchy" Desprez left the Land of the Morning Calm to return to anticipated and not-so-anticipated trips and reunions, then to face hard work, regimentation, and more chances to balk and fight back.

How the images of friends drifted through his head, along with the women and others he encountered along the way: Raul, Morgan Jones, Hank Sauer, Dago Joe, Bingo, Noonan, McNulty, Mason, Murch, Burley, Anne, Amanda, the Fontenots, Solstice Weathers, Mayor Finkle, Alice Perrers, Dave Davis, Bill Cosby, Father Mal, the Rabbi, Dr. Beck, Cowboy Rich, Soddy, Otto, Marcin, Pods, Willis, Mudge, Forrest, Hypes, Sylvia, Snuffles, Webber, Lee-Mo, Kim, Young-No, Ace.

By the way, Sgt. McNulty did attend the Great Lakes Marine Academy and wrote stories of his navy, army, and boat experiences.

Friends were the big thing, friends everywhere, with no real stinkers that he wanted to recall; anyway, to heck with them. It had happened so fast, it was like a big blur, all in all, an incredible time, and he had truly come of age as a warrior in just ten months of active duty and just two months in the war theater.

We can be confident that his award for valor in the shootout was raised to the Distinguished Service Cross. Thus, he received:

> The Distinguished Service Cross,
> The Silver Star,
> The Bronze Star with "V" attached,
> Two Purple Heart Medals,
> The Korean Service Ribbon,
> The Good Conduct Medal,
> The United Nations Service Medal, and
> The Republic of Korea Presidential Unit Citation.

That is not counting the Expert Marksman Medal or the Baby Nambu, semi-automatic handgun, received from Col. Young-No, who would, himself, soon reach the well-deserved rank of major general in the Republic of Korea Army and later serve in the National Assembly. Think of Cadet Desprez, trying to wear all those awards along with the customary Military Academy regalia!

After Frenchy departed, there was almost another year of war, some of it horrendous, with many infamous and heartrending battles yet to be fought in 1952: Old Baldy, Bunker Hill, Outpost Kelly, Sniper Ridge, the War's largest air strikes, and T-Bone Hill on Christmas Day.

President-elect Eisenhower fulfilled his campaign promise and went to Korea, where he had a good visit with the troops. He lunched with Cpl. James A. Murray, who, sadly, was killed in action a few days later.

Then, the War actually stepped up in 1953, as both sides seemed to have an "I'll not be pushed" attitude. Frenchy's old dislike—patrols in the DMZ—continued, actually expanded. There were two battles for Pork Chop Hill with heavy losses, including a fire for effect on the command bunker quite like the fire on Cuspid, yet that tiny outpost was also in the DMZ, and of doubtful value. After all the bloodshed, by orders of Gen. Maxwell Taylor, Pork Chop Hill was finally abandoned by U.N. Forces.

In April 1953, sick and wounded prisoners were exchanged in Operation Little Switch; however, the stumbling block at Panmunjom remained, as it had since 1951—what to do with Chinese and North Korean prisoners who did not wish to go home.

On 13 July to 20 July, the Chinese launched a six-division attack on IX Corps. The 555th Field Artillery Battalion (the "Triple Nickel") was overrun with three hundred casualties, part of the Battle of the Kumsong River Salient. Then, on 24–26 July, a total of 3,000 Chinese attacked U.S. Marine regiments in the last actions of the War. In those last sixty days of combat, the enemy fired 700,000 artillery rounds at U.N. Forces who fired 4,700,000 rounds back, and, in that mad sixty-day finish, approximately 100,000 Communists and 53,000 U.N. troops were killed, wounded, or captured.

It was the greatest artillery war of all time with more rounds fired than in all theaters of the Second World War.

As the conflict wound down, the end could be described as inconclusive but certainly not a Communist victory, as they claimed. After all, they had been chased back above the Parallel with extreme loss of life—probably losses in the millions; North Korea had been pulverized. The Domino Theory—a concern at the time—had ceased to operate: the South Korea domino tile did not fall. Still, men on both sides had to "die for a tie." We suffered 157,530 casualties, including 54,246 fatalities.

The cease-fire finally came on 27 July 1953, with the exchange beginning 5 August, through the Neutral Nations Repatriations Commission, consisting of five neutral countries. This turnover to neutral nations should sound familiar. Remember that back at Oakland Army Base Frenchy asked his new friend, Dave Davis, about the POW problem, wondering, "Why don't they ship 'em off to some third-world country and let it be unsnarled there?"

Dave laughed, "Why not? They should send you to Panmunjom."

Acknowledgements

I dropped some old habits back in March, 2008, when I started work on Frenchy: I stopped playing *Sudoku*, and limited golfing, bridge-playing, sculpturing, jewelry-making, and traveling; but, most of all, I changed my reading habits to convert to the study of the Korean War. See the Bibliography at the end of this part; more than forty of those books—literally all I could lay my hands on—are directly related to the war.

Also included here is a section by Col. Arthur, which serves as a briefing on the twenty-first century army.

Since I lived through the thing, part of the time in the army, and therefore knew the main events to begin with, all that reading tended to bring things back to mind and to put many new details swimming around in my head. For the most part I can't say where this or that idea sprang from; nevertheless, certain sources were revelations—expressions of totally new facts, ideas, and opinions that changed my thinking substantially.

I was very moved by S.L.A. Marshall's *The River and the Gauntlet*. His second book, *Pork Chop Hill*, is the better known of the two and was made into a good movie, starring Gregory Peck, but *The River and the Gauntlet* affected me in a special way: I was appalled by our inept leadership, horrified by the loss of life,

429

and bewildered by what is said to be the longest retreat in the history of our Armed Forces. Slam Marshall's Chapter, *Murch's Battalion,* which I read after I had been in Murch's Leadership School, of course added to the book's significance.

Appleman's *South to the Naktong, North to the Yalu* furnished a straight, non-critical account, as did *The Korean War: Years of Stalemate.* Gen. Paik Sun Yup wrote *From Pusan to Panmunjom*—a vivid account from the standpoint of a great Korean general; I read it twice.

But for new and critical ideas, Halberstam's *The Coldest Winter: America and the Korean War* was in a special category. There, MacArthur's attitudes were revealed and criticized, along with the short-comings of various generals, including Almond's repeated miscalculations. Along the same critical lines are: Higgins' *Korea and the Fall of MacArthur;* Manchester's *American Caesar;* Costello's *Days of Infamy;* and James' *Refighting the Last War: Command and Crisis in Korea.*

In my historical accounts, I avoid quoting or paraphrasing; however, my reference to "an arrogant, blind march to disaster," "an insane plan," and to MacArthur's "sycophants" are from Halberstam (pages 438 and 613), and the quote in praise of Lt. Col. Murch is from Hackworth's *About Face* (page 109).

I have many to thank: I will first mention three and then list some others in alphabetical order:

My wife, Jane Arthur, was the technician, computer expert, and primary critic.

Col. Julia Arthur wrote the introduction and steered me to needed information.

Kate Sloan Fiffer served as copy editor and guided me away from technical writing and toward fiction writing.

Now, for the rest:

Curtis Aronson kindly replied to my email to veterans of the 61st Field Artillery Battalion where he served as Wire Chief in

Headquarters Battery. I was interested in his route: San Francisco to Camp Drake to Inchon, to Uijongbu.

Dr. Russell Becker got me started in the study of Carl Gustav Jung. He went through psychoanalysis at the Jung Institute and advised me on Dr. Beck's Camp Drake analysis of Frenchy's black moose dreams.

Roland Calhoun—an old navy man—for straightening me out on the monkey fist.

Paul Chasey and his wife Ellie live in Palm Desert, California, and Pont De Boyon, France. Their French home is in the Maconaise, a lovely part of Burgundy—home of the world's most famous wines. I'm very nostalgic about this region, having driven down the Loire Valley in 1956, eventually to rendezvous with my future wife in Venice. Paul served in the Army Signal Corps, stateside, back in the 1950s. He is a retired Director of American Friends of our Armed Forces, and I mention him because he helped me with the French passages—mostly amatory dialogue between Frenchy and Amanda.

Robert F. Comeau, retired army colonel and West Point graduate, put me in touch with Bob Murch, son of Col. Gordon E. Murch, as explained in the Preface.

Mike Gershbein is a librarian at The Glencoe Public Library and frequent aide to me in locating some of the books listed in the Bibliography. Let him serve as a symbol for all the help I received from all the folks at that library—many thanks to all! One coincidence is that Mike retrieved a copy of William Russell's **Stalemate & Standoff: The Bloody Outpost War** from a library in Florida, where the author was serving as a volunteer. Bill Russell was an army combat correspondent in Korea from 1951–1953, earning the Bronze Star for his reporting. I had a nice telephone visit with him.

Stan Grote was a lieutenant in the 61st Field—a brilliant FDC man and FO. We got reacquainted at reunions, and he helped me recall the cannoneers' hop. Stan went on to become a bird colonel in the Reserves.

Murray Hirsh entered service in August 1952, after graduating from NYU. With his accounting degree, he was sent to Quartermaster eight-week Basic Training, then Leadership School, troopship to Japan, then Inchon in May 1953, finally to Headquarters Battery, 12th Field Artillery Battalion, 2nd Division. He ended up Supply Sergeant in this 155-howitzer outfit. Murray furnished useful information on battery life and supply procedures.

Joseph E. Jannotta is a special case. He went to New Trier High School and Williams College, graduating in 1951, immediately joining the navy and going to Preflight School at Pensacola, then to Corpus Christie, earning his wings in October 1952. Joe flew Corsairs off the Carrier *Champlain*, stationed in the Yellow Sea. His squadron furnished close-air support, worked with Air Controllers (FACs) and L-19s, fired 50-caliber machine guns, napalm, 1,000-pound bombs, etc. On one mission his squadron encountered foul weather and searched for their carrier for five hours, finally locating it with "just enough petrol for one pass." He confessed that he was so exhausted they had to lift him out of the Corsair. Joe reached the rank of Lieutenant, Senior Grade. Interestingly, his brother, Ned, flew the AD-Skyraider, and their uncle was an admiral in the Pacific War. Anchors aweigh, my boys!

Dick Kasperson and I were classmates at Northwestern University School of Law. To my surprise, at lunch after golf in the summer of '08, he said his family came from Grand Haven, Michigan, and generations of Kaspersons worked on Great Lakes boats. The lore of swinging on booms, going uptown, ice breakers for winter runs, voyages to Murmansk, everyday boat life, unloading the ore, and death on the Lakes came with help from Dick.

Will Kellogg is another special case—a classmate of mine at Central School in Glencoe and New Trier High School. Will went through Artillery Basic Training at Camp Chaffee, Arkansas, and had sad stories of endless KP duty and of taking the northern route to Yokohama with everyone sick, sick, sick. He served as Supply Sergeant in the 423rd Field Artillery, an eight-inch howitzer outfit, fighting in the Iron Triangle near Kumhwa—as he said, "opposite 300,000 Chinese." With inadequate clothing—just fatigues— they endured twenty-below weather, having to keep the prime movers, trucks, and generators running twenty-four hours a day. They endured counter-battery fire, night attacks by the Chinese, and cold, cold, cold. Their tents were burned, and they suffered hemorrhagic fever—carried by the plentiful rodents—a sorry, miserable, dangerous time in combat.

George Lecornu from Ft. Smith, Arkansas, joined the marines in 1951, age eighteen, took Boot Training in San Diego, and advanced training at Camp Pendleton, California. He shipped out on *USS Polk* to Kobe, Japan, then to the famous 1st Marine Division. Becoming sick with pneumonia, George was sent to Pusan and worked there for a while on mail detail, after which he ran the post office at the 7th Marine Regiment, where he served for thirteen months. He remembers the time Marine Fighter Pilot Ted Williams crash-landed his Corsair at a nearby airbase. George was on active duty for twenty years, later worked very successfully for McDonalds and as a franchisee.

Moonja Yoo, working at Evanston Hospital, suggested use of some tricky Korean phrases—*Kamsa Moonja!*

Robert G. Murch of Arlington, Virginia, and son of Col. Gordon E Murch, was discovered by Col. Bob Comeau (see above and in the Preface). Bob Murch sent me a batch of information on his father: pictures, history, award citations, and newspaper clippings. The following is a quote from Bob's email dated September 7, 2008:

Many years later after his retirement, my dad and I were driving by the Pentagon where he had worked several years. We were on our way to visit my mother's grave at Arlington Cemetery. He said: "We thought we were doing the most important thing in the world." Then he said: "Maybe we were."

Armand Norehad, a good friend gave me valuable ideas for the Great Northern chapter.

Fred Nothdurft is a real get-up-and-go guy, with many interests; indeed, the only problem I have with him is spelling his name! Drafted in September 1951, he took Basic and Ordnance Training at Camp Breckenridge, and then was sent to Fort Lawton, Yokohama, Camp Drake, Inchon, and Uijongbu (sound familiar?). Fred served in Service Company, 17th Infantry (the "Buffalos"), 7th Division, where he drove a deuce-and-a-half for the Regimental Food Service. He was in Korea from April 1952 to May 1953—overlapping with Frenchy! Fred's team picked up food sent from Seoul to the Regiment, divvied it up, and brought it to the units, including to the foot of the hills on the MLR—a scary delivery service! The mess sergeants would pick up the food, and they became adept at making sure there was plenty of it. My interview with Fred was good background on this vital aspect of army life; as Napoleon allegedly said, "An army marches on its stomach."

Jack Robinson worked for Modar—a Division of Motorola Corporation, Schaumburg, Illinois. He was Manager of Marine Products, and gave me a description of the radios likely deployed on the ore boat, *Hawkeye*, even suggesting the use of a competitor's radio (RCA).

Dr. "Sid" Rosenberg is a bridge-playing buddy, a graduate of the University of Manitoba Medical College who came to the U.S. in 1963 and practiced emergency medicine—no better person to help me with Frenchy's operation at the MASH unit, including especially the use of the Penrose Drain. Sid served as a gunner in the Canadian Air Force during World War II.

Ray Sauve was the Recon Sergeant, A Battery, 61st Field, when I arrived at Camp Chitose. We were reunited in 2002 at the Pueblo West Reunion, by which time he had married Bernice, had seven children, was a retired county engineer, and lived in Bemidji, Minnesota. I interviewed Ray by telephone and gathered information about his Korean experiences; among his many service medals, he was awarded the Bronze Star.

Barron Schoder, originally from Westfield, New Jersey, attended Dartmouth College and Marine Officer Candidate School at Quantico, Virginia. He served as a rifle platoon leader in the Imjin River area. Lt. Barry described disturbances and problems along the DMZ just after the Armistice.

John Sivright, originally from Silver Spring, Maryland, graduated from the Naval Academy in 1950 and elected to go in the marines. John married a lovely lady from my home town, Glencoe, Illinois, and through this connection we met at Fort Sill when I was a Red Bird (upper classman) in OCS and he was a first lieutenant, back from Korea and teaching gunnery. John served in the 11th Marines, 1st Marine Division, as Battery Executive Officer, Battery Commander, and Advisor to the Korean Marine Corps. He later had a distinguished career with The Harris Trust and Savings Bank in Chicago, serving as Executive Vice President. John gave me many ideas and put me in touch with two marine books: Nolan's *The Run-up to the Punchbowl: A Memoir of the Korean War* and Cooper's *Cheers and Tears: A Marine's Story of Combat in Peace and War. Semper Fi!*

Steve Slavin, a golfing friend, and his wife, Carol, gave helpful comments on the Great Northern chapter.

Lawrence Stein got to Korea in 1954—more than a year after the ceasefire. I latched on to him after his wife, Joan, said, "Larry ran a whorehouse in Korea!" Well, not quite. He was in the ROTC Program for Army Military Police at the University of Wisconsin, attended the Basic Officers' Course at Camp Gordon, Georgia, and reached Korea in November 1954. He was sent to the 24th Division as MP Operations Officer. As he explained, "Everything off-the-road was off-limits; all hookers had ID cards and were checked weekly." It seemed very likely to me that this same situation existed two years before; so I came up with the communications expert,

Cpl. Hiram Spachek, based on Larry's story and Joan's somewhat twisted explanation of his duties in Korea.

Cheryl Stereff, teaches writing at the California State University, San Bernardino Branch, Palm Desert Campus, where I have been in three of her classes. She had a struggle on her hands when she read and commented on a draft of the Great Northern chapter, which she pretty well panned.

The Rev. Bobbie Taylor helped me with the Sermon and actually helped me present it at The Glencoe Union Church on a Sunday morning in September 2008.

George Grady Tucker, Jr., was in command of Baker Battery when I arrived at the 61st Field in 1953. Grady had served in the navy 1944–1947, and then graduated from the ROTC program at the University of Florida as a Distinguished Military Graduate in 1951. He was sent to Fort Sill, then Fort Hood, finally Camp Drake, Sasebo, and Pusan. Assigned to C Battery, 143rd Field Artillery Battalion, he served as Forward Observer during the battles in the Iron Triangle at Chunchon. I interviewed Grady at our Reunion in Colorado Springs, September 2008, learning about his life in combat on an OP. We covered the following: spotting and shooting at various enemy targets, use of base-point and check-point registrations, working in a bunker with his Recon Sergeant and Wireman, living in a hoochy, opportunities for hot meals, and reliance on C-Rations. After Korea, and the 61st Field in Japan, Grady Tucker went into the army's guided missile program; he retired with the rank of full colonel. *'Sta Bueno*!

Jim Vogel, from Evansville, Indiana, graduated from The University of Evansville in 1952, was drafted August that year, and sent to eight-week Artillery Basic at Camp Chaffee. Jim took a troop ship to Sasebo, Japan, and from there flew to Kimpo, just west of Seoul. After serving in the ranks at the 155 Howitzers of the 12th Field Artillery Battalion, he became Chief of Firing Battery—a very significant achievement for a man who was not a career soldier. His battery encountered counterfire from mortars.

Jim White, also of Glencoe, Illinois, was a Navy Lieutenant Commander who made many useful suggestions, including the types of ships used by Frenchy and starting from Oakland Army Terminal.

Jim Wood is another old friend from Central School, Glencoe, and New Trier High School. He also went through Field Artillery OCS at Fort Sill; but from there our paths changed: he went to L-19 flight school—like Capt. Forest (get it: Wood/Forest?). When I had the Red Tail L-19 crash in the DMZ and hotshot pilot Wiggins go to the rescue, I called Jim Wood and asked if an L-19 could take off with four people. The answer came back: "Heck, yes, but where would you put 'em?" I indicated: "Not to worry—I'll stack one on a lap and hang our hero from a strut."

This book is not a memoir, much less an autobiography, but there are some events and people based on my experiences.

Harvey Brothers was an actual store in Iowa. My uncle, like Pierre, worked there for my aunt's family and went to France in World War I. Similarly, my father, like Guy, left town, went to college, and led quite a different life. Pierre's war record in France is based on Arthur's *Holding the Colonel's Horse: PFC Thompson and Col. Reeves of the 353rd Infantry Regiment*—Thompson was my father-in-law.

Capt. Birdsall and Sgt. Noonan represent how I think a Basic Training Company should be operated, unfortunately, not how my unit was run.

The character Otto Rentner III is based on a man in my OCS class—a master sergeant and great guy—who simply washed out because of the gunnery requirements late in the program and much to my chagrin. He would have been a fine career officer. He gave me a solid-gold shoulder bar on his sad departure. So, in the book, why not, I had him make it! It gave me a lift. As for the name, I had a friend named "Pug" Rentner (Northwestern Wildcat and Chicago Bear) who pointed out that, spelled backward, his name was still Rentner.

I went through the motions of cleaning Battalion Headquarters during a storm while the dingbat sergeant led the troops in the rain. My quote, "I'm not your (bleeping) chaplain" is exact, perfectly recalled. That guy was just what the army didn't need.

I gave the class on Hannibal and the Battle of Cannae at Fort Sill.

Other early happenings, which resemble my experiences—all with names changed—include the following:

"Hit him with a brick" (my mother); the Duprez Family's favorite books; skating on the rivers; smutty jokes from WWII vets; Hank Sauer; peeing in a cup; the tuckpointer and the punch card guy; the Isle of Guam Sergeant; the stockade; the fallout drill as corporate punishment; McNulty, Bratton, Heusting, and drummer Weinman; officers with different shaped butts; the entire curricula of Basic and Leadership School; the Chief Warrant Officer instructor; hiding an unauthorized car at Fort Knox; the stolen entrenching tool; the black and white fight; the Easy Eight; the Tank Leaders' Reaction Course; map-reading class and inspection by Turkish Officers; the Cheshire cat; the circus; going AWOL; USO dances; trip to Mammoth Cave; the nasty mess hall corporal.

Then, later on we have:

Dave's mother (reference: my mother); the Hungary i and Bill Cosby; ciopino and abalone at Fisherman's Wharf; the 38 Police Special; ashore at Adak; inspections and seasickness aboard a MSTS vessel; ashore at Wake Island; speaking euphemistically of the surrender on the battleship *Missouri*; C. G. Jung and dreams; God, be my helper; a Dear John letter; the Tokyo Onsen; touring Tokyo, including the Dai-Ichi Building and the Imperial palace; Sukiyaki on the Ginza; "Play it cool, do it right . . ."; of course, the sermon; short-arm inspections; the five islands in Tokyo Bay; Williams College and Newport Line Officers' School (T. Taylor); Yale ROTC; Otto Rentner; descriptions of Officers' Club and

BOQ (Chitose); widow with ten thousand dollars; Black Tooth in Wyoming; dude ranch near Sheridan, Wyoming; the Colonel Boogie; seeing the Pope; the Minimax; and speaking Japanese.

There is a reference to "To a Mouse: On Turning up Her Nest with the Plough, November 1785," by Robert Burns (1759–1796). Also, didn't Frenchy pick a great one when he recited "To Lucasta on going to the Wars" by Richard Lovelace (1618–1658)?

Finally, I wish to relate the source of the name Desprez. Robert W. Service wrote **Rhymes of a Red Cross Man** (Barse & Hopkins, 1916), based on his experiences as an ambulance driver in World War I. The poem, "Jean Desprez," tells of a peasant boy who becomes a tragic victim when war reaches his little village. He comes to the aid of a dying French soldier, called "the Zouave," and, as punishment, the little boy is directed by the evil Prussian Major to kill the Zouave. As the horrid major put it: "the dying dog he fain would save shall perish by his hand." They gave "the lad a rifle charged, and set him squarely there. . . ." The Zouave says, "shoot, son, 'twill be the best for both . . . I will murmur *Vive La France!* and bless you ere I die."

So, the boy, Desprez, stands there, the shining rifle in his hands, as the poem concludes:

> Shoot! Shoot! The dying Zouave moaned;
> "Shoot! Shoot!" the soldiers said.
> Then Jean Desprez reached out and shot . . .
> **The Prussian Major dead!**

The 21ˢᵗ Century Army
By Colonel Julia Arthur

The army is very different today than it was back in the 1950s, even apart from changes in technology. Most significantly, it has been a volunteer force since the 1970s. My father, TA, and our hero Frenchy were both drafted; the current force serves by choice. We may not get as many of the highly educated scholars (like little Bingo), however, we don't get the deadbeats and malingerers who would rather be anywhere else instead of serving their country. We don't have "smoke breaks" and we do not tolerate drug or alcohol abuse.

Artillery is not my area of expertise. However, I've checked around and can make a few observations.

Frenchy's time was pre-microchip and pre-satellite. He did not have the benefits of computers, GPS, and guided missile technology. His tedious days of slip sticks, deflection fans, aiming circles, logarithmic tables, aiming posts, bulky radios, and L-19 observation aircraft are all in the past.

Still, Frenchy's time did advance from the Second World War weaponry by introducing such innovations as combat helicopters, jet aircraft, flak jackets, MASH units, counter-battery radar, six (instead of four) howitzers to a battery, the L19's, the 3.5 Bazooka, and many, many others. On a strategic level, one big difference was that, after February 1951, the Korean "Stalemate" settled into trench warfare, mostly in the mountains, which is often compared to 1918, rather than the 1940s.

All the weapon systems are new since Frenchy's time; his Garand was replaced by the M-16 in the 60s and the L-19 has been replaced by Unmanned Aerial Vehicles (UAVs). Over the years the 105 and 155 howitzers have continued to evolve. A towed version of the 155 can even be lifted for insertion or extraction by the army's Blackhawk helicopter. That would certainly surprise Frenchy! The self-propelled version is called the "Paladin." It has on-board digital communications and fire control plus a positional and directional determining system.

One of the greatest combat multipliers created in the 1980s is the Multiple Launch Rocket System, called MLRS. With guided missiles the System is called ATACMS. More than ten thousand of these rockets were fired in Operation Desert Storm. One version can fire thirty-five miles with pinpoint accuracy, and with adaptations, another version can fire over 180 miles.

The High Mobility Artillery Rocket System (HIMARS), the newest, highly mobile version of MLRS, was first introduced in 2005 during Operation Iraqi Freedom. HIMARS can fire and move away (shoot and scoot) before it can be detected by an enemy. A new fire control system was added in 2008. It can be aimed in sixteen seconds and operates with a crew of three.

The navy is coming out with a new smart missile, the SM-6, which can autonomously identify targets, enabling ships to shoot at targets beyond radar range and destroy ballistic missiles. It's due out in 2011.

Perhaps more interesting to the reader of this book is our present understanding of the concept of "limited war." In 1950, our leaders could only look back at two World Wars with no model of a limited war. Recent history gives us plenty of examples including Korea, Vietnam, Grenada, Panama, Desert Storm, Somalia, Bosnia, Kosovo, Afghanistan, and Iraq.

TA was very interested in this limited war concept, which he tried to analyze and to have his characters discuss throughout the book. Our military continues to learn about limited wars, and with those lessons come changes in how we interact with the local civilian population.

While I was teaching at the reserve Command and General Staff College (CGSC) in 2005, counterinsurgency, known as COIN, was added to the curriculum. Gen. David Petraeus had served in Iraq, commanding the 101st Airborne in 2002 and 2003. He was the driving force behind understanding the enemy and working with the local population to defeat the insurgents. Some of the COIN principles include: get to know the people; help them; learn their language; leave your area of operation better than you found it; walk, don't ride; and be patient—you are there to help, not hurt. The new COIN manual was prepared at the CGSC and released December 15, 2006. A new Foreword states,

"The field manual was widely reviewed, including by several *Jihadi* Web sites; copies have been found in Taliban training camps in Pakistan. It   was downloaded more than 1.5 million times in the first month after its posting to the Fort Leavenworth and Marine Corps Web sites." (Lt. Col. John A Nagl, *Forward to the University of Chicago Press Edition, The U.S. Army-Marine Corps Counterinsurgency Field Manual, 2007, p. xvii).*

Our governmental leadership has always struggled to determine the balance between current and future requirements. In a tough economy with ongoing operations, the Military must make sharp choices between research and development for state-of-the-art weapons for future wars and the boots-on-the-ground preparations needed for the counterinsurgencies we have been facing in places like Iraq and Afghanistan, where weapons for major theater wars are ineffective against a relatively lightly-armed but determined enemy that blends in with the local population. Field artillery is a prime target of debate between major theater war and insurgency funding. Limited funding forces choices between mobile mortars with limited range and mechanized artillery. The prospects of longterm insurgent battles vs. the less-likely possibility of theater wars will make the argument for continued development of artillery more difficult.

A different global thought: Great Lakes ore boats are now one thousand feet long, and they still ply the waters from mine to mill; however, steel production in China (those folks who unkindly surprised us at the Gauntlet and the Reservoir) is now five times as great as ours!

Julia Arthur
Colonel, United States Army Reserves

Glossary

Readers of drafts of this book got after me to include a glossary. I resisted and now advise the reader that most military hardware is described where it is first mentioned and need not be remembered in detail anyway. Some repeated technical terms (always as used in 1952) seemed to be particularly arcane to my early readers, so here is a short list.

caliber—Bore size in decimal inches, thus 50-caliber is one-half inch.

CCF—Chinese Communist Forces.

DMZ—Demilitarized Zone, still there sixty years later and still a no man's land.

FDC—Fire Direction Center where FO information is processed and sent to the guns.

FO—Forward Observer, one of the world's most dangerous jobs.

HE—High Explosive projectile, the most common artillery shell.

L-19—Small two-passenger observation aircraft.

MASH Unit—Mobile Army Surgical Hospital.

MLR—Main Line of Resistance, each side having one, no man's land in between.

mm—Bore size in millimeters, thus a 105 howitzer has a bore of 105 millimeters.

MOS—Military Occupation Specialty, such as Chief of Firing Battery—MOS 1844.

MSR—Main Supply Route.

NK—North Korean army.

OP—Observation Post, sometimes on the MLR, sometimes forward in the DMZ.

ROK—Republic of Korea (South Korean) army.

TO&E—Table of Organization and Equipment, used at all unit levels.

VT—Fuse variable time, also called victor tear, causes rounds to explode in the air.

WP—White phosphorous projectile, also called willy peter, creates fire and smoke.

In 1952, the highest ground unit in Korea was the **8ᵗʰ Army**, commanded by a **Lieutenant General**, consisting of several Corps. A **Corps** was a large unit of army and, sometimes, marines, consisting of a number of divisions. From Corps down, the units were triangular—two units on line, one in reserve.

A **Division** consisted of three infantry regiments and supporting units, commanded by a **Major General**. A **Regiment** consisted of three infantry battalions and supporting units, commanded by a **Colonel.** An infantry **Battalion** consisted of three infantry companies and supporting units, commanded by a **Lieutenant Colonel,** second in command was the **Executive Officer**, a **Major.** A **Company** was commanded by a **Captain.**

However, in an artillery battalion, each of these three attached units was called a **Battery**, not a company. Second in command of a battery was the **Executive Officer**, a **First Lieutenant.** A battery **FO Team** was commanded by a **Second Lieutenant.** At the high end, artillery supported the infantry division with **Division**

Artillery, called **Divarty,** and commanded by a **Brigadier General.**

Companies and batteries were the smallest fully equipped units capable of independent deployment with their TO&E, including a full complement of assignments in small arms, certain heavier weapons from mortars to howitzers, headquarters, communications, mess, aide stations, supply, etc. Companies contained four **Platoons** of four **Squads** and, in a battery, **Sections** for six-gun crews. These smaller units were led, in the case of platoons by **Second Lieutenants.** Other units were led by **Non-Commissioned Officers (NCOs),** including **Corporals** and various levels of **Sergeants. NCOs** held key subordinate jobs at all the higher levels as well. On a day-to-day basis, army and marine routines were run by **Sergeants.** God bless 'em!

Bibliography

Acheson, Dean. *Present at the Creation: My Years in the State Department*. New York, New York: W.W. Norton & Company, Inc, 1969.

Appleman, Roy E. *South to the Naktong, North to the Yalu (June–November 1950)*. Washington, D.C.: Office of the Chief of Military History, Department of the Army, 1960.

Arthur, Tom and Jane. *Holding the Colonel's Horse, Pfc. Thompson and Col. Reeves of the 353 Infantry Regiment*. Glencoe, IL: Not Published, 2000.

Berry, Henry. *Hey, Mac, Where Ya Been?: Living Memories of the U.S. Marines in the Korean War*. New York, New York: St. Martin's Press, 1988.

Birtle, A.J. *The Korean War: Years of Stalemate, July 1951– July 1953*. Washington, D.C.: Center of Military History, United States Army, U.S. Government Printing Office.

Blair, Clay. *The Forgotten War: America in Korea 1950–1953*. Anapolis, Maryland: Naval Institute Press, 1987.

Bove, Bob (with Lou Angelloti). *Accordian Man: The Legendary Dick Contino.* Tallahassee, Florida: Father & Son Publishing Company, 1994.

Brady, James. *The Coldest War: A Memoir of Korea.* New York, New York: Thomas Dunne Books, St. Martin's Griffin, 1990.

Carroll, Lewis. *Alice's Adventures in Wonderland & Through the Looking Glass.* New York, New York: Bantam Books, 1916.

Chang, Jung and John Halliday. *MAO: The Unknown Story.* New York, New York: Anchor Books, 2005.

Clark, E.F. *The Secrets of Inchon: The Untold Story of the Most Daring Covert Mission of the Korean War.* Itaska, Illinois: Putman Publishing Company, 2002.

Clayton, J.D. *Refighting the Last War, Command and Crisis in Korea.* New York, New York: The Free Press, A Division of MacMillan, Inc., 1993.

Clede, Bill. *The Practical Pistol Manuel: How to Use a Handgun for Self-Defense.* Ottawa, Illinois: Jameson Books, Inc., 1997.

Clubb, O.E. *China & Russia The "Great Game."* New York, New York: Columbia University Press, 1971.

Cocklin, Robert F. (Lt. Col.). "Artillery in Korea." *Combat Forces Journal, Vol. 2, No. 1,* August 1951.

Cooper, Charles G. *Cheers and Tears: A Marine's Story of Combat in Peace and War.* Victoria, British Columbia: Trafford Publishing, 2002.

Costello, John. *Days of Infamy (WWII Background).* New York, New York: Pocket Books, 1994.

Cray, Ed. *General of the Army.* New York, New York: W.W. Norton & Company, 1990.

Dehuai, Peng. *Memoirs of a Chinese Marshall.* Beijing, China: Foreign Languages Press, 1984.

Deparrtment of the Army. *Field Manual (FM) 22–5.* Fort Benning, Georgia: Department of the Army, 1986.

Drury, Bob and Tom Calvin. *The Last Stand of Fox Company.* New York, New York: Atlantic Monthly Press, 2009.

Dutton, Fred W. *Life on the Great Lakes: A Wheelman"'s Story.* Detroit, Michigan: Wayne State University Press, 1981.

Edwards, P.M. *The Korean War: An Annotated Bibliography.* Westport, Conneticut: Greenwood Press, 1998.

Gammons, Stephen Y.L. *The Korean War: The U.N. Offensive.* Washington, D.C.: Center of Military History, United States Army, U.S. Government Printing Office.

Garfield, Brian. *The Thousand Mile War: World War II in Alaska and the Aleutians.* Fairbanks, Alaska: University of Alaska Press, 1969.

Gavin, James M. *Crisis Now.* New York, New York: Random House, 1968.

Goulden, J.C. *Korea: The Untold Story of the War.* New York, New York: Times Books, 1982.

Hackworth, Col. David H. and Julie Sherman. *About Face.* New York, New York: Simon and Schuster, 1989.

Halberstam, David. *The Coldest Winter: America and the Korean War.* New York: Hyperion, 2007.

Hanford, William B. *Dangerous Assignment: An Artillery Forward Observer in WWII.* Mecnanicsburg, Pennsylvania: Stackpole Books, 2008.

Hanley, C.J.H. and M. Mendoza. *The Bridge at No Gun Ri: A Hidden Nightmare from the Korean War.* New York, New York: Henry Holt and Company, 2001.

Harrity, P.D. *A Forward Observer Reports From Korea. Combat Forces Journal, Vol. 1, No. 9,* April 1951.

Haskins, Sonya A. and Cathy A. Hawkins. *Images of America: Soddy-Daisy.* Charleston, South Carolina: Arcadia Publishing, 2006.

Hastings, Max. *The Korean War.* New York, New York: Simon and Schuster Paperbacks, 1987.

Herbert, Anthony B. *The Making of a Soldier.* New York, New York: Hipppocrene Books, Inc., 1982.

Higgins, Trumbull. *Korea and the Fall of MacArthur: A Precis in Limited War.* New York, New York: Oxford University Press, Inc., 1960.

Inderdahl, Howard K. (Master Sergeant). *In the Hills of Korea.* Scandinavia, Wisconsin: Watson Graphic Designs.

Insight Guide: South Korea, Eigth Edition. London, England: APA Publications, 2007.

James, C.D. *Refighting the Last War: Command and Crisis in Korea 1950–1953.* New York, New York: The Free Press, 1973.

Johnson, Haynes. *The Age of Anxiety—McCarthyism to Terorism.* New York, New York: Harcourt, Inc., 2005.

Jung, C.G. *Man and His Symbols.* Ljubljana, Yugoslavia: Miadinska Knjiga, 1964.

———. *Memories, Dreams, Reflections.* New York, New York: Vintage Books, 1961.

Kammerer, Judith l. *History of Hamilton, Illinois.* Carthage, Illinois: Journal Printing Company, 1984.

Kennan, George F. *Memoirs (1950–1963).* Boston, MA: Little, Brown and Company, 1972.

Knorr, Klaus. *Limited Strategic War*. Princeton, New Jersey: Princetron University Press, 1962.

———. *On the Uses of Power in the Nuclear Age*. Princeton, New Jersey: Princeton University Press, 1966.

Macksey, Kenneth and John H. Batchelor. *Tank: A History of the Armoured Fighting Vehicle*. New York, New York: Ballantine Books, 1971.

Manchester, William. *American Caesar*. New York, New York: Dell Publishing Co. Inc., 1978.

Marshall, S.L.A. *Pork Chop Hill*. New York, New York: William Morrow & Company, 1956.

———. *The River and the Gauntlet*. New York, New YorK: William Morrow & Company, 1953.

McGrath, John J. *The Korean War: Restoring the Balance*. Washington D.C.: Center of Military History, United States Army, U.S. Government Printing Office.

Merriam-Webster's French-English Dictionary. Springfield, Massachusetts: Merriam-Webster, Incorporated, 2004.

Mikaelian. *Medal of Honor: Profiles of America's Military Heroes from the Civil War to the Present*. New York, New York: Hyperion, 2002.

Miller, John, Owen J. Carroll, and Margaret E. Tackley. *Korea: 1951–1953*. Washington, D.C.: Center of Military History, United States Army, U.S. Government Printing Office, 1947.

Mossman, Billy C. *Ebb and Flow: November 1950–July 1951*. Washington, D.C.: Center of Military History, United States Army, U.S. Government Printing Office, 1990.

Nolan, John. *The Run-Up to the Punchbowl: A Memoir of the Korean War, 1951*. Philadelphia, Pennsylvania: Xlibris, 2006.

Paik, Sun Yup. *From Pusan to Panmunjom.* McLean, Virginia: Brassey's (US), Inc., A Division of Maxwell MacMillan, Inc., 1992.

Palmer, Donald E. *The Memorable Fifties: An Unforgettable Decade.* Miami, Florida: Live Your Dream Enterprises, 2004.

Parker, William (Editor). *Men of Courage.* Chicago, Illinois: Playboy Press, 1947.

Pocket Dictionary Korean. Berlin, Germany: Langenscheidt KG, 2006.

Reserve Officers' Training Corps. *Field Artillery Gunnery 1941 Edition, Book 161.* Fort Sill, Oklahoma: Field Artillery School, 1941.

Ricks, Thomas E. *The Gamble.* New York, New York: The Penguin Press, 2009.

Rieth, John K. *Patton's Forward Observers.* Richmond, Virginia: Brandylane Publishers, Inc., 2004.

Russ, Martin. *The Last Parallel.* Kingsport, Tennessee: Kingsport Press, 1957.

Russell, Major James. *The Memories of an Artillery Forward Observer, 1944–1945.* Manhattan, Kansas: Sunflower University Press, 1999.

Russell, William. *Stalemate & Standoff: The Bloody Outpost War.* Deland, Florida: EO Painter Printing Company, Inc., 1993.

Sanford, John A. *The Man Who Wrestled with God.* Ramsey, New York: Paulist Press, 1974.

Smith, W. Thomas, Jr. *Alpha, Bravo, Delta Guide to the Korean War.* New York, New York: Alpha Books, 2004.

Sobieski, Anthony J. *Fire For Effect!: Artillery Forward Observers in Korea*. Bloomington, Indiana: AuthorHouse, 2005.

————. *Fire Mission!: The Story of the 213ᵗʰ Field Artillery Battalion in Korea 1951–1954*. Bloomington, Indiana: 1st Books Library, 2003.

Stephenson, June. *Poisonous Power: Childhood Roots of Tyrany*. Diemer, Smith Publishing Company, Inc., 1998.

Steves, Rick. *French Phrase Book & Dictionary*. Emeryville, California: Avalon Travel Publishing, 2003.

Stewart, Richard W. *The Korean War: The Chinese Intervention*. Washington, D.C.: Center of Military History, United States Army, U.S. Government Printing Office .

Stokesbury, James L. *A Short History of the Korean War*. New York, New York: William Morrow and Company, Inc., 1988.

Thompson, Mark L. *A Season Aboard Great Lakes Freighters*. Detroit, Michigan: Wayne State University Press, 1999.

Tobin, James. *Ernie Pyle's War*. New York, New York: The Free Press, 1997.

Toland, John. *In Mortal Combat: Korea 1950–1953* . New York, New York: Quill William Morrow, 1991.

Trotter, William R. *A Frozen Hell: The Russo-Finnish Winter War of 1939–1940*. Chapel Hill, North Carolina: Algonquin Books of Chapel Hill, 2000.

Tuchman, Barbara W. *Stillwell and the American Experience in China, 1911–45*. New York, New York: The MacMillan Company, 1970.

"Weapons at War: Big Guns." The History Channel. New York, New York: Greystone Communications Inc., 1993.

Webb, William J. *The Korean War: The Outbreak*. Washington D.C.: Center of Military History, United States Army, U.S. Government Printing Office.

Wehrwein, R.E. *Deck Hand on the Great Lakes*. New Ulm, Minnesota: Wehrwein, 2006.

Westover, John C. *Combat Support in Korea*. Washington, D.C.: Center of Military History, United States Army, U.S. Government Printing Office, 1987.

Whitson, William W. (with Chen-Hsia Huang). *The Chinese High Command*. New York, New York: Praeger Publishing, 1973.

Wilhelm, Richard & Cary F. Baynes. *I Ching or, Book of Changes* . Princeton, New Jersey: Princeton University Press, 1950.

Winchester, Simon. *The Man Who Loved China*. New York, New York: HarperColins Publishers, 2008.

"Yearbook, 1953, Battery A, 67th Armored Field Artillery Battalion." *Third Armored Division*. Fort Knox, Kentucky: Albert Loove Enteerprises, Atlanta, Geogia, April 1953.

About the Author

Tom Arthur grew up in Glencoe, Illinois, where he lives with his wife, Jane Arthur. After graduating from Hamilton College in 1952, he was drafted and then went through Infantry Basic Training, Armored Leadership School at Ft. Knox, Kentucky, and Field Artillery Officers' Candidate School at Ft. Sill, Oklahoma. In the summer of 1953, just after the Korean truce, he was commissioned Second Lieutenant, Artillery, and served in the 61st Field Artillery Battalion, 1st Division, in Hokkaido and Northern Honshu, Japan. He had extensive experience as a forward observer, adjusting artillery fire, and as a battery executive officer. He also attended the Far East Command Mountain Training School and taught at the Winter Training School.

After completing his military service, Tom attended Northwestern University School of Law and was a partner in the Chicago firm of Gardner, Carton & Douglas, with a corporate securities practice. He retired in 1997.

In addition to tennis and golf, Tom and his wife have hiked and climbed in Mexico, New Zealand, Europe, East Africa (Kilimanjaro—19,340 feet), and throughout the Western United States, especially in the Grand Canyon.

In addition to writing, Tom paints, sculpts, and makes silver jewelry. He has also enjoyed making furniture, mountain dulcimers, carving songbirds, and blacksmithing.